Max

By Marjorie Joseph

Higher Ground Books & Media
Springfield, Ohio.
http://highergroundbooksandmedia.com

Printed in the United States of America 2020

CHAPTER ONE

"What happened to Stanley Morris was a terrible mistake. That error costs the hospital millions in lawsuits," Dr. Max Kane censured hospital staff during a biweekly hospital meeting in October of 2019. Max was the Director and Chief of Staff of Fairfield Hospital out in Seattle, Washington. "Medication imprudently administered resulted in a Code Blue," he reprimanded.

Irritation shaded Max's face, and he shook his head contrarily. "We *will* eventually live down the scandal, but we've all got to do better when it comes to caring for the elderly. Stanley Morris's death is one life too many lost to negligence. We *are* Seattle's leading hospital, and we definitely have a reputation to uphold. There might be room for mediocrity at other facilities, but there is no margin for it around here."

"Dr. Kane, a quick segue. You said that two badges will soon become mandatory for hospital staff, and that the second badge is to obtain access to certain restricted areas on hospital grounds?" Jane Orr, a nurse who worked through the hospital questioned. Jane was finding it difficult to stop gawking at the handsome doctor. In fact, every woman-married and single alike-who worked through Fairfield Hospital, had their eye on the doctor, director and chief of staff.

Max Kane had only been working through Fairfield Hospital for a few months. During that early morning meeting, for Jane, sizing up Dr. Kane in his dark gray business suit, made it difficult to focus on his bullet points. She found herself doting on him, and tripping over her words. Jane could tell, as she skimmed over the meeting hall, she wasn't the only one struggling. Most of the women were ogling and seemed oblivious to anything he had to say about hospital policy. They were all engaged in watching him speak, and enrapt in scrutinizing his well-formed mouth.

Max Kane was something of a wonder. Standing at about 6'1, the illicitly handsome Indian doctor had caused quite a stir at the hospital. With his sandstone-colored skin, thick raven hair, muscular upper build, pecan-colored eyes, he was storybook princely! Max also had perfect hands, and a flawless mouth, which appeared to be dripping honey. However, because Doctor Kane was immersed in his work, it seemed he was unmindful of all of the women who had their eye on him. Even if Jane was married, she had to admit that being around Dr. Max Kane intimidated her. Being around him often made her feel *school-girlish*.

Max addressed Jane's question. He nodded affirmatively. "In a matter of weeks, special badges will be issued to *select* members of our staff. The original badges will remain in use, but the new one will facilitate access to certain parts of the hospital. Those select badges will also expedite finding hospital personnel whenever needed."

"Will the new badges interfere in any way with the effectiveness of the old ones?" Doctor Sandy Middleton, a Cardiologist who worked through the hospital inquired.

"Not at all. Both badges will have distinct features for specific functions. You can say that one is an extension of the other. Again, these changes are being implemented to better serve our patients, and for the hospital to track all medical-related activities," Max expounded.

"If there are no further questions in respect to the new badges, I'd like to address a very important matter," Max redirected. Annoyance strained his usually temperate mien. "I can't stress this enough. It is mandatory for staff to come into work at least half an hour prior to starting their shifts. Giving report to the doctors, nurses and or to the Physician's Assistants is vital. Are we all clear on that?" Max looked from one end of the room to the other. Everyone seemed to be in agreement.

"Are there any more questions?" Max stared all around the expansive hall at everyone who'd assembled for the meeting. When silence permeated the room, he realized there wasn't very much left to say at that juncture. There were biweekly meetings held to address concerns, and to keep medical personnel aware of impending changes. Max was about to adjourn the meeting when Doctor Tim Eckhart raised his hand.

"Yes, Tim?" Max addressed the man.

"Just wanted to double check that *Rapha Nine* will be implemented as the latest in hospital software in a matter of weeks?"

Max nodded in affirmation. "*Rapha Nine* will probably go into effect before Christmas," he informed. "So, once *Rapha* is the new software, there will no longer be the need to browse patient's records through computer files. Each of you will carry a small tablet connected to the database. The moment there is facial recognition, that patient's information will be displayed-all of their history from the most recent, so on and so forth."

"I can only imagine that the application of this new software will increase hospital activity, and also its potential revenue," Dr. Eckhart speculated.

Max issued a faint smile. "Absolutely, and that can't hurt to any capacity." He perused the entire room once more. "Anything else?"

Nurse Ava Thorne pursed her lips, all poised to ask a question, but she felt too timid to ask Max Kane anything. Even if she occasionally worked through the hospital's Emergency Room with him, she struggled with insecurity. Whenever Max was around, she often felt self-conscious, taciturn and reserved. Similar to someone suffering from a medical condition, her heart raced, she got butterflies in her stomach and her palms got sweaty. In the presence of Max Kane, she wasn't the strong confident woman she wanted to project. Rather, she was totally demure. More often than not she felt completely inept.

For a while now, Ava had noticed how Max had shut himself up in some impenetrable world. He seemed to be sequestered in a fortress, which kept the general public at bay. Max Kane was extremely affable and polite, but totally absorbed in running the hospital. Ava had concluded that nothing else seemed to really matter to the man. Even if they often worked together, she sensed that he was unaware of her existence. Ava wanted her *boyfriend* to be more like Max Kane, but that was just wishful thinking on her part.

Ava assented to the fact that many of the women who worked through Fairfield probably had a crush on Max. She often wondered who would be lucky enough to get Max to tear down all of his walls, and finally win his heart. Ava had wanted to ask him a question regarding to the new inventory of scrubs scheduled to come in but desisted. Rather, she continued making notes on her phone in respect to the points covered in the meeting.

"Ladies and gentlemen, I appreciate your time this morning. I hope to see some of the matters we've discussed rectified moving forward. So, if there are no further questions, this meeting is officially adjourned," Max addressed hospital personnel.

As soon as the meeting was over, Max moved quickly through the meeting hall. His aim was to get out of there as soon as possible. So, he evaded medical staff who were chomping at the bit to connect to him on a personal level. As he made his way outside of the hospital, he breathed in the crisp air. The sun was a haze of white pasted to light gray skies. Max hiked over to the hospital parking lot, and accessed his SUV, which was parked in his private space on the grounds. He had just enough time to make it over to the gym for a quick workout.

Hopefully, after his workout, he'd get to go home for a power nap. Later, he had to return to the hospital to work a shift through the ER. Nowadays, it seemed that the hospital had become his new home. Max had only been living out in Castle Horn, Seattle for a few months. He was now both the Hospital Director and Chief of Staff for Fairfield Hospital.   There were many things to be said about his responsibilities, but *mundane* wasn't one of them.

Practically running the hospital *and* being part of its medical team was indeed challenging. His duties at Fairfield were even more demanding than when he'd worked as the Medical Chief of Staff for Bainbridge Hospital out in Colorado. Max had worked there for a short while after leaving Silver Water, Georgia for the first time. Max had made the biggest mistake of his life. He'd agreed to take world-renowned billionaire Kayden Bohm up on his offer to end the relationship with his then girlfriend, Kennedy Proctor. So, Max left Georgia, and had distanced himself from her.

As Max drove out onto the expressway, he relived the gaffes which had brought him out to Castle Horn. Once again, regret gnawed away at him. He'd had it all with Kennedy. She was beautiful, intelligent, witty, kind and so much more. Most importantly, they shared faith in Jesus Christ. In that respect and many others, Max and Kennedy were on the same page. At the time, both Max and Kayden Bohm were vying to win her heart. However, Kayden Bohm, being illicitly rich, had offered Max ten million dollars to walk out of Kennedy's life. Sadly, Max made the irrevocable mistake of accepting the deal.

For a little while, Max lived in the lap of luxury, and practically ran Bainbridge Hospital in *Crystal Canyon, Colorado*. However, it was one of the most miserable times in his entire life. The pain and despair he experienced over losing Kennedy was too hefty a price to pay. Max eventually came to his senses and gave the money back to Kayden Bohm. Soon after, he returned to the town of Silver Water in order to set the record straight with Kennedy, but the damage was already done.

Things went south pretty quickly for Max. Upon returning to Silver Water, he'd resumed his position at Grandview University Hospital. All of this was done for the sake of trying to get Kennedy back. However, by then, it was much too late. Kennedy had someone else in her life. Assistant to the DA, Oliver Wright, was standing by to help her pick up the pieces after her relationship with Kayden fell apart. Oliver Wright had waited for quite some time for chance with Kennedy. So, after Kennedy broke off her engagement to Kayden Bohm, Oliver stepped in just in the nick of time.

Kennedy told Max that there was no going back. Also, at the time, she and Oliver had just begun dating. However, at the end of the day, Kayden was the one who won Kennedy's heart. Shortly after Kennedy and Kayden married, Max couldn't see himself living in the same town. It would have been too much for Max to handle to occasionally see the power couple around town. So, when Fairfield Hospital called and propositioned his new work detail, Max jumped at the chance.

Now, everything that transpired out in Silver Water seemed so far removed from his reality. Living out in Georgia was a vague memory. However, the one thing that remained current was his love for Kennedy. Losing Kennedy to Kayden Bohm had left such a comprehensive wound in Max's heart, he couldn't see himself opening up his heart to anyone else.

Max recounted the run-in he had with Kennedy at the airport on the morning he left town. Seeing her was so poetic. She looked positively breathtaking! For a while after Kennedy married Kayden, Max had felt dead on the inside. However, seeing her that morning had in some way brought him back to life-if only for a few minutes.

Forced to say goodbye to Kennedy at the airport that morning, took something away from Max. Since then, he'd shut down completely. Being a man of faith, Max trusted God with his whole heart. Still, the mistakes of his past in respect to his romantic connections, had landed him into a dark lonely pit. When Max moved out to Colorado, one of the nurses who'd worked through Grandview University Hospital out in Silver Water had followed him.

Raven Glass had found Max, and he'd hired her to work through Bainbridge Hospital. Hence, his short-lived relationship with Raven had wreaked havoc upon his life. Max discovered much too late in the game that the relationship with Raven wasn't God-ordained. So, one mistake had compiled into a slew of others. Yet, as a man of faith, Max was trusting God for healing, even if finding true love ever again seemed implausible.

His love for Kennedy was so profound. So, Max was dubious that the kind of love they'd shared-or at least *his* love for her-would come around a second time. Furthermore, it wasn't something he was actively looking for. His life now consisted of work through Fairfield Hospital, and attending *Light of Glory Church* on Sunday mornings. With a full schedule, there was very little time for much else, and Max rather liked it that way.

***

Max pulled into the driveway of his house at about a quarter to nine a.m. Leaving the car running, he dashed up the steps and sprinted inside of the expansive house. In the foyer closet he found his gym bag. Soon after, he rushed into his bedroom. Rummaging through the closet, he found appropriate gym attire and his sneakers. Taking a moment to change, he peeled off his dress suit. He was tying up the laces on his sneakers when his cell when off. Standing upright, he floated over to the bedroom dresser where he'd set his phone. His heart thudded nervously, as the considered that the hospital was calling for one reason or another.

He sighed, relieved that the call was from his friend and work colleague, Doctor Dalton Davis. Dalton was one of the few friends Max had made out in Castle Horn so far. "What's up, Dalton?" Max answered hurriedly.

"Are we meeting up at the gym like we planned?" Dalton checked. He had the day off from the hospital, and he and Max had made tentative plans to meet up at the gym.

"Yep, we're still on. I was just about the leave," Max confirmed.

"Did I miss very much with the meeting earlier?" Dalton asked, pertained.

"Nothing that I can't fill you in on. Not a big deal."

"I see you couldn't wait to get out of there. You're home actually earlier than I thought you'd be."

"I don't particular enjoy those meetings. They are a little too boring for my taste, but I guess they're necessary."

"You *guess*…?" Dalton razzed. "There are no guessing games here, Mr. Hospital Director/Chief of Staff."

"Shut up, Dalton," Max said, shaking his head nonsensically.

"Ouch, I'm really offended by that," Dalton joked.

"Whatever… Look, I'm just about to leave. So, I will see you in a few."

Max shut down his phone and finished dressing. Drifting into his modern state-of-the-art kitchen, he opened up the fridge, and grabbed a Premier Protein shake. Ensuing, he got his gym bag,

hopped back into his SUV, and drove off meet Dalton over at the
Castle Horn Gym.

***

"Hello," the pretty young lady greeted Max in a beguiling
manner. "What's *your* name?" She had wandered over to the
weight training area of the gym, while Max benched pressed
weights.

Startled by her sudden appearance, Max set the weights down,
and reflexively sat upright on the bench. It was then he got a proper
look at the pretty blonde with the sea blue eyes. "How are *you*? My
name is Max!" Max said affably-taking a short break, in order to
give her his undivided attention.

"I've seen you in here a few times, *Max*, and I've been
meaning to introduce myself," she said with an alluring smile.

Max issued a friendly smile, but anticipated a moment, so that
he could interject what he wanted to say.

"I'm Deanna Wilson," she said perkily.

"It's nice to meet you, *Deanna*!" Max declared. Inwardly, he
was just a little annoyed for the intrusion, but he didn't believe in
being rude to any capacity.

"So, I'll just cut right to the chase. I've noticed you for a while
now. I was hoping that maybe we could go out for drinks or
something one of these days after our workouts." Deanna had a
hopeful smile on her face, as she explored Max's pecan-colored
eyes. She assessed how beautiful and mysterious his eyes were. His
pupils were outlined in a deep gray tint.

"Deanna…?" Max tested at first to ensure he got her name right. The young woman nodded. Max couldn't help noticing how beautiful she was. However, there were two major issues. For one, if he was *ever* going to be romantically involved again, that person had to be a follower of Jesus Christ. Secondly, in light of all he'd gone through, beautiful women did very little to elicit a reaction from him. "Deanna, first of all, thank you for coming over and saying hello. That was very sweet of you, but I'm afraid I *can't* go out with you."

Deana frowned. "Oh, alright… I didn't notice a wedding ring. Still, I'm assuming that you have a girlfriend," she speculated.

Max neither confirmed nor denied her words. Rather, he offered an amiable smile. "I apologize for being so forthright."

"No, it's alright. I get it. I've got to respect a man who is serious about his relationship," she stated with an earnest smile pasted to her sweet face. "Well, if you and your girlfriend ever break up…" She winked at Max.

Max smiled temperately at Deanna. "Sure."

"It was nice meeting you, Max," Deanna said demurely, turning to leave.

"Likewise," Max replied, watching the young woman saunter away.

"Max, my man!" Dalton said, having just gotten off of the elliptical. "That was brutal," he commented, and shook his head in disapproval and incredulity.

"*What* was brutal, Dalton? What on earth are you rambling on about now?" Max shook his head nonsensically.

"Do you have any idea how many times I've watched you annihilate some unsuspecting woman who had the nerve to ask you out?" Dalton's green eyes narrowed in inquisition. His tan skin was ruddy. Beads of perspiration rolled down his face and issued from his pores.

Max kept shaking his head in the negative. "Me?" Max pointed at himself. "I've never annihilated anyone. In fact, I'm usually too nice," he argued.

"You may be nice to everyone, buddy, but you're hard on women. You know they call you *Shutter Island* over at the hospital, right?" Dalton edged in closer to the bench where Max rested.

"And what's *that* supposed to mean?" Max inquired warily.

"It means that you live on your own island, and no one knows how to *shut* women down faster than you, my friend. And, it's such a shame, because there are so many women over at the hospital looking to connect to you." Dalton shook his head in the negative. "Man, if I had it like *that* I'd be all over them."

"*Really*, they're calling me *Shutter Island*? I can't believe that." Max's face wrinkled, disconcerted. It bothered him that his reputation was that of a coldhearted, heartbreaking recluse. That was the last thing he wanted. He was by nature a very warm and friendly person. He'd also experienced a great deal of hurt, so the last thing *he* wanted was to inflict pain upon anyone. He kept a health healthy distance from women, because in that way he couldn't hurt anyone, and neither would he know the devastation of heartbreak again.

"Yeah, and rightly so, Max. You're probably not aware of this, but I've been made privy to one- or maybe even a dozen of those scenes you just had with *Deanna*. Why are you so anti-romance?" Dalton asked, nonplused.

"Dalton, I'm *not* anti-women or romance," Max maintained, hurt. "It's just that I don't have the time-"

"Max, I doubt *time* has anything to do with it. Just from the look on your face before you sent that girl away, you were chomping at the bit to tell her to get lost. It's almost as if you didn't want to hear *anything* she had to say. Before she even said a word, you'd already made up your mind that you weren't going to give her a chance," Dalton evaluated.

Max's face wrinkled in perplexity, and his heart knotted up in offense. Dalton was the only person who'd made any comments about his love life or lack thereof. It was sobering to hear what other people were thinking about him. Max's heart softened over the realization that Dalton was probably right. Perhaps, he *was* on a mission to hurt anyone before they hurt him. That wasn't the person he wanted to be. "*Really-Shutter Island?*" he queried, baffled. "Is that the way I've been coming off?"

Dalton nodded. "Look, Max, I know that it probably isn't any of my business, and maybe I am overstepping here. All I can say is that all women shouldn't have to pay for the sins of the *one* who hurt you…just saying…"

Max sat there quietly mulling over Dalton's words. Dalton was a bit of a jokester. So, because he'd taken a moment to seriously share his opinion with Max, his words resonated. Max had no idea that he was punishing anyone who came his way, because his heart had been broken. At that moment he said a prayer. Max asked God to make him more mindful of the times where he lashed out from a place of hurt.

After Dalton had said his peace, Max watched him hike over to one of the other weight-lifting machines. Max was left feeling bewildered, and totally humbled by his friend's opinion. As he sulked, Psalms 147:3 came to mind. "He heals the brokenhearted and binds up their wounds." (NIV)

Max meditated on that passage of scripture and prayed for God to make that a reality in his life. He direly needed a healing touch from the Lord. It wasn't always easy to see one's own shortcomings. It hadn't occurred to him that he'd withdrawn from life and from people. The last thing Max wanted was to be a source of pain to anyone's life. He had in the past been on the receiving end of hurt, so he resolved to be more mindful of when *he* himself was the one inflicting it.

***

"Keith, let go of my arm," Faith wailed, "you're hurting me." Tears flooded her eyes, as she tried to dodge the abuse from her live-in boyfriend of close to two years.

"I don't want you talking to any of those cafeteria guys," Keith bellowed, scowling in fury. "Are we clear?" His face turned ruddy, and his hazel eyes were swimming in a pool of red.

"I've already told you that Ken Ames was just asking me questions about the work. He's new over at the school." Faith grimaced and groaned in pain as a result of Keith's affront.

"You're a lying witch," Keith berated. Pulling away enough to obtain leverage, he forcefully backslapped her.

"No, no, no. Keith, please don't hit me again," Faith entreated, shrinking away. "I promise that there's no one else. I haven't even *talked* to anyone else since we've been together. Please, don't hit me anymore."

"You'd better *not* talk to anyone else over at the school, Faith. I'm not playing any games here." Keith grasped hold of both of Faith's shoulders and shook her. "Look at me," he demanded.

Timorously, Faith's tear-filled eyes connected to her boyfriend's. Her face radiating in pain where she'd been struck.

She couldn't stop shaking and shuddering, because of Keith's violent outburst and assault.

"Even if some guy were to come up to you with questions about the job, tell them to go talk to your supervisor, or someone else who works through the cafeteria. Are we clear?" he admonished.

Erratically, Faith shook her head in agreement. "Yes...," she said hesitantly, terrified.

"We'd better be clear, Faith. You are *my* property, and no one else will ever have you," Keith delineated heatedly, shoving away from the vise grip hold he'd kept on her arms.

Faith had been all set to leave for work before Keith had jumped her. Now, she felt shaky and uncertain. She had also planned to stop by her dad's place for a brief visit. James Langhorne had been sick for some time now. At only sixty-two, the man had a daily nurse. And, because Faith was the only one of her siblings who still lived out in Seattle, she was responsible for overseeing his care. Faith cautiously distanced herself away from Keith's volatility. There was no telling if he'd hit her again. Her heart hammered in angst to even be in the same room with him.

"You're supposed to be stopping in to see your dad, right?" Keith asked suspiciously, glowering over at Faith.

"Yes. I'm going to stop by before going into work," Faith said, swallowing hard. Her face felt hot, and it throbbed where Keith had just slapped her. Faith wondered if another bruise would surface. There were a number of purple, black, and blue contusions on her face and arms that were still on the mend. She kept them hidden using makeup concealer and wearing long-sleeved sweaters. But the cafeteria school uniform did very little to cover up all of the marks.

"You'd better call me just as soon as you're over at the school," Keith warned.

"I *will* call you," Faith said compliant.

Standing in front of the door all set the leave, Faith noticed Keith's glare hot on her. She could tell that there was more he wanted to say. However, Faith didn't want to stick around for round two. Eager to get away, she abruptly said goodbye. "I will call you later."

"Get over here now!" Keith ordered.

"What…?" Faith asked, tremulous, heart dipping down to her feet.

"You better give me a kiss goodbye."

Literally trembling, Faith ambled over, and bridged the gap between them. With very little animation, she inched up and pressed a quick kiss to Keith's mouth.

However, Keith violently snatched her into his arms, and held on acquisitively. "You love me right?" he tested.

"Yes," Faith squeaked out, petrified.

"You better love me," Keith exacted. Slightly pulling away, his lips fused to Faith's, and he virtually ingested her.

Faith felt numb but tried to reciprocate Keith's forceful kiss- knowing that if she didn't Keith would go totally ballistic.

"Bye, baby," Keith said finally letting Faith go.

"Bye," Faith said sullenly.

She drifted over to the living room couch, grabbed her pocketbook, and stepped outside of the apartment. Not having time to wait for the elevator down the hall, Faith took the stairs. Before long, she strode outside of the building. Drifting through the complex parking lot, she found her 2009 Nissan Pathfinder truck and slipped inside.

Turning the key in the ignition, Faith stalled. She started shaking all over again, and tears pooled in her eyes. Faith quiescently rested her head on the steering wheel and wept with abandon. How had things gotten so off course in her life? She kept reviewing the choices in her life which had brought her to this dismal place.

Faith Langhorne had had so many goals, ambitions and dreams in the past. The twenty-seven-year-old school cafeteria worker had wanted to become a nurse. She'd gotten good grades in high school. After graduation, she'd taken courses over at Somerset Ridge Community College. Things were on the up and up for Faith until Danny Gaines happened on the scene. She'd met Danny at a campus party. Even if Danny *wasn't* a college student, he'd been invited by friends. He'd instantly taken a liking to Faith.

Fast forward a few months into their relationship, Faith wound up pregnant. Danny had seemed supportive when she'd first told him the news. However, it didn't take very long for him to skip town, and to disappear from her life soon after. Faith had tried to continue taking courses through the college, while pregnant, but the pressures got to be too much. So, she wound up dropping out.

At the time, she'd lived with her parents, and had their support. She had a baby boy and named him Matthew Brandon. By then, Danny was for all intents and purposes a deadbeat dad. He never got to know his son. As a single mother, Faith was left to fend for herself-determined to give her child a good life, even if she and her family didn't have very much. So, she took odd jobs to ensure Matthew had everything he needed. Faith's mom Rita was a hotel housekeeper. And, when her dad had enjoyed better health, he'd driven school buses for the town of Somerset Ridge.

Needless to say, money was scarce. So, Faith worked hard to provide for Matthew. By then, she had abandoned all career-related goals. Furthermore, her parents were both heavy smokers. So, Faith had lost her mom, and Mathew had lost his grandmother to cancer. Matthew was only four when his grandmother passed away.

Left to raise a child on her own, and losing her mom, were only the onset of tragedies which would permeate Faith's life. At the pinnacle of those misfortunes, was losing her son Matthew. He'd died in his sleep as a result of a congenital defect, unbeknownst to Faith and her family when he was born. Matthew was only eight years old. Faith was absolutely devastated. The level of grief she suffered just could not be summed up.

After Matthew's death, Faith shut down. She'd built her life around her son, even putting her goals and dreams on hold, and he was gone. In the wake of losing Matthew, she couldn't seem to find the motivation to return to college to pursue her goal. So, Faith kept working through the cafeteria of Somerset Ridge Middle School in the town of Somerset Ridge. Two years ago, the school was in process of undergoing construction. Keith Wendt was one of the men working with the construction crew.

He *seemed* nice enough when he'd asked Faith to go out with him. Faith honestly believed that her life was finally moving in the right direction after meeting Keith. However, she could not have been more wrong. Moving in with Keith after a month of dating seemed ideal. They'd found an apartment out in the area. During their courtship, Keith had exhibited jealous and possessive tendencies. Notwithstanding, he'd manhandled Faith in the heat of a few arguments.

Yet, Faith could not have foreseen becoming a statistic-a battered woman. Keith was violent and hurt her almost every day.

Faith was much too ashamed to tell her father that the man she'd moved in with was abusive. Her dad had COPD and chronic Emphysema. How on earth could she tell him that she was trapped in an abusive relationship without further compromising his health? Furthermore, Keith had been out of work for the past three months. So, all of their financial burdens had fallen onto Faith's shoulders.

Faith had seen her share of troubles, but could not have imagined her life turning out this way. Keith cheated on her and brought a variety of women over to their place while Faith was at work. Needless to say, it was adding insult to injury whenever he chided *her* for even *speaking* to another man. She was growing more resentful of the man by the day.

Something had to be done, but Faith didn't have a set plan yet. One thing she knew for sure was that she wasn't going to solve all of her problems in one morning. Neither was there any time on the schedule to cry. She had to go see about her dad, and then it was off to work. The bills weren't going to pay themselves. So, Faith pulled herself together. Wiping the tears away, she freshened up, and pulled out of the building parking lot.

***

"Morning, Ruth," Faith greeted, stepping into her dad's apartment later that morning. "How are you?" She forced a smile.

"I'm good, Faith. How are you?" Ruth Tandy said perkily. She was the Nurse sent over to care for James Langhorne on the regular.

Even if Faith kept a smile glued to her face, it still seared from where Keith had hit her. "Well, you know… Same old, same old... How's my dad?" she said, evading any more small talk with Ruth.

"He seems to be doing okay. We just finished his oxygen treatment. He was just a little bit more congested than usual," Ruth informed.

Faith frowned, concerned. "Did he say he had chest pressure?"

"Not as much as before. He's out in the living room if you want to talk to him," she prodded. "He *did* say that you'd be stopping by."

"Yeah, I promised to check in when we talked on the phone last night. Thank you for taking such good care of him."

"You're welcome, dear!" Ruth offered Faith an earnest smile.

Faith turned, hauled away from the kitchen area, and crossed over into the living room. "Dad...?" Faith called out, as she stepped through the living room entryway.

"Morning, sweetheart," James Langhorne's voice was gravelly, but a slow smile curved over his lips.

"Morning, Dad." Faith ambled over. Hunching down, she pressed a kiss to his cheek, then settled down on the armchair adjacent to his. Faith could still see the oxygen tube set up close by. "How are you feeling this morning?" Faith took his hand in hers, and brushed on it sensitively. She searched his honey eyes compassionately.

"I'm doing okay-all things considered," James said, taking exaggerated breaths. "How are *you* doing?" he questioned, trying to meter out his breathing.

"I'm okay, dad. Just came by to make sure *you're* okay before I go off to work this morning." Faith was nervous, and agitatedly stared all about the room. She did not want her father to notice the bruises on her face.

"Sugar, look at me," her father enlivened. Worry creased on his distinct features.

Faith inched her head up deliberately, and she established eye contact with her dad. "Something wrong, dad?" she asked quietly.

"That's what *I* want to know," James said, miffed. He paused for a moment, and took deep, measured breaths. "I don't like that Keith character. He isn't right for you."

Faith flinched, instinctively pulling away, after what her father said. She and Keith had been together for almost two years, and Keith had only visited her dad's place a few times. During those visits he'd been on his best behavior. "You don't like Keith?" Faith verified.

"He isn't right for you, sweetheart. You're a good girl, and you deserve someone kind," James said through labored breathing. It seemed as if his breathing was growing shallower every second.

Faith was at a loss for words. *How on earth could she explain to her dad-who could barely breathe-just how miserable she **really** was? How could she admit that Keith was an abuser who hit her on the regular?* She blinked back tears again, as she considered just what a dark turn her life had taken. "Keith's just fine, dad," she defended. "He's actually been looking for a new job." Her eyes wandered away again.

"Faith...?" James's expression was that of appeal. "Things being what they are, I don't know what's going to happen to *me*. God forbid that anything does, I need to know that my youngest, my baby, is in good hands."

Faith's eyes affixed to her dad's again. Exploring them, she shook her head in the negative. "Please, don't talk like that, dad. I can't deal with it," her voice undulated. "Nothing is going to happen to you, alright?"

"Faith, I need to know that you're going to be alright," James reasoned, puffing between every other word. "A man like Keith doesn't deserve my daughter." He coughed, but that was just the beginning. James found it difficult to stop coughing.

"Dad, please don't get upset." Faith bounded to her feet, alarmed. Reflexively, she began to stroke on her father's back in a gentle rhythm in order to alleviate the coughing.

Ruth Tandy rushed into the living room, hearing Mr. Langhorne coughing. "Is he alright?" Panic creased on the older woman's face.

"He's fine, Ruth," Faith reassured. "Dad, I've got to get going to work now." Faith turned towards her dad. "Please take it easy. I promise to give you a call later." She hunched down, and pressed a kiss to her dad's face. "Bye dad."

"Bye, sweetheart," James said, as the coughing subsided.

Faith fleetingly stood in the living room entryway watching Ruth tend to her dad. She was concerned, but she had to leave for work. After a while, she checked the time indicator on her smart phone, and realized she had just about twenty minutes to make it over to the middle school.

***

Later, Keith stared out of the apartment window, and watched Faith step out of her truck. She had just pulled into a parking space in the building lot. Knowing Faith's work schedule, Keith had just ushered the woman he'd just slept with out of their place. Faith usually got home at around half past four. Keith frowned when he saw the new tenant smile and wave at Faith. Darren Peyton took a moment to talk to her as well. He'd just moved into an apartment on the first floor. He was a good-looking, single teacher, who also worked through Somerset Middle School.

Keith's face reddened in irritation seeing Faith smile at Darren. As Keith examined their interactions, he could tell that Darren was attracted to Faith. Keith was livid, because he'd warned Faith not to spend time entertaining other men. He considered that maybe his message wasn't coming in loud and clear, because it was obvious that Faith wasn't getting it. For that very reason, he resolved to provide full and total clarification, once she stepped through the front door.

Faith made her way up to the fourth floor and stepped out of the elevator. Feet ahead, she saw Keith standing outside of the door of their apartment. His hands were crossed over his chest, and his face was cardinal. Faith's heart immediately began hammering inside her chest. Her skin tingled in fear, and her legs were wobbly as she ambled down the hallway. Shakily, she met him at the door. "Hi, Keith," she said timorously.

"Hey, Faith," Keith said through clenched teeth, forcing a smile.

"How was your day?" Faith's voice wavered. Heat rose to her pores, and her heart trounced more loudly than jungle drums.

"My day was just great!" Keith's smile cemented on his face. He opened up the apartment door, and let himself back in, with Faith following behind him. The moment Faith stepped fully inside; Keith shut the door after them.

"Did you speak to the foreman in charge of the new building construction about a job?" Faith's voice undulated, and she was frozen to her post in front of the closed apartment door.

"No, I didn't," Keith snarled, yanking Faith's arm. Crushing it in his hand, he slapped her repeatedly on the face. "Didn't I tell you not to entertain other men?" he reproached, striking her more vehemently.

Faith flinched and tried to use her free hand to protect herself, but to no avail. This time around Keith punched her to the side of her left cheek and made her see stars. She felt like a helpless rag doll, as she pleaded. "I didn't entertain *anyone*, Keith. There is no one else. Please…" She grimaced in dismay, as tears automatically rolled down her cheeks. "There isn't anyone else," she wailed like a wounded fawn. "Please, believe me."

"I saw you talking to that new teacher who lives here."

"He was just telling me about upcoming events having to do with work. The schedule's going to be changing for Thanksgiving," she miserably explicated, trying to distance herself.

"I don't want you talking to him." Keith hauled Faith cogently into his arms and crushed her to himself as a Cobra would its victim.

"Okay, okay…," Faith cowered. "I promise not to talk to him ever again. Please, just don't hit me anymore," she implored. "Please…"

Keith finally released his hold on Faith. However, he watched her like a hawk, as she drifted over to their bedroom. Faith shut the bedroom door, doing all she could not to fall apart. She was terrified and didn't know how to continue in such a humiliating relationship. There was no doubt in her mind that if she tried to leave Keith, he would find her and kill her.

But, what was she going to do? She hated the person she'd become. She wasn't weak, neither was she needy. In the past, she would have never allowed someone to treat her in that way. As she peeled off her work clothes, she kept thinking about her mom and about Matthew. Faith's face warped in mortification and shame, as she considered what they would have thought of her. It was a deplorable situation. Faith assented to the fact that she needed help but didn't know where to turn. Something would have to give. It was either she would be free from this abuse, or she would die trying to free herself from it.

***

"So, Mrs. Thompson, your husband has Diverticulitis, and he's being admitted to the hospital tonight," Max delineated. Mrs. Thompson had been at the hospital with her husband since the very early evening.

"For how long, Dr. Kane?" The woman frowned in concern.

"It all depends on how he does with the antibiotics. Pending how he does with the meds, we will be able to determine how soon he's discharged, and tentatively work out a modified diet plan," Max explained.

"So, for the next few days or so?" Mrs. Thompson asked warily.

"At the very least," Max confirmed. "Now, if you'll be so kind as to go out to the registration area and sign your husband's admission forms." Max offered Mrs. Thompson a comforting smile.

Mrs. Thompson nodded in agreement, and Max guided her over to the registration area, keeping his hand protectively on her small of her back. "I will return in a little while to go over a few more details with you." Max smiled again, turned away, and closed the registration office door, while Lila Thompson filled out her husband's forms with the Registrar.

The moment Max crossed back over into the ER, he was pounced on by the PA's and the nurses. They had a gazillion questions. However, some were more urgent than others.

"I wouldn't recommend such a high dosage. The side effects would only exacerbate his condition," Max told Dennis Billings a PA on staff that night, who needed to verify the proper dosage of medication for one his patients.

Max sat in front of his desktop inside of the nurse's station. He made necessary changes to his patient's charts and put in admitting orders for a few others.

"Dr. Kane," Ava Thorne addressed Max, as she floated over to his desk.

"Hey, Ava." Max smiled, turning to give her his undivided attention. "What can I do for you?"

Ava's heart dipped to the bottom of her feet the moment Max's chestnut eyes fastened to hers. Her heart whisked in insecurity, and her palms were sweaty. For Ava, it was always that way whenever Dr. Kane worked through the ED. She felt completely inept and silly. Max Kane was *just* a man-an extremely gorgeous one, but still *just* a man.

So, Ava willed herself to pull it together, and to put on her professional hat. She had a question regarding one of her patients being admitted that night. Clearing her throat, she asked, "About Mr. Winters…?" her voice undulated. "Should I wait for the shift change, or should I administer his second dose of Warfarin now?" Ava tried to maintain eye contact.

"I would wait until shift change," Max said plainly. "You can tell the relieving nurse just as soon as she gets here." Max offered Ava a genial smile.

"Okay-will do," Ava acquiesced. She pursed her lips to say something else, but Max abruptly stood to his feet.

"If you'll excuse me, Ava," Max said politely, hiking out of the nurse's station. His shift was all but over, but there were still so many lose ends he needed to tie up. So, Max's hands were full.

"Okay… thanks… Bye," Ava's voice trailed, seeing Max dash away. It was obvious that Max was extremely busy. Still, she felt frustrated for not showing more confidence around the illicitly handsome young doctor.

"How long have you been experiencing chest pain?" Max examined a young man who'd been rushed into the ER. Using his stethoscope, he cautiously listened to the patient's heart.

"Since this afternoon, Dr. Kane," Scott Moore admitted.

"Sounds pretty good," Max said, after checking Scott's heart. "I'm ordering an EKG, and then we can run a number of other tests," Max settled.

"Alright. Thanks, Dr. Kane," Scott said.

"You're welcome!" Max issued a reassuring smile before leaving the room.

Max then crossed back over to the nurse's station and accessed the computer. "Ava," he addressed the nurse, "would you kindly go over to room 12? Scott Moore needs a quick EKG."

Startled that Max had singled *her* out for the task, Ava smiled awkwardly at him. "Sure, Dr. Kane."

"Thank you. I really appreciate it."

"You're welcome!" Ava set out to leave right away.

Max remained at his desk for a while. He made notes in several of his patient's charts, made a few more calls to the hospital's East and West wings, and put in prescriptions through the hospital pharmacy. The ER was packed and staying busy was paramount.

***

Max made it home a little after nine p.m. Aside from his stint spent over the gym, and an hour power nap earlier on, he'd spent most of the day over at the hospital. He and the ER staff had ordered Greek Food from a nearby restaurant for dinner, but that was hours ago. In any event, even if Max was a little hungry, he was much too exhausted to raid the fridge. Changing out of his hospital clothes, he washed up for bed. Ensuing, he got down on his knees, worshiped and had devotions.

"Lord, earlier on, Psalms 147:3 came to mind. Your word says you heal those with a broken heart, and you bind up their wounds. Well, I need for you to step in and do that for me. My life hasn't been the same since I lost Kennedy. I've come to terms with the fact that she's married now. Still, falling in love with, and losing her broke my heart.

"Dalton told me that I'm *mean* to women. Lord, the last thing I want is to hurt anyone. Please, help me not to be insensitive to others just because *I've* been hurt. It isn't fair to those on the receiving end. I also pray for wisdom to run the affairs of the hospital. I love you with my whole heart, Lord! I have made egregious mistakes in the past, and I don't want to repeat them. Lead and guide me in the way you see fit."

Moments later, Max turned on the T.V. There was a lively game of basketball on. Wiped out, he quietly slipped under the covers. Before long, he was asleep with the game playing in the background. He'd been invited to a very important event. This forum would require a great deal of energy, so he needed to rest up.

CHAPTER TWO

It was Career Day over at Somerset Ridge Middle School. Max was invited as a keynote speaker. He'd promised the middle school principal a Q & A in respect to his career, and the medical field for grades 5-7. Before stepping out of his SUV, Max checked the time indicator on his phone. It was twenty after eight. That meant, he was early with a little time to spare.

Max hopped out of the automobile and stepped out into the busy parking lot. The brisk November air struck his face, as he made his way up to the school's entryway. It was an overcast day, but the sun was fighting its way through the haze. Seattle weather was something Max was still *trying* to get used to. It was such a dichotomy from Silver Water, Georgia. Max smiled as he noticed that the parking lot was almost filled to capacity. So, he concluded there were a number of guests invited to the special assembly. Needless to say, the parents had also come out in droves to support the school's career day celebration.

Walking through the school's entrance, Max was halted by the woman who worked the reception booth. "May I help you, Sir?" she asked politely.

"I'm one of the keynotes speakers for your special assembly this morning," Max informed.

"Your name?" she asked.

"Max Kane," he answered. Max watched the woman peruse a guestbook.

"Oh," she smiled openly, "*you're* Doctor Max Kane." She stepped out of the glass booth.

"Yes," Max affirmed.

The young woman handed Max a name tag, and the assembly program. "Here you go! The auditorium is all the way down the hall, across from the stairwell doors. Those doors will be to your left-hand side." Her smile brightened.

"Thank you." Max waited for the buzzer to go off, clearing him to enter the school building.

"You're welcome!" the young woman said.

Max could feel her stare hot on him, as he navigated down the hallway. However, he didn't allow the scrutiny to make him feel in any way uncomfortable. As he strode through the hallway, he perused the posters, bulletin boards and school-related paraphernalia. It was always interesting to revisit a place such as a middle school as an adult. More often than not, those places often appeared considerably smaller. Max smiled musingly as he considered that the building probably looked bigger than life to the kids.

He made an abrupt left turn in order to get to the auditorium. However, at that moment, someone else issued from the stairwell door at that corner. Max was caught off guard when he bumped into the cafeteria lady, carrying a tray of cups, napkins, paper plates and plastic utensils. Luckily, the items were still sealed, because they went flying up in the air, before he even got the chance to pull back.

"Oh no," Faith cried, seeing the items she'd just brought up from the cafeteria scattered all over the floor.

"I'm so sorry," Max said, reflexively huddling down in order to help gather up the material.

"It's okay," Faith reassured, as she genuflected, and scooped up some of the items.

"I'm such a klutz this morning," Max said, cautiously placing the items back on the tray, which the young woman had set on the floor.

"No, don't worry about it. It isn't your fault." Faith stood upright. Mesmerized, she temporarily abandoned the task at hand, and took a moment to scrutinize the stranger. She was captivated and found it impossible to look away.

"I'm truly sorry. I hope I haven't ruined breakfast for everyone," Max said ruefully, standing up to full stature. It was then that he got a good look at the young lady. "Forgive me," he entreated. Max couldn't help noticing how pretty she was, in spite of the hairnet she was mandated to wear for her job. She was about 5'7", butterscotch-colored skin, tiny waist, curvy hips and shapely.

In Max's estimation, this woman made *even* her pink and white cafeteria uniform look stylish. Although she was indeed very beautiful, Max remarked a few darkening bruises to the sides of her face, on the bridge of her nose, and even on her chin. The discolorations immediately set off an alarm.

"You didn't do anything wrong." Faith guffawed, waving a dismissive hand. She wanted to stop gaping at the man, but found it difficult to. Faith had never seen anyone so handsome! This was a Native American man about 6'1", a perfect, full head of raven hair and eyes the color of mocha. In his deep blue business suit, he looked incredible, and he smelled spicy and clean.

Moreover, he had a beautiful body, with just enough upper body brawn. Faith forced herself to stop gawking at the way his muscles rippled through his dress suit with every move he made. She was suddenly feeling flustered and completely self-conscious. The good-looking stranger stared curiously at her. It was awkward to say the least, and Faith felt out of sorts. The man looked like a movie star! She, on the other hand, could just as well had been wearing a nightgown and curlers in her hair.

"Are you alright?" Max asked, pertained. Reflexively, he arched down again in order to accrue the rest of the items that had flown a good distance away. Picking the tray from off of the floor,

Max smiled at the woman, and handed it to her. It was then that he noticed that she had marks on her arms as well. Affected, his eyes lowered compassionately into hers.

"I'm fine," Faith said, inching away from Max. "Sorry for the trouble."

"Not at all," Max told her. "I'm Doctor Max Kane. I'm one of the keynote speakers for the assembly this morning!" He extended his hand in greeting. Max inspected the young woman, concerned but utterly amazed.

Faith was surprised by how affable Doctor Max Kane seemed to be. There he was extending his hand out to her in greeting. As happy as she was to hear that he was a part of the school's special assembly, Faith was terrified that Keith would get wind of their encounter. So, in a perfunctory manner, she quickly shook his hand. The sooner she could introduce herself, the faster she could make a dash for it. "My name's Faith," she said reticently, inching away from him.

"*Faith…* That's a beautiful name!" Max complimented with an earnest smile. For reasons unknown he was worried about Faith. There was such a sad aura around her. Max perceived that she'd been hurt a great deal. It seemed that her external bruises were only a manifestation of what going on inwardly. "Well, it's nice to meet you, Faith!" Max searched her eyes. Faith kept pulling back and made him feel as if he were under quarantine, or as if she feared he might in some way hurt her.

"It's nice to meet you too, Doctor Kane," Faith said uneasily. She kept her distance, but couldn't keep her eyes off of Max Kane. He was spectacular! Faith couldn't say she'd ever seen anyone as good-looking who wasn't on television.

"So sorry for the blunder," Max emphasized, delving her big soft sienna eyes. "Would you like me to carry that stuff into the auditorium?" Max's face creased conscientiously.

"No, I'm fine. And again, no worries," Faith said hurriedly. "I hope the kids enjoy your segment in there." She nervously stared over at the auditorium doors.

"I hope so too. It was nice meeting *you*," Max told Faith, rushing ahead to get the door for her. "Ladies first." He swallowed hard, as he continued to stare at Faith. Max deemed that she was just as sad as she was beautiful.

"Thank you." Faith secured her hold on the tray and stalled in the doorway of the opened door. She hesitated and stared up into Max's gingerbread eyes. Max smiled as their eyes fastened, and at that moment, Faith felt her entire world turn upside down. The moment was transient, but she found herself slipping into the enticing pools of Max's perfect eyes. Outlining his well-formed mouth, she took a mental snapshot. However, when she recounted Keith's fury, she hastily redirected and kept it moving.

"You're welcome!" Max said kindly, watching Faith float inside of the auditorium. Carrying the tray of plastic cutlery, she walked to the left-hand side of the room. Max followed her gait, until he heard bustling activity out in the hallway. There were a number of teachers gathering out in the hallway with their classes. However, the auditorium was still virtually empty. So, Max figured he would go inside of the auditorium, and take his place in the row of seats reserved for guests.

Max ventured inside hoping that he'd see Faith again, but he doubted that he would. The young woman had disappeared behind the stage curtains. He wondered if she was alright. There was an internal alarm telling him that Faith was in trouble. Nevertheless, he perceived Faith probably didn't particularly care for him. For starters he'd knocked down all of her things. Then, she had behaved as if he were diseased, and could not get away fast enough. However, Max wasn't taking it personally. After all, they were perfect strangers. Still, it was difficult to escape the sadness Faith exuded. So, Max made a mental note to keep her in his prayers.

"Dr. Kane, is it true that you see blood and gore all the time?" one of the 6th graders asked Max during the Q & A.

Max was on the stage behind the podium. He laughed and shook his head nonsensically. "Being a doctor isn't always about blood and gore. There *are* times where that *is* a part of the job, but many of the things that take place at a hospital aren't always the way they show it on T.V. Mostly, it's about helping people who are sick and hurting. Those people are depending on you to make them better," he explained.

"My parents say that I should become a doctor, because doctors make a lot of money," another child said boldly. "Is that true, Doctor Kane?"

Max's cheeks flushed crimson, and he shook his head incredulous. "Well, the medical field is very important. It *is* possible to make money, but that should be secondary. A person shouldn't become a doctor *because* they want to make a lot of money. A person should go into medicine, because they love helping others. Being a doctor is more than just a job. It's about being responsible, and making a promise to take care of others," Max delineated.

"What's *your* favorite part about being a doctor, Doctor Kane?" one of the fifth-grade boys asked.

Max smiled reflectively, pleased by the question. Taking a moment to weight his words, he confidently spoke, "I would have to say that my *favorite* part of the job is hearing a patient or a member of their family tell me how much better they're doing, because of something I did to help them. That part *never* gets old…"

Faith stood behind the stage curtain to the side. Refreshments would soon be served, so she had to be prepared. Nonetheless, at that moment, she was awestruck, as she watched Max Kane on the podium. Faith had heard all of his responses in respect to his career, and she had hung on his every word. There were so many wonderful impressions about Max Kane. Not only was he insanely good-looking, hot and successful, but he seemed quite nice.

Faith was impressed by the way Max addressed the children, and how thoroughly he answered their questions. She assessed that he was wise and unmistakably humble. Regret overwhelmed Faith to consider that she *could have* been with someone like Max Kane, if things had gone differently in her life. If she'd fulfilled her career goals, perhaps she and Max could have been work colleagues. It warmed Faith's heart to imagine working alongside someone like Max Kane.

However, just then, Faith heard the jarring voice of her supervisor. Mr. Aubrey reminded her to go down to the cafeteria and bring up extra coffee fixings. "I'll go get them now." Faith shook herself free from the trance of watching Max Kane.

"And don't forget to bring up some more ice," he added.

"Okay."

Faith took one last long look at Dr. Kane, who was still engaged in his segment of the Q & A. "You're totally out of his league, Faith. You only attract men like Keith," she muttered, forcing herself to look away from the handsome and successful doctor.

Max was all smiles, as he made his way out of the school building in the late morning. The kids had enjoyed his segment of the Q&A during the assembly. So, Max felt a sense of gratification, and hoped that he had in some way positively impacted their lives. Max found his car and hopped in. Now, he had to get over to the hospital for a meeting with some of Fairfield's newest doctors. Faith pressed on his mind as he rolled away from the school's parking lot.

Veering away from school grounds, Max made a right turn at the light ahead. Trying to adhere to the speed limit, he drove cautiously down the street. However, about a quarter of a mile away from the school, he saw Faith. However, she wasn't alone. She was with some burly and brawny Caucasian guy, who looked to be about 6'2". Max could only define the expression on Faith's face as sheer terror. The sizable man was tugging forcefully on her arm and talking down to her. Max's heart sank to the floor. "What on earth…?" he said quietly. "Take your hands off of her, you sleaze," Max railed, perturbed.

Max figured that Faith probably had no idea what his car looked like, so he pulled over to the side of the road in order to watch their interactions. His SUV was parked behind at least three other cars. Faith and her friend were just a few feet away. Max was unsettled, and his face wrinkled in concern.

"I need a hundred dollars right now, Faith," the beefy white guy told her.

"Keith, you *know* that I don't get paid until Friday, and we have just enough money to cover our bills. We can't take a hundred dollars out of the account, because our rent is due," Faith argued with a strained and distressed expression.

"Faith, I need that money. You can borrow a hundred from your dad," the guy exacted.

"I can't take money from my dad. He's barely making ends meet with his disability and Social Security payments," Faith disputed.

The guy yanked her arm, and Max saw Faith flinch in misery. It took all of the restraint he had not to jump out of the car, and tear into the guy who was manhandling her. Max had to keep reminding himself that the matter wasn't any of his business. However, he daunted the guy to do one more hurtful thing to Faith.

"Come on, Faith. Your dad *can* spare a hundred dollars," Keith harassed, squeezing Faith's arm.

Tears flooded Faith's eyes as she surrendered. "I only have fifteen minutes left on my break," her voice broke, and tears meandered down her cheeks. "We can swing by the ATM," she acquiesced.

"Now, *that's* my girl!" The husky man took Faith up in his arms and crushed her to himself.

Max was sickened by all he'd just witnessed. He watched Faith hop into a silver Nissan Pathfinder with the offensive man. Conflicted, it was an exercise in self-control not to follow behind them. Max needed to know for sure that Faith was going to be alright. She seemed like such a nice woman, and Max was irritated because she had such a miscreant for a boyfriend. Moments later, Max pulled away from the area. Following behind the couple just wasn't an option. Max was frustrated, but there was very little he could do. Knowing that his hands were tied, bothered him all the way over to the hospital.

***

"You're such a liar, Brian. I've seen your phone, and you *have* been Direct Messaging that Kayla girl for weeks. And I heard you talking on the phone with her last night when you thought I was sleeping," Ava recriminated her boyfriend Brian. She was stressed to the max, because in less than three hours, she had to report to Fairfield Hospital for the evening shift.

"Come on, Ava. You *know* you're the only girl for me," Brian coaxed, slipping his arms about Ava's waist. "Don't be mad. I'm not interested in anyone else."

Ava kept shaking her head in total incredulity and hurt, and tears formed in her eyes. "How could you do that to me, Brian? We've been together for almost three years, and this is how you repay my loyalty? This is such a slap to the face!" Ava shoved away from Brian's arms. "I want you out of here just as soon as possible."

"What…?" Brian's face twisted in surprise and bewilderment. "No way, Ava, you can't possibly mean that."

Ava took measured steps away from Brian, glaring at him. "I'm working the evening shift over at the hospital. So, by the time I get back, I want you gone. "

"Come on, Ava," Brian cajoled. He moved in close again and tried to take her into his arms. However, Ava shoved away even more forcefully this time. "No, Brian," her eyes speared through him, "I mean it. I want you gone. I want all of your stuff out of house by the time I get back. If I find you here later, I'm calling the cops."

"Are you serious?"

"I'm as serious as a heart attack? Do I *look* like I'm kidding here?" Ava's face twisted in indignation. "We're done. I've tried so hard to be a good girlfriend to you, but you've been playing me for a fool. I'm *so* done." Ava turned away. She had a few errands to run before going into Fairfield to work 4-12.

"Ava, come on," Brian argued, looking dazed. He couldn't believe that his live-in girlfriend of three years wasn't only breaking up with him, but she was kicking him out of her place.

"I want you gone by the time I get back, Brian," Ava said again, not even bothering to look back. She opened up the front door, dismounted the steps, hopped into her car and drove away. It didn't take very long for her to break down in tears. Despite the strong façade she'd presented with Brian, she was deeply hurt by his betrayal.

It took all of the strength she had to power through mundane routines like going to the supermarket, paying bills, and stopping in to the post office. Before long, she would have to report to Fairfield with a smile pasted to her face to take care of her patients. Ava had to tuck away the sadness in order to do her job effectively. So, falling apart wasn't on the schedule.

Nevertheless, there was *one* bright spot in her day. Max Kane was working through the ER on her shift. So, above the despair of her ashes, there was a spark of hope. Something about having Max around brought about the sunshine to everyone's overcast world. Ava realized that Max probably had no idea he possessed that quality.

So, even as she cried, and mourned the breakup with her boyfriend Brian, Ava was encouraged because she would be working with Max later on. So, instead of focusing on her current troubles, Ava tried to keep her focus on how great it would be to see him. After months of pining after him, she was finally free to explore his bronze eyes, and to outline the curves of his well-formed mouth. Max's good looks were *criminal* to say the least. Fantasying about Max got Ava through the hurt and the disappointment of her failed relationship.

***

"Are you making dinner tonight?" Keith welcomed Faith the moment she got home from work. He'd spent the entire day at home, and entertained yet another one of his girlfriends, while Faith had worked through the middle school.

"Okay." Faith drifted into the living room. "I will make dinner just as soon as I change," she acquiesced. She was exhausted from her job. The special Career Day Assembly had left her absolutely drained. It was a huge success, but cafeteria staff had to work twice as hard. Not only did they have their regular detail of serving lunch to the children, but they had to serve refreshments to the teachers, the parents and the guests.

The highlight in Faith's day was meeting Doctor Max Kane. Max had never once left her mind since they'd literally bumped into each other that morning. Contemplating how handsome and nice Max seemed, was a wonderful detour from the reality of her wretched world. However, she wasn't even free to fantasize about a true *dream man*, because she'd barely gotten through the front door, and Keith was hot on her heels.

"Faith…," Keith summoned, standing at the center of the living room. His arms were cross over his chest. Mistrust and perplexity strained on his face.

Faith's heart dipped down to the floor, as she turned to address him. "What is it, Keith?" Fear and angst immediately knotted up her stomach.

"Can you come over here?" He appeared annoyed.

Faith set her pocketbook down on the edge of the sofa, and diffidently walked back over to him. "What is it?"

Roughly pulling Faith into his arms, he complained, "You never give me a kiss anymore when you come home. You used to greet me with opened arms when we first started going out. What's the matter? Don't you love me anymore?" He squeezed Faith like a child would a favorite stuffed animal.

Eyes falling away from Keith's lethal stare, Faith muttered, "Of course I still love you, Keith."

"Look at me when you say that," Keith exacted, tightening his grasp.

"I…I still love you, Keith," Faith stammered looking directly into his eyes. Faith was frightened as to where Keith was taking this little powwow. It made her shudder to think that Keith knew about the brief conversation she'd had with Doctor Kane at the school that morning. Faith flinched in dread and expected him to hit her.

"Do you still love me, Faith?" Keith coaxed, kissing her. "I love you so much! You're my heart, baby." He fondled and caressed Faith in a familiar way.

Faith quivered in trepidation. Keith was having one his rare amorous moments. She wasn't sure what repulsed her more, when he struck her, or when he tried to show affection. She was equally repulsed by both. Faith felt nauseated. Furthermore, she couldn't even bring herself to wrap her arms around Keith. There was so much resentment and bitterness there.

"Can you hold me, baby?" Keith requested, entranced. In a forceful manner, he gripped Faith's arms, and physically set them about his own waist.

"I thought you wanted me to make dinner? I was just about to change and get dinner started," Faith reminded him, utterly sickened by Keith's touch. Her face twisted in disgust and fear.

"We can hold off on dinner for a while. Right now, I need to have you close to me." Keith took Faith by the hand and guided her over to their bedroom.

It was almost 7 p.m., and Faith lay next to Keith on their bed feeling totally disconnected. Even if Keith *was* her boyfriend, she felt as if she'd just been taken advantage of. The tears rolling down her cheeks irritated the sides of her face and dripped over onto her pillow. For all intents and purposes, she was a piece of meat which had been tenderized by a butcher. There was no love lost for Keith on her end. Still, she had no idea how to get away from the nightmare. As she lay there, Faith kept thinking about Max. *How had her life veered so off course that she had evaded meeting someone as wonderful as he seemed to be?*

Faith had made her bed with a monster, and now she was trapped. Being with someone like Max was so far removed from her reality, but at least Faith could dream about him. However, hearing Keith snoring loudly behind her on the bed was a wakeup call. Faith wiped the remaining tears from off of her face. She inched away, slipped out of the bed, and wandered into the kitchen. No matter how she *felt* she *had* to make dinner. Quite soon, the bear would awaken from slumber, and she would be mauled for sure if she didn't have a hot dinner waiting on their kitchen table.

***

"Based on test results, Mr. Morrison's Troponin levels are elevated. I'm concerned that this might be problematic down the road. Elevated Troponin is present whenever someone has *had* or is close to having a heart attack. That's why he complained of chest pain and shortness of breath. We're going to be monitoring those levels for the next few days. Sometime later tonight, he will be transferred to a room up on 3East," Max detailed to Mr. Gerald Morrison's family. The sixty-eight-year-old man had come pretty close to succumbing to a heart attack.

"Will I be able to stay with my husband up on that floor?" Mabel Morrison asked Max, frowning in apprehension.

"Yes, of course-provided that it's *only* you," Max told her. He then turned to address the rest of the family, "I'm afraid that everyone else will have to wait until the morning to visit." Mr. Morrison's two sons and his daughter, along with their spouses, had been camped outside of the ER waiting area for hours.

"Thank you for everything you've done, Dr. Kane," Mabel Morrison said, grateful.

"You're welcome! I'm just glad that his symptoms did not escalate into something far worse." Max offered Mrs. Morrison and the family a comforting smile.

"We appreciate all you've done, Dr. Kane," the rest of the family took turns thanking Max.

"You're all welcome! Goodnight." Max veered away from the family and drifted back over into the ER.

Max crossed back over to his desk inside of the ER. He had some loose ends to tie up in respect to a few of his patients. So, he settled down at the desk in front of his desktop. It was almost midnight, and his shift was just about over. Taking a moment to put in medical orders, Max finalized his admissions. Moreover, he properly verbalized the results of tests run on patients earlier on. As Max worked, Faith came to mind...again. She had been on his mind since they'd met over at the middle school that morning.

The hopelessness on her face and in her eyes, as she was manhandled by a monster, still haunted Max. Max presumed that the reprobate was Faith's boyfriend. Regardless, Max wanted to find the guy who'd hurt her, and pound him into oblivion. It bothered him whenever men used brute strength to mistreat and undermine women. Women were meant to be loved, cherished and protected by men. They were not around to be victimized, taken for granted and abused.

The more Max evaluated the circumstances, the more compelled he felt to get to the bottom of what was going on with Faith. Minding his own business and steering clear of the matter, had been his initial response. All things considered; Max couldn't see himself remaining neutral. He had to at least *try* to help. Perhaps, if he hadn't been made privy to the infraction, he could have walked away. Therefore, because he was aware of the matter, he couldn't in all good conscience ignore it.

"Dr. Kane," Ava stepped into the near empty nursing station. Many of the doctors, nurses and PA's were setting out to leave, and waiting on their shift-change relief.

"Ava...?" Max looked up with a startled expression. He'd been a hundred miles away immersed in work and consumed by thoughts of Faith. "What can I do for you?" He gave Ava a friendly smile.

Max's buddy and colleague Dalton Davis was working that night. He'd just seen his last patient and had returned to the nurse's station. Dalton drifted over to his desk, but kept a curious eye on Max. Dalton knew that Ava Thorne had the hugest crush on his buddy. So, in light of the fact that they were the only three people inside of the station, he was anxious to hear what she wanted to say to Max.

Ava was hesitant to address Max, because his friend Doctor Davis had returned to the station. However, even with a hammering heart, and feeling totally flustered, she had to try. She was determined invite Max out on a date. Throwing her boyfriend out of the house earlier on, fanned the flames of courage and bravery for Ava.

"Something wrong, Ava?" Max examined the pretty dark-haired nurse with a concerned expression.

"Uh, no, not at all," Ava said with an awkward smile. She issued a spontaneous laugh as her eyes connected furtively to Max's. The fact of the matter was that *thinking* about asking Max out, and actually *fulfilling* the task, was a lot harder than she'd anticipated. Ava took a deep breath and tried to redirect. "My friend got tickets to see *A New Wave* in concert this weekend-front row seats. She's not going to be able to make it," Ava informed.

"Okay...?" Max allowed. "I think they're awesome!" His face lit up.

"Well, I was thinking maybe *you'd* like to go to the concert with me?" Ava found herself asking-skeptical she'd found the courage to verbalize the words.

"Right... You're asking *me* to go with you?" Max restated, perplexed and frowning in uncertainty. Ava inviting him out was the last thing he'd expected. For starters, he'd been under the impression that she had a boyfriend. Furthermore, it had become an unspoken rule that no one was to *ever* ask him out. Even if he'd never outwardly discouraged anyone from trying, Max acquiesced to the fact that those were the vibes he gave off.

At that moment, Dalton suddenly developed a nervous cough. He coughed out the words, *"Shutter Island."*

Understanding, Max shot him an incredulous look. He remembered their conversation a while back. Dalton had told him that he had a reputation. It seemed his work staff and colleagues referred to him as *Shutter Island*. Apparently, Max was a recluse who systematically shut down the women who were brave enough to ask him out. Max had prayed on the matter and resolved to try to do better. It had been over a year since the poignant breakup with Kennedy Proctor-Bohm. Even if the breakup had left him in pieces,

Max realized how unhealthy it was to keep holding on to the past. And so, perhaps it was time to move on.

"Wow!" Max smiled and looked into Ava's eyes. "Thank you so much for thinking of me. *New Wave* is actually one of my favorite R & B groups."

"Really...?" Ava speculated, hopeful.

"Yes. 'Can't give you my love if I can't get it back...'" Max began to croon out playfully.

"'*Can't Give you my Love*' is one of my favorites on their new album," Ava admitted. "That was actually pretty good," she told Max, smiling. Her heart pulsed more loudly than ever.

Max chuckled. "You're much too kind, Ava. That was terrible," he joked.

"No, seriously, if this gig as a doctor doesn't work out, you can totally rock that voice," she quipped, feeling a bit more at ease with Max at that point.

Max released laugher from the hollow of his throat. "Okay... If you say so... In any event, it would be *lovely* to attend the concert with you!" Max found himself agreeing.

"What? You're going with me?" Ava questioned, surprised

Just then, both Max and Ava's heads whipped across the room, because Dalton had almost fallen out of his chair.

"Everything alright over there, Dalton?" Max quipped, winking at his buddy.

"Everything's good," Dalton told him, shaking his head incredulous. He was over the top happy that Max had said yes to Ava.

"So, I will call you with the details," Ava said, redirecting towards Max.

Max gave her an approving nod. "Sure. I look forward to it."

"I can't wait," Ava said with scarlet cheeks. She couldn't believe she'd just invited Max Kane to an event, and he'd said yes. It was all she could do to keep from jumping for joy. The moment felt surreal. Since Max had transferred over to Fairfield Hospital from Grandview University Hospital out in Georgia, he'd caught the eye of practically every woman at the hospital. Max had never said yes to any of them, and so Ava felt in some way favored. "So, I guess I'll see you in a bit," she said reticently to Max.

"Okay," Max said with an amiable smile.

Ava turned and headed out of the nurse's station. Midway, she veered and offered Max an alluring smile.

Max held Ava's stare and smiled back at the pretty brunette. He shook his head in skepticism over what had just occurred. Had he *really* just agreed to go out on a date with one of the nurses on his staff? Max was skeptical. However, Dalton crossing over to his desk to have word, solidified the fact. There was a Cheshire cat grin on Dalton's face. Max shook his head comically over his friend's ridiculous humor.

"Max Kane, my man!" Dalton raved, and held his hand up for a high five.

Max couldn't help laughing. "You need help, Dalton," he joked.

"What...? Are you *really* going to leave me hanging?" Dalton's hand was still up in the air.

"I'm totally leaving you hanging," Max quipped.

"I'm really proud of you, Max. Good job!" Dalton told him.

"Well, thanks, Dalton," Max quipped. "I'm glad you approve."

"You keep this up, and they might just change your name around here."

"Words to live by…," Max heckled, looking away, and tuning into the computer monitor.

***

Max pulled into the parking lot of Somerset Ridge Middle school the next morning. He was all dressed up for work. He had a meeting with a group of doctors from neighboring hospitals to discuss the implementation of **Rapha Nine**-a breakthrough in medical computer software, which had taken the medical world by storm.

However, before going into the hospital, he decided to stop in to the school to see Faith. She had pressed on his mind all night. In fact, Max had a nightmare that her boyfriend had beaten her up so badly that she'd wound up in the ICU Unit of Fairfield Hospital. Max had never done anything like this in his entire life. It was unlike him to get involved in other people's drama. Moreover, the last thing he wanted was to make trouble for Faith. It was clear that her boyfriend was overly possessive and *dangerous*. Regardless, Max couldn't ignore the fact that Faith was in trouble.

Max floated into the school building and saw Hazel behind the glass-encased front desk.

"Dr. Kane, you're back!" Hazel announced, smiling. "To what do we owe the pleasure?"

"I'm just as surprised as you are that I'm back today, Hazel," Max said chummily. "It's nice to see you again!"

"Likewise, … What can I do for you today?" Hazel asked.

"I realize that it might be a little unorthodox to ask, but is Faith here today?" Max's face crinkled in both curiosity and uncertainty.

"Faith? You mean the lady who works downstairs in the cafeteria?" Hazel tested, bewildered.

"Yes," Max said plainly. "Is she working today?"

"I believe she is. So, you're here to see her?" Hazel asked, confused.

"Yes, if that's alright," Max affirmed.

"Sure. I can buzzer you in, and you can go down to the ground floor kitchen to see if she's available," Hazel informed.

An encouraging smile curved over Max's lips. "That would be great."

"Okay then," Hazel assented. "Come on through."

Just as Hazel had instructed, Max walked down the familiar hallway. However, he stopped short of the auditorium, and went through one of the stairwell doors. Max took the stairs leading down to the basement. Hazel had said that Faith worked through the cafeteria kitchen. After going down two flights of stairs, Max opened up the door leading out to the basement. It felt strange being there. There were echoes of every activity taking place down there, and voices carried. Moreover, the ambiance was just a little depressing, despite the fact that it was surprisingly well-lit.

There were a number of different locations, but Max followed the blue arrow which indicated the staff kitchen. Soon after, he came to a set of double doors. They were wide open. Max stood there and scanned the room for Faith. He could see some of the other workers wearing their obligatory pink and white uniforms, and prepping school lunches. Max didn't budge from his spot at the doors. However, a tall, middle-aged gentleman with hazel eyes, and sandy brown hair walked over to him.

"Is there someone you'd like to see?" the gentleman asked Max.

"First off, I apologize for interrupting your work." Max's face creased, pertained. "Is Faith around?"

"You're here to see *Faith*?" the man questioned, bewildered.

"Yes-I mean if that's alright."

Without saying a word, the man wandered away. Max hung out in the entryway struggling with feelings of uncertainty and nervousness. "What are you doing, Max? You shouldn't be here. This is none of your business," he chided himself.

Faith just got done stacking sandwiches for the first lunch period when Mr. Aubrey came to get her. "Faith, there's someone here to see you," he said plainly.

Surprised, Faith's heart immediately dipped thinking it was probably Keith. No doubt he'd come by to harass her for money to buy random and unnecessary things. She suddenly felt flustered and nauseated. Nevertheless, she offered Mr. Aubrey a genial smile. "Thank you. I shouldn't be too long."

Faith drifted over to the kitchen's entryway. However, she froze in her steps. Her eyes widened in shock, and her mouth gaped to see Max Kane standing there. Faith was convinced that he was a figment of her imagination. Surely, she'd dreamed him up, because Max hadn't left her thoughts since they'd met yesterday morning. *But what on earth was he doing down there, and what did he want?*

Timorously, Faith willed her legs to move, as she walked towards him. She was completely captivated by how amazing he looked in his designer coffee-colored dress suit. She had assessed his flawlessness the day before. However, that earth tone did something to Max's smooth, even bronze skin and his mocha eyes. His amazing body was highlighted, and his stalwart arms and chest were accentuated again.

Faith's heart raced, but this time around, it wasn't because of the terror instilled by Keith's wrath. Rather, it had *everything* to do with Doctor Kane. Yet, Faith knew that she couldn't get carried away. Keith was watching her every move, and entertaining Max Kane was potentially dangerous. Faith wasn't sure why he was there, but she knew she had to keep their interactions extremely brief.

A sense of peace and also relief permeated on the inside for Max, seeing Faith again. As she walked over to connect to him, it was difficult not to scrutinize how truly pretty she was. Her lengthy highlighted hair was pinned up underneath a hairnet. Faith's pink pants and pink and white uniform top accentuated her curves. She had a small waist, but her hips fanned out like the base of a guitar. Not staring was a real challenge, even if Max *didn't* see Faith in that way. He was just a concerned bystander who wanted to make sure she was okay. All things considered; Max couldn't say he blamed her boyfriend for being possessive-even if the man was bordering maniacal.

"Doctor Kane," Faith stood in the doorway, "what are you doing here?" she asked, unsettled. She fought back feelings of intimidation, because she was up close and personal with Max Kane again. Faith evaluated that he was even better looking than she'd originally assessed. Moreover, Max's clean musky scent, though understated, was a trip to paradise.

"Faith," Max's face wrinkled pertained, "I'm probably the last person you expected to see, but it was *really* important that I have a word with you," his voice was guttural in appeal.

"I don't understand. *Why* is it so important for you to talk to me?" Faith frowned, befuddled.

"Look, I'm just going to come right out and say it. Faith, I saw you yesterday afternoon down the road as I was leaving the school grounds. You were with someone," Max said lowering meaningfully into her honey eyes.

Faith flinched in shock but tried not to lose composure. "You saw me down the road with a friend yesterday-and what of it?" she asked brashly, with a mistrustful expression.

Max inched in closer and delved her eyes. "I saw you with that guy. He was hurting you, and you were crying," Max said directly, exploring her sweet face.

Sheer horror veiled Faith's face at that point, and she tried to counter Max's words. "He's my boyfriend, and we're fine. He wasn't hurting me." Faith's eyes veered down to the floor.

"*Yes*, he was," Max countered, leaning in even closer. He gently took Faith's hand in his, bringing her attention to some of the darkening contusions on her arm.

Faith shrank back in fear, because Max's touch had left her stunned. "Those are marks I've gotten here through the kitchen," she lied. "Keith and I are fine." Tears shone in her eyes, and she began to tremble.

"Faith, I know that it isn't any of my business, but I haven't been able to stop thinking about you since yesterday. No one has the right to touch you that way," Max argued.

Faith pushed away forcefully. She distanced herself from Max, even if for a fleeting moment she'd experienced bliss being close to him. It was suddenly cold now that his hand no longer seared sensitively on her skin. Faith realized that there was trouble brewing, and she really didn't need to borrow anymore. She had enough trouble with Keith.

Notwithstanding, if she didn't nip the matter in the bud, Max would *also* be in danger. "Look, *Dr. Kane*, I appreciate that you've taken time from your busy schedule to come here this morning. But let's get this straight. You don't *know* me, so please stay out of my life. You're certainly right about one thing," she said cheekily, as her eyes knifed through the handsome stranger's.

"And, what's that?" Max prodded, searching her face and eyes with involvement. His heart rent in half, because he vicariously felt the pain radiating from Faith. She was terrified, and he wanted to reassure her that she didn't have to be. However, the last thing he wanted was to upset her any more than she already was.

"You're right in saying this is none of your business, so please stay out of it." Faith's face warped in vexation.

"Faith, please…. I know you're probably afraid, but you don't have to be. I can help if you'll let me," Max made a dire appeal. "Please…"

Faith kept shaking her head contrarily. "I'm sorry. I've got to get back inside." Her face twisted in remorse, as her eyes fastened critically to Max's.

"Alright," Max allowed, removing a card from the inner pocket of his suit jacket, "I'm sorry to have shown up here unannounced. But, in the event you should need my help, you can reach me over at Fairfield Hospital."

"I *won't* need you," Faith muttered, with tears pooling in her eyes. "Please leave me alone, and don't come back here." Faith was terrified that Keith would find out about Max Kane's little visit. How on earth could she even begin to explain to Keith that she'd done absolutely nothing to solicit Dr. Kane's attention?

Max sighed, feeling utterly defeated. It killed him Faith was pushing him away, and there was nothing he could do. She'd asked him to leave her alone, and so he had to respect her wishes. "I'm sorry that I've upset you, Faith." Max stopped moving in closer and kept a respectable distance. He was convinced that he was creating even more drama for her. "I apologize for showing up here. I won't bother you again." He held both hands up in a ceasefire.

Faith's breathing was labored as she glared at Max. She felt like such a horrible person for blasting him when he was being so kind. It was the first time *anyone* had ever shown such concern for her wellbeing. So, the last thing she wanted was to hurt him. And yet, she had to cut all ties for fear of endangering both of their lives. There was so much she wanted to say. However, Faith remained standoffish with her arms crossed over her chest, glowering at the incredibly handsome and apparently *good-hearted* doctor.

"Alright then," Max acquiesced, gaping intuitively at Faith, "I guess I'll be going now." The desire to protect her only intensified, as Max's scrutiny virtually burned through Faith. He didn't want to leave her but realized that he had no choice in the matter. "Take care of yourself." Compunction and melancholy wrinkled his face, as he hesitantly turned away.

Max drifted out into the hallway, but turned back to look at Faith, who was still standing in the kitchen entryway. There was a rueful expression on her face. Max swerved and picked up his pace just before finding the stairs again.

Faith waited until Max disappeared. She then rushed over to the ladies' room at a corner down the hallway. Stepping into one of the stalls, she buried her face in her hands, and wept with abandon. *What on earth just happened? And what did it mean for later?* Keith would tear her to pieces for having entertained Fairfield Hospital's director and chief of staff. Faith hadn't taken Max's card, but she'd glanced over it.

As she cried, Max's mellow voice, and his clear concern for her resonated. Faith's skin still seared from his tender touch on her arm. She yearned to be close to him again, but then realized the impossibility of the circumstances. Dragging him into her mess, would only get him hurt, and wind up getting her killed. In spite of the arguments, Faith was totally captivated. How would she be able to talk herself into not wanting to see and to be around Doctor Kane? Even so, Faith justified vehemently pushing him away for his own good.

CHAPTER THREE

"'Can't give you my love if I can't get it back...'" Max and Ava sang, as Max opened up the car door for Ava. They were still snapping their fingers, and on a total high from *A New Wave's* concert which had just ended with a bang. Max secured Ava inside of his SUV. Inhaling the brisk November air, Max caught sight of the deep night sky studded with clear crystals in the panorama.

Walking around to access the driver's side, Max hopped into the vehicle still smiling. "That was actually a lot more fun than I thought it was going to be," he celebrated, looking over at Ava.

Ava was beaming. Her heart raced, and her skin felt flustered just being in such close proximity to Max. During the concert, they'd remained close, and had danced the night away. "That *was* a lot of fun," Ava commented, unable to stop gaping at Max. He looked amazing in his dark jeans and stylish black shirt and leather vest. She had only seen him a few times away from the hospital in casual clothes, and she was ready to admit that he looked even more smoking hot *dressed down*. "Who knew you could move like that, *Doctor Kane*," Ava razzed.

Max gave Ava a farcical look. "Thanks, but **Really**? You're calling me *Doctor* Kane tonight?" He shook his head nonsensically.

"Well, that *is* your name," Ava quipped, giggling.

"Whatever you say, *Nurse Ava Thorne*," Max jested.

Ava shook her head humorously and laughed.

"So, *Nurse Thorne*, you're not planning to tell hospital staff that I totally cut loose tonight, are you? They might not look at me the same. It might compromise my reputation as an authority figure." Impishness shaded Max's face.

"Right…" Ava snickered. "We wouldn't want that. Trust me when I say your secret's safe with me," she told him, totally fascinated. Ava was doing all she could to quiet her racing heart.

"I would have *liked* to be able to take you out for drinks, but I *do* have a very early morning," Max said as he pulled out onto the open road. He gave Ava a curious sidelong look.

"Oh, no worries. You'll just have to make it up to me *next* time," Ava said boldly.

"Oh, listen to *you* being all bossy." Max smiled at her, as he came to a stop light.

"Me, *bossy*, never…," Ava trifled. "I'm really glad we went out tonight, Max. I didn't think I'd ever see *this* side of you." She examined him with a playful expression on her face.

"You mean my wild and crazy side?" Max quipped.

"No, I mean your easygoing, laidback and funny side. You're always so serious at the hospital," Ava told him.

"Well, the hospital's a very *serious* place," Max said facetiously, frowning.

Ava laughed. "Yeah, I guess it *is*, but you surprised me."

"And how have I done that?" Curiosity crinkled Max's face.

"Well, ever since you started working at the hospital, you've been a little antisocial-aloof even," Ava admitted, admiring Max.

"Ouch, is *that* what I've been?" Max questioned, incredulous. "Believe me it hasn't been intentional. Honestly, my focus has been on running the hospital to the best of my ability."

"And you *are* doing an amazing job, Max, but that shouldn't be your *only* focus." Ava stared down for a moment and fiddled with her fingers. "I've often wondered if someone has broken your heart." Ava looked up and connected to Max's riveted stare.

Max was quiet for a moment. Just then, a thousand memories of being with Kennedy overwhelmed him like powerful ocean breakers. In silent contemplation, he looked over at Ava and smiled. That was an aspect of his life he wasn't quite ready to share with anyone. Perhaps, given time, he'd be able to talk about how he lost her. "Hey, you *did* say to make a left on Pine, right?" Max evaded, verifying her street address.

"Yeah, you're going to make a right at the light, and then turn into Pine Circle," she reminded. Ava felt out of sorts for prying too quickly into Max's personal life. So, for the remainder of the short ride over to her house, she tried not to create any more ripples in the water.

"I really had a great time hanging out with you tonight, Ava!" Max avowed, standing at Ava's front door. "Thank you for sharing those tickets with me!" He searched Ava's bright blue eyes.

"You're welcome, Max. Anytime…" Ava's heart thudded in her chest, and her stomach sank like shifting grains of sand on the beach. "It was so worth it to see *you* in your element."

Max chuckled. "I'm glad you got to see that I'm *not* the grumpy old doctor who lives under the bridge." He winked.

"I get that, Max." Ava smiled quietly. "*One* more round for the road?" Ava humored, suggesting they sing their favorite *A New Wave* song.

"Can't give you my love if I can't get it back… If you can't get onboard with my heart, you might as well just up and pack…," the two sang in concert, laughing up a storm.

"Wow! So, Ava, you're *really not* allowed to tell anyone on staff I spent most of the night singing that song," Max bantered.

"Oh, I don't know about that. I can only make that promise if *you* do something for me," she vamped. Ava set both hands on Max's chest just then.

"And what is that?" Max asked, intrigued.

"That you make good on your promise for us to have drinks."

"Oh, that…?" Max shook his head farcically and chuckled. "Alright then, if that's what it takes." Max winked.

"That's the *only* way to ensure my silence." Ava reached up and pressed a fond kiss to Max's cheek. "Goodnight, Max," she said softly, searching his eyes as she pulled away.

Surprised by her display, Max stared at Ava with a sense of wonder. "Goodnight, Ava," he said throatily as he watched her turn away. Ava opened up her front door and waved at Max one last time. Max gave her a pleasant smile and waved back at her.

Ava slipped into the house feeling conflicted. *Why didn't you kiss him on the lips? Why are you so intimidated, Ava? You're not the only woman over at the hospital who wants Max. If you don't step up your game, you might lose this once in a lifetime chance.* Ava sighed, feeling totally disappointed in herself for a number of reasons. At least, she was encouraged that there would be a next time. She could only hope that their second date would be better. The truth was that even if she felt a little bit more confident around Max, he still intimidated her.

Max jumped back into the SUV and headed away from Ava's. As he drove out onto the expressway headed back over to Castle Horn, he evaluated his date with Ava. Max readily acknowledged that it was something he'd needed. It had been a while since he'd gone out with anyone-let alone with a beautiful woman to a fun event. It felt nice to have had some *adult* conversation, but Max was still anxious about moving forward. Casual dating didn't scare him, but the thought of opening up his heart again did.

So, until his heart was a hundred percent, Max had to press in closer to God in prayer. Ava was a nice girl. So, Max didn't want to offer her false hopes, especially because it seemed as if she *really* liked him. Therefore, he knew that the same God who'd brought him this far, would continue to outline the path he was to take. His steps were being ordered by his Lord and Savior, and God would heal his broken heart, and bind up all of his wounds (Psalms 147:3).

Later, Max said his prayers, and quietly slipped into bed. There was a lot to consider in respect to upcoming hospital events, but Max had managed to set those thoughts aside. However, he couldn't seem to lock Faith Langhorne to a corner of his mind. In fact, Max had just prayed for her. It had been a couple of weeks since he'd taken the initiative to go over to the school.

Max wondered how she was doing. More importantly, had she found a way to escape from the grasp of her *horror show* of a boyfriend? Thanksgiving was coming up, and Max wondered if Faith had plans. There was an overwhelming desire to reach out to the young woman. In spite of his good intentions, Max realized he couldn't help anyone who didn't want to be helped.

Faith had asked him to leave her alone. So, for all intents and purposes, Max's hands were tied. Besides, the last thing he wanted was to create even more drama for Faith. Her deranged boyfriend was a ticking time bomb. Max tried to sleep but couldn't get Faith off of his mind that night. It was almost four in the morning, and he found himself staring up at the ceiling. Reminded to commit his cares to God, Max said a prayer. He released his worries to the only one strong enough to shoulder them. Soon after, he drifted off to sleep.

***

"I need to go inside to be with my dad," Faith told the EMT workers, who'd just rushed her father over to Fairfield Hospital's Emergency Room. Faith had stopped over at her dad's before going in to work that Tuesday morning-just two days shy of Thanksgiving. James Langhorne had been struggling with shortness of breath since the very early morning. Mrs. Tandy had called for the ambulance.

"I'm afraid you're going to have to stay out in the waiting room. Your dad has to see the doctor first," one of the rescue workers told Faith. "Give the medical staff a chance to examine him, then I'm sure they'll come out to you."

Faith didn't answer. She frowned in sullenness and angst. There were tears in her eyes, as she twisted nervously on her hair.

"Just give them a few minutes to help your dad, Faith. He's going to be alright," Ruth said softly resting her hands on Faith's shoulders.

"I hate when it gets cold. It makes it twice as hard for my dad to breathe," Faith groused. "The weather has *really* taken a toll on his breathing lately."

"He's going to be fine," Ruth reassured. Her face creased in concern, as she supportively rubbed on Faith's arms.

Faith turned towards Ruth and buried her face in the woman's shoulder. "Oh, God, please… Please, don't let anything happen to my dad." Faith cried and breathed spasmodically.

Ruth wrapped her arms around Faith in support. She tried to silence all of the young lady's fears, but Ruth herself *was* alarmed. James Langhorne had lived with the COPD for quite a few years, and he was at the end stages of his Emphysema. Still, the last thing Ruth wanted was to create any more angst for Faith. So, instead of verbalizing those concerns, she resolved to remain prayerful.

"He's *got* to be okay," Faith said, robotically pulling out of Ruth's arms. Tears caked on her face, as she agitatedly took to pacing the floors of the ER's waiting lounge. "God, please let my dad be okay. Please, God…" Faith kept shaking her head in the negative, as she petitioned God's help. "He's the only family that I have left out here."

"What are we looking at here?" Max asked, rushing over to the scene. A call had been dispatched from Castle Horn Emergency services that a sixty-eight-year-old COPD patient was being rushed over for severe shortness of breath and obstruction.

James Langhorne lay on a stretcher unable to get enough air to his lungs. He was surrounded by medical personnel, who were all trying to help in one way or another.

"Get oxygen treatment going stat for Mr. Langhorne," Max ordered. He took a moment to check the man's heart. Hearing whistling and wheezing in Mr. Langhorne's chest, Max concluded that there was indeed severe congestion, quite possibly due to Bronchitis. And in light of the fact that the man had Emphysema, they needed to act quickly. "You're going to be alright, Mr. Langhorne. You just need to take it easy right now. We're doing all we can to alleviate your breathing," Max placated, deeply concerned for the older man.

James was terrified, and his breathing was growing shallower. The wheeziness had become more audible with every labored breath. His butterscotch skin suffused red, because he was clearly agitated.

"You can't panic right now," Max told Mr. Langhorne. "Relax…" Max set his hand on Mr. Langhorne's chest, and stroked it in a pacifying manner, as Oxygen was administered. "That's right. Don't let yourself get all worked up. You're going to be just fine. There you go…" After a while, Max noticed a huge difference. They were succeeding in bringing the man's breathing under control.

Moments later, after Mr. Langhorne's breathing was stabilized, Max took a moment to familiarize himself with James Robert Langhorne's history. Even if the man was doing a lot better, he was by no means out of the woods. Max made a connection in respect to the *Langhorne* name. Was the man related to Faith? No sooner after making that association, Max scrolled down on the computer page, and saw that Mr. Langhorne's health care proxy was his daughter Faith.

Max shrank back when his suspicion was confirmed, and his thoughts raced. *If Faith was James's daughter, and his health care proxy, she was probably at the hospital that morning.* Max immediately rushed away from his desk and headed out of the ER. However, before he even got the chance to make it out to the waiting area, he was halted by Dalton Davis.

"Max, I thought you should know that James Langhorne's daughter is out in the waiting room with his nurse. She wants to know when she can go in to see her dad." Dalton's face creased in urgency.

Max was both surprised and perturbed by Dalton's announcement. The thought of seeing Faith again created such inner conflict. Faith had asked that he leave her alone the last time they'd seen each other. So, for him to be the doctor on staff on the morning her father was brought in, was more than just a little bit awkward. Max had misgivings about seeing Faith. All the same, he had to set them aside, so that he could address her professionally. Still, Max realized it would be challenging *not* to react or say anything, if he saw anymore bruises and contusions.

"Max…? You okay?" Dalton tested, staring warily at his friend.

"Yeah, I'm fine," Max said distracted. "Thanks for letting me know. I was just headed over to speak with Mr. Langhorne's family now," Max affirmed, trying to stay in the moment.

Dalton gave Max a faint smile and patted his arm. He then walked away, opened up the ER door with his badge, and slipped inside.

Taking a deep breath, Max strolled over to the waiting lounge. Feet away, he could see Faith. She appeared tense and restless, sitting on the edge of the armchair. It was the first time Max had seen her in regular clothes. So, he took a moment to admire how gorgeous she looked in her black jeans, rust-colored sweater and stylish black boots. Her lengthy hair was pulled up in a ponytail. She also had on a pair of brown quartz crystal loop earrings. It occurred to Max that Faith was probably headed over to work when the crisis with her father ensued.

Max smiled musingly, because she looked so pretty. He concluded just how *different* she looked when she wasn't wearing the pink and white work uniform. However, the smile on Max's face was transient as he wandered over. The closer he got to her, the more he was able to decipher the fading bruises on her face. And even if she had on the sweater, Max noticed black and blue marks on her caramel skin above her clavicle bones. He was livid.

Furthermore, he had no idea how he was going to address her father's condition, without also pointing out the obvious.

Faith's heart whisked, and her thoughts raced, as she waited to speak with the doctor. Her dad had had a terrible bout with his Emphysema earlier on. Mrs. Tandy had gone down to the hospital café for coffee. However, Faith's stomach was in knots, and she was petrified. She couldn't move an inch until she knew how her dad was doing. She had already lost her mom and her son years ago, and her father was the only family she had left in Seattle. And so, if anything happened to her dad, she would be devastated.

Just then, it dawned on her that she had not called Keith. So, he had no idea that she hadn't gone into work as planned. Faith frowned over the thought of even speaking to him. Lately, Keith had grown even more suspicious and jealous of other men. Thus, every time a man even *looked* in her direction, she became his punching bag for the day. Reflexively, she reached for her phone in order to call him but desisted. Faith was already struggling, so she didn't want to bring *his* kind of drama into the mix.

As Faith sat there fretting, she didn't realize that the doctor had come out to have word. She made a sudden turn, and saw Max Kane standing to her right-hand side.

"Faith...?" Max said throatily, not wanting to startle her.

Surprised, Faith immediately stood to her feet. Shock shaded her pretty face. "Doctor Kane?" she questioned shakily. She marveled as her eyes knifed through his. "I didn't know that you....," her voice trailed, and her face twisted in apprehension and uncertainty.

"I'm on staff this morning," Max told her. His eyes searched hers intuitively. "I was just with your father."

"How is he?" Faith asked, anxious, and eyes widened in ambiguity.

"He's doing a little better since his Oxygen treatment. We've also administered a few Bronchodilators in order to alleviate the obstruction." Max's face wrinkled in concern as he moved in on Faith. Standing in close proximity, their eyes fastened. Max wanted to ensure Faith that he was doing everything in his power to help her dad.

Faith sighed with a sense of relief. "So, he's breathing a lot better, and his airways are clear?" Worry strained her pretty face.

Max gently set his hands on her shoulders, with a pertained expression. Faith flinched, but her reaction didn't startle him in the least. Staring meaningfully into her eyes, he took time to weigh his words. "His breathing is somewhat bettered since he's gotten here. However, Faith, you should know that I'm recommending that he be admitted. We need to monitor his COPD for the next few days. There is severe inflammation of his lungs due to Bronchitis. We're going to be working on getting that under control."

Tears were in Faith's eyes. "So, he needs to be monitored for the next few days..." Sadness shaded her face as she mulled over Max's words. And yet, it was difficult to process anything, because Max's strong, beautiful hands were on her shoulders. Faith had never felt anything more wonderful. Max's touch was gentle and caring-a total contrast from the way Keith touched her. She wanted to shove away but couldn't bring herself to. In fact, the desire to be in his arms was relentless. Faith longed to be comforted, because the pain of her circumstances screamed so audibly on the inside.

"I'm afraid so," Max affirmed. "But, he's going to have the very best care in the ICU. The doctors over there are excellent...I promise." Max's eyes lowered compassionately into Faith's. Touching her and speaking to her up close was all he wanted. Max wanted to wrap his arms around her and reassure that everything was going to be alright. For reasons unknown, he wanted Faith to lean on him, because he cared. Just then, he was hit with the realization that he actually did. "He will be in good hands," he added with an encouraging smile.

Max flinched when he saw purple streaks to the sides of Faith's clavicle bones. He tried not to react just then. Rather, he kept comforting her in respect to her father's condition.

"So, can we go and see him?" Faith asked, captivated by Max's mocha eyes. They were like garnets.

"We...?" Max's face wrinkled in uncertainty.

"Yes. My dad's nurse is here. She went upstairs to the café for coffee," Faith informed. It was difficult not to be affected by her closeness to Max.

"Yes of course. You can go into the ER to see him, but just for a few minutes." Max removed his hands from touching Faith's shoulders. Thoughts of her *monster* of a boyfriend returned with a vengeance. Max didn't want to make trouble for Faith, but he wanted to keep her close. Moreover, the urge to locate her boyfriend Keith, and pulverize him was intensifying by the second.

"*I* need to see him now. I guess my dad's nurse can follow when she gets back," Faith delineated, exploring Max's eyes. Taking in his perfection left her spellbound. It didn't seem to matter if he was wearing a dress suit or a hospital lab coat, he was still the most beautiful man she'd ever laid eyes on. Faith had to keep reminding herself that even if Keith wasn't in the picture, she would still be out of Max Kane's league. Accepting such a sobering reality, she pulled back from their little moment of intimacy.

"Of *course*. You should go in now to see you dad," Max said. It dawned on him that he and Faith were reconstructing the walls they'd constructed to remain distant strangers from the outset. It bothered him, but Max had to remain professional.

Faith nodded. "Thank you, Doctor Kane," she said, as she followed behind Max in the direction of the ER.

"You're welcome, Faith." Before he used his badge to open up the ER door, Max veered back towards Faith. "I really think you should call me *Max*." He offered Faith a warm and open smile.

Faith's smile was awkward, and she guffawed. "Alright then, thank you, *Max*." Their eyes fastened.

Max shook himself free from the trance, opened up the door, and led Faith over to her dad's room inside of the ER. The room was just an opened space partitioned by curtains. "If you need anything at all, please don't hesitate to ask," Max told her just before he wandered away.

"I will. Thanks again, Max." Faith followed Max's gait all the way across the spacious ER. She saw him slip into the nurse's station and take his place behind a desk. Just before pulling back the curtain to see her dad, Faith caught Max's eye from across the room. Their eyes locked for a moment. Faith looked away, adrift and mislaid, as she pushed back the curtain. It seemed her dad was a lot less agitated than before, but he was still undergoing treatment. His eyes were closed, so she didn't want to alarm him in any way.

Faith diffidently crossed over to the armchair at her dad's bedside. Quietly, she sat down and examined him. Some wheezing and whistling could still be detected. However, Faith was grateful that her dad no longer seemed to be struggling to get enough air to his lungs.

She issued a quiet sigh as fresh tears shone in her eyes. Clasping her hands together, she thanked God that her dad appeared to be okay for the most part. Faith also thanked God that Max Kane was working through the ER that morning. Having Max there made all the difference in the world to Faith. Given their brief history, the one thing she knew for sure about Max was that he was full of compassion.

It was almost one in the afternoon, and Faith and Mrs. Tandy had been in the ER of Fairfield Hospital since the very early morning. Faith was immensely grateful that hospital staff had not asked them to leave her dad's bedside. Rather, they'd worked around them in order to tend to his medical needs. Faith perceived that Max had probably asked his staff not to give them a hard time. Occasionally, Faith stepped outside of the curtain, and had watched Max navigate his affairs through the ER. He was indeed a dynamic doctor and administrator, and she was totally impressed by his authority.

Faith also couldn't help noticing how the women who worked through the ER doted on Max. It was obvious that most of them were in love with him. How on earth could she blame them, when it seemed that she herself was beginning to succumb to the same affliction? Her heart had thrummed, and she'd gotten a sinking feeling in her stomach every time a doctor, nurse or a specialist had stepped through the curtain to see her dad.

Faith's heart had jumped, because she'd expected Max every single time. But Max had disappeared. No doubt he was extremely busy and sought after at his workplace. Faith grasped that as the hospital's Director and Chief of Staff, Max's duties weren't just limited to the Emergency Room.

"Are you hungry, Faith? It *is* after all lunchtime," Ruth brought up. She noticed that Faith had stepped outside of the room for the umpteenth time. Ruth surmised that the young lady wanted to peruse the activity, and bustle taking place inside of the ER. Mr. Langhorne was resting soundly at that point.

"I'm sorry?" Faith's face wrinkled in confusion as she turned to address Ruth.

Ruth shook her head humorously. "I asked if you were hungry, because it's lunchtime. By the way, I think your doctor friend might have gone up to the first floor. I saw him slipping into the elevator when I was looking for the ladies' room earlier on." Ruth gave Faith a curious smile.

"*What* doctor friend?" Faith asked coyly with reddened cheeks.

Ruth pursed her lip in order to answer faith. However, at that moment, someone stepped through the partition, startling them both.

"Max…?" Faith said, surprised to see him. This time around, Max held white paper bags. The bags appeared to come from a restaurant in the area.

"Hey," Max smiled, "I thought you might be a little hungry, so…" He held up the bags. "I don't know how you and Mrs. Tandy feel about meatball subs. I also didn't know if you wanted cold drinks or coffee, so I got both. I was just down the road, and I thought…" Max searched Faith's face and eyes with a pleasant expression on his face.

"Max," Faith kept shaking her head contrarily, "you really shouldn't have."

"Yes, he *should* have," Ruth countered. "Thank you so much, Doctor Kane."

"You're welcome," Max told Mrs. Tandy, only shifting his gaze over to the older woman for a second. Otherwise, he was totally absorbed by everything Faith. "Your dad will probably be resting for a while. So, feel free to use the staff lounge to have lunch. It's empty right now, and I doubt anyone will come in there to bother you." Max smiled more openly at Faith.

"I don't know what to say," Faith said delicately, with wobbly legs. That was definitely a first. Her stomach lurched, and she was literally swooning. "That was very thoughtful and sweet. Thank you, Max." Faith stared into his eyes, and smiled back in earnest.

"You're welcome, Faith! Now, if the two of you will follow me...," Max invited.

Closing the partition, Faith and Mrs. Tandy stepped outside of the hospital room, and followed behind Max.

Max opened up the staff sitting room door using his badge. He waited for Faith and Mrs. Tandy to step completely inside of the lounge. He then set the food on the table. "Ladies, enjoy..." He smiled, with his eyes affixed to Faith.

Faith couldn't contain her smile, as she watched Max tread back over to the door. "Thank you again," she said meekly.

Max smiled and nodded understandingly. "I hope to see you in a while. I will come and find you once your dad's admission orders are complete."

Faith nodded. "Okay. When does your shift end, Max?" she found herself asking.

"Seven," Max said. His gaze was intense into Faith's eyes. However, Max redirected, and hesitantly twisted the doorknob leading outside of the room.

Max made an abrupt turn after having closed the staff lounge door and bumped right into Ava. "Hey, lady, you *really* need to watch where you're going," he teased, taking a firm grasp of Ava's shoulders. She seemed just a little bit disoriented.

"I should say the same about *you, doctor*," Ava razzed. The truth was that she'd followed Max out to the staff lounge. She had notice how he'd paid *special* attention to James Langhorne's daughter. Mr. Langhorne still struggled with complications in respect to his COPD and end stage Emphysema.

Ava had inspected Mr. Langhorne's daughter and Max together all day. The two had exchanged pining looks in every corner of the ER. Ava wasn't sure what it was all about, but she wasn't having it. She had waited for a while to be able to connect to Max-suffering in a loveless relationship with her ex-boyfriend Brian. So, she was ready to go to war over Max Kane.

"You *are* still coming over to my place when your shift ends on Thanksgiving right?" Ava reminded Max, dreamily sizing him up. She yearned to touch him, but had to pull back, because they were at work.

"I said I'd swing by, so *yes*, our plans remain intact." He gave Ava a warm smile. "And thanks again for inviting me over. You must be a glutton for punishment."

"Why would you say that?" Ava shook her head comically.

"You want to hang out with *me* again." Max winked at her.

Ava gave Max an alluring smile. "I absolutely *adore* punishment." She winked back.

"Oh, I told Mr. Langhorne's daughter and his nurse that they could have lunch in the staff lounge," Max told Ava-realizing that she was headed in there.

"No worries," Ava said pleasantly. "I was only going to my locker. So, I won't bother them."

"Thanks, Ava."

"Sure… Where are *you* headed now?"

"To boardroom three for a workshop," Max gladly told her.

"So, I *will* see you later. Oh, by the way, I will text you to let you know what you should bring over for dinner," Ava told Max, watching him walk away.

"Absolutely…" Max veered back towards Ava, smiling.

Ava followed his gait until he disappeared. She then used her badge to access the lounge. Ava wanted to get a good look at the woman who had kept Max captivated all day. She slipped inside of the breakroom with the widest smile painted on her face.

Faith was startled when the nurse came through the lounge door. Her heart dipped to the floor, because she felt uncomfortable being there. She deemed how awkward it would be explaining to staff why she and Mrs. Tandy were having lunch in *their* lounge.

"Oh, don't mind me," Ava said, breezing in, "Doctor Kane already told me not to disturb the two of you." The smile on Ava's face had fossilized at that point.

"That's alright. It *is* after all *your* lounge, so Mrs. Tandy and I will just get right out of your way," Faith told the nurse. She couldn't help thinking how pretty the woman was. She was about 5'6", slender, pretty dark hair and bright blue eyes. Faith presumed that this was the type of woman Max could go for. Nevertheless, the notion saddened Faith a great deal.

"No, not at all, please take your time," Ava insisted, and waved her hand dismissively. She got the chance to examine the young woman. She assessed that this was a very pretty African American woman. Ava had seen the woman inside of the ER, and thought she had a nice shape. With the exception of a few blotches, her skin was flawless. Furthermore, she had long hair, highlighted with layers of brown that complimented her honey eyes.

"Thank you," Faith said perfunctorily.

"Oh, you're quite welcome," Ava returned. "I'm Nurse Thorne by the way," she introduced herself. "If you or Mrs. Tandy should need help with anything at all, please don't hesitate."

"My name's Faith," Faith told her, feeling a little bit more at ease. She evaluated that Nurse Thorne was pretty nice.

"Oh, *Faith*…? That's a very pretty name," Ava uplifted. Even talking to Faith created internal conflict for Ava. The woman was gorgeous, a lot pretty than she'd originally given her credit for. Ava resolved to do everything in her power to limit Faith's interactions with Max.

"Thank you-and thanks for being so nice to my dad," Faith added.

"It's part of the job detail. Besides, your dad is lovely!" Ava enlivened. She hated being phony. However, there were times where a woman had to fight for what she believes to be hers. And Ava wanted Max to be solely hers. So, if she *had* to be a little catty in the process, it was a means to an end.

"I think so," Faith said smiling.

"Again, if the two of you should need anything at all," Ava extended, as she floated over to another door towards the back end of the staff lounge.

"Absolutely." Faith smiled graciously. "And thanks again."
She watched Nurse Thorne walk through a door down the hall, and
all the way in the back of the room.

"Well, *she* seems nice." Faith turned towards Ruth.

"If you say so," Ruth said with a skeptical expression on her
face.

Ava walked into the ER staff's locker room stewing in
jealousy. Faith Langhorne was beautiful, but Ava evaluated that the
woman just wasn't good enough for Max. So, Ava made up her
mind to pull out all of the stops. At the end of the day, she *had* to be
the one on Max's arm come hell or high water.

Faith stepped out of the ER and drifted over to the waiting area
in order to call Keith. If she'd worked that day, she would have
almost been home. Faith knew that if she didn't call Keith, there
would be a heap of trouble. She dreaded telling Keith about her dad,
because he was likely to come storming into the hospital to create
unnecessary drama. Faith could only hope that she would be able to
talk him into *not* coming out there.

She had enjoyed interacting with Max all day. The back and
forth between them had encouraged her a great deal. Even if Max
had a gazillion other responsibilities and had been pulled away a
number of times from the ER, Faith loved the moments where he'd
popped up out of nowhere. Thus, she wasn't in a hurry to have Keith
burst the bubble of her pretend world with Max. No doubt her
riotous boyfriend would be waiting in the wings with his evil *pin*.

There was such a sense of conflict there, but Faith understood the reality of the matter. If she didn't autodial Keith's phone in a matter of minutes, she herself might be brought back to Fairfield Hospital on a gurney. So, she sighed, looked heavenward, and asked God for strength before pressing the talk icon on the keypad of her smart phone. Faith's heart whipped in trepidation as the phone rang. She waited for an answer, but oddly enough, it went straight to voicemail.

Undoubtedly, Keith was still entertaining one of his bevy of girlfriends over at their place. Doing the bare minimal, Faith decided to leave a brief message. "Hey, Keith it's me. I'm with my dad over at the hospital. He had some breathing issues earlier on, so Mrs. Tandy and I brought him over to Fairfield. Don't worry he's doing a lot better now. I'll be here with him until about nine tonight. That's when visiting hours are over. I'm sorry I didn't tell you earlier on. Things have been so crazy over here. So, I will call you later," Faith detailed, and quickly hung up the phone.

She was relieved that she had not gotten to talk to Keith personally. In Faith's heart and mind, she'd bought herself a little time. Keith would probably call her back when his hands were *less full*. Faith ambled through the ER waiting area. She turned towards the entryway leading back inside of the ER, when Max stepped out through the doors. Winded and totally captivated, Faith's heart took to hammering in her chest, they'd practically bumped into each other. "Max," she acclaimed, surprised as her eyes locked urgently to his.

"Just the person I was looking for." Max stood only inches away and explored Faith's soft amber eyes. Sidetracked, he found himself utterly fascinated, as he drank in every inch of Faith.

"You were looking for *me*?" Faith marveled. Her heart thrashed so loudly she swore that everyone inside of the ER and beyond it could hear it.

"Yes." Max shook off the trance and tried to remain focused. "Mrs. Tandy said that I could find you out here. Are you alright, Faith?" His face wrinkled in concern as he gazed meaningfully into her eyes.

"I'm okay," Faith said softly, mislaid. Never in her entire life had she experienced this kind of attraction to anyone. Faith knew she was being weird, because she was ogling. For all intents and purposes, Max was a paranormal manifestation which had just materialized out of thin air. That was to the extent to which she was awestruck. "I just had to make a phone call," she said adrift, rapt by Max's perfect face.

"Well, I just wanted to let you know that your dad is going to be transferred over to the ICU in just a little while." Max gave Faith an open smile. "Maybe within the hour," he added.

"Oh, they found a room for my dad!"

"Yes, they have." Max chuckled.

"That's great news!" Faith exclaimed. Her face twisted in sentimentality and appreciation. "I just wanted to thank you for everything you've done for us today," her voice was velvet, as she gazed dotingly at him.

Max issued an empathetic smile. "It was my pleasure. I'm glad that I was here today!"

"So am I. It made things so much easier for us." Faith looked away, feeling self-conscious. However, she built up the nerve to look into Max's eyes again. "There's something very comforting about having you around."

Max beamed delightfully over Faith's comment. He was suddenly a lightbulb, and Faith had just turned on the switch. "Thank you so much for saying that. It means a lot." Concern suddenly changed Max's smile, as he examined the discolorations outlining Faith's clavicle bones. "How have *you* been?" he suddenly brought up.

"Oh, *me*…?" Faith set her right hand nervously on her neck. She had noticed Max frowning, as he'd skimmed over some of the contusions on her skin. Faith was surprised that Max wanted to know how she was doing. She had put him on blasts and had been unkind the last time they'd seen each other over at the middle school. "I've been okay." Faith's head slumped, and she looked down with a sense of shame.

"Faith," Max said, cupping her chin, "look at me."

Faith flinched, stunned by Max's tender touch. It was bizarre that the way in which Max touched her made her wince, while she no longer shrank back over Keith's savagery. "I've been okay," Faith said unconvincingly, eyes shimmering with tears.

"I'm sorry that I just showed up at the school that morning. I was just concerned for you. You've got to know that was my *only* motivation," Max explained, pulling back from touching Faith. It occurred to Max that he enjoyed connecting to her in that way far more than he should.

Faith nodded in compliance. "I realize that now. I'm sorry that I was so rude to you."

"You weren't rude, Faith. Showing up at your workplace out of the blue was *weird*. I own that." Max searched her eyes intuitively. "I was concerned about you then…, and I *still* am." Max held his hands up in a disarming manner. "You don't have to say anything, Faith, and you certainly don't have to agree with what I'm about to say. But will you *at least* listen?" Max's face strained in concern and appeal.

Faith quiescently nodded in agreement, mesmerized and completely at Max's mercy. She couldn't fight him even if she wanted to.

"I want you to know that if you should ever need my help-for any reason at all-please don't hesitate to ask. I know that there are things you can't tell me right now, and that you might even be too scared to confide. Still, Faith, I am begging you not to remain in a situation where you're endangering your life. The thought of *anyone* hurting you that way kills me," he admitted, shrinking back from his own candor and transparency.

Max paused for a moment and weighed his words. The magnitude of his disclosure was highlighted by the look on Faith's face. She seemed completely taken aback, flabbergasted even.

Faith gasped in shock over Max's words. *Had she just heard correctly?* He'd said that the thought of anyone hurting her killed him. Stirred beyond all comprehension, she remained speechless, and examined him in utter amazement. *Was it even possible for someone like Max to care in the way that he had come to?* "Max…," Faith began to say with tears brimming over in her eyes.

"I'm sorry. I guess I'm overstepping again," Max assented, staring down for a moment. However, his eyes reconnected urgently to Faith's again. "Please, don't stay in that relationship." Tears glimmered in his eyes parallel to Faith's. "If he's hurting you on a regular basis-and I would bet my life that he still is-you need to walk away from that abusive situation."

Faith's face twisted in remorse and despair. "I don't know how to leave, Max. I wouldn't even know the steps to take to be free of him." Tears rolled down her cheeks.

"Oh, sweetheart," Max's voice broke, as he drew Faith into his arms, and hugged her in comfort. "It's alright. It's alright, I promise. You don't have to face any of it alone." Max pulled back in order to look into Faith's tear-filled eyes. "I'd like to help-that is *if* you'll let me." His arms still encircled Faith's waist. Something about having her close felt familiar. It was almost as if he was coming home from a faraway place.

Faith kept shaking her head contrarily, trembling. "Max, I can't. I can't get away from Keith. He would find me and kill me. He will kill *you* if you get involved," she said, traumatized. Despite the misery of her circumstances, the moment felt totally surreal to Faith. Even if it was short-lived, she would always remember how it felt to be in heaven. Being in Max's arms was a safe haven, and sheer paradise.

Max gently cradled Faith's face in his hands, and tenderly brushed her tears away. "No one is going to kill *you* or me. I can promise you this much. Please, let me help, Faith. Don't go home tonight," he implored.

"I only have one other option. I could go over to my dad's, but Keith would find me there," Faith argued.

Max kept shaking his head in the negative. "You don't have to go back to your dad's. Just give me a chance to figure something out for tonight. Then, we can work on a temporary solution, huh?" He cupped her chin again. Everything inside of Max screamed to protect Faith. He was ready to obliterate anyone who tried to hurt her.

"I can't, Max. Please, give *me* the chance to figure it out. I couldn't just suddenly up and leave." Faith subtly inched away from the bliss of being close to Max. For a moment she had seen an *out* of her life of sorrow and pain. Max had given her a vision of a whole new world, but now she had to face her reality. There was no way Keith was ever going to let her go.

"So, you're going back to *him* tonight?" Max's face turned florid in utter frustration. "Faith, the longer you stay in that situation the more you're at risk." Tears now shone in Max's eyes. "I don't want anything to happen to you," his voice was guttural.

"Oh, Max…," Faith said, incredulous. She kept shaking her head in total disbelief. "How on earth can you be this wonderful?" Fresh tears meandered down her cheeks. "I have read about people like you in storybooks, but those were fairytales." Faith reached up, and set her hand to the side of Max's face. "But *you're* real."

"Yes, Faith, I'm real. I'm just a *real* man who's worried about you. I will do my best to come up with a solution in the next couple of days. I promise that we're going to get you to a safe place where *Keith* won't be able to find you," Max avowed.

Faith shrank back again, stunned beyond all comprehension. "You would do that for *me*?" She kept shaking her head in utter skepticism.

"I would do whatever it takes to make sure you're safe," Max admitted, surprised by the weight of his disclosure. "Please, let me help you, Faith."

Faith grimaced with a sense of despair and cried. She could no longer hold back the emotion. Before long, she found herself anchored by Max's caring arms again. Only, this time around, she buried her face in his chest, and allowed herself to weep.

"It's alright, sweetheart. I know you're scared. It probably won't be easy, but it isn't impossible." Max rubbed on Faith's back in mitigation and tried to silence her fears. He vicariously felt the pain she grappled with, and he longed to take it all away. "It's alright, honey." Tears escaped the corners of Max's eyes as well.

"Max, please give *me* the chance to work it out," Faith muttered, pulling away. However, her head still rested on Max's chest, as her sad eyes inched up to connect to his. "Will you give me a chance to work it out? I have to figure out a way to leave my situation peacefully," her voice wavered.

Max ceded. "Alright, but I will be keeping close tabs on you for the next couple of days. Faith, it can *only* be a couple of days, alright?" Max's eyes lowered urgently into hers. "If he even *touches* you too forcefully *I* need to know about it," he outlined. "Is that fair enough?"

"Yes," Faith found herself agreeing. She couldn't believe any of it was happening. How had she come out to Fairfield for her dad's illness, only to wind up in Max Kane's arms? Notwithstanding, Max was issuing an ultimatum, demanding that she leave Keith. Not only did the experience feel dreamlike, but it was totally out of left field. "I will slowly start to pack up my things. Keith is usually asleep in the morning when I'm getting ready for work. So, I can start carrying things out to my car."

Max nodded. "Good plan. And, I promise you will have a safe place to stay within the next couple days." He delved her eyes meaningfully.

"What about my work over at the school?" Faith asked, panicked.

"I'm not sure how attached you are to that job, Faith, but we can find something else. We can even work on getting your dad and Mrs. Tandy away from the town of Somerset Ridge," he contrived.

Faith examined Max in awe. "Why would you do all of that?" She was both incredulous and bewildered.

Max smiled, collected her face in his hands and pressed a kiss to her forehead. "Faith,"

Max opposed in a nonsensical manner, "Why *wouldn't* I? I don't want you to worry about anything. Just promise me that you *will* take me up on my offer," he settled.

Faith wrapped her arms around Max and squeezed him devotedly. She had to make sure he wasn't an illusion that would quickly fade away. All she'd known was heartache and pain, so it was difficult to interpret what Max's role was or would be. What Faith was certain of was that she would do her best to hang on to this dream for as long as she could. "How can I ever thank you?" Faith breathed into his brawny chest.

"You can thank me by letting me walk you through this." Max tenderly brushed back wisps of her hair.

"Alright," Faith agreed, too overcome by gratitude and appreciation to say no.

Max cradled her face in his hands. "Thank you. You have no idea how worried I've been," his voice broke.

Overwhelmed, Faith just gaped at him, mystified. She shook her head befuddled and offered a sentimental smile.

Max quietly smiled back and stared yearningly into Faith's eyes.

Overwhelmed, Faith threw her arms around Max again, and squeezed him with a sense of gratitude. Reflexively, Max set his arms about her waist, and crushed her endearingly to himself.

"Dr. Kane, they're ready to move Mr. Langhorne over to the ICU...," Ava's voice trailed, because she'd stumbled upon Max holding Faith Langhorne in his arms. Ava's heart immediately fell in hurt and disappointment.

Max gently released his hold from about Faith's waist. He then directed towards Ava. "I should be right in," he told her.

Ava forced a smile. "Sure." She then turned away and reentered the Emergency Room.

Even if commonsense told Ava that Max was probably comforting Faith over her father's condition, all she saw was *green* and *red*. There was the green-eyed monster of jealousy, and the red of fury. Ava refused to roll over and play dead while this *Faith girl* stole Max away. She had worked too hard in the past six months. It was totally unfair.

"So, let's go back inside." Max turned towards Faith. "They're about to move him over to the unit."

"Alright," Faith said, following Max back into the ER. The two drifted over to James Langhorne's room. Faith stood back, and watched Max oversee her father's transfer to the ICU. A few transporters from the ICU Unit had come to get James Langhorne. They moved him from the ER bed to a gurney to facilitate the transfer. Faith and Mrs. Tandy gathered up their things from the small ER room.

"I really don't want to stay overnight at the hospital, sweetheart," James argued as the transporters began rolling him away.

"I know, dad, but it's necessary. The doctors want to make sure that you don't have any more breathing issues and obstructions to your lungs," Faith upheld. She had to follow the transporters out of the ER and leave Max for a moment. Faith hoped that he would come out to the ICU to find her. She also prayed that he wouldn't finish out his shift without saying goodnight.

"I have Mr. Langhorne's jacket and his hat with me," Mrs. Tandy said, trailing behind Faith and the nurses rolling her father's stretcher through the hospital's hallway.

"Alright, thanks, Ruth," Faith turned to tell her. "I've got all of the rest of his things in my pocketbook."

"Good," Ruth told her as they tried to keep up.

CHAPTER FOUR

It was forty minutes after 7 p.m. when Max finally got the chance to take a walk over to the ICU. Since the life-altering conversation he'd had earlier on with Faith, they had not seen each other. Max had been needed on another wing of the hospital. He'd just taken off his lab coat and was just about ready to leave for the night. However, he didn't want to leave without first looking in on Faith and her dad.

Max knew that James Langhorne had been transferred to ICU Room 201. So, Max found the room. Not wanting to startle Mr. Langhorne or Faith, he knocked gently on the wooden door.

"Come in…" Max heard through the door.

"Hey there," he said, popping his head through the ajar door, and offering Faith a winning smile.

"Max!" Faith beamed, immediately standing to her feet, and rushing over to him.

"How is he?" Max stepped diffidently into the ICU room. Looking over at Mr. Langhorne, Max realized the man was fast asleep. Out of habit, he scanned over the vitals on the man's monitor.

"He's exhausted," Faith said. She was awestruck seeing Max in Jeans, and a rust-colored cardigan, with a black T-shirt underneath. He looked positively dreamy. "It's been a really long day for him." Faith looked over at her dad.

"It certainly has," Max agreed, smiling. "I just came by to say goodnight."

"I thought you might have left because it's almost eight," Faith said in earnest. Max had told her that his shift would end at seven.

"There's never really a set time for me to leave this place. It feels as if I live here sometimes," Max joked. "Besides, *me* leave without saying goodnight?" He smiled into Faith's eyes and shook his head contrarily. "I would never do that."

"That's good to know. I'm glad you stopped in before leaving." Faith's face turned scarlet. "Thanks again for everything." She opened up her arms inviting Max in for a hug. *What on earth was coming over her? She had never done anything so reckless. However, with Max, there were several **firsts** on that day alone.*

"You're so welcome!" Max pulled Faith affectionately into his arms and squeezed her devotedly. "Are you going to be alright?" he asked pulling back to look into her eyes.

Faith nodded. "Yes, I believe that I will be. I will start packing up my things just as soon as I can."

"Promise…?" Max searched her face and eyes, pertained, with his arms still encircling her waist.

"I promise," Faith said softly, basking in the joy of being in Max's stalwart arms again.

"Can you tell me just what the hell is going on in here?" Keith's roar preceded him as he burst into the hospital room. He'd seen Faith with another man through the glass slot at the top of the wooden door. "Hey, get your hands off of my woman," he bellowed at Max.

Max and Faith were overcome by shock. Both were unsettled by Keith's sudden intrusion. Keith immediately began his affront. Tearing into Max, he threw punches everywhere. "Who do you think you are?" Keith railed, and shoved into Max. For a moment, he had Max pinned to the left-hand side of the door, and his right forearm at Max's throat.

"Keith, stop it. Get your hands off of him. What are you doing? This is the ICU Unit. You can't behave this way... Doctor Kane is the hospital director and chief of staff. He was just concerned about my dad. Please, stop it, Keith. Take your hands off him," Faith pleaded with tears in her eyes. "Keith, please..."

"You're the doctor, director *and* chief of staff for this hospital? What right do you have to *comfort* my girl with your hands all over her?" Keith criticized, and tried to hit Max on the face again.

Incensed, Max shoved out of that corner. Blocking Keith's unruly strikes, he tore into him. Undaunted, Max pushed back, and hit Keith momentously on the face. "So, you're looking for a fight? You *want* to fight me? Well, let me tell you something. I might be a doctor, but don't get it twisted. I can just as easily land you a spot in here," Max remonstrated, with clenched fists and a cardinal face.

"Max, don't. Please, don't," Faith made a dire appeal. Her heart whisked in dread. Keith wasn't going to stop, and she didn't want Max getting hurt.

Enraged, Keith lunged into Max, swinging everywhere, but aiming mostly for his face.

Max gripped Keith's arms, and literally threw him across the room. Keith went flying into a corner to the side of the hospital room door.

"Had enough yet?" Max walked over ominously-fists clenched to his sides, his face scarlet in paroxysm, and his eyes darting out venom. "Faith," he then turned toward Faith, "please go out to the nurse's station, and ask that they send security up here right away," Max requested, still glowering at Keith. Despite the fact that he was peeved, Max was shocked that he'd retaliated.

"What kind of doctor are you, anyway?" Keith asked acrimoniously, as he staggered to get to his feet. "You're going to be sorry you went there with me today." His face gnarled in bitterness and rage.

"The way I see it, you're *already* sorry, and you need to leave. This is *my* hospital, and no one comes here showing such blatant disrespect," Max recriminated, standing his ground.

"I don't care about being in your stupid hospital. Thank God this isn't the only hospital in Seattle. You just need to keep your hands off of Faith. She's mine."

"Well, you're going to have to leave this hospital, or security will escort you out," Max disputed, critically.

"Don't think that I didn't notice the way you were *holding* and *talking* to my girl. You need to get those ideas out of your head, because she belongs to me."

"And I see that you're *so* good to her," Max indicted, fearlessly closing in on Keith.

Keith flinched in shock. "What the hell are you talking about?" His expression was surly.

"I'm talking about the marks, the bruises and contusions all over her skin." Tears of rage pricked Max's eyes to even bring it up. "I *know* you hurt her regularly, but that's going to stop," Max threatened. "If you need to hit someone, why don't you try hitting *me* instead?"

"I don't know what you're talking about," Keith said coyly, looking away from Max's glare. "I love Faith."

"You love her so much that you can't keep your hands off of her. You keep hurting her. I've got your number, *Keith*, and it's up. Not only are you leaving here tonight, but you're going to stop putting your hands on Faith," Max delineated.

"Faith is *my* woman, and she's going to stay with me. The only way I will lose her is over my dead body," Keith challenged, dauntingly moving closer to Max.

"I hope and pray that it doesn't come to that, but I'm game if you are. Keep your hands off of her," Max emphasized.

"What are *you* going to do?" Keith scowled, inching in even closer.

Max was about to answer, but hospital security stormed into the room just then. Faith stood outside of the ICU room, surrounded by hospital staff and onlookers.

"Dr. Kane are you alright?" security asked. Four of Fairfield's top security personnel infiltrated the room. By then, most of the people on the unit had wandered over to the area to see what the upheaval was all about.

"I'm fine." Max was sidetracked. "I want this man removed from hospital grounds immediately. He is not to return here again," Max ordered.

Keith glared at Max, as security surrounded him. When they set their hands on him, he shoved away in hostility. "Get your hands off me." Keith dropped a string of expletives, as he stepped outside of the ICU room. Security hemmed him in, as sharks would surround a blood-soaked body found in the middle of the ocean.

"*You're* coming with me," Keith said, grabbing hold on Faith's arm.

Max shrank back in anger seeing Keith's forceful grip on Faith's arm. He wanted to react, but desisted, as his heart hammered, and veins pulsed at his temples. Max realized he needed to get his feelings in check. He'd already lost his cool once that night, and he didn't want to continue going down that slippery slope.

"Keith, I have to stay with my dad," Faith argued, with a face warped in misery and fear.

"No, Faith. You *need* to come home. You've been with your dad all day. He's been admitted, and he's asleep. What more can you do for him?" Keith disputed as security closed in on him.

Faith shook her head contrarily, with tears in her eyes. "I need to stay here for a little while longer."

Keith gave Faith a knowing and daunting look. "You have to come home *sometime*," he reminded her. "I'll be up waiting for you." Artfulness shaded his scowled face.

Faith turned and looked away. Her eyes connected to Max's, who was still inside of the room watching her interactions with Keith.

"Okay, suit yourself, Faith," Keith said, as security led him away from the unit.

The moment Keith disappeared; Faith rushed back inside of the room into Max's waiting arms.

"Oh, honey, I'm so sorry." Max folded her protectively. "I'm so sorry." He cradled her face in his hands.

"Max, *I'm* the one who's sorry. He came in here and attacked you." She cried. "He hurt you."

Max shook his head contrarily. "No, honey, he didn't hurt me. I'm fine," he reassured, delving her eyes. "But I know that *you* won't be if you go home to him tonight."

"Max, if I *don't* go home, it will be far worse. He's not going to give up," Faith groused.

"And neither am I. I'm *not* giving up until you're safe." Max gently brushed tears away from Faith's eyes. "Faith come home with me tonight," he propositioned. "He will hurt you for sure if you go back out to Somerset Ridge." Max frowned in concern and urgency.

Faith flinched in shock. "Max, you want *me* to come home with you? I don't want to create any more trouble. You've *already* gotten into trouble tonight because of me." Remorse veiled her face.

"Faith, what kind of man would I be if I let you go back out to Somerset Ridge tonight?" Tears shone in Max's eyes. "Keith is outraged, and he will definitely take it out on you. I couldn't…" Max shook his head in the negative.

"What…?" Faith questioned, overwhelmed.

"I can't bear the thought of him hurting you anymore. Please, come home with me tonight. We can figure things out in the morning. We can find a place for you…for your dad," Max petitioned.

Faith surrendered to a slow nod. "Okay… I don't have any of my things, but okay."

Max smiled genuinely for the first time since having gotten into the fist-fight. He nodded quiescently, as he explored Faith's sad eyes. "We can get anything you need in the morning." He cradled her face in his right hand and stared meaningfully into her eyes. "When you're ready, the police can escort us over to your place out in Somerset to get your belongings. But, for now, the goal is to keep you safe, alright?"

Faith was trembling but wasn't sure why. There had been so much sadness and despair in her life, that she couldn't wrap her head around Max's kindness. She kept waiting for the other shoe to drop. She had learned that if something or someone seemed to be too good to be true, they probably were. Still, she found herself surrendering to Max's arms. There was no place else she *could* go. "Will you go with me in the morning?" Faith breathed, pressed up to his chest.

"Of course, I will. I wouldn't let you go out there alone." Max crushed Faith in his arms. Feeling so protective of her was totally unexpected. And yet, there he was, ready to fight wolves for her. Max challenged anyone to lay one malicious finger on her.

"Alright," Faith acceded, too overcome by pain and exhaustion to argue.

Max hung out on the unit until visiting hours were officially over. He'd remained by Faith's side until she'd pressed a goodnight kiss to her father's forehead. He was amazed that Mr. Langhorne had remained asleep during all of the commotion which had taken place earlier on. It was about half past nine when Max walked Faith out to his SUV. Opening up the door, he secured her inside. There was such a tremendous sense of satisfaction that she was safe with him.

Soon after, Max took his place behind the wheel. Seeing the fretful expression on Faith's face, Max gave her a reassuring smile. "Hey, are you okay?" He examined her with a sense of involvement.

Faith forced a smile. "I think so."

"You're going to be just fine. I promise." Max took her hand in his and stroked it caringly. "You don't have to be scared, Faith. I won't let him hurt you anymore," Max emphasized, sensitively searching her eyes.

"Somehow when *you* say it, I believe it. How can I thank you enough for all you've done?" Faith asked, setting her free hand on Max's in reciprocation.

"You can thank me by allowing me to help you through this, huh?" he enlivened.

"Why would you do this for a complete stranger?" Faith questioned, taking in just how truly perfect Max was. The dim lights out in the lot made him look positively beatific.

Max chuckled and shook his head contrarily. "Faith, I know how it feels to be totally alone. There have been times where it's felt as if no one's in my corner. And it's something I wouldn't wish on my worst enemy, much less would I wish it on someone I'd like to think of as a *friend*." His eyes smiled into hers.

Setting aside her insecurities, Faith offered Max an encouraging smile. "A *friend*, huh?" she quizzed.

"A *wonderful* new friend," Max emphasized. Bringing Faith's hand up to his lips, he planted a kiss to it.

Faith was totally taken aback by Max's kindness and warmth. She had never met anyone like him. And yet, in spite of his affectionate nature, she perceived that he wasn't trying to put the moves on her, neither was he romantically inclined. He was just a wonderful man! Still, as kind and compassionate as Max was, Faith's heart whisked in angst over the circumstances.

As they drove away from the hospital, she kept expecting Keith to pounce at any given turn. There was a sinking feeling in the pit of her chest that she wasn't truly safe. Even so, for a moment, it felt good to nurse the illusion that Doctor Max Kane was her knight-in-shining armor. Max was whisking her away from the sadness and despair she'd known for far too long.

"His name is Doctor Max Kane," Keith talked over the phone through clenched teeth. Having a second key for Faith's Nissan truck, he'd asked his buddy Sal to drive him over to Mr. Langhorne's place, where Faith had parked the car. After getting the truck, Keith had driven back over to the hospital. Finding a spot in the ICU parking lot, he'd waited for Faith.

However, when Faith finally *did* come out, she was with Doctor Kane. Max Kane's SUV had been parked in a reserved spot for doctors on the opposite side of the expansive lot. As far as distance went, Doctor Kane was parked on Mercury, and Keith was parked on Saturn. So, even if he saw Faith and Doctor Kane from a good distance away, they were unaware of his presence there. That night, Keith thought it wise to remain incognito, in light of the fight he'd gotten into with Max Kane earlier on.

Keith was more than peeved, as he spoke over the phone to his buddy Sal. "Yeah, Faith just got in his car." His face reddened in fury. Frustrated, he punched the steering wheel.

"What you gonna do, Keith?" Sal asked.

Sal had been released from prison a few years ago. He'd served a fifteen-year sentence for manslaughter. He and Keith had been friends for a while. So, Sal didn't appreciate hearing that some doctor guy was trying to put the moves on Keith's woman. "We can take him *out* if you want-you just say the word," Sal said routinely, as if he were offering Keith a cup of coffee.

"Nah, we don't gotta do that. I *know* how to handle Doctor Max. If he thinks I'm going to roll over and play dead while he takes Faith away, he's already a dead man walking. He ain't no punk though. He got in a punch or two before asking hospital security throw me out of *his* hospital. Seeing he's the bigwig over there at Fairfield, I guess it *is* his hospital. He the director and chief of staff or something like that."

"I don't care if he's Chief Indian or Hiawatha himself, I don't appreciate what he did tonight. Let me know how you want to handle this, Keith. *We* not punks, so we can't let no straitlaced doctor think he can walk all over us."

"Yeah, Sal, you're right, but let *me* handle it. I will let you know if I need your help at some point. Right now, I just can't wait to get my hands on Faith. I'm going to teach her a lesson she will never forget," Keith plotted. "She got to show up to the apartment sometime. She got all her stuff over at our place. So, when she does, I'm gonna be there waiting for her. She's going to be sorry for siding with that Max Kane for sure."

"Oh, no doubt, Keith, no doubt… Call me if you need me. "

"I will, man."

Keith pulled out of his parking space in the ICU lot. After a few twists and turns on hospital grounds, he was out on the main road. He had wanted to trail behind Doctor Max and Faith, but they were long gone by then. For a number of reasons, he *had* to lay low that night. So, he was temporarily down but definitely not out of the game. Nothing and no one was going to stop him from finding out where Doctor Max was taking Faith, neither would anyone stop him from getting her back.

***

"Do you want a little bit more of the stirred fried noodles?" Once back over at his house, Max tried to coax Faith into eating a little bit more of her dinner. They'd just ordered Thai takeout.

Faith shook her head in the negative and moved the food around on her plate. She had taken a few bites but didn't feel very much up to eating anymore. She gave Max a vague smile. "I'm not very hungry, Max." Faith was still trying to process the events of the day. Furthermore, it was taking a minute to wrap her head around the fact that she was at home with Dr. Kane. Max's house was more like a mansion-by far the most lavish place she'd ever been.

"Would you like something to drink?" Max's face wrinkled in concern. He perceived how afraid and out of sorts Faith felt being there with him. The situation was extremely challenging. It also didn't help matters that her dad was at the hospital.

"No, I'm fine," Faith's voice was gravelly.

"No, you're not," Max countered intuitively. "I know it's been one long and rough day. I get that you're scared about how things are going to play out." He reached across the kitchen table and took Faith's hand in his. His eyes explored hers sensitively. "That's why I'm here, sweetheart. You're not in this alone." His eyes lowered into hers in reassurance. "We're going to walk it out together, okay?" He stroked her hand fondly.

Faith nodded in agreement, growing increasingly more aware of Max's heavenly touch. Despite the ambiguity of the circumstances, she didn't want the fragile illusion of being with Max to fade away. Faith wanted to remain close to him for as long as she possibly could. "I appreciate all you've done." She felt completely inept in thanking him.

"You don't have to keep thanking me, Faith." Max smiled. "When you're okay, *that* will be thanks enough for me." He stood to his feet and began gathering up the silverware on the table. Before he took her plate away, Max hovered over Faith and asked, "Would you like for me to save this for later? You might feel up to eating something in a little while." His eyes searched hers sensitively.

"Okay," Faith agreed. Pushing out of her chair, she stood to her feet, and helped Max clear off the table. Faith followed him over to the sink. Max scraped off the remainder of his food into a bin to the side of sink. He then set their plates and glasses inside of the sink. Squeezing clear dishwashing liquid into it, he turned on the water faucet.

Faith stood at his side, and silently studied him. Max was totally fascinating. She'd observed him over at the hospital being an effective doctor and administrator. Then later, she had watched him assume the role of a protective big brother. Moments earlier, Max was a concerned parent trying to get her to eat her dinner, and now he was doing the dishes.

"You're awfully quiet," Max said, turning to give Faith a quirky sidelong look. "I know that I'm not the most exciting person in the world…"

"You *are* by far the most fascinating person I've ever met, Max Kane," Faith said dreamily, marveling.

Confused, Max said, "If I didn't know any better, I would think you *actually* meant that."

"That's because I *did* mean it," Faith affirmed, giving Max her most genuine smile.

"Thank you for saying that Ms. Faith. Ah, but you *really* need to get out more." Max gave her a playful wink. When he got done drying up the dishes, he set them gingerly into a compartment inside of the cupboard.

"Well, I've been around long enough to know that it doesn't get much better than you," she said, sizing him up with great admiration.

"Aw… Thank you, Faith." Max's heart melted. He and Faith locked eyes in that little span of time.

"You're welcome!" Faith was captivated by Max's pecan-colored eyes. However, she flinched in dread when she imagined Keith finding them. "You said that you laid some things out on the bed for me in the guest bedroom?" she asked, shattering the intense undercurrents between them.

"Yeah," Max said distracted and spellbound, "I have pajamas, socks, a towel and a toothbrush. There's soap and shampoo in the adjourning bathroom. Please let me know if you need anything else."

"I will. Thanks, Max," Faith told him.

"Are you *ready* to call it a night?" Max asked a little disappointed. He had hoped to spend a little bit more time talking to Faith and getting to know her.

Faith nodded, feeling somewhat mislaid. The truth was that she *wanted* to stay up with Max. However, something about having him near her was intimidating and a bit scary. The circumstances weren't conventional, and Keith was like a lion lurking and marking its prey. So, Faith figured that it was wise to keep her distance. She had acceded in allowing Max to help her, but she didn't want to create any more unnecessary drama. "It's been a long day, and I'd like to see my dad in the morning."

Max nodded in agreement, with a pertained expression on his face. "Of course, … You should definitely get some rest. We will figure things out in the morning." He smiled warmly at Faith.

"Are you working tomorrow morning?" Faith asked.

"I have tomorrow morning off, but I do have to be at the hospital tomorrow afternoon. I *am* working 4-12," Max informed.

"Well, I wouldn't want to put you out on your morning off."

Max shook his head contrarily and chuckled. Setting his hand compassionately to the side of Faith's face, his eyes lowered kindly into hers. "Figuring things out together in the morning is hardly putting me out," he settled. "You get some rest okay?" Max searched her face sensitively. "Let me know if you're warm enough."

"I'll be fine," Faith's voice was velvety, as she stared devotedly up at Max. *What on earth was she going to do now?* In a subtle way, Faith distanced herself. "Good night, Max," she said quickly.

"Goodnight, Faith," Max said, and watched her cross out of the kitchen.

After getting ready for bed, Faith slipped under the covers of the King-sized bed in one of Max's spare bedrooms. In the stillness, Faith received an epiphany. She was in love with Max Kane. Granted, she had suffered so long at Keith's hands that it was hard to decipher love from gratitude. However, as the shadows hung over her in that room, she longed for the sensation of Max's arms around her. So, she concluded that it was the former. She *had* indeed fallen for Max.

Max had devotions and was finally ready to turn in for the
night. Pushing back the covers, he quiescently got into bed. He
sighed as he considered the kind of day he'd had. If anyone would
have told him that Faith would be under his roof by the end of the
day, he would have said they were certifiable. And yet, that's
exactly what had occurred. Bits and pieces of his interactions with
Faith throughout the day inundated Max's thoughts. Summing up
his fight with Keith Wendt in the ICU, Max realized just how much
Faith had suffered at his hands. So, the only thing Max cared about
at that point was keeping her safe.

Keeping her away from Keith was paramount. There wasn't
anything Max wasn't prepared to do to ensure her safety. "Lord, am
I doing the right thing? Should I have gotten involved in this
situation? I pray that you would grant me the wisdom not to do
anything out of turn. The desire to hurt Keith Wendt is so all-
pervasive, Father. I resent him for making Faith's life a living hell.
For that very reason, I am asking for your help to tread cautiously in
the matter. All I want is for Faith to live a life free of his abuse.
Please, help me find a way to help her," Max prayed.

As he lay there in the penumbra of his room, he received an
impression from the Spirit of God. He was reminded not to be
overtaken by anger. Ecclesiastes 7:9 "Be not hasty in thy spirit to be
angry: for anger rests in the bosom of fools." (NKJV) Max asked
God to help him not to be reactive when it came to dealing with
Wendt. He also asked for forgiveness for losing his temper over at
the hospital. Eventually, he was able to drift off to sleep, after such
a long and trying day.

***

Max smiled expectantly when he saw Faith stand in the kitchen
entryway. As he'd hoped, the smell of bacon, hickory and maple
syrup, had enticed her to come out to him. "Hey there," Max

welcomed the moment he saw her. He was in process of scrambling eggs. "Good morning!" He smiled, watching her cross over.

"Good morning!" Faith told Max, perusing the stack of pancakes, and the plate full of bacon strips Max had ready. Faith inched in closer and came to stand to Max's left hand side. "You've done all of this?" She marveled with an irrepressible smile.

"I thought you might be hungry, seeing that you hardly ate anything at all last night," Max said thoughtfully, searching Faith's eyes.

"Max…" Faith's eyes shone with tears.

"What's the matter?" Max questioned, affected. He turned down the burner, and veered towards Faith, giving her his undivided attention. "What's wrong, honey?" He set his hand to the side of her face and brushed it softly.

Faith shook her head nonsensically, incredulous. Her head slumped before she looked up and reconnected to Max's intent stare. "It's just that you've been so kind. I really didn't expect anyone…" Her eyes gleamed more intently.

"Faith, I haven't been kind *enough*," Max argued, eyes lowering caringly into hers. "I feel as if I should have done something weeks ago. I should have done something that day when I saw Keith down the road from the school hurting you. I was so worried," Max admitted. "I hated seeing him put his hands on you, and not be able to do anything about it." He explored her eyes urgently.

"But we hardly know each other," Faith countered, befuddled.

"We *do* know each other now," Max refuted. "And we're getting to know each other a little more with time."

Faith laughed lightly and set her hand over the one Max had cradled to her face. "You *would* say that wouldn't you?" she teased. "I certainly want to know *you* a lot better, Dr. Max Kane!" Faith's heart skipped a beat, and she gulped, as her eyes fastened to Max's garnet ones. Butterflies danced in the pit of her stomach just to be near him.

Max smiled warmly at Faith. "That's good to know, because I'd certainly like to know *you*, Ms. Langhorne. Now, how did you sleep last night?" Max gently set his hand back down to his side.

"Remarkably well," Faith said spiritedly. "You have the most comfortable bed, and the most beautiful home," she uplifted. Faith drifted over to the cabinet and pulled out plates for them.

"I'm glad you like it. This house is my haven away from the craziness of my work," Max admitted.

"Well, you've created a charming living space," Faith commented, staring all about Max's expansive state-of-the-art kitchen.

"Thank you for saying that. You are welcome to be here anytime," he extended.

Faith turned to look at Max. Nostalgia veiled her sweet face, and she smiled. "That's awfully good to know," her voice undulated.

"Absolutely…" Max gave Faith a meaningful smile as well. "I hope you like scrambled." His cheeks reddened, as he returned to the task at hand.

"I love scrambled eggs." Faith crossed back over and went to stand close to Max again. She then floated over to the counter and set their plates down. "What time did you get up?" Faith leaned over the counter, and stared admiringly over at Max. He was a dream in his jeans and a dark blue T-shirt. His skin was as creamy as butterscotch pudding. Max's slick head of raven hair looked freshly washed, and soft hairs curved around his forehead and temples. In short, he was the most beautiful thing Faith had ever beheld.

"I've been up since about six thirty." Max gestured for Faith to hand him a plate.

Faith handed him one of the plates and watched Max pile on fixings of the scrumptious breakfast he'd cooked on it. "That's pretty early," Faith remarked, unable to stop gawking at Max's amazing body. Max was buffed but looked deceptively smaller in his business attire. In that T-shirt, his broad shoulders, and biceps had greater definition.

"That's the time I usually get up anyway-even earlier depending on my schedule. My body is its own alarm clock. It doesn't discriminate on days that I'm not working early," Max humored. He walked over and set a plate on the table for Faith. "Is this okay?" he tested searching her honey eyes. Max thought she looked adorable in his PJs. They swallowed her up.

Faith's pretty hair cascaded down her shoulders and back and framed her striking features. It was the first time Max was seeing her with her hair down. She looked amazing! Max was tickled that the sleeves to his pajamas covered Faith's hands and hung down as clothes would on a line. He smiled endearingly over the cuteness of it all. "You're welcome to dig in if you'd like. Coffee's almost done," he told Faith.

"No, that's okay. I will wait for you." Faith found herself transfixed, ogling the dream guy who'd just cooked an amazing breakfast for them. It was something she'd never experienced before. With Keith she was *always* the one cooking for him. He'd never once cooked *anything* for her. "I'll get creamer and sugar and set them on the table," Faith offered, excitedly walking over to the fridge.

"Sure. Thanks, Faith." Max watched every move she made with keen interest. It warmed his heart that Faith was with him, and she was safe for the moment. Max wanted to ensure that she remained that way. "I have almond milk, if you like that with coffee."

"I've never had it before," Faith admitted, opening up the fridge.

"It's pretty good, but that's *my* thing. I also have pumpkin spice creamer."

"Ooh...pumpkin spice, you *really* like to live on the edge don't you?" Faith razzed. She held the fridge door opened for a moment, staring at Max for a reaction.

"I'm a total *madman*," Max said rising playfully to the occasion. He turned and gave her a clever smile and wink. "Sometimes, I actually take Irish Cream."

"*Scandalous*," Faith teased, shaking her head humorously.

"Breakfast was great, Max!" Faith raved.

"I'm glad you enjoyed it," Max told her. "It was good to see you *actually* eating," he admitted. Max stood to his feet and began to clean up.

Faith drifted over to the sink in order to wash dishes. She set the water running and squeezed dishwashing liquid into it.

"Don't even worry about those. I will set them into the dishwasher in a little while," Max told her. He stood only a few inches behind Faith. There was something incredibly appealing about her hair falling over the nape of her neck. Max was tempted to touch her but desisted.

"Are you sure?" Faith asked, startled by their sudden closeness. She found herself gaping at his perfect mouth and exploring his mocha eyes. It was all too easy to get lost in them.

"I'm sure…," Max said adrift, captivated by Faith's sweet face and her intoxicating eyes. For all intents and purposes, he was about to slip into a state of hypnosis. "Um…," Max redirected, "I highlighted a few places on my phone that we can look at later." Max shook himself free from the trance and took the phone out of his jean's pocket. Accessing the images, Max pressed in even closer to Faith. He'd screenshot a few apartments he thought she might be interested in seeing.

"Wow!" Faith marveled over some of the places Max had highlighted. She leaned into him in order to get a better look. In that instance, Faith's right shoulder pressed up to Max's forearm. It felt nice to be connected to him in that way. Faith examined Max's picks. "Max, these places are much too expensive. I can't afford…"

"Faith, I don't want you to worry about it. All I care about is getting you away from *him*."

"But *Castle Horn* is your area, and much too expensive," she argued feeling conflicted.

"I know. I didn't want you to be too far away in the event you should happen to need me. These apartments are located down the road, and part of the Castle Horn building complex," Max informed. "Now, I don't want you to worry about it, okay?" Max settled, delving her eyes.

"Max…?" Faith tried to argue, but Max surprised her.

He playfully set his finger over her lips. Max chuckled and shook his head humorously. "Not another word."

The two were transiently locked in that moment. Faith's lips were so velvety to the touch that Max found himself wanting to lean in and kiss her, but he refused to go there. She was already going through so much. Furthermore, Faith was still entangled in a terrible relationship with a very dangerous man. The last thing she needed was to be taken advantage of in her fragile state.

"Now, I need for you to go and get dressed," Max ordered. "Feel free to search through my things for a sweater, a T-shirt or anything else for that matter. We're going to swing by the hospital to see your dad first-if that's alright. Then, we're going to find you a place," he delineated.

Faith nodded compliantly, and tried not to laugh, but it was useless. She wound up bursting into laughter. "Can I speak now?" she asked, because Max had removed his finger from off of her lips.

"No, I wasn't finished." Max laughed as well.

"Okay then, *Mr. Bossy*, finish," Faith badgered, staring wonderingly into Max's eyes. Just then, it dawned on her that the condition was getting worse. Her feelings for Max were growing exponentially, and she was getting sucked in even deeper. All things considered, that should not have been such a terrible thing.

However, her life was a total mess, and she was totally out of Max Kane's league. Faith estimated that someone like Ava Thorne was more his speed. Faith had to keep reminding herself of that reality, because it wasn't hard to fall for Max. She *was* falling fast and hard, and it was difficult to stop the landslide.

"Thank you very much," Max said with a quirky expression on his face. "Now, go get dressed, and I'll finish up in here and wait for you. Alright?" he tested, staring pleasantly down at Faith.

"Okay, Okay… I guess I can't argue with that." Faith smiled up at him. "What time it is by the way?"

"It's half past eight. I wanted us to get an early start, because I have to work a shift tonight," Max said more urgently. "By the way,

I've already contacted the authorities. They will escort us over to your place when you're ready to get your things out in Somerset Ridge."

Jeopardy and apprehension shrouded Faith's face. There was a sinking feeling in pit of her stomach that things were going to play out in an ugly way. She couldn't see Keith giving her up without a fight. She began to quaver, and tears immediately pooled in her eyes. "Oh, Max, I'm so scared," she admitted.

"Oh, honey…" Max collected her in his arms and crushed her devotedly. "You don't have to be scared." He rocked her in his arms and stroked her hair. "I won't let him hurt you ever again. I promise. It's going to be alright," he silenced her as she wept in his arms.

"You're going to be okay, and you don't have to live in fear anymore." Max pulled away, cradling Faith's face in his hands. His face warped in commiseration. "Please, don't cry. Don't cry, sweetheart." He pressed a comforting kiss to her forehead.

***

Hospital staff was surprised to see their director and chief of staff dressed down. It was Max's morning off, and he had on a pair of jeans, a T-shirt and a teal blue hoodie. His work buddies had seen him in civilian clothes before, but the shock factor was always the same.

Max was friendly to his staff and work colleagues, as he and Faith made their way into the ICU Unit to visit her dad. "How is Mr. Langhorne doing this morning?" Max asked Dr. Wain Brice. He was the one working through the ICU that morning. Faith stood by Max's side anxiously waiting to hear what Dr. Brice had to say.

"Mr. Langhorne is doing a lot better. There is far less congestion to his bronchial passages, and his breathing is a lot less labored," Dr. Brice told Max. Max looked over at Faith and offered an encouraging smile. "That's really great news," he told Dr. Brice, but with his eyes affixed to Faith.

"Do you think he can go home for Thanksgiving tomorrow?" Faith asked hopefully.

"We're not sure of that yet, Ms. Langhorne, but we will continue to monitor his progress," Dr. Brice told Faith.

Faith's heart lurched in disappointment, because her dad really wanted to be home. The admission had already thrown him off, and so Faith dreaded having to tell him that he wasn't getting discharged, and probably wouldn't be home for Thanksgiving.

"Hey, it's alright." Max nodded affirmatively, turning towards Faith. "We've got to make sure he's one hundred percent when he *is* discharged," he uplifted. "Are we ready to go in to see him?" he asked furtively, exploring her eyes. Faith had on one of his dark T-'s and a flattering pale yellow sweater. Once again, his sweater dipped down to her knees, and covered up her arms and hands. Max thought she looked amazingly pretty in yellow. She had pinned up a portion of her hair, but tendrils cascaded down her shoulders and back, and framed her sweet face.

Faith nodded hesitantly. "We're ready," she ceded. Her face wrinkled in uncertainty, as she and Max crossed over to her dad's ICU Room. "He's going to be so disappointed, Max," Faith said, worried.

"It'll be alright," Max enlivened. "You'll see. Everything's going to work out." He told Faith just before they ventured into the room.

Faith nodded again and tried not to get too worked up. The last thing she wanted was for her dad to panic in addition to his already exacerbated COPD.

Max and Faith opened up the ICU Room door to find that Ruth Tandy was already there. "Good morning, Mrs. Tandy!" Max greeted properly as he drifted inside.

"Morning, Ruth," Faith said, with eyes affixed to her dad.

"Good morning, Faith, Doctor Kane…," Ruth acknowledged.

"My dad's still asleep?" Faith asked, crossing over to stand to the right-hand side of the hospital bed.

"He was up a little while ago, but I guess the treatments have tired him out," Mrs. Tandy said.

"Yeah, he's probably still wiped out." Faith's face twisted in sadness. She was choking back tears, as she placed a cool hand on her father's forehead.

Max stood back and watched Faith with her dad. Just then, he said a prayer for Mr. Langhorne's total and complete recovery. It pained him to see how heartbroken Faith was, because he was so frail. It also didn't help matters that Mr. Langhorne would probably be spending Thanksgiving at the hospital.

"Is that my Faith?" Mr. Langhorne's voice was gravelly, as he slowly opened up his eyes.

It's me, dad," Faith said, smiling. She was encouraged that her father's eyes were opened.

"Hey, sugar, how are you doing?" James asked shakily. Slight wheezing could still be detected when he spoke and took metered breaths.

"I'm here to ask *you* that question, dad. How was your night?" Faith perked up, heartened that she was speaking to her dad.

Max stood to a corner of the hospital room, and quietly observed Faith's interactions with her father. He found himself smiling sentimentally from time to time.

"I'm sorry, dad, but Dr. Brice thinks you should spend another night," Faith finally found the courage to say.

Mrs. Tandy sat in the armchair on James's left-hand side, and quietly mulled over the way Dr. Kane was staring at Faith. She also observed the way Faith intermittently searched for Max's eyes around the room. It warmed her heart to see it. Ruth sensed the beginning of something special. She truly hoped it was. She knew all about Faith's abusive relationship with Keith Wendt. The man was a total terror. Ruth perceived Mr. Langhorne would have been stronger if he wasn't constantly worried about Faith. She hoped and prayed that this extremely good-looking-and seemingly kind doctor-was Faith's silver lining after a prolonged season of overcast skies.

"So, I have to stay *here* another night?" James asked, frustrated. He sighed heavily, but then began to cough.

Max immediately rushed over, and got his oxygen started again. "You're alright, Mr. Langhorne," he pacified.

James Langhorne was surprised to see Dr. Max Kane. Max Kane had been extremely kind to him when he was brought in by ambulance the day before. James couldn't say for sure what the young man was doing there, but having him there, made him feel a lot better. James doubted that Doctor Kane was even on call, but it didn't matter one way or another. His presence was extremely comforting. James hoped that Doctor Kane would in some way help his daughter.

"I'll come back a little later, Ruth. Please, give me a call-in case there is any change to dad's condition," Faith detailed to Mrs. Tandy. The two stood just outside Mr. Langhorne's hospital room.

Max stood a few feet away and tried to respectfully give Faith her space. All the same, nosy hospital workers were prying into their business. They were already whispering about his connection to Faith, because he'd escorted her over to the hospital. Everyone on the unit-and probably beyond it-would be looking at them as if they collectively had four heads.

"Your father's going to be fine, Faith. You go on and do what you need to. You're not working over at the school today are you?" Ruth checked.

"No, I called in. There are a few matters that I needed to handle."

"I see...?" Ruth said, as her eyes drifted over to Max Kane. "Such beautiful matters..." Ruth gave faith an inquisitive smile.

Faith in turn gave her a nonsensical look. "Ruth, are you serious? Max and I are friends. He's just a wonderful man."

"Yes, I know," Ruth razzed, "Max is certainly that...wonderful." She winked at Faith.

Faith shook her head, incredulous. "It's so not what you think." Her cheeks turned scarlet. However, at that moment Keith's face flashed in her thoughts, and she shuddered. "I've got to go. I will call you in a little while," she redirected.

"Okay, but your father should be just fine," Ruth reassured.

"Thanks again," Faith told her.

"You're welcome. Go on... Dr. Max is waiting for you," Ruth goaded.

Faith crossed over to where Max was standing, and he issued a warm smile. "Are you all set?" Max searched her face and eyes, pertained.

Faith nodded and smiled back at Max. "I'm all set."

As they drifted off of the ward, Faith couldn't help thinking how surreal it felt to have Max Kane by her side. He was her partner in crime, fighting diligently to keep her safe. Faith was totally captivated, as Max helped her into his SUV. She doted on him the entire time, staring devotedly at him when he took his place behind the wheel.

"What...?" Max asked as he smiled over at Faith.

"Oh nothing...," Faith said looking away with reddened cheeks.

"Come on, you're really *not* going to tell me?" Max prodded, intrigued.

"Nope," Faith said with a playful expression. "Will you keep your eyes on the road, Dr. Kane?" she heckled.

"That's just mean," Max told her, unable to stop smiling.

"*Mean* is my middle name."

"Okay... If you say so..." Max shook his head humorously. From time to time, their eyes met, causing both to issue quiet and contented smiles.

Keith waited until Max and Faith pulled out of the hospital parking lot, and he drifted down the road after them. He and Sal had switched cars. Sal had the Nissan Pathfinder, while Keith was driving Sal's dated 2005 black Jeep Cherokee. Keith was aggravated and annoyed. He couldn't believe Faith had carried things this far. She'd spent the night away from their place. It was difficult for Keith to process, but Faith had spent the night with Doctor Kane.

From the way she was dressed, it was obvious. Faith had on her own jeans, but she was wearing a T-shirt and sweater which were undeniably Max Kane's. Keith was infuriated, and his face turned cardinal as he followed behind them. "That's what you want to do, Faith? You want to play it out this way? Well, you got it, babe. If you think for one minute that I'm going to give you up to that prude, straitlaced punk, you better think again.

"You're not going to mess up my life. I didn't sleep a wink last night. I had to go out for breakfast, and I'll probably have to order dinner in tonight. Besides all of that, you belong to me. You, Faith Kendra Langhorne, are mine-locked, stocked and barreled.

"I'm going to teach you that very important lesson once and for all." Keith's face constricted in rage. "I can't wait to *school* you, my dear sweet girl." He bobbed and weaved out on the expressway, with only one car between his and Doctor Kane's SUV. Keith refused to change lanes, despite the fact that he was obstructing the flow of traffic.

"Max, I think Keith followed us here," Faith said panicked. She kept looking back nervously from the front passenger's seat of Max's car.

"It's alright," Max reassured, seeing the horrorstricken look on her face. "It's alright, Faith." Max reached for her hand. "I need for you to trust me right now, alright?" His eyes lowered meaningfully into hers. "Do you trust me?" he tested.

"Yes," Faith said, trembling. She took deep breaths in order not to hyperventilate. "I trust you, Max."

"Alright, then, there's no reason to be afraid," he reassured, squeezing her hand. "So, here's the plan. We're going to do a little shopping inside of the Target. Alright? This is a huge lot, so I'm going to leave my SUV parked right here.

"After we've shopped, my buddy, Dalton Davis, is going to swing by, and pick us up on the other side of the strip mall. He and I will switch out cars. I will drive his SUV, and he will take mine," Max explained calmly. "Alright?" His eyes delved Faith's.

Faith nodded in compliance, and wiped tears away from her eyes. "Max, I'm sorry about all of this. You shouldn't be involved," she groused.

Max gave her a sympathetic look just before hopping out of the car. He walked around in order to get the door for Faith. Taking her hand in his he gently helped her out. "It's much too late for that, Faith." He set his arm protective around her shoulder. "I'm already in waist deep." He gave her another reassuring smile. "Come on, sweetheart." He squeezed her closer to his side, as they headed for the doors of the Target convenience store.

Keith pulled into the parking lot of the Target on the *Broad Avenue* strip mall. He parked his car in the row of spaces twice removed from where Max Kane had parked his. Keith felt vindicated, because Faith and her new boyfriend, Dr. Max, had been discovered. Keith was hot on their trail, and it was only a matter of time before he closed in on them. When he *did*, there was no telling what would happen. What he did know was that when it was all said and done, he would be the last man standing. It really didn't matter what he had to do to make that happen. If it meant eliminating the good doctor once and for all, he was prepared to do just that.

"I don't think he followed us in here," Faith told Max, as they drifted up and down the aisles inside of the target. They had actually shopped and had picked up a few items.

"I *doubt* he followed us inside here." Max stared warily around the store. "He's probably waiting outside for us to get back into the SUV, so that he can continue tailing," Max figured.

Halting the cart for a moment, he stared into Faith's eyes in concern. Max tenderly took hold of her shoulders. "It's alright, Faith…it *really* is," he uplifted. "This is only temporary, I promise." Max cupped her chin. "Don't worry. If Mr. Keith Wendt keeps pushing, he's going to wind up a very sorry and broken man." Max's expression took on an icy quality just then.

Faith shrank back, surprised by Max's resolve. "I feel as if we're in this together," she admitted.

Max affectionately stroked her chin. "That's because we *are*. I don't want you to forget that," he emphasized

Overwhelmed, Faith threw her arms around Max, and squeezed him devotedly. "How can I ever thank you for what you're doing?" her voice broke.

"Oh, sweetheart, you don't have to thank me." Max buried his face in her shoulder. "You're going to be alright. In fact, we're *both* going to be okay." Max squeezed Faith closer to himself. It felt wonderful to hold her that way. Max was beginning to understand how much he needed to protect her and to have her close. However, understanding how critical the circumstances were, he playfully shoved away. "So, while we're here, we might as well pick up some of the things you need."

Faith felt cold all over because Max had pulled away. Still, she recognized that it was his way of keeping their connection uncomplicated. The situation was convoluted enough. "Okay," Faith ceded.

"Let's pick up a few things. We might not be able to make it out to Somerset Ridge for a couple of days. Maybe, we can go the day after Thanksgiving," he figured, frowning in uncertainty.

"I'm not looking forward to going back there, but it has to be done," Faith acquiesced. "I guess I can pick up some PJ's and a few changes of clothes," she agreed, staring up into Max's perfect face. "But, I don't have my credit card. Keith has it." Shame and embarrassment shaded her face, because she only had that one debit card, and Keith had taken it. She kept thinking how lucky she would be if Keith didn't squander away the two thousand dollars she had in the bank. It was her entire life savings.

"Faith...?" Max shook his head humorously. "Just pick up the things you need." He draped his arm about her shoulder and used the other to navigate the shopping cart.

"Max...?" Faith whined and tried to argue.

"Do you need for me to silence you again?" Max addressed Faith and stared down at her with a disarming smile.

"No, *please* don't silence me again," Faith told him, feigning dread.

Max watched Faith pay for their purchases up at the register, as he stood to the side, and had word with Dalton. "Yeah, we're just about to come out. Are you all set?"

"Yeah, of course, Max. What's going on?" Dalton questioned, worried.

"I'll get into the details later," Max told him. "My car's parked out on the east end of the lot. So, we're making the transition very quickly," he told Dalton, keeping his eyes protectively on Faith. Max passively observed how they'd picked up a few things for Thanksgiving. They'd bought a Turkey, a ham, a few pies, cranberry sauce, fixing for Macaroni and cheese and so forth. Max smiled endearingly as he contemplated Faith. She had told him that she was a great cook and could whip up a Thanksgiving dinner at the drop of a hat. So, Max was excited over the prospect.

"Max, you're so lucky you caught me on my day off," Dalton reminded. "You owe me big time for this one."

"Of course, man. I've *got* you," Max assured. Just then, he saw Faith pull away from the register with their bags all packed up. "I've got to go. I'll be outside in like a minute," he told Dalton.

"Sure, I'm ready to make the switch. I'll even help you with your stuff."

"Thanks a lot, Dalton. I appreciate it."

"Sure, Max."

Moments later, Max secured Faith inside of Dalton's wine-colored BMW SUV. He and Dalton had efficiently packed up their purchases to the trunk of the automobile. Now that Dalton had Max's keys, Max was free to pull away from the parking lot. It was a tremendous source of relief when he and Faith managed to make it out to the expressway. "Hey, how are you doing over there?" Max asked checking to see if Faith was alright. She was actually smiling.

"I can't believe we pulled that off," she said marveling. Her face radiated joy and excitement. "Max Kane, are you sure you're not espionage?" she teased.

"I can't say, because then I'd have to..." Max winked over at her.

"You wouldn't kill me," Faith countered playfully.

"Oh, no, I *could* never do that to my new best friend," Max said, catching her eye sporadically.

"Aw, you're so sweet."

Max shook his head contrarily. "It's *really* nice to see a smile on that pretty face," he told her openly when they stopped at a red light.

Faith was taken aback by Max's words. *Did he just say she was pretty? Did he really think that?* She questioned, totally stirred. Faith quickly checked the car console, and saw that it was a quarter to one p.m. "Do we still have time to look at a few of the apartments?" she evaded, entangling herself all the more into Max's loving web.

"Yes, as a matter of fact, there is a realtor waiting to meet with us at one fifteen," Max informed. "First, we'll swing by my place again, so that I can bring our groceries inside."

"I want to help," Faith told him.

"No, sweetheart, it's okay. The less visible you are, the safer you'll stay. Please, let me bring our things inside," he insisted.

"Alright." Faith was overcome by devotion and appreciation for Max. It was a scary place to be, but she was totally captivated. Somewhere along the road she had slipped and fallen. And now, it was impossible to get up. She was in love but had no idea what she was going to do about it. In Faith's assessment there was nothing she *could* do.

She'd gotten into a heap of trouble and had entertained the devil for far too long. At that point, Faith regretted some of the choices she'd made in life. If she'd known that someone like Max Kane existed, she evaluated that she would have made better choices. However, the damage was already done. Her less than stellar decisions had disqualified her to entertain someone like Max. And, as painful as it was to come to that conclusion, it was something Faith had to live with.

"If you like this particular apartment, we can have it all set and up and ready for Ms. Langhorne on Friday," the realtor told Max and Faith. Joseph church had shown them two other places, and this was the third out in the Castle Horn Apartment Complex.

Faith was mystified and totally speechless. The apartment was spacious, fully furnished, and had all new high-end amenities. There was a huge master bedroom with an adjourning bathroom, and one spare bedroom. Her head was spinning as she considered the possibilities. Mostly, she considered that her dad could move in, and she'd be able to take better care of him. Like a little kid lost in a vast amusement park, Faith was overwhelmed as she sized up the lavish apartment.

"Faith," Max drifted over to her, and set his hands on her shoulders, "how do you feel about this one?"

Faith turned to face him. Max still had his hands on her shoulders, as he excitedly delved her eyes. "Max, I love it! This is the best one we've seen today!" Enthusiasm chimed in her voice and danced in her eyes. "I can't believe all of the conveniences. There's even a new washer/dryer," she marveled.

Max couldn't help celebrating the Joy he saw on Faith's face and in her eyes. "So, I'm going out on a limb, and taking a guess that you *really* like this one." His face wrinkled in mischief. "Joe says that it can be ready the day after tomorrow."

"Wow, that soon, huh?" Suddenly worry wrinkled Faith's face. Moving in meant having to go out to Somerset Ridge again.

"The sooner the better," Max prompted. "By the way, if you don't want to go back to Somerset Ridge, I can go out there for you," he offered.

"Max," Faith argued, "I would never send you into that situation alone. Just promise that you'll be with me when I go over there."

"Of course, sweetheart. Just try and stop me," Max affirmed. "So, are we ready to tell Mr. Church the good news?" he tested, lowering urgently into Faith's eyes. "This *is* the place you want?" he affirmed.

"Yes. This is lovely, Max! At least, let me help with the down payment," Faith argued, feeling totally guilty. The last thing she wanted was to abuse Max's kindness.

"Faith, look at me," Max urged, "don't worry about it."

"Please, tell me how much the down payment and security fees are," Faith petitioned.

"Absolutely not," Max razzed, smiling. "By the way, Joe says that there's a communal gym down the hall if you're interested in that kind of thing," he evaded.

"Yeah, he told me," Faith said with a quiet smile.

She instinctively draped her arms about Max's neck and squeezed into him devotedly. Pulling back, she reached up, and pressed a kiss to his cheek. "Thank you," her voice broke. Faith realized that she liked having her arms draped around Max's neck. So, for a brief moment she didn't move. Rather, she pressed yet another kiss to his cheek. "You're wonderful!"

Taken aback by her display of affection, Max found his heart melting as his eyes explored Faith's. He was stirred beyond words by Faith's tender touch and kiss. "You're welcome," his voice was gravelly as their smiles melded. In a subtle way, Faith pulled back. Her withdrawal left Max feeling ice cold. Still, he was moved by her sentimentality. Max could see the apartment through her eyes, and it warmed his heart to see her so happy. Seeing Faith in such good spirits, made him realize that it was paramount to keep that sweet smile on her face at all times.

Faith waited in the car, while Max finalized the paperwork with the realtor. Faith wasn't sure if Max was aware that she'd had word with the realtor earlier on. Faith had asked how much the down payment and security fees were for the new place. He'd told her that Max had paid up to twenty-thousand dollars, and that her rent was paid up for the next six months. Tears were in Faith's eyes as she internalized the sacrifices Max had made for her.

She worried that she would never be able to pay him back. And being indebted to anyone wasn't something she was comfortable with. Faith had been there before. Some men felt as if a woman owed them the world if they bought her a nice dinner. Faith wondered what Max wanted in return for his kindness. She kept expecting the other shoe to drop. Maybe, Max would want *things* or *favors* in return. Faith hated thinking that way, but it was what she was used to.

"Are we all set to leave?" Max asked Faith, taking his place behind the wheel. He couldn't help noticing the worried expression on her face. "Faith...?" he coaxed in order to get her to look at him. "Are you alright?"

"I'm fine, Max," she said quickly.

"There's something off," Max concluded. He was beginning to know her just a little and picked up on alarming undercurrents. "What's going on in that head of yours?" Concern wrinkled his face.

"Max, I would need to pay you back for everything," Faith resolved, staring over at him with a conflicted expression on her face.

"Alright," Max acquiesced, not wanting to make Faith feel any more uncomfortable. "I'm not keeping tabs, but if you feel you need to..."

"No strings attached?" Faith asked, bewildered.

"Now, *there's* the real issue," Max pinpointed. "Faith, the only string I'm concerned about is the one Keith has on you. Aside from that, sweetheart..." Max kept shaking his head contrarily. "I'm not sure about the types of friendships you've had in the past, but please make no mistake about it. *Everything* I do is from my heart, and motivated by the love of God," he delineated. "Understand?" His face wrinkled in urgency. It was important for Faith to see who he truly was.

Faith flinched, bewildered, but nodded quiescently. She was more than taken aback by how attuned Max was to the way she felt. *How was it that he'd addressed her biggest concern?* If she had marveled before over the *wonder* of Max Kane, Faith was even more riveted. At that point, things were beginning to make sense. Max was a man of faith. That knowledge endeared him all the more to Faith, and she direly wanted to know more. "I'm sorry for being so prideful," Faith told him, as they set out to leave the apartment complex.

"It's okay to be prideful, but *everybody* needs somebody at some point in their lives," Max assessed wisely, staring sidelong over at Faith.

"I'm beginning to realize that," Faith admitted, catching Max's eye.

"Then, don't be afraid. Trust that God brings certain people into our lives when we really need them."

"I'm beginning to realize that too," Faith's voice undulated.

"So, allow God to use *me* to be a friend right now. Hopefully, down the road I will desperately need *your* friendship in return," Max reasoned.

"I sure hope so, because I'd like to be there for you too, Max."

Max issued a fond smile at Faith. "I think you already are there for me, Faith." He winked at her.

Faith smiled devotedly over at the man she loved. There was no doubt in her mind that she loved Max. Again, what would be done about it remained to be seen. "Max, look at the time? We don't have much time to get you home. You've got to get ready for your shift," Faith evaluated.

"It shouldn't take too long for me to shower and change," Max reassured. "Faith, I know you wanted to come with me when I leave for the hospital."

"I *did* want us to drive in together, but I know that it isn't the best idea," Faith reasoned.

"I'll take a Lyft over to the hospital, and I will leave Dalton's SUV for you so that you can visit with your dad. Later, we can figure out how to leave together under Keith's radar," Max strategized. "It will work out," he encouraged.

"I know. This has all been so strange," Faith assessed. "One minute I'm with Keith, and then the next..." She looked over at Max devotedly.

"I'm just glad that you're letting me walk you through the transition." Max gave Faith a heartening look.

Faith's smile brightened as Max helped her out of the car. The building complex was only five minutes away. "I'm really glad too, Max. I'm so happy that I met you!" Faith cradled Max's head in her small hands and stroked fondly on his cheeks.

"I'm *equally* glad to have met you, Ms. Langhorne." Max pressed a kiss to the palm of Faith's hand.

***

"What the hell?" Keith questioned, confused. "What's going on?" Max Kane's SUV was finally on the move, but something was very wrong. Keith had been sitting outside of the Target for the past couple of hours waiting for Faith and Doctor Kane to come out. However, did his eyes just deceive him? Some other guy had come out of the Target and had gotten behind the wheel. *Was it possible that Faith had seen him following behind them?* Keith couldn't wrap his head around that concept, because he thought he'd been so cautious.

"I can't believe this..." Keith dropped a string of expletives, as he grudgingly followed behind the SUV from a distance. Even if he'd lost Faith and Dr. Kane...*again*, whoever was behind the wheel would bring him closer to finding them. Keith felt like a fool, because he'd been tricked by Faith and Doctor Kane. He vowed to teach Faith a critical lesson, and to make Dr. Kane pay dearly for *playing* him, and for messing with his woman.

CHAPTER FIVE

It was almost 9 p.m., and Max was on his first real break on a very busy night in the ER. Slipping into the staff lounge, he thought about grabbing a bite, but was much more concerned about how Faith and her dad were doing over in the ICU. For Max, it was paramount that he rush over to the unit to check in on them.

Upon starting his shift at four, Max had dropped in briefly to check in on Faith and her dad. Since then, Faith had texted him to let him know they were alright. Max was grateful that she had made it over to the hospital uneventfully in Dalton's car. Later, he and Faith would meet on the hospital's ground floor, at the north end of the lot, and drive back over to Castle Horn together.

Max was frustrated over the circumstances, and direly wanted to confront Keith. However, Max understood that a person like Keith Wendt was well-past reasoning with. To Keith, Faith was property, and he would stop at nothing to ensure that she was back in his hip pocket. What Keith failed to understand was that Max was just as determined to shut him down.

Keith had no right to put his hands on Faith, or any other woman for that matter. Max wanted to ensure that this was the end of the line for Keith. He refused to keep playing musical cars in order to dodge a madman. He and Faith had discussed it briefly, but they were both in agreement to have an emergency order of protection filed against Keith.

Notwithstanding, Max was ready to utilize his clout as the director of the hospital. Along with that status came a few privileges and warranted special favors from the authorities. Max would see to it that the authorities stayed on top of Keith, until the man had no choice but to dig a hole in the ground and go into hiding indefinitely.

However, Max would stand by Faith, as she courageously took one step at a time.

Max wasn't feeling much up to eating anything at that point. However, he crossed over to the fridge to see if he still had any protein shakes left there. It was usually hit or miss on that front. Hospital workers in general often behaved like scavengers. If they were hungry enough, they were in habit of taking things that did not belong to them on any given late-night shift.

"Well, would you look at that," Max said, marveling. One of his vanilla Premier proteins shakes had remained untouched. Max shook his head in irony, because he'd sworn there were three inside the fridge. Still, he refused to complain. "Thank you, Lord!" Max praised. "I'm just grateful there's one left." He smiled.

Max shook the container, and he was about to twist off the cap, when Ava slipped inside of the breakroom. Max set the shake on the lounge table for a moment. "Hey, there," he greeted Ava with a friendly smile.

"Just the man-or should I say the *doctor* I was looking for," Ava heralded, breezing in and allowing the lounge door to close.

"Is that so?" Max queried curiously.

"Yes it is," Ava's voice knelled, as she eliminated the space between them. Decisively, she edged in close to Max, and set her hands strategically on his chest. In cadences, her arms inched up to his shoulders until they clasped around his neck.

Max was a bit confused but didn't want to overtly pull away. He liked Ava, and thought she was very nice. He had sensed that she liked him a great deal. Wary of making any abrupt moves, Max smiled in uncertainty. "Is there something you wanted to tell me?" He explored her eyes, pertained.

"Yes," Ava said alluringly. She eliminated all spatial boundaries, then reached up and linked her lips to Max's. For a few seconds she massaged his lips fondly with her own. She then pulled away and stared dreamily into Max's face. "I wanted to do that on the night we went out to the concert," she admitted. "I just didn't have the nerve." Her cheeks turned scarlet, and her head slumped.

Max sighed, and gently took her hands in his. "Ava, I'm flattered," he confessed, searching her face and eyes intuitively. "That was really nice, but the truth is that I'm not at a very good place right now. Don't get me wrong, I would really like to get to know you. However, I think it's important to keep building on our *friendship*," he explicated wisely. Max wasn't sure what to say at that point. Ava had kissed him, and she seemed ready to move on to the next level.

Things being what they were, Max was still trying to process the painful breakup with Kennedy Proctor-Bohm. It was hard to decipher whether or not he was ready to offer up his entire heart. There were times where he felt as if he could, but those instances were few and far between.

Ava smiled, reclaimed her hands, and draped her arms about Max's neck again. She reached up and pressed a kiss to Max's cheek. "That's all I'm asking for, Max. I'm asking for a chance to build on our friendship. I didn't mean to be pushy or insistent just now," she assented.

Max shook his head contrarily in order to reassure her. "You didn't do anything wrong-well except for choosing the wrong place." He winked with a quirky expression on his face and gestured to their surroundings. "But it's fine. I'm truly flattered that you like me. I like you, Ava," he disclosed.

However, Max telling Ava that he liked her felt in some way off. He'd been romantically dormant for a while, and for all intents and purposes dead. Even so, he was ready to admit that he'd felt more alive in the past couple of days than he had in a very long time. Being around Faith; having her stay over at his house, making sure she had a good breakfast, visiting her dad in the ICU, dodging Keith, shopping together at the strip mall, and finding her a new place, had in some way sparked new life in him.

In fact, being around Faith and looking into her eyes often made Max's stomach sink, and his heart drum. It was a wonderful roller coaster ride whenever she was anywhere near him. Still, Max was finding it difficult to define what it meant. Had he found the missing pieces of his heart again, or was it something else? Only time would tell.

"Great, because I *really* like you, Dr. Kane," Ava said overjoyed. "I'm sorry again." She cautiously removed her arms from about Max's neck. "Are you still coming over tomorrow after your shift?" she reminded him.

"Oh, right…," Max deliberated. He'd agreed to Thanksgiving dinner over at Ava's, but that was before Faith had stepped into the picture. There was so much to consider. Mr. Langhorne was still admitted to the hospital. Faith had promised to cook Thanksgiving dinner, and to bring it over to the hospital for her dad. Max had looked forward to helping her cook, then later going over to the hospital with her, because he was only working for a few hours tomorrow.

Ava frowned in disappointment. "Something's come up?" she asked warily.

"Not exactly, but I don't think that I can make it for dinner. I can stop by for a minute, because I've already picked up a few things for your dinner party," Max said in all honesty. He *had* picked up a fine wine and dessert for Ava's gathering. "I'm sorry. I have a dear friend who is going through a tough time right now, who truly needs my help. It would be wrong of me to pull away, while they're dealing with so much," he reasoned.

Ava was totally put out to hear Max say those words. She was tempted to ask Max if his friend was Faith Langhorne but desisted. Rather, she smiled and forced herself to understand. Max had just said he liked her. So, she figured that even if the progress was slow, it was better than no progress at all. She wouldn't be playing the role of the possessive girlfriend-at least not yet. She first had to obtain the status. "I understand," Ava said quiescently.

"I'm so sorry, Ava. I promise to make it up to you, as soon as things are a little bit less crazy," Max heartened. He refused to commit to anything else until he was certain that Faith was safe, well-adjusted and thriving.

Ava nodded understandingly. "I get it. You're a great friend, Max. One of the things I admire most about you is that you genuinely care about people."

Max smiled openly, stirred by Ava's words. "There really is no point to life if we're apathetic to the needs of others," Max said insightfully.

"You know you're right," Ava told him, and fondly rubbed his arm.

"Well, it's my moral code." Max tenderly set his hand on the one Ava had on his arm.

"Can we see your ID, Sir," hospital security questioned Keith on the hospital's the main floor Wednesday night.

"Uh, I don't have my license, but I'm here to see James Langhorne in the ICU," Keith told them through gritted teeth. He had on a hat, a hooded sweatshirt, and reading glasses, as not to be recognized. Lucky for Keith, the guards who'd thrown him out last night weren't there. Furthermore, the one working the booth had absolutely no idea who he was. So, Keith had a plan. He would wait out in the ICU until Ruth Tandy went home, and until Max Kane wasn't buzzing around Faith. Then, he'd find a way to connect to Faith, and force her to come home.

"Sir, I'm going to let you in *this* time, but for future reference, please bring a picture ID whenever you present at this desk," the dark-haired, middle-aged Caucasian security guard told Keith.

"Of course, Sir. I understand," Keith quickly feigned compliance. "I'm so sorry that I forgot to bring my ID tonight."

"That's alright, Sir. I will clear you to go up to the ICU Unit. Do you know the room number?" Keith.

"Yes, I *do* know the room number, thank you," Keith said with a cunning smile.

The level of gratification Keith felt at that moment was indescribable. He'd been granted access to the ICU where he could get close to Faith. It was the night before Thanksgiving no less. Keith figured that if he grabbed her that night, he'd have her back just in the nick of time. Faith would cook him a nice Thanksgiving dinner tomorrow. This scrumptious meal would ensue a critical lesson he needed to teach Faith in respect to the repercussions of walking away from him.

Faith had to remain in her dad's ICU room until her dad returned. Mr. Langhorne had been transported to another floor of the hospital for bronchial treatment. Mrs. Tandy had gone home for the night. So, Faith sat quietly in one of the armchairs, mulling over whether or not to cross over to the ER to see Max. However, she decided not to act on her impulse. She had heard ICU staff discussing how busy it was over in the ER. Besides, they had to prep a number of ICU beds for the influx of admissions being transferred over from the ER.

Faith refused to behave familiarly with the hospital's director, chief of staff and head doctor. Even if Max didn't take himself very seriously, Faith wanted to show him the utmost respect at *his* hospital. Still, Faith hoped that Max would steal a few moments to come out to the ICU before his shift ended. As soon as Max's shift did end, he'd come find her, and they would go home together. Faith couldn't believe how drastically her life had changed in just a few days.

Not only had Max Kane taken her away from Keith's violent grasp, he had secured a brand new place for her to live. Faith was overwhelmed by love and gratitude, as she considered just how wonderful Max was. Helping her wasn't something he *had* to do, but he'd embraced the job wholeheartedly. Faith wanted to tell Max that she loved him, but she figured she didn't stand a chance. Guys like Max Kane had all of the women at the hospital crushing on and pining for him. So, Faith strove to tuck in her strong feelings. If she entertained her feelings for Max, she would irrefutably be setting herself up for hurt.

There was a light rap on the ICU room door. Faith stood to her feet and crossed over to see if it was the doctor, or even one of the nurses coming in to see about her dad. Through the clear, glass slot posted to the top center of the door, she didn't see anyone. Nonetheless, Faith went ahead and opened up the wooden door. Her face immediately changed, and her heart plunged in sheer terror when she came face to face with Keith. To Faith, he looked bigger than life. Keith grimaced menacingly, warning her not to react. He set his finger over his lips-indicating she should *not* make a sound.

Misery strained on Faith's face, and her heart hammered in angst. She instinctively retreated away from the door, as Keith pushed his way into the room. At that point, they were both only a few feet away from the door when Keith grabbed Faith's arm and pulled her in forcefully. "Well, if it isn't my long, lost girlfriend," he said mockingly. His eyes darted out venom as he applied pressure to her arm.

"Keith, you need to leave right now. The nurse and the aid should be back with my dad any minute," Faith censured, tremulously and flinched in dread. "You need to go," she said again with a wavering voice.

"I'm not going anywhere. Do you hear me?" Keith compellingly took hold of Faith's shoulders and shook her mercilessly. "You witch! You had that Dr. Kane call security on me, and they ushered me out of the hospital like I'm some criminal."

By then, Faith was already in tears, terrified, and shrinking beneath Keith's aggressive affront. "Keith," her face twisted in hopelessness, "let me go."

"I'm not letting you go anywhere, Faith. You belong to me," he thundered. With his right hand, he hostilely slapped her on the face. "You went home with Dr. Max. I *know* you've been staying over at his place. I don't know where that is, but I *know* you've been with him." He hit her yet again on the face.

"Keith, stop, please… Please, just leave me alone. I don't want to be in this relationship anymore," Faith muttered with tears bristling over her eyelids. "I don't want to be with…" She didn't even get to finish her train of thought, because Keith shook her so vehemently, it felt as if she had slipped into a state of vertigo.

"I don't care what you want, Faith. Don't you get it? You're mine. You are *my* property, and no one else can and will have you." Keith's face twisted in rage, and his eyes were cardinal, as if he were demonically possessed. "You don't *get* to walk away from me. I know you slept with him," Keith ranted, shaking and smacking Faith.

Faith sobbed in anguish but couldn't pull away from Keith's potent grasp. "I didn't sleep with Max. He *isn't* that kind of guy," she defended, with a face searing and radiating in agony, where Keith had repeatedly struck her.

"What..? Is he gay? I *know* he's not gay, so you're lying. You slept with him, and I can't believe you did that to me. Do you *know* what it was like for me to spend the night alone?"

"I'm sorry, Keith," Faith tried to pacify. She reasoned that appeasing Keith was the only way she would make it out of this situation without getting killed. "Okay... I'm sorry. I didn't mean to walk away from you. I'm also sorry that I didn't take *your* side over Max Kane last night," she pacified, saying all of the things she knew Keith wanted to hear. "Please, forgive me for being distant." She shuddered and winced in distress, as the tears flowed unremittingly down her cheeks.

Keith mellowed out a bit and loosened his grasp on her. "Well, alright, as long as you recognized how *you* messed up. Now, Faith, I'm not playing any games. We're going to walk off of this unit together-you and me. There's not going to be any drama, and you *will* not make eye contact with anybody out there." Keith pointed over to the door. "You're going to keep a great big smile on that pretty face, and you're coming home with me tonight. Are we clear?" He yanked on her right arm, lowering ominously into her eyes.

Broken and terrified, Faith surrendered to a slow nod. She hoped and prayed that Max would find them and stop Keith in his tracks. Going home with Keith that night was a guaranteed death sentence. Faith knew that if she *did* go home with him, he would continue to take his anger out on her for walking away. Faith was afraid that when Keith got done, her very life would be snuffed out. And yet, she perceived that if she didn't comply, things would be far worse. "Alright, Keith, I will go with you," she assented, putting both hands up in surrender.

"Good...cause we're leaving now." Keith jerked on Faith's right arm and began hauling her over to the hospital room door. Before opening it up, his foreboding eyes connected critically to hers again. "Remember what I said, act natural or else it's not going to be pretty once we're alone."

Disheartened, Faith nodded compliantly, as Keith opened up the door, and proceeded to usher her outside. An elastic smile stretched over her face, as Keith placed his arm around her shoulder. He was smiling as well, in an effort at exhibiting a happy and united front.

Faith was brokenhearted and felt completely powerless. She also felt like a fool having to parade around the hospital as if everything was coming up roses, when she was in danger. As Keith dragged her through the hospital's corridors, her heart twisted in knots. There was a real sense of dread that she had in all likeliness lost her connection to Max for good. That concept hurt even more than the abuse she'd just suffered at Keith's hands.

"I've been waiting for this moment all night," Max said spiritedly, opening up Mr. Langhorne's ICU room. However, he was totally surprised and taken aback, because neither Faith nor her dad were around. "Alright..." Max drifted in fully into the room, confused.

Just then, warning bells went off. So, Max stepped out of the room again. It was at that time that he saw the nurse and her aid bringing Mr. Langhorne back over to his room. Max instinctively rushed over to them. "Good evening, Mr. Langhorne," he said affably. Max had a sinking feeling in the hollow of his stomach.

"Good evening, Dr. Kane," James Langhorne said with an earnest smile. His voice was a lot stronger after his treatment.

"If I may ask, is your *daughter* anywhere around?" Max's face wrinkled in urgency, and his heart whipped in angst.

"Faith should be inside of the room. She stayed behind while these lovely young women conveyed us over to another part of the hospital for treatment." James frowned in concern. "Have you checked inside of the hospital room?"

"Yes, I *did* check." Max offered a faint smile-not wanting to alarm Mr. Langhorne. The man was already struggling with health issues, and Max didn't want to exacerbate his symptoms by making him worry.

"That's odd, because she *should* be in there."

"Are you talking about your daughter, Mr. Langhorne?" Tanya Perkins, one of the nurses who stood by, and had heard the conversation asked.

"Yes, he's looking for her." Max veered towards Tanya.

"Well, she just left with a *friend*," the nurse informed.

"A friend...?" Max questioned going into panic mode. "Tanya, get security. Tell them to cover every square inch of the hospital. Please, instruct them to look out for anyone leaving the hospital using the cameras posted at every viable exit. Also, they are to comb through every area in and around the stairwells," Max ordered Nurse Perkins. "Do it now." He rushed away from the ICU nursing station, and off of the unit like a madman.

"Is something wrong?" James Langhorne asked, confused. "Where's my daughter?" he asked, but Max had already disappeared.

Max explored every floor of the hospital, taking the stairs by leaps and bounds in search of Faith. His heart hammered in his chest, and tears of rage and frustration were in his eyes. It was dark out, so if Keith *had* taken Faith off of the grounds, it would be a lot more difficult to discern, even if cameras were set up at virtually every corner of the hospital.

He had remained in close communication with hospital security the entire time. Max had asked that they keep him posted if they happened to spot Faith before he did. "God, I failed her," Max groused, brushing his fingers agitatedly through his hair. "I was doing all I could to keep her safe, but I dropped the ball. It's *my* fault if anything happens to her... God, please don't let anything happen to her. I would never be able to forgive myself." Max cried in brokenness.

Just then, his cellphone went off, and Max immediately recognized the number as hospital security. "What's going on?" he demanded.

"Sir, we've spotted the gentleman and Mr. Langhorne's daughter. They are approaching the ground level towards the east end of the parking lot," security told Max. "Security staff is headed over to that part of the hospital right now," security informed.

"Thanks for letting me know." Max hung up, distracted. He then literally jumped a few flights of stairs in order to make it to the ground floor. "Not if I get there first," he affirmed, outraged. He was on a mission, determined to find Keith Wendt. Max prayed for God's temperance not to explode, but it was difficult not to be incensed over what was happening. The realization that Keith had put his hands on Faith that night burned him up.

Max stepped out into the chilly night with the onyx sky looming above and hiked through the hospital's lot on the ground floor. It had rained earlier on, so the ground was still soaked through with rainwater. Max had taken multiple flights of stairs down in order to get to that part of the lot. It took forever, so Max feared that Keith had already taken Faith away.

Undaunted, he ran across the expansive lot until he got to the east side. Once there, Max continued until the very end of the lot. Suddenly halted, his heart leaped in his throat by something he saw feet away. Max was all the more incensed when he saw Keith trying to force Faith into the same stupid black Jeep they'd seen earlier in the day. Max rushed over like a man on fire in order to get to Faith. The look on her face broke his heart.

"Max…!" Faith called out, both surprised and relieved. She veered away from the Jeep, because up until that very moment, Keith had been doing all he could to shove her inside.

Max stood only a few feet away facing Keith. His breathing was labored, and his skin seared just beneath the surface. Faith immediately darted away from Keith and rushed over to his side. Max took his place protectively in front of her. Faith trembled, and tears were in her eyes as she clung to his arm. Max's caramel skin flushed red with blood, and his fists were balled to his sides, similar to the night before.

"You again…," Keith griped, inching in closer to Max. "Do you *really* want to do this?" Keith challenged. His tan skin was redder than a crab's, and his eyes were black, as if demons had possessed him.

"Just give me a reason," Max daunted. The sound of Faith crying behind him, and the fact that her trembling rippled throughout his entire body set off an alarm for Max. "I warned you to stay away from her. I told you that if you *ever* laid a hand on her again that there would be repercussions. Did he hit you, Faith?" Max asked, as his lethal eyes speared through Keith's shadowy ones. Faith's silence told him all he needed to know, and Max was furious.

"Bring it on, *Doctor*. I can take you. In fact,..." Keith tore into Max, and began swinging punches.

"I *told* you to give me a reason." Max was as immovable as a cement structure, while Keith continued to issue strikes. Max grabbed Keith by the collar with one hand-as easily as one would a ragdoll. Lowering at him, Max hurled a number of defining blows to Keith's face until Keith's legs gave way. "I warned you." Max hunched down and continued his ministry of retribution. On a mission, Max beat Keith to a pulp while the man was sprawled out on the ground. "How does *that* feel, huh?" he taunted. "How does it feel to be hit repeatedly?"

"Max, it's alright. It's okay. Please, stop it," Faith pleaded, with a face warped in sadness, misery and fear. "You don't have to go there."

"I promise you a trip to one of the *other* hospitals you're so fond of if you *ever* lay hands on her again..." Max shook his head contrarily, totally peeved. Even if Keith had been rendered incapacitated, and there was blood issuing from the base of his nose, Max wanted for him to feel the repercussions of what it means to hit a woman. He wanted for Keith to feel as powerless as he made his victims feel.

"Go to hell, Dr. Kane," Keith spat out in recrimination. "You're going to pay for this."

"You," Max alighted from off the ground and hovered over him, "need to get it through your head that Faith no longer wants to be in a relationship with you. It's over. So, you need to learn to how take *no* for an answer, or else I will continue to *school* you," he retorted.

At that moment, security permeated the east end of the parking lot. Three precinct police cars also pulled into the area and obstructed the general exit. All at once, they pounced on Keith, and began hauling him away.

"We asked this man to stay off of hospital grounds. Last night he attacked our hospital director and chief of staff. He had the nerve to come back tonight to make trouble," security staff explained to the authorities.

Max turned towards Faith and edged in close to her. Tenderly cradling her head in his hands, he searched her face and eyes pertained. "Are you alright, honey?" Emotions were still running high, and tears shone in his eyes.

"I'm alright, Max," Faith acquiesced. "I'm going to be okay."

Max noticed swelling to Faith's right cheek and saw the darkening contusions on her right wrist. His face twisted in remorse, as he collected her in his arms. "I'm so sorry, Faith. I'm so sorry I wasn't there." Max was grieved, and tears rolled down his cheeks.

Faith trembled in his arms and cried as well. "It isn't your fault. You had no way of knowing that he would show up again after what happened last night." Faith allowed herself to breathe into Max's chest and held on to him for dear life.

"I *should* have known," Max railed, tussling with guilt. "I'm *so* sorry that I wasn't there. Please, forgive me, honey." He pulled back and held Faith's face in his hands. "He hurt you, and *I* wasn't there." His face bridged critically to Faith's. "I'm so sorry…" He crushed her protectively to himself.

"It's okay, Max. It's okay. I'm just grateful you found me before it was too late. Please, don't beat yourself up about it.

Please, don't break my heart that way," Faith grumbled, as they clung acquisitively to each other. "It's not your fault," she reassured.

Max kept shaking his head in the negative. Supporting her face in his hands again, his eyes lowered meaningfully into hers. "I promise never to fail you in this way again. Even if I have to handle the matter myself, I will make him back off and leave you alone." He pressed a kiss to Faith's forehead. "I promise."

Faith could finally breathe again after all she'd endure at Keith's hands that night. She felt safe and secure in the folds of Max's arms. She couldn't stop trembling, and she realize that it was Max's strength that kept her from faltering. "It's alright, Max. I *know* I can trust you," she uplifted, as Max kept a secure hold about her. She had suffered so much that night but reconnecting to Max had undoubtedly alleviated her agony.

"Do you want us to press charges, Doctor Kane?" one of the police officers questioned Max a few moments later.

Max gently released his hold from about Faith but stood closely to her side. "Yes, I want him arrested. You might want to check his record to see if he has a history of violence. He's been abusive to his ex-girlfriend," Max detailed. Slipping his arm protectively around Faith's waist, he refused to let go. Faith in turn propped her head up to his shoulder.

"You got it, Doctor Kane. We apologize for not getting here sooner," the officer said.

"That's alright," Max glared over at Keith, "it gave me the chance to address the matter *personally*."

The officer gave Max a knowing wink and offered a faint smile. He then nodded and drifted off. Feet away, Max and Faith heard the police reading Keith his Miranda Rights.

"Hey, honey, are you *really* alright?" Max tuned in to Faith after Keith was taken away, and hospital security had dissipated. His face strained in empathy and concern.

Faith gave him a reassuring nod. "I'm alright, Max. Thank you for finding me." She swallowed the chunk lodged in her throat.

"I'm so sorry that I wasn't there when he got to the ICU room. I'm *so* sorry, Faith," Max emphasized. Fresh tears shone in his eyes.

Faith eyes gleamed affectively, as she offered him an encouraging smile. Taking Max's hands into hers, she reached up and pressed a kiss to his cheek. "Thank you so much, Max. Please, don't blame yourself for what happened tonight."

"It's hard not to, sweetheart." Max sighed and shook his head in the negative. "I'm so grateful that he didn't get the chance to take you away." He set his hand to the side of her face and tenderly caressed it. "Are you coming back up to the unit?" Max still grappled with guilt.

"I'd like to, but only for a few minutes to say goodnight to my dad. Honestly, I'd like to go home if that's alright," Faith's voice broke. "I know you have to finish out your shift."

Max shook his head contrarily. "No, I *can* take you home. It's already half past ten, so I'll call Noel Amos. He's the doctor who's coming in to relieve me. I'll ask him to come in a little earlier."

"Are you sure?" Faith tested, still worried.

"I'm sure. I've done it for *him* a dozen times." Max smiled. Taking Faith's hand in his, he began to guide her away from the east end part of the lot. Max knew a shortcut. If they took the steps up to the second level, they would access the elevators that would transport them over to the general part of the hospital. Max had never felt so possessive of anyone in his entire life. In fact, he refused to let Faith out of his sight.

He walked her back up to the ICU, where he watched her kiss her father goodnight. Max could tell that James Langhorne was concerned for his daughter. It killed Max that Faith had to put on a strong front for her dad. He'd promised to protect her at all costs. And even if Max had no idea how far Keith planned to take the matter, Max determined never to allow him to hurt Faith in that way again.

***

"Are you feeling a *little* better?" Max asked Faith, gingerly administering soothing ointment to her face. The swelling had gone down a bit where Keith had hit her. However, the redness and the irritation were still visible. Faith sat on a barstool at the kitchen counter, while Max hovered over her, and smoothed the medicine on her face.

"I'm feeling a *lot* better, Max," Faith reassured. Max's tender and caring hands on her skin alleviated the bruises. Everything about Max mitigated her pain and offered hope. "Thanks again for everything. I'm sorry that you had to cut your shift short," she said sounding guilty.

"Oh, don't even worry about it." Max brushed over her face lightly, finishing up what he started. There was a reassuring smile on his face. "I'm sure that I'll have another atrocious shift just like tonight soon enough." Max pulled back and cupped her chin. "How does that feel?" He searched her eyes sensitively.

"So much better," Faith said smiling up at him. "Max, I can't stop apologizing for getting you mixed up in all of my drama." Tears shimmered in her eyes.

"Hey, look at me," Max said throatily, stroking her chin, "there's nothing to apologize about. I walked into this situation with my eyes wide open." He gave her a reassuring smile. "Getting you away from that monster is something that I *unconsciously* submitted to the moment I saw you with him down the road from the middle school."

"I can't believe you came by the school the very next day," Faith assessed, sentimentally gazing into Max's eyes. "I wasn't very kind to you that morning." She frowned in remorse.

"You were perfect," Max uplifted. "In fact, you *are* perfect, huh?" Max took Faith's hand in his and pressed a kiss to it. "You didn't know me."

"Well, I'm *so* glad I got to know you. Max, I also can't believe you beat Keith up." Faith shook her head incredulous and nonsensical. "You didn't even hesitate stepping in, and defending me against him. You don't even know *me*." Faith looked away for a moment, and tears meandered down her cheeks.

"Faith, look at me," Max gently prodded. They were in close proximity, as their eyes fastened. "I know enough to know that you're quite special. I know that you're *worth* fighting for," Max delineated. "I also know that I will *never* let Keith put his hands on you that way again. It's my solemn promise," his voice broke. "I *dropped* the ball tonight, but I promise you, Faith. No one will ever hurt you like that again." Tears were in Max's eyes.

"Max...?" Faith marveled. She threw her arms around him and hugged him comfortingly. "What happened tonight wasn't your fault. Please, let it go. Please, don't punish yourself over it, because…," her voice trailed.

Max inched away enough to lock into Faith's shining eyes. "What is it, honey?" he asked, concerned.

Faith cradled Max's face in one hand and raked her fingers through his thick raven hair with the other. "You're the most wonderful person I've ever known in my entire life," her voice undulated.

Max smiled warmly and pressed a kiss to both of Faith's palms. "Like I said before, Faith, you *really* need to get out more." He winked.

"I don't need to travel the world to know that it's rare to find someone like you. You're the kindest!" Faith brushed her fingers through Max's hair, submitting to how much she enjoyed being close to him.

Faith's grasp around his neck was intoxicating, and Max loved the feel of her fingers sweeping through his hair. It was the most wonderful sensation he'd experienced in quite a while. And yet, there was nothing overtly sensual or romantic about it. Max recognized that they were building on a very special friendship, and this was Faith's way of being affectionate. "You're awfully sweet, Faith," Max told her. "But can I tell *you* something?"

Faith nodded in agreement. "Of course."

"It isn't difficult to be kind to you, because I happen to think you're amazingly kind yourself." His eyes explored hers in earnest.

"Oh, Max, what am I going to do with you?" Faith stared dotingly up at him, as she rhythmically plowed her fingers through his silken mane.

"Hopefully, you will trust me *again* to guide you through this crisis in your life," Max said meekly.

"Max Kane, I've never once stopped trusting you. I need for you to get that," Faith gently chided. "I never have, and I never will lose my faith in you," she affirmed.

"Will you look at that? Faith has *faith* in me," Max teased.

"She sure does," Faith emphasized.

Max smiled meditatively, as Faith gently removed her arms from about his neck. He felt cold as ice after she withdrew her tender touch. But he powered through the vulnerability. "I've already drawn your bath. I put in Epsom salt, lavender, and a bunch of essential oils into the water. That should help you to relax a bit, and you'll sleep better," Max evaded, as his heart raced.

He'd drawn a bath for Faith. Max hoped that it would alleviate the pain and discomfort after all she'd suffered that night. "So, whenever you're ready…." He offered her a warm smile. "Oh, by the way, I also set the clothes you purchased today on your bed. So, you'll be wearing your own PJ's tonight." He winked.

"Thank you, Max," Faith said softly, mesmerized. "I guess I *should* be glad to have my new PJ's, but quite honestly, I kind of liked *yours*. They were so comfortable," she admitted.

"Oh, okay…" Max's cheeks turned ruddy. "I have another pair in blue if you're interested." He chuckled.

"It's alright. I will wear my own pair tonight." Faith hopped off of the stool and turned to leave.

"Are you sure? I really don't mind," Max encouraged.

"I'm okay…" Faith stalled for a moment just staring mawkishly over at Max. She was stirred beyond words. In fact, she was having a hard time believing that he was even real. Max was the storybook prince little girls read and dreamed about. Faith couldn't believe he'd been thoughtful enough to draw her bath. He'd thought of everything.

"Let me know if you change your mind about the jammies," Max razzed, watching Faith drift further away.

"I will," Faith called out, as she neared the kitchen entryway. However, before she disappeared, she turned to look at Max again. He was still standing by the kitchen counter. "Max…?" Faith said softly.

"What is it, sweetheart?" Max asked, concerned.

"Thank you so much for everything!"

"You're very welcome!" Max smiled. Sentimentality masked his face, as he watched Faith turn a corner out of the kitchen.

It was close to midnight, but Max *had* to ensure that certain things were handled with the authorities. It was paramount for him to know that Keith Wendt was detained. He was hoping that a few nights in jail would be a wakeup call. Also, having Keith jailed would buy Faith a little time. Max wanted to secure an emergency order of protection against the man. So, when Faith was ready to go get her things out in Somerset Ridge, she could do so without any interference from her miscreant ex-boyfriend.

"Yeah, I *know* you can't hold him there for too long, but you *can* certainly detain him for a few days. Assault, illegal entry, trespassing… I don't care how you pull it off," Max told Detective Aaron Fennimore over the phone. "He's an abuser. The only reason why he was at the hospital was to harass his ex-girlfriend," Max explained. "He's been such a thorn in her side."

"Is she willing to press charges over his abuse?" the detective asked.

"I'm sure she *would* be willing to. Still, she needs a little time to figure things out. Keep him in that jail cell for the next few days," he exacted.

Max didn't want to promise that Faith *would* press charges against Keith. Max realized that Faith was terrified of him. Sadly, it didn't matter one way or another whether Keith was distant or in close proximity. The fear factor was still the same. Such was the kind of psychological damage abusers wielded over their victims. It was the kind of intimidation that followed, even if the abused were geographically removed from the predator.

"Alright, Max. We will detain him for as long as it's *legally* possible in the county jail. It should be easy enough if we make it almost impossible for him to make bail."

"Great thinking, Aaron. *Make* that work," Max emphasized.

"Don't worry, Max, we've got it all under control. Still, in regards to the physical abuse, you should encourage the young lady to press charges."

Max frowned in concern as he considered Faith. "I will do everything in my power to ensure that she does," he settled. That being said, he got off of the phone with the detective.

Sometime later, Max drifted over to Faith's room carrying a tray of food. Max had just made toasted turkey and cheese sandwiches, and hot chocolate for Faith. Balancing the tray in his left hand, he knocked softly on the door.

"Yes…," Faith said, simultaneously opening up the door to Max. She timorously sized up how handsome Max was. He'd changed out of his work clothes and had on a pair of dark blue sweats and a smoke gray T-shirt. He looked positively dreamy. Faith had seen Max dressed to the nines. And she'd seen him in casual gear, but she couldn't decide which look she liked the best. Max styled them both with equal finesse. He was just beautiful!

"I *thought* you might want something," Max informed, eyeing Faith in her pink, faux-silk pajamas, which she'd purchased at the Target convenience store earlier on. There was something about the color pink that made her look irresistible. Her lengthy hair was out, and graciously tumbled over her shoulders and back. Also, the soft pink material emitted a special light around her angelic face. "You look pretty." Max swallowed hard.

"What, in *this* old thing?" Faith teased.

"Yes…in *that* old thing." Max winked. "Pink is *definitely* your color."

Faith smiled with reddening cheeks. "Thank you, Max. Let's see. What do you have there?" she evaded, and curiously examined the food on the tray.

"Turkey and cheese sandwiches," Max announced. "I hope you're a fan," he enticed.

"I'm a *total* fan. Turkey and cheese is a favorite!" Faith cheered.

"I'm glad. By the way, Faith, you look *so* much better. I think the ointment helped a lot on your face." Max scrutinized Faith's face. The swelling was down, and some of the bruises were already beginning to fade.

"Yeah, I think the ointment helped a lot. And, by the way, *Doctor Kane*, thank you for putting so many awesome things into the bathwater. It really helped. I'm feeling so much better!"

"I'm overjoyed to hear that. Are you ready to turn in for the night?" Max asked, concerned. "Well, actually it's after midnight. So, I guess I should ask if you're ready to turn in for the morning. I'll just set the tray on the nightstand," Max offered.

"Can *we* eat together out in the family room?" Faith suggested. "I just need to wind down a bit. I'm still a little wired after everything that happened tonight. Will you sit with me for a little while?" she asked with a vulnerable expression and tone. Faith was still struggling with feelings of angst and uncertainty.

"Of course... You don't have to ask me twice." Max smiled. "I'm a really great listener," he told Faith as they walked through the expansive house and crossed over into the family room.

"I'll only eat if you join me." Faith sat on the comfortable sofa in Max's beautiful family room. She had longed to explore that room from the first night Max had given her a tour of his amazing mansion. His family room had every imaginable comfort, including a fireplace.

"Of course,...if you insist." Max set the tray on the center table. "Let me go get some more hot chocolate."

"And extra marshmallows," Faith reminded him, watching Max cross out of the spacious room.

Faith sighed and allowed her back to press into the comfortable sofa. It was the first time she'd had a moment since Keith's affront over at the hospital. Faith quavered to relive what happened, and how close she came to returning to Somerset Ridge with Keith. Tears were in her eyes again, but she blinked them back. She kept reminding herself that she was alright now. She was with Max and being with Max was the best place to be. So, she tried to tuck away the bad feelings, and to pull herself together. She had shed more than enough tears for a lifetime that night alone.

"So, Kennedy Proctor-Bohm decided that it was best to end the relationship?" Faith asked, unsettled after hearing Max's story.

"She chose someone else over *you*?" Faith was incredulous, and she kept shaking her head in the negative. "I can't even *imagine* anyone choosing someone else over *you*," she heartened.

"Well, that's sweet, Faith, but the truth is that I made a ton of mistakes. I became someone *I* didn't even recognize and did things I'm not very proud of. Taking that money from Kayden Bohm was the biggest mistake of all. It ruined my life," he admitted. "When Kayden put out that offer, I should have told him that there wasn't enough money in the world..." Max kept shaking his head nonsensically, recounting the life-altering decision he'd made. That awful choice had negatively impacted his life.

"But you returned the money, Max," Faith upheld. "It was an emotional decision, but after you thought it through, you did the right thing." Her face twisted in sympathy.

"There *are* times I think my motives were totally unselfish, but there are others where I'm forced to take responsibility for being so self-absorbed. I *really* didn't need that money," Max admitted, with tears shining in his eyes. The memories overwhelmed him just then.

"Max, I haven't known you for very long, but I *can* say this." Faith prompted him to look at her, and Max's eyes connected furtively to hers. "There isn't anything selfish about you. The offer Kayden Bohm made would have been a test for *any* man.

"Most men would not have valued *love* or integrity enough to return Georgia, so that they could make things right." Faith reached for Max's hand from across the sofa and squeezed it devotedly. "What matters is that despite the lapse in judgment, you had enough dignity and bravery to own up to it." Her eyes delved his perceptively.

"Faith, you give me way too much credit," Max argued. He squeezed her hand in return. "Still, you *should* know how much I appreciate that you believe in me so much." He smiled into her eyes.

"I *do* believe in you, Max-wholeheartedly," she inspired. Faith remained pensive for a moment before she met Max's eyes in query. "Do you still love Kennedy?" Hesitation and diffidence veiled her sweet face.

"When you *truly* love someone, there's this part of you that will *always* love them to some capacity. When my heart was initially broken, I didn't think I'd *ever* get over it."

"And *now*…?" Faith's face creased in affect. Her heart thrashed in dread as she awaited Max's answer.

"*Now*, I trust God's purpose and plan for me. Kennedy is a happily married woman, and I begrudge her nothing. She's a wonderful person, and I would always want for her to be happy. It took some time, but I *have* come to terms with the fact that she just wasn't in God's will. She wasn't *mine*," Max disclosed.

"I know how it feels to make choices you're not proud of. I wish that *I* could go back and undo a lot of the mistakes *I've* made." Tears shone in Faith's eyes at that point. "I wish that I could have had the *assurance* you seem to have in respect to your faith in God," Faith admitted.

Max took both of Faith's hands in his and stared at her with involvement. "You absolutely can, Faith. It's never too late to turn things around. God is always available and makes Himself accessible to anyone who cries out to Him in the name of his Son Jesus Christ."

Faith issued a sad smile. "Max, I *would* want that-I would want to know God more than anything else." Her face warped in sorrow. "I just wish that I had known that God leads and guides, and that he keeps his children from making huge blunders."

"Sweetheart, even now, surrendering your life to Jesus Christ, means that God can take all of the broken pieces, put them together, and make them work for your good." (Romans: 28) Max's face wrinkled in compassion and understanding.

"Max, there are times I think that if I didn't have my son Matthew out of wedlock, he might still be alive today." Faith began trembling, and tears filled her eyes. "He was just a little boy. I still don't know why God took him away from me," she muttered.

"Oh, sweetheart..." Max inched in closer to her on the couch. Collecting her into his arms he allowed her to cry. "It's alright..." He buried his head in her fragrant hair as he pacified. "God didn't take your son away because you did anything wrong. We as human beings often try to figure out why certain things happen.

"God allows them for reasons that are often beyond us. The bible teaches that God's ways, and his thoughts are much higher than ours... (Isaiah 55:9). I'm *so* sorry you lost Matthew, Faith. I can't even imagine how devastating that was for you," Max commiserated. "Still, you've got to realize that God isn't trying to get back at you for anything you've done. He didn't take your son away to punish you." He pulled back and cradled her face in his hands.

"I keep thinking that if I had made better decisions, *both* my mom and Matthew would still be here. That's why I'm so protective over my dad." Her face warped in misery. "He's all I have."

"That's not true," Max countered staring meaningfully into her eyes. "You've also got *me*," he established. "Faith, you need to understand that everything happens for a reason. You can't place those types of burdens on your shoulders," he said throatily. "Why on earth would you ever be so hard on yourself?" Fresh tears gleamed in Max's eyes as he evaluated her words.

"One bad decision has led to another. First, Danny, Matthew's father, abandoned us… Then, I get mixed up with Keith," Faith groused, with tears running down her face. "Maybe, that's what I deserve, Max." She looked up into Max's eyes with a sense of despair.

"Oh, honey, you're so wrong." Max gently brushed the tears away from her eyes, as he explored her sad face. "You deserve only the very best of everything, Faith Langhorne. From what you've just told me, you were a wonderful mom. You made so many sacrifices for Matthew. Your brother and sisters didn't stick around shortly after your mom died.

"So, *you're* the one who's remained out here in Seattle helping your dad piece *his* life together after she passed. You also picked up the slack when he got sick. All of this you've done completely on your own. I've seen you with your dad, Faith." Max stroked fondly on her cheeks. "You are so wonderful with him, and he loves you so much!

"Not to mention the fact that you've loved that troublemaker Keith to the point of sacrifice. You've been longsuffering, devoted and loyal to someone who totally doesn't deserve it," Max inspirited. He was quiet for a moment as he weighed his words. There was something he wanted Faith to know. "Faith, does a diamond stop being a diamond because of where it's found?" Max asked critically.

"No," Faith said softly.

"You might be coming from a very rough place, but that doesn't make you a part of that world. It just means that you've been in the wrong places, being mishandled by those who were incapable of seeing how truly priceless you are," Max's voice resonated. "Do you understand?" His eyes lowered pivotally into hers.

Overwhelmed, Faith remained speechless for a moment. She had no idea how to respond to what Max had just told her. Finally, she asked, "Is that the way you see me?" She marveled.

"Uh-huh," Max said smiling into her eyes. "You are such a precious jewel!" he told her, smiling wistfully into her eyes.

Faith was floored, and eerily silent for a moment. She trembled keenly. Taking Max's hands into hers, she shakily requested, "Will you pray for me?" Her face wrinkled emotionally.

"I would be happy to pray for you, Faith!" Max said with a reassuring smile. Joy inundated on the inside over Faith's resolve.

That morning, Max led Faith to salvation. She received Jesus Christ as her Lord and Savior. Moreover, he prayed over Faith regarding all of the misery she'd endured earlier at Keith's hands. Max wanted her to know that true freedom, and healing could only be found in God through a relationship with Jesus Christ.

CHAPTER SIX

Faith wandered into the kitchen on Thanksgiving morning looking for Max, but he was nowhere to be found. However, crossing over to the counter, she saw that he'd made French toast. Max had also set strawberries on and through the pieces of toast. There was also fresh coffee in the maker. Faith smiled, as she picked up the note Max had left for her to the side of the breakfast tray.

"Happy Thanksgiving, Faith! I hope you slept well. I had to go into the hospital quite early this morning. I called a very special meeting with hospital administration and security before starting my shift. I tried not to make too much noise, because I didn't want to wake you. I hope you like French toast with strawberries. If not, feel free to help yourself to whatever you want. I should be back at around noon. If you need anything at all, please don't hesitate to call or text me.

*"Faith, I know that we'd planned on cooking Thanksgiving dinner together when I got home later, then going over to the hospital together to bring dinner for your dad. But I really don't want you worrying about **anything** at all today. Don't be upset with me, but I've already ordered a precooked Thanksgiving dinner for us. Caterers will be dropping by later.*

*"What **I** want for you to do today is to take care of yourself. I want for you to have a very relaxing and uneventful morning. I've taken the liberty to book a salon appointment for you at the **Beauty Town** Strip Mall just a couple of miles away from the house, where you will submit to a massage, get your hair done, and submit to a*

manicure and pedicure-that is if you should wish to. Luckily, each establishment is a few doors down from the next.

Then, I'd like for you to go into any of the boutiques in that area, and shop to your heart's content. Pick out a lovely dress or a dozen. Please lift up your breakfast tray for a moment..."

Faith marveled over Max's letter. As tears glistened in her eyes, she did as he'd instructed.
Cautiously, lifting up the tray she found he'd left several credit cards. "What...? Max...," she said overwhelmed as tears rolled down her cheeks. "You didn't have to do that..." Her face twisted in bewilderment and affect.

"I know you're going to tell me that I shouldn't have done this, but guess what? I'm not going to listen to you, Ms. Faith. So, you need to get dressed and get going. I took a Lyft into work, and left Dalton's car out in the driveway for you. The keys are hung on the key-holder birdhouse out in the foyer. By the way, you're safe for now. Spoke to the authorities, and they're going to keep Keith under ice for a few days. That will give us a little time to go grab your things from the apartment out in Somerset, and to start getting you moved into the new place.

"I should be home by the time you get done being pampered (smiley face). Faith, we're going to have dinner together. Then, we're going out to see your dad if that's alright. From what I understand he's doing a lot better. Dr. Brice says he's pending discharge tomorrow. I'm thrilled beyond words about how much he's improved. Later-that is if you'll let me-I'd like to surprise you. I realize how bossy and presumptuous I sound in this little letter but bear with me. If you'll allow me to, my dear friend, I'd like to take

you someplace special. So, please try to enjoy this day. By the way, Faith, our time together earlier this morning meant the world to me!

"It meant the world to *me* too, Max," Faith said, rereading his letter. She wiped tears away from her eyes. "Oh, God, thank you! Thank you for bringing Max into my life. I've been through so much, but I couldn't even imagine that you'd bring someone like Max Kane into my life. I marvel over the way our paths have crossed." Faith closed her eyes reflectively, sending up silent prayers, and lifting up the name of the Lord.

Since Max had prayed with her earlier on, she'd felt different, empowered and totally anchored. No longer was she bogged down by her burdens and troubles. For the first time in her life Faith felt as if God was real, and that he was with her and cared.

Her smile was irrepressible, as she took hearty bites of strawberry French toast. It tasted divine! On top of being all around wonderful, Max was also an amazing chef. Perhaps, she figured, being on his own for such a long time, had perfected his culinary skills. Faith knew that Max and his family were originally from Mumbai, India. The Kane's were one of the few families which had converted to Christianity in that region.

Maximillian Mordecai Kane was the eldest of four siblings. Max's birthday was February 7, 1985, and he was thirty-four years of age. Max had two brothers and a sister. Both of his brothers were doctors, specialists in Oncology and Cardiology who lived out in Michigan. Max's sister was an attorney who lived in Houston, Texas. Max's parents lived out in New York.

The more Faith learned about Max, the more in love she was with him. However, she struggled to tell him how she felt. Things being what they were, she was already struggling to free herself from the entanglement of Keith's snare. So, Faith didn't know if she should even try. Nevertheless, she was resolved to pray on the matter. For Faith, being free to share her cares and concerns with God, was the most precious gift in the world. It was something she would never take for granted. Faith's only regret was not being more aware of God's presence from the start.

***

Faith strode over to the *Sheer Elegance Boutique* feeling like a million bucks. She'd just gotten her hair done at *Hair Mirage* and had gotten a deep tissue massage two doors down from the salon. It was late morning, but the skies were overcast. Still, not even the gloomy skies could dampen her spirits. Faith walked confidently. Her freshly relaxed, trimmed and styled hair fluttered in the brisk November wind. Curls tumbled graciously over her shoulders and back. Faith especially loved the light brown, honey and red highlights layered into her hair. She hardly recognized herself, as she looked into the mirror inside of the boutique.

It felt strange to be inside such a high-end establishment. It was the first time Faith had been to such an upscale designer boutique. It was the kind of store only the wealthy frequented-the kind she'd never imagined being able to step foot in. Faith was so humbled by Max's kindness and generosity, she struggled with guilt over it all. However, Max had texted her just a little while earlier, farcically warning her to do exactly as he'd said.

"Can I help you?" the pretty blonde saleswoman with bright blue eyes met Faith the moment she stepped into the boutique.

Startled by the woman's prompt attention, Faith smiled, but flinched in surprise. "Hi," she breathed, gasping to catch her breath.

"Oh, you smell nice," the woman complimented. "What is that scent?"

"I'm not sure." Faith smiled. "Maybe, it's my body lotion or my hair." She shrugged in uncertainty.

"Well, whatever it is smells pretty," the woman enlivened.

"Thank you." Faith kept a pleasant expression on her face, as she perused her surroundings.

"Are you looking for something in particular?" the saleswoman asked.

Faith was a little distracted as she got a feel for the establishment. There were a number of patrons scattered throughout the store, browsing the merchandise. Notwithstanding, several of the sales reps were dispersed in various corners helping them. Faith couldn't help noticing how elegantly the sales reps were dressed. It was obvious that they were modeling some of the designs on sale. "Did you say something?" Faith asked, only discerning mumbles.

"Are you looking for a gown, a dress, heels, a coat…?" the woman asked Faith.

"Oh, I'm sorry. I'm just a little overwhelmed. Your store is amazing!" Faith uplifted. "I'm actually looking for a dress."

"Yes, this *is* actually a great place! I'm Jennifer by the way," the woman told Faith.

"It's nice to meet you, Jennifer! I'm Faith."

"Well, then, *Faith*, come with me," Jennifer said with a winning smile. She headed towards the back, veered right, and encouraged Faith to follow.

Faith compliantly followed behind Jennifer. Jennifer led her over to an area of the store with some of the most beautiful, and expensive looking dresses Faith had ever seen.

"I will get a dressing room started for you," Jennifer told Faith. "Feel free to browse, then let me know what your selections are and in what size."

"Alright," Faith acquiesced, totally overwhelmed. She watched Jennifer float away and disappear towards the dressing room area. "Thank you," Faith called out.

"You're welcome!" Jennifer asserted, and continued towards the back of the store.

It seemed Faith had tried on a hundred different dresses. They were all very nice, but only *one* spoke to her. She'd found a beautiful deep green embroidered lace dress with floral print of pink roses. It was modest, and yet very flattering of her figure. The fringed, belled-shaped bottom made her feel like spinning around in it like a dancer. She couldn't wait to tell Jennifer that this was the one she wanted.

"Wow!" Jennifer breezed back into the open dressing room.

Faith had just stepped out modeling her pick. "This is the one I want!" she gladly announced.

"I don't blame you! You look incredible!" Jennifer said in earnest. "I bet your guy's going to go crazy when he sees you in it!" She issued a playful wink.

Faith shook her head contrarily. "I don't... I don't really... I mean I have a great friend," she shared reticently.

"You won't be *friends* anymore after he sees you in *this* dress," Jennifer razzed. She chuckled and got Faith to laugh as well.

Faith shook her head humorously over Jennifer's words, but didn't say anything. She took a moment to admire herself in the beautiful deep green dress and evaluated that she looked perfect in it. Faith sent prayers of thanksgiving up to God. It was fitting to thank God especially on that day, because it was after all Thanksgiving Day.

***

"Wow! Look at you!" Max acclaimed, meeting Faith at the front door. He marveled, and his eyes grew to the size of quarters seeing her with her hair done. Honey, red and gold curls bounced everywhere, framing Faith's adorable face.

"Max!" Faith celebrated, throwing her arms around him.

Max laughed, having gotten the wind knocked out of him. He placed his arms around Faith's waist and squeezed her lovingly. "Alright then," he quipped. "I'm happy to see you too!"

"Thank you so much for everything!" Faith crushed him lovingly in her arms. For a moment she just basked in their closeness.

"You look absolutely amazing! So, my guess is that you had a great morning."

"I *did*," Faith said, reluctantly letting go of Max. She could tell he was happy to see her too. "I had the best morning and afternoon!" She stepped into the house and shut the front door.

Max took a moment and fiddled with the alarm pad not too far away. He then tuned in to Faith, giving her his undivided attention. Taking her hand in his, they walked through the spacious house. "I'm so glad you enjoyed your day! I *really* wanted you to," Max addressed Faith. "Are you feeling better?" His face strained in concern.

"I'm feeling wonderful!" Faith cheered.

"That's wonderful, honey." Max began guiding Faith over to the dining room, where he'd already set up their Thanksgiving dinner. He stared at Faith sidelong, taking in just what a rare beauty she truly was. Something about her freshly set hair, highlighted and layered, softened her sweet features. Max was thrilled that Faith had had a relaxing and stress-free morning, in spite of all she'd suffered the night before. He wanted to make Faith forget all about the pain, and the demoralization of being under Keith's oppression.

"How was *your* day?" Faith asked, gladly allowing Max to direct her.

"My dad was okay. I had that meeting with hospital security early this morning. The crux of the meeting was to emphasize the importance of keeping our patients and their families safe. So, as of next week, security staff over at the hospital will have to complete a mandatory training course," Max expounded. Delving Faith's eyes, he attested, "What happened at the hospital last night with Keith will *never* happen again. I am taking measures to ensure that."

"I trust you, Max. I know that you're doing the very best you can. No one works harder." Faith reached up and pressed a kiss to his cheek.

"Aw… you're so sweet, Faith. Would you look at that?" Max's face flushed red. "I just got a kiss from a *very* pretty lady." He winked.

"Max, *I* just kissed you. I don't know who this *pretty lady* is," Faith razzed.

"Well, her name is Faith Kendra Langhorne, and she's amazing!" He squeezed her hand.

"Max…," Faith whined, embarrassed.

"Let's go, *pretty lady*." Max took her hand, as they walked through the house.

Before long, they were in the dining room. Max was deeply stirred by Faith's reaction to his surprise.

"Max!" Faith gasped and cupped her mouth in shock.

Max had set up the dinner table so elegantly. White linen tablecloth, napkins, the best crystal, china and silverware embellished the spread. Candles and fine wine also added a dash of flair. In addition, Max had created a fall-themed centerpiece with orange, gold, burgundy and rust-colored flowers. A sizable harvest orange candle was at its center. Furthermore, the food looked incredible and smelled divine! The turkey and ham had been baked to perfection and looked mouthwatering.

"This is *so* beautiful!" Faith marveled. "It looks as if…"

"It looks as if *we* worked on it together," Max inserted. Seeing the celebration on Faith's face and in her eyes made him happy. "Since it's almost three, I thought we'd have an early dinner, and then go over to the hospital to see your dad. By the way, I stopped into the ICU before leaving the hospital, and I saw him." Max pulled out Faith's chair at the dinner table.

"How is he doing?" Faith stared up at Max, as she sat in the chair he'd pulled out for her.

"He looks great, actually. He said he can't wait for the Thanksgiving dinner we're going to sneak over to him later." Impishness shaded Max's face, as he took his place close to Faith at the table.

"My dad is *so* excited about this dinner. The last thing he wanted was to be stuck at the hospital for Thanksgiving."

There was a musing expression on Max's face. "Your dad and I got a chance to talk. He's worried about you." Max stared over at Faith, frowning.

Faith pouted. "He told you that?"

"He wants for me to look out for you," Max informed. "He said he thinks that I'm good for you." Max smiled pensively, reticently searching Faith's eyes.

Faith's cheeks flushed red in embarrassment. "I can't believe he said that." She shook her head incredulous and mortified.

"What...? You *don't* agree with him?" Max flirted, uncertain as to why.

Faith shook her head comically and with wandering eyes. "Are we ready to say grace?" she eluded with scarlet cheeks.

Max smiled contemplatively. He then took Faith's hands into his. The two bowed their heads and said grace over the scrumptious meal they were about to enjoy.

"There's just one more tradition we need to cover before we dig in," Max said with a pleasant expression on his face after they said grace.

"And what's that, Doctor Kane?" Faith asked properly, sizing up just how incredibly handsome Max looked in his deep green cardigan and dark dress slacks. His hazelnut skin radiated, and his gingerbread-colored eyes glistened in affect. So much love inundated her heart, Faith hardly knew how to contain it all.

"We *have* to say what we're thankful for." Max propped his chin with his right hand and stared devotedly over at Faith.

Faith's cheeks were still scarlet, as she offered a timid smile. "Well, that's easy. There's so much to be thankful for this year! First and foremost, I'm thankful to God for revealing Himself to me. A relationship with God is exactly what's been missing in my life.

"God has used an incredible person to lead me to faith in Jesus! In addition to God's spiritual blessings, I'm thankful for this extravagantly set table, and this amazing meal we're about to enjoy. I'd also like to add just how grateful I am that the hairdresser got my hair just right, and that I found this amazing shade of nail polish. It's going to go perfectly with the new dress I bought," she rambled on facetiously.

"Are you done now?" Max asked chuckling. "You're grateful for nail polish on Thanksgiving Day huh?"

"I wasn't finished Mr. Know-it-all." Faith rolled her eyes teasingly.

Max acceded and gestured for her to finish.

"What I'm *most* grateful for is that God brought Doctor Max Kane into my life," her voice undulated, and tears filled her eyes.

"It's such a blessing to be in his presence on this very special day!" Tears escaped the corners of her eyes.

Stirred beyond words, Max's eyes glimmered in affect as he stared at Faith.

"I don't know what I would have done without him. He's actually kept me alive these past few days. I'm so thankful to be alive, and to be in such a safe place with such a wonderful friend. This amazing man has shown me what true friendship means. He's embodied everything unselfish and sacrificial," Faith's voice broke.

"Oh, Faith," Max's voice was guttural, and he shook his head incredulous over her accolade. Tears brimmed over in his eyes, and he was temporarily speechless.

"It's true, Max. You've shown me what *real* friendship is all about. You've sacrificed your time and your resources. You've brought me into your home, and you're risking your life just to make mine a little better. I can't believe how much you've fought for me." Faith's face warped emotionally.

Max reached for Faith's hand. Holding it devotedly, he searched her eyes. "Some people are definitely worth fighting for. Do you want to know what *I'm* thankful for?" he reversed.

"What are *you* thankful for?" Faith asked softly, as her heart stirred with love and admiration. She wondered if she'd ever find the right moment to tell him how she felt.

"I'm thankful for *our* friendship. I'm thankful that God has brought you into my life as well, Faith. I know you said that *I've* kept you alive. The truth is that's what *you've* done for *me*. Before you came along, I was living a pretty selfish life. Everything was about me."

"There's nothing selfish about you, Max. You're the most wonderful person I've ever met! Besides, I know how much you've been hurt. So, you've been a little bit guarded," she defended.

"Thanks for believing in me, Faith. Still, you came along, and reminded me that life should never be just about me." Max smiled in earnest. "Can I tell you something else?" His eyes lowered meaningfully into hers.

"Anything….," Faith encouraged, heartened.

"Making sure you're safe is essential to me. I won't let you down again…" Max held his hand up haltingly because Faith tried to interject. "I *know* you've told me a dozen times that what happened last night wasn't *my* fault, but I can't help feeling as if it was." Fresh tears shimmered in his eyes. "The thought of anyone putting their hands on you…" Max shook his head in the negative. "Well, it should *never* have happened."

"Max, please don't blame yourself," Faith petitioned. "Promise that you'll stop beating yourself up about what happened, okay?" She squeezed his hand. "I know that there isn't anything you would not have done to keep it from happening.

"Still, as wonderful as you are, Max Kane, only *God* can protect me every second of every day." Faith sensitively caressed his hand as she explored his eyes. "Can we *not* focus on the negative, and just be thankful that we're together on this awesome day?" Faith enlivened with a cheerful smile. "Can we just enjoy this wonderful meal?"

Max smiled through the tears. "Of course, we can," he inspired. "We can definitely focus on all of the positive things in our lives on this *very* special day." Max brought Faith's hand up to his lips and pressed a fond kiss to it.

"Max, thank you." Faith stared over at him with a sentimental expression on her face.

"What are you thanking me for *now*?" Max teased.

"Thank you for this awesome day of pampering, and for being the closest thing I've ever had to a best friend!"

Max gave Faith a devoted look. "You're welcome, Faith! I feel the same way." Their eyes locked at that moment. "Well, I think dinner's getting cold. Shall we eat?" Max tried to work past the muddled emotions brewing on the inside.

"We should definitely eat as if food is going out of style," Faith joked, laughing.

Max shook his head humorously and chuckled. "We should *definitely* do that."

Taking the initiative, Max carved into the turkey and the honey ham. It was a total pleasure to serve Faith, and to enjoy such a delicious Thanksgiving meal together. Max genuinely liked being around Faith. They could and usually *did* talk about everything.

Also, having a little downtime from the hospital felt great. And, for Max, there wasn't anyone else he would have wanted to spend such precious time with.

After dinner, Max and Faith cleared off the dinner table, and set the house in order. As they did, they took time to pack Thanksgiving dinner into Tupperware for Faith's dad. When they got done with those chores, Max encouraged Faith to go and get ready. He'd promised to take her someplace special after they left the hospital later. Max also planned to dress a bit more formal for their special rendezvous.

Dressing formally all of the time was commonplace for Max. Still, he knew that his colleagues over at Fairfield were for the most part very nosy. And Max didn't want them spreading any rumors about his friendship with Faith. His work associates were like ravenous wolves when it came to sifting through his private affairs. However, that evening, he could care less. For the sake of time, he and Faith *had* to be in formal attire by the time they left the hospital later.

Max's jaw dropped to the floor, and he was temporarily thunderstruck, when Faith drifted over into the living room to join him. It was half past four p.m., and they had to leave for the hospital. Captivated, Max found it difficult to verbalize all of the impressions he had just then. Seeing Faith in her new dress had left him both winded and speechless. Faith looked ravishing. The deep green dress hugged her curves. The style accentuated her small waist, her shapely hips, and highlighted her amazing legs. Faith's mane tumbled in curls over her shoulders and back and framed her exceptional face.

Faith was uncertain what Max was thinking, and uncertainty creased her face. "Do you like the dress?" Her hands brushed modestly over the skirt. Faith felt self-conscious, because Max was gaping. "Should I go change into something else?" she asked insecurely.

Max shook free of the trance but found himself unable to stop ogling. "Faith, you look incredible!" He was utterly transfixed as he took in every inch of Faith. "I love the dress! Is this the one you picked out today?"

Faith nodded. "It's the one I couldn't leave the store without," she said reservedly.

Equally enticed, Faith sized up just how amazing Max looked in light gray slacks, a black shirt, matching tie, and a casual black jacket. For all intents and purposes, he'd just stepped out from a men's catalogue. Max's broad shoulders and stalwart arms had greater definition in his ensemble. Again, Faith evaluated just what a beautiful body Max had. She swallowed hard, and tried not to swoon, as she took steps closer to him.

"Well, I'm glad you didn't leave the store without this amazing dress. It's definitely the right one," Max appraised. "Although, I had hoped that you would have picked out more than just one."

Faith smiled timidly. "One is fine, Max," she said softly. "By the way *you* look nice!" she evaded, staring diffidently up into his eyes. "You also smell wonderful!"

"Well, thank you. Coming from such a beautiful lady that means a lot." Max issued a playful wink.

Faith's cheeks turned scarlet, and her eyes wandered away. "Max…," she whined timidly, surprised by his open admiration.

Realizing he might have embarrassed her, Max changed the subject, "I've already packed everything into the car, so we're all set to go." It was still difficult to get his bearings. Faith was so beautiful he couldn't look away. From the day they'd met over at the middle school, Max had evaluated just how gorgeous Faith was. Nevertheless, that afternoon, he was entranced.

"So, I guess we should go." Faith's eyes wandered. She was suddenly shy and nervous around Max. Having spent the past couple of nights at his house, Max had seen her in her nightgown and in her PJ's. He'd seen her wearing his T-shirt and sweater. Furthermore, he'd seen her with her hair up in a ponytail, when she'd worn it out, and when it had looked disheveled. So, there was no reason for her to feel self-conscious. Still, Faith perceived that something was changing between them. All of the sudden she was reserved and timid.

"Well, then, let's go pretty lady." Max took Faith's hand in his, and stared sidelong at her, as she looped her arm through his. There was a sense of dignity having her next to him. For one reason or another, he couldn't wait for everyone to see the beauty on his arm. Max felt a sense of pride when he opened up the car door for Faith and secured her inside. Suddenly, it was difficult to express himself around Faith, and he found himself staring unrelentingly at her.

"Max, you're still *not* going to tell me where we're going after we leave the hospital?" Faith asked, as silence hummed between them on their way over to the hospital.

"Nope. You couldn't even *beat* it out of me." A waggish smile was on Max's face, as he turned to address Faith's question at a stop light.

"You are *so* mean," Faith razzed. There was such intense energy between them, Faith was overwhelmed.

"You think *I'm* mean?" Max quipped.

"Heartless," Faith said farcically.

"Well, you *know*," Max shrugged, "I do what I can."

"Whatever, Max," Faith said, feigning hurt feelings. "Not even a hint...?" she goaded, with an enticing smile.

"As beautiful as that smile is-and don't get me wrong-it's perfect-you're not going to get a thing out of me." Max chuckled. "Give up yet?"

"Never..." Faith crossed her arms defiantly over her chest, and feigned exasperation. Max refused to tell her where they were going after they left the hospital. Honestly, she was curious to know why they were dressed in formal attire. Still, her heart raced in anticipation, because with Max, the possibilities were endless.

Max liked that Faith was curious about where they were going, but he enjoyed torturing her even more as she tried to guess. There was a sense of contentment he had not felt in a long time. Being around Faith sparked hope in his heart, and Max realized how much he wanted to keep a smile on her face. It was paramount to him that she never cried tears of despair again.

***

"Sweetheart that was the best Thanksgiving meal I've ever had!" James Langhorne praised, staring devotedly at his daughter.

"You should *really* thank Dr. Kane, daddy." Faith winked at Max. Max stood to the opposite side of the bed, to her dad's right hand side. "He's the one who called the caterers."

"Dr. Kane, thank you." James Langhorne's eyes linked to Max's, and he offered an amiable smile. His eyes shone in affect. "Thank you so much for *all* you've done!"

"No thanks required, Mr. Langhorne. Faith told me how much you were looking forward to Thanksgiving at home, and we didn't want you feeling as if you missed out." Max nodded reassuringly.

"Dr. Kane, the meal was wonderful, but that's not the *only* reason why I'm thanking you."

"Daddy…," Faith raised her voice, and stared at her father incredulous. Her cheeks reddened in embarrassment.

"No, sugar, please let me say this," he refuted.

"Dad…" Faith shook her head in skepticism, blushing.

Max chortled, stirred by Faith's interactions with her dad, but he didn't say a word.

"Dr. Kane, you've gone above and beyond for me and for Faith. I can't thank you enough!"

Max held his hand up in a halting manner and shook his head in the negative. *"Really*, Mr. Langhorne, no thanks required. Faith and I are just grateful to God that you're doing better. We're even more excited that you're being discharged tomorrow," Max uplifted.

"I *am* looking forward to leaving this luxury hotel," James bantered.

"No doubt," Max acceded, chuckling.

"Sugar," James redirected towards his daughter, "you can look at me now," he prodded.

Faith's eyes connected briefly to her dad's, but then veered towards Max. He was staring sentimentally and smiling.

"Dad, I'm sorry, but..." Faith started to say, feeling uneasy about her dad's disclosures.

"Sugar, I told Dr. Kane how happy I am that the two of you are such great friends!" James went on to embarrass his daughter.

"I agree one hundred percent, Mr. Langhorne!" Max's smiling eyes connected to Faith's. "In fact, I hope that Faith and I will be friends for a very long time," he mitigated, realizing how horrified Faith was by her dad's transparency.

"I hope so too, Max," Faith said quietly, diffidently staring into his eyes. "Dad, what time did Mrs. Tandy leave?" Faith segued away from the subject at hand. She looked over across, and saw Max snickering, and shaking his head humorously.

"She left at about a quarter to five. Her family is visiting from Baltimore." James continued staring between Faith and Max.

"Oh, that's nice. I hope she has a wonderful holiday. She's been a real godsend these past few years," Faith added.

"I have to agree with you there, Sugar. God could not have sent a better nurse to help me."

"So, how are *you* feeling overall, Mr. Langhorne?" Max asked, on a more serious note.

"I can honestly say that I'm feeling a lot stronger than I have in a while. Being admitted to the hospital hasn't been fun, but I guess it was necessary. Thank you for acting so quickly the other day, Dr. Kane."

"I'm just glad you're feeling so much better. So far, I haven't picked up on any wheezing and whistling. Based on what Dr. Brice has told me, your bronchial passages are a lot clearer than they were a couple of days ago. That is amazing news!" Max smiled, encouraged.

"Carrying out a conversation with my beautiful daughter, and her *new* friend without coughing, wheezing or struggling for air *is* a miracle!" James looked over at Faith and winked.

Faith's head slumped in shame, and she wanted to sink to the floor. However, when she looked over at Max, he was staring curiously at her. Faith gave him a reserved smile-doing all she could not to get too bogged down by feelings of mortification.

It was obvious that her dad was eager to see a romantic connection form between Max and herself. Even if that *was* what Faith wanted too, she didn't know if Max felt the same way. Max had made it clear that they were friends. She was barely out of the woods with Keith, so it wasn't fair to bring Max into the mayhem.

Before she could entertain anyone else, the matter with Keith had to be sorted out. Yet and still, Faith had no idea how to contain the profundity of the love she felt for Max. It was so staggering it often overwhelmed. Trying to tuck it away was like trying to contain a gorilla in a breadbox. However, none of it mattered if Max didn't see *her* as a romantic prospect.

It was after six when Max and Faith set out to leave the ICU. Faith encouraged her dad to hang in there for one more night, because he was pending discharge on the on the following day. "So, I will come by the hospital tomorrow afternoon to pick you up. Mrs. Tandy will be with you in the morning, and she'll also be there when you get home, daddy," Faith explained.

"Of course, Sugar. Don't worry about me. I'll be just fine. Are you working tomorrow?" he asked.

"No, I'm off from work tomorrow, but I *do* go back on Monday." Faith squeezed her dad's hand in support.

In the upcoming week, Faith would tell her boss she planned to quit her job. Max promised to tag along to ensure her safety. They both knew that once Keith made bail, he would try to find her over at the school. Because of Keith's volatility, Faith was skeptical of extending a two-week notice. Nonetheless, she resolved to cross that bridge when she got to it.

Faith hovered over her dad, hunched down, and pressed a loving kiss to his forehead. "I love you, and I will call you a little later," she said sweetly.

"I love you too, Sugar. Now, go on. Get out of here. Don't keep Dr. Kane waiting," James said in a hushed tone.

Max stood to the side of the hospital room door, shaking his head humorously. It seemed Mr. Langhorne didn't realize that he could hear his and Faith's exchanges. Max found Mr. Langhorne's unadulterated honesty cute. What he found even *more* adorable was how embarrassed Faith was over the matter. It was obvious that her dad was trying to establish a romantic connection between them. However, Max resolved not to take advantage of Faith in that way. She had suffered unspeakably in a horror show of a relationship, and the last thing she needed was to jump headlong into another.

Although, as Max scrutinized how gorgeous Faith looked that night, he was ready to admit that he was utterly captivated. It was the first time in a while he'd felt so drawn to anyone. It was a miracle he never thought would occur in his life again. Max evaluated that he felt strongly for Faith-stronger than he'd ever felt for anyone else. Still, he couldn't be selfish. He would be the friend she needed until she was strong enough to piece her life back together again.

When Mr. Langhorne drifted off to sleep, Faith crossed over to Max. "Did you want to stay for a little while longer?"

There it was again. Max was completely mesmerized. Ogling Faith, he was slipping into the honey of her eyes. Realizing that he was losing ground, Max shook off the trance and smiled. "No, we should definitely get going now that your dad's asleep."

"Okay." Faith gave him a curious look.

"I hope you don't mind, but there is actually *one* stop I need to make before we go over to *the place*...." He winked.

"We're stopping off someplace first?" Faith asked, confused.

"Yeah, well, I kind of promised Ava Thorne we'd have dinner over at her place today, but…"

Faith's heart fell in disappointment. Nonetheless, she worked past feelings of disillusionment and forced a smile. "Max, why didn't you tell me you had plans? You really didn't have to hang out with me for the entire day," her voice undulated, and she fought back tears. The thought of Max dating Ava Thorne was tearing Faith apart, but she couldn't react. Max wasn't *her* guy. He didn't belong to her, even if she wanted him to.

Max moved in closer to Faith, and gently set his hands on her shoulders. Delving her eyes, he affirmed, "Faith, I *wanted* to spend this day with you. In fact, it's one of the best days of my entire life!" he emphasized, exploring her sweet face.

"Are you *sure*?" Faith tested, with a hammering heart. There were butterflies in her stomach, and her heart had dipped to the floor, because Max's beautiful and strong hands were on her skin.

"And, this day is only going to get better," Max affirmed, smiling into her eyes. "Alright?"

Faith nodded and smiled up into his eyes, feeling encouraged. "Alright. For the record, Dr. Kane, this is the *best* day I've ever had!" she inspired.

"You enjoyed yourself at the strip mall?" Max speculated.

"I did, but that isn't why. It's the best day because I got to spend it with you," she said openly.

"Aw, Faith… You're much too sweet." Max's cheeks turned cardinal, and his eyes shied away in reticence for a moment.

Faith inched up and pressed a fond kiss to Max's face. She felt totally possessive of him. That kiss was an inadvertent reminder that he had her heart, even if she couldn't tell him yet. The kiss was also playing damage control for when Max went over to see Ava in a little while.

Max felt flustered all over, his heart raced, and his stomach sank, as Faith's lips pressed to his cheek. It was a reaction he had not anticipated. His entire body chemistry had changed upon contact, and Max didn't know what to make of it. If he'd doubted before, he could no longer deny that he was attracted to Faith. However, being drawn to Faith wasn't difficult, because she was stunning.

What got Max in a pinch was wanting her in his arms, and the potent desire to kiss her. Max perceived that he was in a great deal of trouble. The way he was beginning to feel for Faith was something he needed to pray about extensively. Fortunately, he would be helping Faith settle into her new place tomorrow. Somewhere along the road things had changed, and Max was struggling with strong desire for his new *friend*.

***

"Max!" Ava beamed the moment she saw Max standing at her door. "I didn't think you were coming anymore." Her smile was irrepressible.

"I *did* promise, didn't I?" Max extended a bag to Ava containing the desserts and the bottle of wine he'd promised. He could hear music and conversation in the background inside of the house.

"And *you*, Doctor Kane, are a man of your word. It's one of the things I love most about you!" Ava gladly took the bag and set it on her foyer table. "Are you *sure* you can't come in for a just a minute?" she tempted. Ava's eyes drifted over to Max's SUV parked out in her driveway. She saw Faith Langhorne sitting snugly inside.

"So sorry, Ava. I can't tonight, but we can do a raincheck." Max's face strained in uneasiness. "But I hope you enjoy dessert and the wine," Max redirected, and offered Ava a warm smile.

"Thank you so much for remembering and for stopping by!" Ava impulsively threw her arms around Max. However, she reflexively cradled his head in her hands, reached up, and linked her lips to his. Ava's mouth flowed over Max's like ripples on a lake. "Since we're not hanging out this evening, I thought I should take a moment," she murmured in between kisses.

Max was completely taken aback by Ava's display. It took a moment to get his bearings. Not wanting to be abrasive, he subtly began to edge away. Max presumed Ava wanted to solidity a romance, but he couldn't say that they were on the same page. He liked Ava a great deal. Although, if he wanted to be totally honest with himself, the only person he could see as a romantic prospect was Faith. "Goodnight, Ava," Max said, respectfully pulling away. "Happy Thanksgiving!"

"Good night, Max." Ava felt conflicted. "And Happy Thanksgiving to you!" Her heart twisted in knots, because she perceived that her impulsive kiss was ill-received.

"Night, Ava." Max smiled uneasily.

Max felt sick at heart, because he was certain that Faith had witnessed the kiss. Why he was so worried about it was beyond him. Furthermore, Max understood that even if *he* felt strongly for Faith, there was no guarantee that *she* felt the same way. Not to mention the fact that she was still in process of emancipation from Keith Wendt's violent grasp. Despite the former arguments, Max still felt guilty. There was a sense of shame over the display, because Faith had a front row seat. He didn't want to feel out of sorts, but it was difficult not to. Faith thinking less of him, to any capacity, bothered him a great deal.

Faith's eyes deluged with tears, and she trembled while waiting in the car for Max. She was torn up on the inside, because she'd just witnessed Max and Ava kissing. If she'd had any doubts before, it was now crystal clear that Max was *only* interested in being friends. He wasn't romantically interested in her. To the contrary, Faith surmised that Max had probably taken her on as a project. It was his civic duty to help out the needy girl in trouble.

Faith's thoughts raced as she sat there. And yet, she had to find a way to pull it together, because Max would soon return. Prior to making this little pit stop with Max, Faith had been enjoying the best Thanksgiving of her entire life. However, seeing Ava's mouth pressed up to Max's a moment ago, had shattered her perception of the perfect day.

Faith had to feign total aplomb, and act nonchalantly, even if all she wanted was to find a quiet and secluded place to cry. Suddenly, she was reminded that God's presence was there with her. She no longer had to carry the heavy burdens on her own. As she strove to pull herself together, she sent a prayer heavenward, "Jesus, I'm brokenhearted. I love Max so much, but it's obvious that he doesn't feel the same way.

"I'm totally out of his league. A woman like Ava Thorne is the type everyone expects to see on his arm. I never finished college; I had a baby out of wedlock... I'm not good enough for Max." Faith was overwhelmed by sadness. It grieved her to internalize the fact that she'd never know Max intimately enough to be in his arms, to hold him and to kiss him.

"Please, help me, Jesus! Max has been great to me, so he doesn't deserve the cold shoulder. It isn't his fault that I'm in love with him. Please, take away the strong feelings that I have for him. It's killing me to feel this way, and not be able to…" Faith swallowed the chunk lodged in her throat.

Looking through the windshield, she saw that Max had turned away from Ava. He was dismounting her front steps and headed back over to the car. Faith quickly used tissues to wipe under her eyes and to blow her nose. Reaching into her pocketbook, she accessed her makeup bag and freshened up. She didn't want Max seeing her in such a state. Applying facial powder and concealer, Faith worked on the under-eye puffiness. Furthermore, she retouched her eyeliner and mascara. Luckily, her mascara was waterproof. Max was almost to the car door, when Faith set everything back into her pocketbook, and tried to look poised.

"Sorry that took a little longer than expected, but we're still making great time." Max hopped back into the SUV and took his place behind the wheel. He stared curiously over at Faith. "Are you okay?" Concern wrinkled his face. Max prayed that she didn't think any less of him, because of what had just occurred with Ava. Ava's inconsiderate behavior still gnawed at him. Even if he and Ava *had been* an item, Max would not have shown any PDA's, while Faith was in the car waiting for him.

"I'm fine, Max," Faith said, smiling until her face hurt.

"Are you sure?" Max tested.

"Uh-huh," Faith said pertly, trying to work through tangled emotions.

"You *do* still want to go with me, right?" Uncertainty masked his face. Inwardly, Max's heart rent in half.

"Of course, I want to go with you, Max. I've been excited about attending this event with you all day," Faith said in earnest, perking up. She still struggled with jealous and insecure feelings over the kiss Max and Ava had shared, but Faith was trying to move past them.

"Faith," Max said searching her eyes, in the penumbra of twilight, "I'm so sorry about…" Max shook his head contrarily, and his face warped in remorse.

Surprised, Faith's eyes widened, and her mouth gaped. "What are you sorry about, Max?" she asked nonplused.

"I didn't plan what just happened. I'm sorry for the display up there with Ava. She sort of caught me off guard, and I would never…"

Faith smiled musingly, realizing just how attuned Max was. Was he actually apologizing for what happened with Ava? Max hadn't said it was *wrong* that Ava had kissed him, he'd just apologized for the display. Still, Faith was moved, because he was so considerate of her feelings. His intuition and kindness only intensified her love for him.

"You don't have to apologize to me for anything, Max Kane," Faith argued, genuinely smiling. In her estimation, if Max felt the need to apologize about the kiss, then he truly cared about her as a person. Maybe, Max *didn't* feel anywhere near the way *she* felt for him, but hope sparked in her heart that he *did* care.

"Yes, I do, Faith. I'm sorry you had to see that. I would never engage in behavior like that knowing you're out here waiting for me. It was done in poor taste," he concluded. Max eyes explored Faith's. "Forgive me," he emphasized.

Faith marveled, totally floored by his insightfulness. "There's nothing to forgive, Max. It's okay." Faith stared devotedly at him, utterly stirred. There was such a strong inclination to ask him about his connection to Ava Thorne, but Faith was too nervous to broach the subject.

"Alright then." Max gave Faith a genuine smile. He wanted to expound on the matter and reassure her that Ava was the one who'd taken the initiative to kiss him, but Max didn't see the point. Regardless, he was still conflicted in regards to setting the record straight. The more time he spent around Faith, the stronger his feelings were growing for her.

"Is Ava your girlfriend?" Faith divulged, as Max pulled away from Ava's. Nowadays, Faith wasn't sure why it was that she kept blurting things out. Putting it all out there had not been her intention. So, she regretted asking the question the moment the words slipped out of her mouth.

Max smiled quietly and contemplatively over Faith's question. He wondered if she was beginning to develop feelings for him as well. He was a bit surprised by her bluntness, but her reaction gave him hope that she might like him just a little. "No, Ava isn't my girlfriend." Max stared sidelong over at Faith, as they lingered at a stop sign.

Faith's face flustered in embarrassment. She felt like kicking herself over being so direct. She couldn't believe she'd just asked Max that question, and hardly recognized herself for doing so. "I'm sorry, Max. I really shouldn't have asked you that." She frowned in remorse.

"No, it's fine. You can ask me anything, Faith. The truth is that Ava and I went out on *one* date, and we've talked on the phone a few times. We were supposed to be spending today together, but…"

"Is it *my* fault? Am I keeping you from spending time with her?"

"Faith, I'm exactly where I *want* to be today. Spending the day with you has been so wonderful and rewarding!" Max told her emphatically, searching her eyes. "And getting to spend time with you and your dad…" He shook his nonsensically. "Priceless…"

Faith smiled. "That's such a sweet thing to say, Max." Tears shone in her eyes, and her heart inundated with even more love for him.

"It's the truth. Also, Faith, for the record, if I *did* have a girlfriend, you would be the first person I would share the news with," Max voice was throaty, as he stared penetratingly into Faith's eyes.

Faith gulped, stunned by Max's disclosure. Tears spilled over her eyelids, and she shook her head dubiously. "Oh, Max…" Her

eyes fastened to his. It was all she could say, because she was all
choked up.

Max stared unwaveringly at Faith. As their eyes fastened, it
dawned on him that his feelings were growing by the second. It was
just like a landslide. There was nothing he could do to stop it.
Despite the slippery slope, he *had* to try to take things slow. There
were still so many obstacles to overcome. However, for the first
time since his poignant breakup with Kennedy Proctor-Bohm, Max
was actually hopeful. And being hopeful again was a great feeling!
"Are you all set for your surprise, beautiful?" he asked
enthusiastically.

"I'm *not* happy that you've held out on me all day, but I *am*
ready for my surprise," Faith affirmed. She was totally spellbound,
and on a cloud because Max had just called her *beautiful*. Moments
ago, she'd been falling apart, because she'd been under the
impression that Ava Thorne was Max's girlfriend. However, after
praying, God had opened up her eyes and cleared the air.
Hopelessness and insecurity had evanesced, and Faith was actually
optimistic.

"I'm positive that you *will* forgive me for holding out on you
once we get there." Max winked.

"Okay, I trust you, Max." Faith stared fondly at him.

"I'm glad you do. I hope you know that you can, Faith,
because I would never hurt you." Max's eyes shone in affect.

"I know that, Max," Faith said softly, marveling. It was
difficult to grasp how this perfect man, who'd taken her breath away,

cared so much about her. Faith also couldn't help noticing how perfect Max looked in the haze of dusk. He was truly a wonder!

"Are you cold?" Max asked Faith, as they slipped out into the expressway.

"Just a little." Faith shuddered.

Pulling over to the side of the road, he slipped off his jacket, and draped it over Faith's shoulders.

"Thank you." Faith smiled and took refuge in Max's snug jacket-relishing the heavenly scent of his clean and musky cologne.

"You're welcome!" Max smiled back. Then, fiddling with dials on the console, he put the heat up a bit. Before long, they were rolling back out onto the expressway.

CHAPTER SEVEN

Max and Faith had orchestra seats for the Christmas extravaganza musical in downtown Seattle at the *Warrington Theater*. It was the very first presentation of *A Christmas Epiphany* of the season. Each year the theater made it a point to kick off their season on Thanksgiving Day. The musical was always centered on a married couple facing difficult times. Amidst their struggle, the pair rediscover true love, and meaning during the most wonderful time of the year.

In the interim were great vocals, amazing dancing-comparable to that of the Rockets at Radio City Music Hall in New York City. There were also excerpts taken from the Nutcracker-all brought together to create one of the most spectacular presentations. Max was all smiles seeing the performances through Faith's eyes. For the obvious reasons, it was difficult to keep his eyes off of her. Faith radiated brighter than the stars that night. Furthermore, her excitement was that of a child's at the circus. The joy bubbling over was infectious.

Each time their eyes met, Max and Faith exchanged meaningful smiles. Max loved that Faith was so captivated by the show. "Are you having a good time?" Max leaned in close and whispered in her ear.

"I love it, Max!" Faith cheered, taking his hand in hers. She wasn't sure why she'd made such an impulsive move, but it felt right.

Max was startled that Faith was holding his hand. The sensation of her hand stroking his was nice, so Max wanted her to hold on for a while.

"I love the way Raymond's wife Deborah breaks out into song every time they start to argue," Faith whispered in Max's ear during the performance.

Max chuckled. "I think it's her way of stopping the fight before it gets heated," he told Faith quietly. "She has an amazing voice!" he remarked.

"She's awesome!" Faith agreed.

"Raymond, have you ever thought about the true meaning of Christmas?" Deborah from the show asked her husband.

"Of course, I have, sweetheart. Christmas is the most wonderful time of the year. There's trimming the tree, shopping at the mall for hours for family and friends. We get to drink apple cider and Eggnog while sitting by the fire, there's sledding..."

"No, Raymond, you've got it all wrong. Those things are nice, but they are not the true meaning of Christmas. The true meaning of Christmas is God's gift to mankind sending his only Son to be the light in this dark world... Luke chapter 2:11 says that unto us is born this day in the city of David a Savior who is Christ the Lord..." At that juncture, Deborah's character was highlighted on the stage. Her husband Raymond faded into the background, as magnetizing stage lights centered on her.

The melody for *Oh Holy Night* overwhelmed and overtook everyone sitting inside of the spacious and lavish theater.

"Oh, Max, this is beautiful!" Faith's eyes shone with affective tears. She mouthed the lyrics to Oh Holy Night. *"Fall on your knees. Oh hear the angel's voices. Oh, night divine. Oh, night when Christ was born..."*

"It's perfect," Max said, unable to contain his nostalgia and delight. Seeing Faith so happy she was actually singing along stirred his heart. He squeezed her hand devotedly, completely enthralled.

The presentation ended with all of the performers on the spacious extravagantly adorned stage singing *Silent Night*. The performance had so moved Max, he found himself humming along. However, he saw that there were tears in Faith's eyes. "Are you okay, honey?" he asked, pertained.

"I'm great, Max. This is one of the most beautiful plays I've ever seen!" she leaned in closely to him to tell him.

"I'm glad you liked it," Max told her.

"Liked it? Max, I loved it!" Faith inched up and pressed a kiss to his cheek. "Thank you so much!"

You're welcome, sweetheart! So, does that mean you forgive me for holding out on you?" Max asked, touched by her affectionate embrace. It dawned on him that he was beginning to enjoy Faith's kisses a little too much.

"You're totally forgiven," Faith reassured.

"That's good to know." He winked at her.

Every cell in Max's body had reacted to Faith's sweet kiss. It was getting to the point that he wanted to feel her lips on his. Max longed to initiate a kiss-and not just on the cheek. He knew that he was definitely in trouble. There was no way he could continue to deny that he was falling for Faith, and it was happening quickly. However, he wanted to protect her at all costs. So, despite his growing feelings, he didn't want to rush anything.

After meeting and talking to some of the performers from the presentation, Max helped Faith into the SUV. By then, it was almost eleven p.m. "So, what did you think?" Max looked over at Faith, eager to hear her opinion.

"I'm so glad we got to be here for the very first performance of the season!" Faith beamed, and stared affectionately over at Max. "Max, it was amazing! I had no idea that there was such an awesome Christmas presentation right here in Seattle."

"I'm glad you enjoyed it, Faith." Max caught her eye and smiled again. "Maybe, one of these days you and I can go out to New York to see the Rockets at Radio City Music Hall!" Max encouraged, surprising himself. He couldn't believe he'd just put that out there.

"You want to take me to New York?" Faith marveled.

"I would *love* to take you to New York one of these days, Faith," Max said without equivocation.

"That would be great!"

"You would *actually* go with me?" Max was surprised, as he pulled away from the locale.

"I don't think there's anywhere I *wouldn't* go with you, Max Kane," Faith said in earnest, with reddened cheeks. Her taciturn twin had returned.

Max smiled musingly over Faith's words, but didn't say anything. Inwardly, there were a myriad of emotions at play. He was just coming to terms with the fact that he was falling for Faith. It wasn't something he'd planned, but he had no idea how to stop the momentum.

All things considered; it was imperative for Faith to move into her own place as soon as possible. In light of his growing feelings, Max deemed it to be unwise that she was staying over at his place. "Faith, first thing in the morning, we're taking a drive out to Somerset Ridge," Max brought up.

"First thing in the morning?" Faith asked confused. "I thought you were working in the morning."

"I was, but I decided it was best to take the day off. Keith is behind bars at least for another day. I doubt that they can detain him any longer than that. That will give us a little time to obtain the order of protection, and to go out to Somerset for your things," Max reasoned.

"You took the day off because of me, Max?" Faith asked, bewildered, and shook her head in skepticism.

"We've got to sign the paperwork over at the precinct, and get you moved into your new place, right?" Max rationalized, lowering sensitively into her eyes.

"Wow! You amaze me more and more, Max Kane," Faith marveled. "You really didn't have to take the day off."

"I wanted to. I wanted to make sure you're okay," Max argued.

"Are you for real?" Faith stared at Max wonderingly. "I keep thinking that I'm going to wake up, and I'm going to find out that I've only dreamed you up," she admitted.

"Faith, I promise you that this isn't a dream. You've got a friend in me for life-that is if you'll have me," Max related meekly.

"*If* I'll have you…? Max Kane you're totally stuck with me." Faith gave him her quirkiest smile.

"And, I *am* totally okay with that," Max celebrated, as they entered the highway.

***

Later, back at the house, after changing for bed, Max ambled over into the kitchen for a piece of pumpkin pie. It was a quarter to one in the morning. Falling asleep had proven to be a challenge, because Max was consumed by thoughts of Faith. It was almost as if he'd contracted some form of rare disease. Holding Faith in his arms, kissing her, and being close was all he could think about. Max had prayed on the matter and had asked God for help. However, his condition was worsening by the minute. In fact, Max had self-diagnosed and recognized the illness. He was lovesick.

As he rummaged the fridge full of leftovers, Max heard stirring in the kitchen entryway. Looking up from the task in the dimly lit kitchen, he saw Faith standing there. His heart immediately began to hammer, because she was only feet away. However, he tried to feign total aplomb. Faith looked adorable in her floral-print PJ's. Her lengthy freshly-done hair was pinned up, but tendrils cascaded over her shoulders and back, framing her sweet face. "Hey, are you alright?" Concern wrinkled Max's face.

"Just a little hungry," Faith admitted, as she advanced into the kitchen.

"I guess I was too. I couldn't stop thinking about pumpkin pie." Max chuckled.

"You and I are so different. I couldn't stop thinking about the mac and cheese," Faith confessed, crossing over to join Max near the fridge.

"Alright then, let's just find that mac and cheese for you." Max winked at Faith. All of the sudden he was totally self-conscious, because Faith was standing in such close proximity. However, he gingerly pulled out their leftovers from dinner earlier on. Perusing all of the delectable choices, made Max want to sample a bit more turkey with stuffing.

"Let me help you," Faith told Max, setting the entrees on the counter. She crossed over to the pantry and took out plates for them.

Max removed whipped and ice cream from the fridge for his pie. He and Faith had packed dinner away using foil paper and cellophane. At that point, the two stood side by side near the kitchen counter. Max took one of the plates Faith offered and measured out a healthy serving of mac and cheese on it for Faith. "Would you like a bit of turkey with that?" Max asked, staring devotedly at her.

"That would be nice," Faith told him, looking up into Max's eyes.

"So, I guess I can count you in for pie as well?" He chuckled.

"I would like a piece of *apple* please," Faith affirmed.

"Coming right up." Max fixed plates for Faith and himself and nuked them in the microwave. "We should have gone out to dinner after the show," he assessed.

"Why, when there are so many great leftovers right here? Besides, we both have early mornings. Actually, it's already morning." Faith smiled timidly.

"It's pretty early," Max agreed. "You want to sit at the table, or stay right here at the counter?" Max removed her plate from the microwave.

"The counter's fine." Faith slipped into one of the chairs surrounding the Island counter. She anticipated Max coming over to sit beside her. Being close to Max was something she could never get enough of. Whenever he was near, her heart skipped, she felt flustered, and got butterflies in her stomach.

Max took a moment to cut up pieces of pie for Faith and for himself, leaving the ice cream to thaw out on the counter. Being conscious of Faith's eyes on him as his heart whisked, were novel experiences for Max. He struggled to move past the intensity of his feelings. After setting the pie on the counter, he walked back around, and slipped into the chair next to Faith's. "I can't believe you're waiting on me to dig in, Faith." Max smiled over at her, and searched her sweet face.

"Well, it's rude to start without you." Faith timidly explored his eyes.

"It isn't rude, honey. This isn't a formal dinner."

"Still…," Faith argued with a reticent smile.

"I'm glad that you waited for me, but we *can* eat now," he teased.

"Okay…" Faith picked up her fork. "Max, did I say thank you again for how great you made my Thanksgiving this year?" Faith stared at him with fondness and appreciation.

Max guffawed and waved a dismissive hand. "Faith, you have nothing to thank me for. You want to know something?" He propped his chin, and his eyes bridged urgently to hers.

"What…?" Faith's face wrinkled in introspection.

"Seeing you smile and happy means a great deal to me," Max admitted. He was temporarily hypnotized as their eyes fastened.

"Making you smile is so important, because I can only imagine how difficult it's been for you to smile lately."

Tears shone in Faith's eyes. "Max...," Faith said, incredulous. "Why have you made my happiness your responsibility? You don't even know me." She kept shaking her head contrarily.

"I think I know plenty, Faith. It's difficult to explain. When we met at the middle school on that career day, I felt as if I *had* known you for a long time." Mawkishness covered Max's face.

"You felt that way too?" Faith asked, stunned. "There was just something about you, Max. From the very beginning you felt like an old friend."

"Everything about *you* felt familiar to me too. It was all very strange, but I know God makes no mistakes. He leads and guides us to the people who are *supposed* to be in our lives," Max assented in wisdom. "I know He's led me to you and *you* to me, Faith."

"Really...?" Faith marveled. "God knew just how much I needed you. I'd forgotten how to smile, how to have hope, and how to laugh before you came along."

"I can't in all honesty take credit for all of that, but I'm on top of the world every time I see a smile on that beautiful face!" Max reached over, and cupped Faith's chin. "As long as it's in my power, Faith, I want to keep you smiling," Max said hoarsely.

"I smile, and I laugh all the time now, because being around *you* makes me happy!" Faith said softly, with wandering eyes.

However, Max propped her chin, urging her to pay attention. "Is that so?" he asked, stirred.

"It *is*…" Faith's eyes sparkled in optimism.

"Being around *you* doesn't exactly break my heart either, Faith." Max winked playfully at her.

"That's good to know, because I don't want you to be heartbroken." Faith quietly and contemplatively searched his face.

"Do you see now why *I'm* so protective of you?" Max stared at Faith, marveling.

"Are you?"

"I would annihilate anyone who tried to hurt you. Actually, I think I might have," Max humored.

Faith laughed. "I doubt Keith's face will ever be the same." She shook her head farcically.

Max's face twisted in embarrassment. "Yeah, about that… Not my finest moment," he confessed. "I'm sorry that I lost it that night."

"I'm not," Faith said, reaching up, and taking his hand. "I've never had anyone defend me in that way." She explored his eyes.

"Faith, as long as God lends me breath, no one's going to hurt you. I will crush anyone who tries to hurt you, especially Keith

Wendt," Max stated emphatically, with a critical expression on his face.

Stunned and taken aback, Faith remained speechless. *How on earth had she gotten to be this lucky? How had she won Max Kane's complete and utter devotion? And would he ever change?* Faith tussled with those thoughts, until she remembered what Max had just said. God in his wisdom always orchestrated every meeting and encounter.

Furthermore, God determined who belonged in everyone's life. So, Faith was beginning to understand that God had brought Max into her life. As she sat there with Max, in the wee hours of the morning on the day after Thanksgiving, she couldn't stop thanking God for such an amazing connection. Faith vowed never to take her friendship with Max for granted.

"Hey, no fair. You said you wanted apple pie, and that's the third time you've picked at *my* pie," Max razzed on Faith. "If you'd *like*, I *can* get some pumpkin pie for you." Max took his plate and veered in the opposite direction.

"What fun would that be?" Faith hopped off of her chair, and pursued Max to the other side of the counter. "I'm having so much fun picking at *your* piece."

Max playfully turned again, swerving away from Faith's affront on his pie. However, Faith was relentless, and reached for it again. She was close enough, but Max playfully set the plate aside, and grasped hold of her hands. "Faith, you need to respect my pie," he quipped.

Waggishness played on Faith's face, as she tried to justify her mischievous behavior. At that point, she and Max were standing only a few inches away. "I'm so sorry for attacking your pie." Her face wrinkled in false penitence.

Max's heart thrummed in his chest having Faith so close. He gently brought his hands up to her shoulders and stared into her eyes with a farcical expression. "Do you *promise* to stay away from my pumpkin pie, Faith Langhorne?" he tested.

Faith nodded quiescently. "I promise." She gazed into Max's eyes amazed.

"So, you're going to show the utmost respect for my pie?" Max quizzed, chuckling.

Faith held her right hand up, as if making a pledge. "I promise to hold your pie in the highest regard, Doctor Kane," she teased.

"Okay." Max took his hands off of Faith's shoulders. He pulled back for a moment, set the pie on the counter, and drifted back over to the fridge to get a piece for Faith. Max made a suspicious turn and examined the playful expression on Faith's face. He studied her curiously and tried not to burst into laughter. Faith was about to launch another attack, but he was ready for her.

Just as anticipated, Faith made a sudden move. However, Max rushed over, took hold of her and gently restricted her. At that point, he was holding her in his arms from behind. "You promised," he teased, turning her around to face himself. The moment Faith turned to face him, Max found himself holding her securely in his arms. His expression changed from playful to urgent in a split second, as he explored just how beautiful she looked up close.

"I'm sorry, Max, I *really* tried, but I just couldn't resist..." Faith stared guilelessly into Max's eyes, completely awestruck. She found herself feeling totally adrift in the folds of his arms. The moment felt surreal for Faith. She was in heaven! It was a challenge not to reach up and kiss him. The magnetic pull to do so was overwhelming.

Max was winded, as his arms encircled Faith. He found himself automatically hunching down in order to kiss her. However, shaking himself free of the trance, he respectfully released his hold from about her waist. Pulling away from her while wanting to keep her close, was one of the most difficult things he'd ever done. However, above all else, Max feared God.

This wasn't the way to go about things. If he acted on his desire, one thing would definitely lead to another. And, before long, he and Faith would find themselves in a state of compromise. Before expressing his strong feelings for her, Max realized that Faith's life had to be a bit more settled. It was the *right* thing to do, and doing right by Faith was something he was committed to.

"Hey, you can have my pie," he heckled. It was a true exercise in restraint for Max to recover from the aftermath of the sparks flying, and the electricity flowing between them.

Cold waved over Faith because Max had broken away. However, she *did* understand his position. Max was a Christian man. And even if he was very kind for wanting to help her, Max still wanted to do things right in the eyes of God. "Thanks for offering up your pie, Max. I realize what a great sacrifice that is for you," Faith joked. She tried to project a nonchalant stance in respect to what had just transpired between them.

"Giving up my pie is a sacrifice I am willing to make only for *you*, Faith Langhorne," Max said kindly, keeping his distance. If he'd longed to be close to Faith before, he was ravenous at that point.

"Thank you," Faith said, ambling over to the countertop. "But we can share it," she bargained.

Max cautiously stepped over to where Faith was standing. "Okay. Just *one* piece for me."

Faith took a sizable piece of the pie, and fed it to Max. She brushed away crumbs from the sides of his mouth. "How's that?"

"Awesome… Of course, *I* already knew that before a certain *someone* tried to steal it." Roguishness sprinkled Max's face. It felt nice having Faith feed him the pie.

"I'm sorry I attacked you for your pie, Max." Faith's face wrinkled in pretend remorse. "Here, have another bite."

"Well, thanks for being nice and sharing with me," Max heartened.

"Of course," Faith teased.

"So, I've set the alarm for seven thirty, but I will let you sleep until eight," Max told Faith. It was about half past two in the morning. "We're just going to sign a few forms over at the precinct. Faith, do you want to see your dad before we go out to Somerset Ridge?" Max's face wrinkled in urgency.

"No, Max. The earlier we make it over to Somerset Ridge, the less problematic it will be," Faith reasoned. Fear tried to creep up, but she had to keep reminding herself that Keith was still being detained at the county jail.

"Alright, but don't worry. Keith won't be bothering you, I promise." Max set his hand caringly to the side of Faith's face. "Everything's going to work out." He delved her eyes pertained. "I know *you*, Faith. That's why I'm asking you not to worry."

Faith acceded. "I'm not worried, Max. I *am* hopeful that I'm finally going to be free of that abusive relationship."

"You will be, honey… I promise. We're taking steps to ensure that you're free. Trust me?" Max's eyes lowered sensitively into hers.

"You *know* I do." Faith set her hand over the one Max had up to her face.

"So, get some rest alright? Nothing and no one's going to stop you for moving into your new place and from starting over."

Faith smiled and shook her head nonsensically. "Alright, Max. I'm not going to worry about how things are going to play out tomorrow," she agreed.

"Now, that's my girl!" Max softly caressed her cheek. "Goodnight, Faith."

Faith relished Max's soft caress on her face, and quietly mulled over the fact that he'd just referred to her as *his girl*. She offered him a warm smile. "Goodnight, Max."

"Night, Faith." Max watched her turn away.

Faith floated out of the kitchen, and down the hallway in order to find her room.

Max stood in the dimly lit room for a moment and sighed. He was temporarily frozen to that spot. Heat waved over him as if he were on a tanning bed. Never had he felt such strong desire for anyone. He would need to tread cautiously with Faith, because he was on fire.

As he lay in bed that morning, Max prayed for God's wisdom and strength. The intensity of his feelings for Faith had so intensified, he had no idea how to contain it. "Lord, what am I going to do? Faith is still struggling to break free from a maniac. She's been through so much. I can't be that selfish guy trying to put the moves on her, while she's recovering from an abusive relationship…" Max prayed.

"I didn't expect to feel this way. I really didn't think it was possible after what happened with Kennedy. God, help me do what's right for Faith. Help me not to do anything to overturn the healing process from that monster of an ex-boyfriend of hers." Max submitted his worries and concerns to God. He trusted God to order his steps, help him to do what was right by Faith, and to keep them both from falling into a place of compromise.

***

"Are these important?" Max asked Faith. They were inside Faith's old apartment later that morning. Earlier on, they'd gone over to the police precinct to secure the order of protection against Keith. Shortly after, they'd driven out to Somerset Ridge. The pair had managed to pack up most of Faith's belongings into boxes. Max sifted through a few more of Faith's personal effects which she kept in a trunk.

"No, I won't be needing those. I've decided to leave them behind," Faith said glumly. It felt strange being back at the apartment. There were so many horrible memories of the times Keith had brutally beaten her, had humiliated, and had taken advantage of her

"Are you sure?" Max crossed over to Faith.

"I just have to find my shoes and gather up my books. I don't need to take anything else," Faith's voice broke. All at once she began to tremble, and tears were in her eyes.

Max's face warped in sympathy. Without saying a word, he collected Faith in his arms and crushed her to himself. "Sweetheart, it's alright. I promise. It's going to be alright." He hushed her and cradled her head protectively in his hands.

"It's so hard being here. There are so many awful memories." Faith grimaced in misery, as her tear-filled eyes affixed to Max's. "Max, I didn't realize how miserable my life was until I met you."

Max chuckled. "So, okay… I'm going to loosely take that as a compliment." He explored her eyes, and cautiously brushed her tears away with his thumbs.

"I *did* mean it as a compliment," Faith assured. "I meant that you came along and helped me to redefine how a man *should* treat a woman," she admitted.

"Faith, *no* one should be treated the way Keith has treated you." Tears gleamed in Max's eyes parallel to Faith's at that point. "No man should *ever* put his hands on a woman-least of all force her to engage in acts against her will," his voice broke. "You've given me way too much credit. I'm only acting in the way *anyone* else would have under the circumstances."

Faith kept shaking her head in the negative. "You are so wrong about that, Max. There is so much you *didn't* have to do. You've been better to me than anyone I've ever known." Faith delicately slipped her arms about Max's neck and squeezed him lovingly.

"Sweetheart," Max folded her protectively in his arms, "that's because you deserve to be treasured, cherished, loved and cared for." Max flinched for being so transparent.

Faith pulled away and stared dotingly up at him. On impulse, she reached up, and pressed her lips to his. "And that, Max Kane, is the reason why I love you so much!" Faith said. However, she recoiled in embarrassment. And yet, Faith couldn't say she regretted finally pressing a kiss to Max's well-formed mouth. The experience far exceeded all of her daydreams and fantasies.

Max gently released his hold from about Faith. He was both electrified and incredulous over Faith's kiss. The sensation still seared on his mouth, but Max was nonplused. Had he heard right? Had Faith just said she loved him? And if she had, how did she mean it? Did she love him as one would a dear friend, or was it more? Max wanted to respond but wasn't sure how to. "I'm sure you love *all* of your friends," he placated.

Faith was trembling, and terrified because she'd said the *L* word. She had only imagined telling Max that she loved him for the longest. However, she had not expected to express it in that way. So, she tried to downplay what she'd meant. "You're my best friend, so of *course* I love you," Faith teased.

Inwardly, her heart thrummed, because she'd allowed it to slip out that she loved him. Also, she was a little hurt, because Max hadn't responded in kind. Nonetheless, Faith refused to be offended, because she doubted that Max had taken what she'd said seriously. Faith concluded that Max hadn't taken her words to heart, because he had just underscored their *friendship*.

"You're my best friend too, Faith," Max admitted.

"Am I?" Faith asked hopeful.

"You sure are," Max heartened. "Are you going to be okay?" He stared caringly into her eyes. Max feigned an offhand attitude, but there was nothing blasé about the way he felt about her. His strong feelings for Faith ran deep. In fact, he wanted to tell her how deeply he loved her, but he wasn't sure that the time was right. Faith had to be okay first and foremost.

Still, he was reeling over the kiss. Again, it was an exercise in restraint not to pull Faith in for a more meaningful kiss. Nevertheless, he was encouraged that they *would* share a *true* first kiss in the future. Max's lips still scorched where she'd pressed her mouth to his.

Max determined that Keith had to be a nonissue when he told Faith how he felt about her. Max was cognizant of his capacity for loving deeply. Loving anyone casually just wasn't who he was. His love for Faith was unlike anything he'd ever experienced before. Max was ready to lay it all on the line for her. Recognizing that there wasn't anything he wouldn't do for Faith frightened Max.

"I'm fine, Max," Faith said, trying to calm her thrashing heart. "Thank you so much for being my *friend*," she emphasized, as a matter of self-preservation, and offered Max a sincere smile. Faith couldn't apologize for kissing him. It *was* awkward, but the truth was that she *wasn't* sorry for the kiss. She was only sorry that it was so short-lived.

"No thanks required for that. That goes both ways." Max gave Faith a reassuring look.

Faith sighed in relief. "I'm sorry I lost it there for a moment. I promise to hold it together until we're finished." Faith skimmed over the corners of the bedroom she was leaving behind. "We're almost done anyway."

Max inspected every corner of the bedroom as well. "You're not taking any of your linens and comforters?" he asked.

Faith shook her head in the negative. "I'd rather not." Her face twisted in unhappiness.

"That's alright. We can swing by the *Bed, Bath and Beyond* or any of the outlets, and pick up all new things. Oh, you're *definitely* going to need pillows," Max figured.

"Yeah, I guess I should grab a few things," Faith agreed. "Max, did Joseph Church say that the throw pillows are staying with the living room furniture?" Faith was elated that the apartment was fully furnished and move-in ready."

"Of course. They're a part of the décor. Why, don't you like them?" Max questioned.

"No, it's because I *do* like them. I just wanted to make sure."

"They are yours to keep," Max assured. "Should I get started with this closet?" Max crossed over to Faith's personal closet. The other one to the side of the bedroom door was Keith's.

"Sure. My shoes, my handbags and coats are to the right-hand side," Faith told Max, while rummaging through the dresser drawers for her personal items.

In the late morning, Max and Faith hauled the last of the boxes into Max's SUV. Max had switched back to using his own SUV and had returned Dalton's earlier on. It felt good to have his car back, and just in time, because the trunk had more space. "So, that should do it," Max stated as he closed the trunk.

Walking around, he got the car door for Faith. "Are you okay?" he tested, seeing the uncertainty on her face. He could tell she was still struggling with the decision.

Faith nodded quiescently and smiled. She took a moment to peruse the area where she'd lived with an abusive man for close to two years. There were so many feelings at play. There was a sense of regret that she'd allowed herself to be victimized for such a long time.

However, as she watched Max take his place behind the wheel, Faith couldn't help celebrating. It seemed that all she'd endured was worth spending just one day with him. He was such an awesome person, and a great man. Max's faith in God, and a relationship with Jesus Christ made all the difference in the world.

"Are we all set to head over to Castle Horn?" Max asked, pulling away from the apartment building out in Somerset Ridge.

"All systems are a go." Faith gave a hearty thumbs up, and smiled at Max. "Mrs. Tandy says that my dad is being discharged at around three this afternoon."

Max smiled devotedly at Faith. "That's the best news! We should have you all settled in by then. I can have movers bring your dad's things over to the apartment before he's discharged. I know how worried you've been that he's still living out here." Max's face wrinkled in concern.

"No, Max, you've done enough. *I* will work on moving my dad in over the weekend," Faith said hesitantly. Inwardly, she *was* anxious. If Keith went over to her dad's, Mrs. Tandy would be powerless against his aggression.

"Faith, it's not a problem at all. Like I said, we'll go out in just a little while for linens. We can set up the spare bedroom for your dad *today*," Max prodded. It seemed Faith was trying to hide her anxiety from him. "Keith would be a fool to try anything at this point."

Faith nodded in agreement. "I'm praying that he adheres to the boundaries."

"If he doesn't, I will make him," Max said coolly. "It's alright, Faith. I promise."

"I trust you, Max." Faith smiled hopefully.

"It's going to be alright," Max affirmed. "By the way, Faith, we have all that food we bought from Target the other day. I will bring the groceries over to your place, and we can pick up a few more things."

"Max, there's no need for all of that," Faith complained, floored. She yearned to tell him that she loved him for *real* this time. The desire was overwhelming. Faith couldn't wrap her head around how Max had made all of her troubles his own.

"All of what, sweetheart?" Max frowned, nonplused.

"You keep talking about what's best for me and my dad," her voice undulated, and tears shone in her eyes.

Max's eyes fastened urgently to Faith's. "That's because I care a great deal about the two of you," his voice was gravelly.

"Max…?" Faith questioned, overwhelmed. She took hold of his free hand, brought it up to her lips, and pressed kisses to it.

Max's heart somersaulted in his chest, because of the sensation of Faith's loving kisses on his hand. He was overcome by love for her at that point. "So, I guess that's a yes. We set up your dad's room today. We can move all of the necessary items from his place later in the week. I will make sure all of his prescriptions are filled, and that he has a full tank of oxygen for when he comes home later," Max delineated.

"Sounds like a plan, Doctor Kane," Faith heartily agreed. "And Max…?"

"Yeah…?"

"Thank You." Faith pressed another kiss to his hand.

"You're welcome!" Max was enthralled, as he relished Faith's soft warm kisses on his hand.

***

"Thanks for helping me make bail, Sal!" Keith hopped into Sal's Jeep on Friday afternoon.

"I can't believe that doctor did this to you." Sal kept shaking his head incredulous, as he pulled away from the police precinct.

Keith's face turned crimson. He was miffed. Wringing his hands in nervous agitation, he contrived, "Oh, don't worry, Sal. Doctor Max Kane is going to pay dearly for everything he's done. By the time we get through with him, he won't even know his own name."

"Yeah, I'm totally onboard with you, Keith. Doctor Max did all of those messed up things to you, then he took Faith away. That's the one thing. A guy should never mess with another guy's woman. Faith is *your* woman. This doctor put his hands on her and touched her," Sal commiserated. "You're my boy, Keith. Even if I'm not trying to get caught up again, I don't mind helping you out with this *doctor dude*. He got a lot of nerve doing what he did."

"You get in touch with Nick and Les like I asked you?" Keith tested. Nick Chase and Les Morgens were friends from Sal's prison days. They were out of prison but were always available to perform favors if the price was right. Because Keith hadn't worked in six months, all he had was eighteen hundred dollars of *Faith's* hard-earned money. He'd transferred the money into his account when Faith started her scandalous affair with Doctor Max Kane.

Keith figured that he could offer each of the guys five hundred dollars. Their mission was to work Max Kane over so good that his own mother wouldn't recognize him. One good beat down deserved another. Keith was still recovering from what happened over at Fairfield Hospital's parking lot a few days ago. Max Kane had broken his nose, busted his lips, and he'd suffered a concussion. The marks, bruises and contusions were still visible on his face. Keith wanted Max to suffer in every way in which he himself had, but with interest.

"Yeah, I got in touch with them yesterday. They are willing to help you out with your doctor friend," Sal verified. "Don't worry, Keith, *I* got your back. We gonna make that man regret the day he was ever born."

"Now, *that's* what I like to hear," Keith enlivened. "By the way, did you follow behind Faith and Dr. Kane on Thanksgiving like I asked?" He had asked Sal to find out where Max Kane lived, and where he had taken Faith.

"Yeah, about that… I got pulled over by the cops that night. Got an inspection ticket," Sal said, embarrassed by the matter.

"Ah, man… So, you mean to tell me you *still* don't know where Kane lives?" Keith rammed his fist into the glove compartment.

"No, not yet. What I know is that it's one of those ritzy castle areas, *Castle Gate* or *Castle Horn*. Didn't get a chance to make it past the highway," Sal explained.

"That's okay. Now, that I'm out of that jail cell, I'm going to figure things out on my own." Keith's entire demeanor change in calculation and elusiveness. "So, you think you gonna play me like that Faith? You think that Doctor Max is gonna save you? Well, good luck, honey. I'm going to *whip* you into submission. When I'm done, you gonna wish you ain't never played games with me. Guess it's that time. I'm gonna remind you once and for all not to mess with me," Keith ranted, speaking to no one in particular. He was so consumed by rage that steam was figuratively issuing from out of his ears.

CHAPTER EIGHT

"Max, I can't believe all we've accomplished today!" Faith marveled, taking in how perfect the apartment looked. It was almost ten p.m. Max had spent the entire day helping her to move and settle into her new place. He had purchased linens, toiletries, had shopped for groceries, and had bought a few kitchen appliances in order to make the transition easier.

Watching Max set up the spare bedroom for her dad, had warmed Faith's heart in an indescribable way. Her dad was home from the hospital, and sound asleep. Of course, her dad had complained about the change. However, he'd gotten onboard fast once Faith and Max explained the circumstances. Mrs. Tandy was overjoyed over the move and loved the new apartment. In fact, she was looking forward to coming over in the morning.

"We had a very productive day, if I do say so myself!" Max smiled, evaluating the beautiful living space he and Faith had created together. There was just one more thing he had to settle at that point. "Faith, let's test out the alarm system."

Max drifted over to the front door, and Faith followed behind him. Before Max opened up the front door, he turned to address her. "Building security is very efficient. There are cameras at every corner. However, if by chance anyone should happen to get past all of that, I need for you to know how to use this."

Faith nodded compliantly, watching Max fiddle with the keypad of the system. "The code is today's date?" she asked.

"Uh-huh. The alarm sensor will automatically pick up on any activity near this door." Max's face creased in urgency. "The system is also connected to *my* phone, in the event something unusual happens, and if you should happen to need me for any reason at all." Max delved her eyes critically.

"The system is connected to *your* phone?" Faith marveled. She shook her head skeptically over all Max had done.

"Of course. You *really* didn't think that I wouldn't be keeping tabs?" Max shook his head in the negative, and cradled Faith's face in his hand. "I'm only five minutes away, alright?" he reassured.

Faith nodded, floored by Max's thoughtfulness and concern. Because Keith had stolen what little she'd had left in her savings account, Max had taken care of all of her expenses. Max had risked his own neck for her in every sense of the word, and Faith was overwhelmed. "I don't really know what to say, Max," her voice wavered. "There isn't anything you haven't thought of."

"When it comes to *you*," Max's eyes lowered sensitively into hers, "I can't afford to leave any stone unturned." His face wrinkled in solemnity.

Tears shone in Faith's eyes. "How can I ever thank you for everything you've done?" Faith was still incredulous.

"Faith, you *don't* need to thank me." Max cupped her chin and made her look at him. "We're best friends remember?" He winked. "Now, show me again how to activate the alarm," he ordered.

"Alright," Faith agreed. Max stepped out of the apartment in order to quiz Faith on how to activate and deactivate the system.

"Great job!" Max stepped back inside with a pleased expression on his face after they'd tested the system for the fourth time.

"Thank you for teaching me. I think I finally got it," Faith heartened, smiling into his eyes.

Max lingered in the doorway for a moment utterly mesmerized. There was such a tug of war on the inside not to leave Faith. She'd been by his side consistently for the past few days. It was difficult to imagine going home, and not have her be there. The thought of being alone in that huge house without Faith in it, seemed too bitter a pill to swallow. Max considered that up until a few days ago he'd enjoyed the solitude. It was a getaway from the craziness of his work over at the hospital.

But now, the thought of going home to an empty house, overwhelmed him with sadness. However, he had to find a way to work through the debilitating feelings. "Are you going to be alright?" Max asked standing in close proximity to Faith at her front door. "Did we buy enough things for your dad? Maybe, I should swing by Target, and pick up a few more Ensure protein shakes," Max fretted.

"Max, Max….," Faith said quietly, trying to get his attention. "We're fine." She took Max's face into her hands. "You pretty much covered all of the bases. You've even had my dad's prescriptions filled." She smiled wistfully. The realization of Max's impending departure hit all at once. Max had an early morning shift.

And, in the upcoming week, Faith had to return to work. Max had promised to drop her off, and to pick her up during one of his breaks.

"Okay, okay… So, I guess I am still a *little* worried," Max admitted with a faint smile.

"My dad and I will be just fine. Mrs. Tandy should be here first thing in the morning," Faith reassured.

"I know." Max nodded in agreement. "Did you want those paintings we saw at the Ikea?" Max was hesitant to leave.

"Maybe, when *I* can afford to buy them for myself," Faith told him. "I can *at least* do that." She stared endearingly up at him.

"Faith, you have no idea. I love being a blessing to you and to your dad. Please, don't deny me…"

"You *have* been a blessing to me and to my dad, Max." Faith guffawed, shaking her head in skepticism. "You have gone above and beyond…"

"That's because you are so worth it," Max stated emphatically, exploring her face and eyes. How on earth could he say goodnight? And yet, Max knew he had to. "So, you can call and text me any time if you need to," he reminded her.

"I know," Faith said softly, and closed her eyes meditatively. "I will call and text you later to say goodnight." Her eyes twinkled in affect.

"Alright. I won't sleep until I get a call or text from you," Max's voice broke. "Oh, and I will *definitely* call you on Monday morning before I swing by."

"Are you sure it won't be a problem?" Faith's face creased in doubt.

"Not at all. By the way, have you decided whether or not you want to keep working through the middle school? They've issued the order of protection, so Keith has no right to be within feet of you," Max delineated.

"I hope he respect the boundaries, Max, but Keith has never been one to respect the rules."

"Like I said, the order of protection is one thing, but I also have the police keeping an eye on him," Max confirmed.

"That makes me feel a lot better, Max. Still, I've made up my mind. I'm putting in my two-week notice. I live in *Castle Horn* now, so I need to find something closer to home," Faith established, staring meaningfully into Max's eyes.

"That makes sense. Whatever you want to do is fine, Faith. Please, let me know if there's anything *I* can do to help…"

Faith pressed a finger over Max's lips and silenced him. "You've done quite enough for me, Max Kane. There isn't anything else you need to do."

Max smiled and took Faith's hand in his. Squeezing it devotedly, he reminded her, "If there's anything I can do to help in respect to helping you find work, please don't hesitate."

Overcome by love and gratitude, Faith draped her arms about Max's neck. She crushed him lovingly in her arms and surrendered to tears. She truly didn't know how to let him leave that night. They'd been joined at the hip for the past few days. So, she was totally addicted to *everything* Max. "Thank you," she breathed into his chest. "Thank you so much!"

Wrapping his arms about Faith's waist, Max couldn't hold back the tears. "You're welcome, Faith! Anything you need, anything at all…" He buried his head in her hair. Inwardly, his heart screamed *I love you!* Because Faith was still struggling with so many issues, Max didn't think it was the right time to tell her how he felt. "Call or text me if you need anything." He gently pulled away, wiping stray tears away from his eyes.

"I will call and text you," Faith enlivened, agonizing that he was leaving. They'd only spent a few days together, but those few days had seemed like a lifetime. Faith was so in love she could hardly breathe. It also didn't help matters that Max had spoiled her in every sense of the word. He'd cooked her breakfast, had drawn her bath, had made her late-night snacks, and had pampered her in a way no one else had ever thought to. *How on earth was she going to get used to not seeing him as much?*

"Promise?" Max tested just before he turned away.

"Of course. I will call and text you later just to say goodnight." Tears looped over in Faith's eyes.

"Fair enough," Max granted, still reluctant to leave. However, he forced himself to turn away and open up the front door. Max slipped through it but lingered out in the hallway. "Goodnight, Faith."

"Night, Max," Faith said softly. "Get home safe." She smiled sadly, as she watched him plod down the hallway.

Max was almost to the elevator when he veered and waved over at Faith one last time. She was still standing in the doorway. He smiled when Faith waved back to him. When the elevator doors opened, Max slipped inside feeling cold and empty. He perceived that those feelings would only intensify once he got home and had to face the loneliness.

***

"Thanks for dropping me off." Faith stared dotingly over at Max, as he pulled into the parking lot of the middle school on Monday morning. She was captivated, as she sized Max up in his dark gray designer suit. Max looked and smelled incredible! Seeing him in that suit was reminiscent of the first time they'd met.

Even if Max had worked the entire weekend, he and Faith had talked and texted nonstop. For the most part, Keith had stayed off of their radar, and Faith was extremely grateful. Faith had stayed at home the entire weekend. She and Max had talked about visiting *Light of Glory Church*, but Faith wanted Max by her side when they attended together on the following Sunday.

"Not a problem, Faith," Max said, smiling. Spending the past few days apart, had opened up Max's eyes to how much he needed her. He had fallen deeply in love! "So, I'll be back for you at around four," he reminded her. He was awestruck! Faith looked gorgeous in a deep red coat. The collar of her cream-colored sweater was visible underneath the pretty jacket. Faith had on dark slacks, black leather boots, and her upswept hair softened her sweet features.

"Max, you're not getting off work until after seven," Faith refuted.

"I have a meeting or two scheduled for this evening, but making sure you're alright is nonnegotiable," Max settled.

"I'll be fine." Faith explored Max's perfect face. She felt as if she were being a little objectifying, because of the way she kept checking Max out in his dress suit. It was a real challenge not to size up his broad shoulders and stalwart arms. They rippled gracefully with every move Max made. Faith was just as swept away as she'd been the first time she'd laid eyes on him. "I was just thinking…," she started to say reticently.

"What were you thinking, Ms. Faith?" Max rose to the occasion.

"I was thinking you could come over for dinner tonight after your shift ends." Her face creased in uncertainty.

Max smiled with cardinal cheeks, as his eyes searched hers. He took a moment to inspect how stunning Faith looked with upswept hair. Her skin appeared malleable, and her tantalizing lips were painted with a coral shade of lip gloss. The desire to kiss Faith was almost agonizing, but Max prayed for God's strength not to act on his compulsion. He *had* to do what was right for her.

"Faith, I would *love* to have dinner with you and your dad tonight!" he affirmed, stirred by the invite. Max wondered if Faith had missed him half as much as he'd missed her. The truth was that the imposed distance between them was killing him.

"So, okay," Faith said excited. "Eight okay?" she asked elated.

"Sounds like a plan." Max beamed. "Might I ask what we're having for dinner?"

"I will surprise you." Impishness danced on her face.

"Do I need to bring anything?" Max explored her beautiful face and eyes. Inwardly, he wondered if his love for her was obvious at that point. Max didn't think he was doing a good job at concealing how smitten he was by her.

"Just bring your wonderful dashing self," Faith uplifted, excited.

"If you say so, honey. Still, I will probably bring a surprise of my own." He winked.

"I can't wait." Faith's face flushed in rosiness. She was suddenly reserved and shy again, because Max was taking her breath away by degrees. Faith felt like a timid schoolgirl, as Max walked her into the school building. She noticed school staff giving her and

Max the once over. They were totally engaged in watching their interactions at the front door.

For the obvious reasons, Faith felt immensely proud. The expressions on the faces of her work colleagues inferred how surprised they were to see her with Doctor Max Kane. Faith could tell that they were under the impression that he was her boyfriend, and she wasn't in any hurry to correct them. "I'll call you during my break," she told Max, while they stood in front of the school's entryway.

"I look forward to your call, even if I'm busy."

"Well, you can always call me back if it gets *really* busy. I don't like bothering you." Faith's face wrinkled in uneasiness.

"Are you kidding me? You are *never* a bother to me, Faith Langhorne!" Max stated emphatically. "So, don't hesitate to call me."

"Alright, Max, I won't."

"Have a great day, Faith!" Max stared protectively at her.

"You have a great day as well, Max! Bye," she said softly.

"I will see you later," Max reassured, taking a mental photograph of Faith. He stood near the front desk for a moment not budging an inch. "Go on," he encouraged. "I'm not going anywhere until you're downstairs in the cafeteria. Call me if you need me."

Faith nodded. "I will." Faith compliantly turned and headed down the hallway until she got to the stairwell leading down to the basement. She waved at Max.

Max waved back and watched her slip through the door. He didn't want to leave Faith alone to any capacity, but realized he had to. He estimated that she would be alright, as long as she remained inside of the school building. He and Faith had discussed the matter in depth, and they'd concluded that Keith Wendt wasn't the kind of man who respected the law. So, even with the emergency order of protection set in place, they had to be on their guard.

Max considered it his *responsibility* to ensure Faith's safety until she worked her last day there. Worrying about Faith had become something of a bad habit in past weeks. So, Max had to keep reminding himself to submit his concern for Faith to God. He lingered at the front desk for a moment, then hesitantly left the school building. Max hopped into his SUV and pulled away from the school lot.

"Doctor Max driving Faith to work now. He will probably pick her up later too," Keith said to Sal. They were sitting in a car rental in an obscure spot near the school. Keith didn't care one way or another that he'd been served with an emergency order of protection. In his estimation, there was always a way around it.

"Yeah, I get that. That guy won't let Faith out of his sight," Sal evaluated, annoyed.

"Yeah, well, we just gonna have to help him out with that problem. He gonna leave Faith alone, because she ain't his woman." Keith's face reddened in animosity.

"Still, Keith, you gotta be careful. You can't be nowhere near her right now."

"I ain't going near her...yet," Keith connived.

"You pay those guys the money?" Sal quizzed. Keith had said that he would hire a couple of guys to put a serious hurting on Max Kane.

"Yeah, for a few hundred dollars each, they agreed to put the fear of God in him. I'd say I got a good bargain there." Deviousness shaded Keith's face. "I can't wait for them to *jack up* Doctor Max."

"Yeah, the *doctor man* would deserve it. I can't believe Faith would be *into* a guy like that. Like, I get it. Doctor Max is the fairytale prince charming type, but she not used to that storybook nonsense. Faith is used to being with *you*."

"Faith won't find nobody to love her better than me. I mean, we got our ups and downs, but at the end of the day, she got my heart," Keith rationalized.

"You think Faith sleep with Doctor Max?"

Keith's face turned crimson along with his eyes. "Yeah, I think she slept with him. I don't know if she's still staying over at his place though. That's what I'm gonna find out today. I'm going to be right here when *doctor man* comes back to pick her up from work. I'm finally gonna see where he been taking Faith all this time."

"I can't believe her father don't live in that apartment no more." Sal kept shaking his head in disbelief.

"Yeah, they moved him out of there. I got to say that Faith and Doctor Max thought of everything. Faith knows me. If her dad still lived out in Somerset, I would have hit him up for her address. She ain't want me bothering her father, so I'm guessing *Daddy Langhorne* has been staying with her. I *hate* that doctor, and I can't wait for him to be a patient at his own hospital. That's what I'm looking forward to the most."

"When did they say they gonna pay Doctor Max that visit?" Sal asked.

"They is waiting to catch Max Kane alone, so it can happen at any time. They'll jump him and make him regret the day he ever *looked* at my girl," Keith said icily. "Doctor Max pretty face is going to need reconstructive surgery when they get through with him."

"He won't even know what hit him." Sal began to laugh.

"I know that's right. It's going to be so poetic!" An inane peal of laughter erupted from the hollow of Keith's throat as well.

Before long, Keith and Sal pulled away from school grounds, and started following behind Max. However, Keith stopped short when he realized that Max was headed over to Fairfield Hospital.

They already knew where he worked. What they were chomping at the bit to find out was where the man lived. For Keith, learning the doctor's address was key. It followed that if they found Max Kane's residence, Faith wouldn't be too far away.

***

"You wanted to see me, Mr. Aubrey?" Faith wandered into her supervisor's office, located towards the back end of the cafeteria kitchen.

"Yeah, I've been meaning to have a word with you," Mr. Aubrey told Faith. "Have a seat." He gestured and slipped into the armchair at his desk.

Faith slid quietly into the armchair across from his. "Is everything alright?" she asked warily.

"Faith, I asked you in here to address how upset I was that you bailed on us the day before Thanksgiving." Mr. Aubrey frowned in displeasure. "You *know* our policy. No days off prior to school holidays."

Faith's face creased in frustration and incredulity. "I *had* a family emergency, Mr. Aubrey. My dad was in the hospital. He's very sick, and he was actually admitted to the hospital that day," she argued, totally skeptical. It wasn't that Mr. Aubrey didn't know that her dad was gravely ill. "I'm the only family my dad has out in Seattle."

"Well, can you bring in documentation to that effect? I'm sorry to be such a stickler, but last Wednesday was actually a very busy day down here," he groused.

"Of course, I can provide documentation," Faith disputed, surprised. "My dad was brought over to Fairfield Hospital that Wednesday morning. He was discharged on Friday afternoon," she informed.

"Alright, alright. Whatever you say, Faith. I'm really not trying to give you a hard time." Mr. Aubrey's face wrinkled in concern. "I think you're a fantastic worker," he praised.

Faith found the entire matter disturbing. She had called in last Wednesday and had left a message for Mr. Aubrey. She was still incredulous that he was singling her out to discuss the absence. Faith couldn't put her finger on it, but she felt in some way slighted.

It was at that moment she received the epiphany. She had no business working through the middle school cafeteria. "Well, I'm glad you think I'm a great worker, Mr. Aubrey," Faith said staring unwaveringly into his eyes. "You *should* know that I brought in my resignation letter today." Faith nodded in a matter-of-fact manner.

Mr. Aubrey's face fell in horror and disbelief. "What, you're resigning?"

"Yes," Faith said with a little less attitude. Seeing the look on the man's face affected her.

"Are you sure that's what you want to do?" Mr. Aubrey asked, solemnly.

"Yes, I'm pretty sure. The truth is that I recently moved to another area, and the commute…," Faith implied. She refused to get into personal details with her boss.

"I see," Mr. Aubrey said reflectively. Regret and uncertainty shaded his demeanor.

Faith couldn't tell for sure, but she perceived that her boss felt guilty for calling her into his office. She sensed that he felt directly responsible for her decision. "My decision to resign has very little to do with my job here." Faith offered an encouraging smile. "I have enjoyed my job here, but I feel as if it's time to move on," she established.

"I understand." Mr. Aubrey's eyes connected urgently to Faith's. "When are you planning to leave?" His face strained in criticalness.

"As soon as possible," Faith said quickly. She'd wanted to talk about working through the cafeteria for another two weeks. However, she couldn't imagine Max having to drive her to and back from work for the duration of that time. Since Mr. Aubrey wasn't demanding she stay on for two weeks, Faith decided that her last day would be Friday of that week. "Friday will be my last day." Her eyes affixed unwaveringly to his.

"Wow! Alright…" Mr. Aubrey laughed nervously. "If that's what you want to do, Faith," he assented.

Faith remained prayerful the entire time. She had expected her boss to give her a hard time, but he wasn't challenging her decision. "It isn't what *I* want, but what's necessary," she countered wisely.

"Well, I'm sorry for giving you such a hard time. I'm glad your dad is doing better." Mr. Aubrey gave her a sad but resigned smile.

"That's okay. Thank you. I'm grateful that he's better too."

"Well, we're certainly going to miss you around here."

"I'm going to miss you all as well." Sentimentally veiled her face.

Faith was immensely grateful Mr. Aubrey had not delineated that she work through the cafeteria for the next couple of weeks. She evaluated that his reaction was a gift from God. So, Faith quietly worshipped the Lord in her heart. She wasn't sure what her next job would be, but Faith was confident that her new occupation would be an echelon above working through the cafeteria of Somerset Middle School.

***

"That was amazing, Faith!" Max complimented Faith over the meal she'd cooked. Standing to his feet, he helped her clean up.

"You think so?" Faith's face crinkled in uncertainty, as she set plates and utensils into the kitchen sink. She radiated joy, because it was the first time she and Max had shared a little quality time since the move.

"Your Shrimp Scampi was to die for!" Max emphasized, crossing over to join Faith by the sink. "Thank you so much for having me over!" He stared yearningly at Faith. It didn't seem possible to have missed someone as much as he'd missed her.

"Thank you for coming," Faith said softly, as her eyes connected furtively to Max's. "It seems like forever since we've spent a little quality time," she said thickly.

"I know. It *does* seem like an eternity," Max acceded, edging in closer to Faith, as if magnetically drawn to her. He was entranced and couldn't seem to pull back. However, Max feigned total aplomb. "Let me help you with those." He turned the sink water on.

"Don't you dare, Max Kane," Faith teased, and playfully slapped his hand. "You never let me do the dishes over at your place, so..." Waggishness played on her sweet features.

"That isn't true," Max argued, "I *always* let you help me." He smiled and winked.

"Barely," Faith argued, taking Max's hand, and leading him out of the kitchen.

"Alright," Max acquiesced, "no dishes." He held his free hand up disarmingly, while Faith held the other.

"Faith, Max...?" James Langhorne floated out of his bedroom to have word with the pair. "I apologize for not being more fun, but I think I'm going to turn in for the night."

"Alright, dad. Is there anything I can get for you?" Faith asked, concerned.

"No, sugar. After that amazing dinner, I'm good. I took my round of pills a little while ago and should be all set."

Faith wandered over, and lovingly draped her arms around her dad. She pulled away and pressed a kiss up to his cheek. "I love you! Goodnight."

"Love you too, Sugar. Goodnight." James crushed his daughter in his arms.

"Goodnight, Mr. Langhorne," Max told him, just before Mr. Langhorne veered in order to return to his bedroom.

"Goodnight, Max. Take good care of my Faith." He winked. "It was so nice seeing you tonight. You should definitely come over as often as possible." James gave Max a knowing smile.

Max shook his head humorously, while brushing his fingers nervously through his thick dark mane. Mr. Langhorne minced no words. "I will *definitely* make it a point to come over as often as I can," he agreed, smiling.

Faith's cheeks turned scarlet mulling over her dad's words. Her dad never stopped putting it out there how much he wanted for her and Max to become an item. In that regard, Faith wished her dad were a little bit *less* transparent. Still, she truly *wanted* to tell Max how she felt. She wondered if she'd get the chance to that night. She had prayed on the matter and had concluded that coming clean was her only recourse. Faith still struggled with doubts and insecurity. Thus, the thought of putting her heart on the line was scary to say the least. Nevertheless, she had to try.

"Dad, Max is *very* busy running Fairfield Hospital," Faith argued, in an effort to keep her dad from embarrassing her any more than he already had.

"I realize that, Sugar, but *Max* is a young man. He needs to get out there and enjoy life," James countered.

"I can't say that I disagree with you there, dad." Faith's eyes wandered over to Max. He was staring quietly and musingly over at her and her dad. "Max could definitely use some downtime."

Max gave Faith a discreet but meaningful smile. "Max *is* working on it," he said in the third person, and winked at Faith.

"Well, goodnight guys," James emphasized again.

"Night, dad."

Faith watched her dad drift out of the living room. He veered right at the end of the hallway in order to find his bedroom. She was so proud of their living space. Her dad was adjusting just fine to the new place, and Faith was beginning to as well. And they both had Max to thank for it all.

"I'm so sorry about that," Faith told Max. Her face warped apologetically, as she turned to face him.

"What *exactly* are you sorry about, Faith?" Max's face wrinkled in confusion. He closed the gap between them and searched her eyes.

"Well, it's obvious that my dad has been trying to recruit you as my new boyfriend since the day he met you." Faith's face turned florid.

Max chuckled with suffused cheeks of his own. "Yeah, he *hasn't* been very subtle on that front, but that's alright. I guess that's his way of saying he likes me."

"He *really* likes you, Max. Believe me, it's not easy to win over my dad."

"Well, am I not the luckiest, that Mr. Langhorne would actually think I'm good enough for his daughter," Max said kindly, exploring Faith's eyes.

"Max…," Faith whined, embarrassed.

"What…?" Max cradled her face in his hands. "You're so cute!" he said, unable to contain his smile. "Every time you're embarrassed or feeling bashful, you say my name like that," he teased.

"Like what?" Faith asked timidly.

"Max…," Max parodied. "Like that. But don't get me wrong, I love it."

"You love when I whine?" Faith asked jestingly.

"I love when you *breathe*, Faith." Max searched her eyes ponderously.

Faith was speechless and totally overwhelmed. For a silent lapse her eyes fastened to Max's. Both were completely awestruck. Faith tried to redirect, but it wasn't easy. "Would you like to take a walk out by the water?"

She was referring to Castle Horn Park, which was a few miles away from the complex. For the past few days, she had felt like a prisoner. For fear of Keith finding her, she had been antsy about leaving the apartment. She doubted Keith would respect the boundaries, even with an order of protection set in place. However, at that point in time, Keith was the last person on her mind.

"Sure, I'd love to," Max said throatily, gaping unrelentingly at Faith. She looked like an angel in a soft pink sweater, dark jeans and leather boots. Her lengthy hair bounced in curls everywhere, and her beautiful skin radiated with life and vitality. Seeing her so healthy and strong warmed Max's heart. The more he tried to fight his feelings for Faith, the stronger they grew. "I'll go get our coats."

"I just have to tell my dad we're stepping out for a bit," Faith told Max.

"Sure, honey. I'll be waiting by the door," Max acceded. He slipped on his coat and waited for Faith to make her way back out to the foyer.

"My dad fell asleep right away, so I left a little note on his nightstand. "He seems to be doing just fine." Faith crossed back over to the front door.

Max nodded. "He's a *lot* stronger, and I'm so encouraged by that." Max helped Faith on with her coat. He was locked in the moment, as he gently veered her body towards his. Max took a moment to adjust the buttons on her coat and felt winded as his fingers brushed over her.

Faith was breathless, and her stomach dipped to the floor, while Max helped her on with her coat. The feel of his gentle, yet strong hand sweeping against her skin was criminal. Just then, the desire to reach up, and bridge her lips to his was staggering. However, Faith fought the urge. "It's a little nippy out, so…" Faith took the liberty to adjust the scarf around Max's neck. "That's better." She set her hands down to her sides

"Thanks." Max found himself hypnotized. "Are we all set to go?"

"Uh-huh," Faith's voice was satin. She forced herself to move towards the front door.

Max followed behind her. However, he reminded her to activate the alarm system before they left. Taking a moment, Faith fiddled with the keypad. Max tested it before they wandered down the hallway and hopped into the elevator.

Soon after, Max was outside securing Faith into his SUV. There were so many impressions on the inside it was difficult to contain it all. He questioned how it was possible to feel so strongly for her. Loving anyone else had seemed unfeasible in the wake of the failed relationship with Kennedy Proctor-Bohm. Even more mindboggling was that Max had never felt for *anyone* else what he'd come to feel for Faith. It was a quandary. Thus, he had no idea how long he would be able to go on pretending that he wasn't head-over-heels in love with her. Max prayed inwardly the entire time he was around Faith.

***

Typical of Seattle weather, the rain had abated only a couple of hours ago. But now it was brisk out. The night sky hung ominously above Max and Faith, as they hovered over the barricade admiring the ambient glossy river. Despite the tenebrous skies, crystals clustered in the panorama, and illuminated the shadows. The stars also illuminated the dark waters.

"It's really nice out here, Max, even if it's a little chilly." Faith looked out into the vast river meditatively.

"Are you cold, honey?" Max eliminated the space between them. Removing the scarf from around his neck, he gingerly wrapped it around Faith's shoulders, and caressed her arms in a gentle rhythm.

"That feels much better. Thank you, Max." Faith stared devotedly up into his eyes.

Max smiled fondly at her. "Sure, honey."

"By the way, I had a serious talk with my supervisor today," Faith announced. Max's tender touch creating friction on her arms was enough to make her insane. Max was gentle and had an expressive way of showing he cared. "Mr. Aubrey wasn't happy that I missed work last Wednesday." Faith disclosed the incident that took place over at the school earlier on.

"I'm so sorry you had to go through that. I wish I could have been there. Believe me, I would have given *Mr. Aubrey* a piece of my mind," Max stated emphatically.

"I'm sure he wasn't *trying* to be condescending. I just took it that way."

"It's alright if you want to work through for the next two weeks." Max's face creased in concern. "I really don't mind taking you into work in the morning." He stared at Faith, as if she were part of a fireworks display on the fourth of July.

"Max, you've already done so much. You have to report to the hospital quite early most days. It isn't fair that you have to return to Castle Horn to pick me up the moment you start your shift. Then, later, you have to set everything else aside to pick me up." Faith's face wrenched in displeasure.

"Faith, it really isn't that big of a deal. What *is* a big deal is keeping you safe, and off of Keith's radar." Max cradled her face in his hands. "I would do anything to ensure you never cross paths with that man again." Max explored Faith's eyes intuitively.

"Max, you've been so wonderful to me." Tears shimmered in her eyes. "Still, the last thing that I want is to be abusive."

"Faith, I doubt that you would even know how to be abusive. So, please stop talking that way. Friends take care of each other," Max pointed out with a loving smile.

Faith nodded in agreement. "You *are* the best friend I've ever had, Max Kane," she uplifted.

"And you are mine," Max reciprocated.

Max felt conflicted about telling Faith how he felt. He was
deeply in love but didn't want to just blurt it out. Inwardly, he
prayed for the right moment to tell her the truth. "Faith," he
redirected, "I've been thinking…" Max took hold of her shoulders
and rubbed caringly on her arms.

"Uh-oh." Uncertainty veiled Faith's face. "*What* have you
been thinking, Max?"

"I was thinking that you don't have to go back to work right
away. You have options you know. If it's something you still want,
you could go back to school to finish what you started." There was a
critical expression on Max's face. "Actually, there is a nursing
program being offered at the hospital in a month or so. It's due to
start in January. It's a six-month accredited course. The course is
the hospital's way of guaranteeing that our nursing staff has the very
best training."

"Max, what are you saying? I couldn't possibly just go to
school. I would still need to take care of myself and my dad.
Granted, I don't have to worry about rent or a few other bills, but I
can't afford to go back to school."

Max smiled, and his eyes lowered meaningfully into hers.
"Oh, yes you can, Faith. I'm the director of the program, and we can
definitely work on getting financial aid. You shouldn't have to
worry about bills right now," Max evaluated. "You've always
wanted to get a degree in nursing," he reminded. "Now, you have a
chance to follow that dream."

"Max, why on earth would you do all of this?" Faith shrugged,
with a bewildered expression. "I won't be able to pay you back-at
least not for a while." Tears brimmed over in her eyes.

"Faith, don't you know by now? There isn't anything that I wouldn't do for you?" Max's voice broke. "Please, don't worry about having to pay me back for anything." His eyes shone with faith and optimism.

"Oh, Max, I don't know what to say."

"Just say you'll think about it," he goaded.

Faith nodded in the affirmative. "Oh, Max, I love you so much!" Faith admitted, staring devotedly into his eyes.

Max guffawed and laughed lightly. "I *know* you love me, Faith, because I'm your best friend," he rationalized.

Faith shook her head in the negative, as she explored Max's gingerbread-colored eyes. They sparkled like gems against the backdrop. "No, Max, I'm *in love* with you!" Faith grasped his right hand in hers.

"Oh, sweetheart…" Max's shook his head totally incredulous. There were so many impressions at that moment. His heart inundated with joy and hope. Exploring Faith's tears-filled eyes, he stated emphatically, "I'm *so* in love with *you*! I love you so much, Faith!"

Max caringly took hold of her hands and drew her into his arms. Fastening his arms about her waist, he hunched down, and bridged his lips with hers. In a delicate, yet avid manner, Max took his time to explore every inch of her mouth with his. As if parched in the desert for many days, he kissed Faith profoundly, extracting sweet cane from the source of her mouth. "I love you!" he kept telling her, as their mouths amalgamated, and broke free at intervals.

The moment felt surreal to Faith. She was immured by Max's caring and secure arms. Being able to savor the honey of his mouth was overpowering. Faith's heart thudded avidly, as she and Max indulged in nectar kisses. The excitement escalated like a crescendo from a powerful piece of music. It felt natural to respond just as ardently to Max's fervent kiss. "I'm so in love with you," she reminded him between meteoric kisses.

In the aftermath of their fiery kiss, Max and Faith's faces bridged in intimacy. "I've missed you so much, Faith!" Max said throatily. "Being all alone at the house these past few days has been unbearable!" he admitted.

"I've missed you *more*, Max. It's been so hard being away from you. You kind of spoil a girl, you know," she admitted, smiling.

Max chortled. "Well, I've missed having you around, so that I can totally spoil you." Tears escaped the corners of his eyes. "I didn't think I could *ever* feel this way," Max confessed, pressing kisses to Faith's face and lips at intervals.

"I didn't know *you* felt that way about me, Max," Faith marveled. "The truth is that I think I fell in love with you the very first time we met," she whispered, pressing a sweet kiss to Max's nose.

"In all honestly, I think I did too, but I've been so scared to show you." The two inched away, but Max kept his arms encircled around Faith's waist.

"Why?" Faith frowned in uncertainty.

"In light of all you've gone through with Keith, I didn't want to be that guy trying to put the moves on you so soon after…" Max gazed adoringly at her. "I didn't want to be selfish."

"Max Kane, I don't think you have one selfish bone in this beautiful body," Faith countered. "Besides, don't you know that your love and kindness have healed me?" Fresh tears shone in her eyes. "You're exactly what I needed. Your kindness has made me whole."

Max smiled sentimentally, as he examined everything about the woman he loved. "Oh, sweetheart, you mean the world to me! Can I tell you something?"

"Of course,…"

"I've already told you how devastated I was after things fell apart with Kennedy."

Faith nodded with a sense of understanding. "I remember," she acquiesced.

"I told her that I'd never love anyone else," Max admitted.

"Yeah, you *did* tell me that," Faith granted.

"Well, *now*, I see just how wrong it was for me to say that. The truth is that I've never felt stronger for anyone," Max confessed, stunned by the realization of his admission.

Faith's smile was irrepressible. She threw her arms around Max and crushed him lovingly in her arms. "I love you more than anything, Max Kane! You are my heart." She pulled away and covered his face with tender kisses.

Max laughed, overwhelmed by love and happiness. Faith had knocked the wind out of him, but he squeezed her just as potently. "Turns out all I needed was a little *Faith*."

Faith smiled lovingly. "I think we both needed a little faith, Max." She squeezed Max affectionately and buried her face in his chest.

Max held Faith in his arms against the starry backdrop in total celebration. It was difficult to interpret everything he felt at that moment. However, Max could not stop thanking and praising God for such an unexpected but sought-after breakthrough in their relationship. Discovering that Faith loved him as much as he loved her was indeed a miracle from God! It was a miracle he would never take for granted and vowed to protect at all costs.

CHAPTER NINE

"The ruby and diamond bracelet is perfect for Mrs. Tandy. Is that the one you were telling me about?" Max affirmed, at the *All that Glitters Jewelry Store* inside of the Castle Horn Mall. It was a Friday afternoon in the middle of December. Max slipped his arms possessively around Faith's waist, as they perused items through the display case.

"Mrs. Tandy's birthstone is the ruby. So, I *know* she's going to love this bracelet." Faith tried to shy away from Max's addictive touch. Max's affectionate nature was making her completely insane, but in a good way. While Mr. Langhorne and Mrs. Tandy were over at the hospital, Max and Faith were Christmas shopping for them. Faith's dad had an outpatient follow up visit at Fairfield's Respiratory Treatment Center.

"Well, which one do *you* like, babe?" Max asked Faith, pressing a kiss to her cheek.

"Max, you *really* don't need to get *anything* for me," she argued. "There isn't anything that I need for Christmas this year." Faith turned, slipped her arms about Max's neck, and crushed him lovingly in her arms. "I already have *everything* I was praying for." She pulled back and stared fondly into his eyes. Inching up on her tiptoes, she pressed her lips repeatedly to his.

Max cradled her face in his hands, and planted kisses to every corner. "Is that so? Well, everything on *my* grownup Christmas list is in my arms. Still, can you please humor me?" he coaxed. "I want my girlfriend to have something really special."

Faith's smile was irrepressible. "Is *that* what I am...your girlfriend?" she teased. Being with Max in this way still felt surreal. The couple had confessed their love for each other just two weeks ago. Since saying *I love you*, Faith had been living on a virtual cloud. The days she'd spent with Max had been the best of her entire life. She could not imagine that such joy and happiness could be found on this side of heaven. Most of her life had been shaded by misery and sadness. However, Max had come into the picture, and had shown her paradise.

There was a mawkish expression on Max's face, as he stared tenderly into Faith's eyes. "You are *so* much more than my girlfriend. It's difficult to put into words all you've come to mean to me..." Tears shone in his eyes. "Now, tell me which one of the bracelets *you* like, Faith," he prodded.

"Max, I know you've already gotten me a gazillion other things..."

Max gave Faith an illogical look, then redirected over to the store manager. "We're taking all three," he settled in respect to the jewelry.

The store manager's eyes widened in shock. "Are you sure, Sir?" Skepticism masked his face.

"Max, no," Faith argued. "I don't need any of that stuff. All I need is you."

"I know you don't need any of it, but it is my *solemn* duty to spoil you," his voice broke. "I've been waiting for quite a while now indulge the woman I love."

Tears gleamed in Faith's eyes as well. Max considered it an honor to pamper her. It was his way of expressing his heart. "Max Kane, I love you!" Faith reached up and pressed another kiss to Max's mouth. "I'll take this one here." Faith pointed at the diamond tennis bracelet. "We don't *have* to take all of them," she told the manager.

"Are you sure, Ma'am?" the store manager tested.

Faith nodded. "This is the one I want." She highlighted the diamond bracelet again.

Max crushed Faith in his arms from behind and watched her try on the bracelet. He'd already purchased a number of different items for her for Christmas. What she didn't know is that he'd already selected *four* of the pieces they'd browsed at the store that day.

In fact, Max was actively praying about asking Faith to become his wife. However, he perceived that it was a little too soon to ask. Furthermore, all loose ends had to be tied before they could take such a momentous step. More than anything he wanted to put a ring on her finger. Max cradled Faith in his arms from behind and pressed a sweet kiss to her shoulder blade. "That looks amazing on you!" he celebrated.

"You think so?" Faith turned to face him.

"I like it a lot." Max winked. "It looks perfect on your arm," he delighted. "In fact, you're absolutely perfect!" He gave her a loving squeeze, totally enamored.

Typical of Seattle weather, the temperature had dipped by the time the couple made it outside of the mall. Max was content, and generally excited about life. Things were finally at a good place. The last thing he'd expected upon moving out to Seattle was to find love again. A romantic relationship was something he'd closed himself up to completely. So, he could not have imagined meeting Faith, and falling head-over-heels in love. In that regard, he assented to the fact that God's ways were truly past finding out.

Keith had pulled back for a minute, so Max and Faith were enjoying a little stint of peace. However, they weren't foolish enough to count Keith out indefinitely. Both realized that the quietness was probably the calm before the storm. Max was definitely expecting to come to blows with Keith at one point or another. He evaluated that men like Keith seldom knew how to pull out when a relationship soured.

Keith considered Faith his personal property. So, Max and Faith knew without equivocation that the man would rear his ugly head again at some point. Despite the imminent danger, Max resolved to be ready for whenever Keith decided to issue the strike. Max was in constant communication with the police. Keith's activities were being monitored at every given turn. As a result of Max's connection to the authorities and because of the order of protection, Keith had backed off for a while. Still, Max and Faith knew that they had not heard the last from him.

"We really did a great job today, Max!" Faith bragged, as they packed their Christmas purchases into the trunk of Max's SUV. "I'm so excited about the things we got for our families. By the way, my dad and Mrs. Tandy are going to love their gifts!"

Max took Faith's hand and guided her over to the passenger's side. Opening up the door, he secured her inside. "I'm *also* confident that your dad and Mrs. Tandy are going to be over the moon happy about our choices." Max smiled and gave Faith a loving wink before shutting the car door.

Max walked around and took his place behind the wheel. "I'm so excited that you allowed me to bless *you* with a little pre-Christmas gift." Max found it difficult to keep his eyes off of Faith. *Was it even humanly possible to love anyone the way he loved faith?*

"Max, you've got to promise me. No more gifts. You must have at least a dozen of them under the tree for me," Faith complained. She reached for Max's free hand and held it hers. "Promise me."

"Okay, I promise no more presents…that is until *after* Christmas." Waggishness shaded Max's face.

"Max…," Faith whined. It was her reaction whenever she was taken aback or surprised by anything Max did. "You've got to promise me," she prompted.

"Are you hungry, babe?" Max evaded the subject.

"I'm starved. How far is the *Fancy Grill Restaurant* from here?" Faith asked. The two had planned to stop in for takeout once they were done shopping.

"It isn't too far away. I can't wait for you to taste their smoked shrimp." Max enticed with a compelling expression on his face.

"That sounds amazing! I can't wait to try it either. But, seriously, Max, no more gifts." Faith gave him a knowing smile. She was used to Max's eluding tactics by now.

"So, I guess talking about smoked shrimp didn't distract you, huh?" There was a quirky expression on Max's face.

"Nope, I know *you* too well, Max Kane," Faith razzed. She brought his hand up to her lips and pressed loving kisses to it.

"It's getting to be that I can't get away with anything with you, can I?"

"Nope. So, you'd better get used to it." Faith laughed.

"I guess I'm just going to have to." Max stared fondly over at Faith with an incorrigible smile.

He waited until they stopped at a red light, then he reached over and pressed a sweet kiss to Faith's mouth. "I love you so much!" he reminded her.

Faith's heart melted in the way it always did whenever Max said I love you. "I love *you* so much, Max Kane!" she said with an undulating voice.

Despite the brisk weather, it was a beautiful afternoon. There were a few fading clouds in the horizon, but the sun beamed potently. Faith still couldn't believe that she no longer had to work through the cafeteria of Somerset Ridge Middle School. For the past week she'd been gainfully *unemployed*. And, in the days ahead, she and Max would finally visit *Light of Glory Church*. Max had been working consistently for the past few weekends.

Faith looked forward to being on his arm when they attended church. She had been reading through the gospels in the New Testament and learning more about the life of Jesus. Faith was over the top excited about her newfound faith. Furthermore, she couldn't seem to stop praising God for all he'd done in her life.

Max drove out onto the expressway headed over to the restaurant, when Faith's cellphone went off. Faith immediately took the phone out of her pocketbook and answered. "Hey, Ruth." Faith recognized Mrs. Tandy's number. "Are you and my dad ready to be picked up?" she asked warily. Max and Faith had to swing by to pick them up from the treatment center.

"Faith, you and Dr. Kane need to get over to the hospital right away," Mrs. Tandy announced with a wavering voice. "Something's happened."

"What's happened?" Faith asked, alarmed. Her face immediately warped in foreboding fear.

Seeing the distraught expression on Faith's face, Max instantly pulled over to the shoulder of the road. "What is it, sweetheart?" His heart hammered.

"What? Keith showed up over at the treatment center. He was pressuring my dad for answers, then dad started having breathing issues," Faith reiterated, incredulous. Her face warped in misery as tears brimmed over her eyelids. "What...? He *is* alright, isn't he? Please, tell me he's going to be alright." Faith cried.

Max moved in closer to Faith. Mirroring her sadness, tears shone in his eyes. "What is it, baby?" His heart rent in half seeing the expression on her face.

The phone slipped out of Faith's hand, and she began to tremble. "No, Max, no.... There must be some kind of mistake. Mrs. Tandy said that dad just died from respiratory distress." Her face contorted in despair. "My dad told Mrs. Tandy he needed a little air, while they were waiting to see the doctor. When they went outside, Keith was there. He started pressing my dad for answers. My dad got freaked out, and all of the sudden couldn't breathe," Faith muttered.

"Oh, sweetheart, I'm so sorry." Max was grieved, as he collected Faith in his arms. "I'm so sorry." He crushed her to himself and sobbed along with her. "Oh, honey...," he pacified, but Faith was inconsolable. For the first time in their history, Max had absolutely no idea what to say or how to make things better for her. He was outraged, because Mr. Langhorne's breathing distress had been triggered by Keith's harassment.

Max had never been a violent man, but he wanted to find Keith. Max wanted to make him pay for all of the suffering he'd brought into Faith's life. He prayed not to act on his impulse. As Max drove a brokenhearted Faith over to the treatment center that afternoon, he felt completely powerless. For Max, if felt personal that something so reprehensible and *criminal* had taken place at his hospital, and Keith Wendt was the culprit.

Faith was absolutely devastated. The tragedy also could not have come at a worse time. Max reasoned that Christmas would forever be a source of unspeakable pain for Faith. His heart lacerated to consider all of the loss she'd known in her life. She'd lost her mom, her child and now her father. The disconsolate expression on Faith's face and in her eyes were indescribable on their way over to the treatment center. James Langhorne had died only two weeks before Christmas.

Mr. Langhorne had been Faith's only family out in Seattle, and Max's heart went out to her. Faith had done everything in her power to ensure quality care for her dad. She had even taken it upon herself to oversee all matters concerning his health. However, Max acceded to the fact that being at the end stages of Emphysema, Mr. Langhorne's condition was touch and go. Regardless, that afternoon, he vowed to make Keith pay for all of the suffering he'd caused.

***

"Thanks for letting me crash here, Sal," Keith said, in a panicked state. It was the day after James Langhorne had passed away outside of Fairfield's treatment center. Mr. Langhorne had been with his nurse when Keith found them. Keith had approached them and had asked for the man's new address. However, the man had gotten so upset he'd started having breathing troubles. Keith had run off. He had no idea that James Langhorne had succumbed to his Emphysema only moments after.

"Yeah, sure, Keith." Sal's face warped in concern. "You *are* moving over to that place on Chapin Road in a couple of days, right?" he verified. Sal had a small studio apartment, and he couldn't see Keith staying with him for too long.

"Yeah, I *am* moving over there. I got some of my money back from them guys. I told them to lay off Kane for now. So, with that money, I paid for one month plus security. But, I gotta wait to move out there. They doing renovations or something. I need to lay low now, cause of that protection order," Keith explained.

Keith was still unsettled by the turn of events. He kept raking his fingers through his dark hair, and his hazel eyes were swimming in a pool of red. He and Sal were sitting at Sal's small round kitchen table with a bottle of Scotch, and two small drinking glasses between them. "I can't believe I'm going through all this mess cause of some chick." He shook his head incredulous. "I ain't expect her dad to die."

"What you gonna do, Keith? You already know that doctor's got the cops watching every move you make. He ain't gonna let you get nowhere near Faith," Sal pointed out.

"I know. I thought it was gonna be a cakewalk to find Faith's new place, but I know them cops on my tail. After I seen *Daddy Langhorne* in Dr. Max's car, I knew they was headed over to the hospital. So, I kept calling until I found out that they drop him off at the treatment center. This girl I know dropped me off over there. That's why nobody was tailing me then. But ain't no doubt Kane got his dogs watching me. It wasn't no coincidence when the cops pull you over the other day, Sal," Keith presumed, angry but also terrified.

"Yeah, I still ain't paid off that no inspection ticket. Listen, Keith, I think you should leave Faith alone. Let it go… Let her go. There's so many other chicks out there. I don't think it's worth it to keep going through all of this mess because of *one* of them," Sal advised. He knew that Keith was a ticking time bomb, so he was being careful not to set the guy off.

"I want to let her go, Sal, but I can't. Faith's a really good girl. She been pretty good to me. Even if I busted her chops about being with other guys, I don't think she ever cheated on me…not until recently." Keith's face warped in acrimony.

"Yeah, but look what's going on, Keith. First off, she with Doctor Max. Then, you had to up and leave your place. Look at you, man. You all freaked out that the police is coming for you, because Faith's dad is dead. You scared that this powerful doctor will get you thrown in jail *again*. Last time they locked you up in that jail, they kept you longer than they was supposed to. And, you *know* that Doctor Max Kane was behind that, Keith. He rich and powerful, so you need to leave him alone."

Keith pounded his fist on the small kitchen table, jostling the alcoholic libation in the bottle and their glasses. "I can't let any of it go, Sal. Don't you get it? Faith is *my* woman! She *was* my woman until this Doctor Kane come along. Just because he rich, and got influence in town don't mean I got to roll over and play dead while he steals my girl.

"I ain't no punk, Sal. Ain't nobody got the right to steal somebody else woman. I'm gonna find a way to get my hands on

Doctor Max Kane, and he gonna regret ever crossing paths with me." Keith seethed with vengeful thoughts.

"Keith, man, Faith's dad is dead. You *really* want to keep doing this?" Sal questioned, incredulous, trying to get his friend to see reason. Sal hadn't been out of prison for too long, so he wasn't trying to get caught up again. Prison life was much too hard. So, as soon as Keith moved out of his studio, Sal planned to distance himself. He didn't need the trouble. Keith was hell bent on ruining his *own* life, so Sal didn't want to be on that ship when it sank.

"Max Kane think he can come in and steal my Faith, but not on my watch. He gonna regret the day he met Faith." Keith's face twisted into a malicious scowl. "And, once I'm done dealing with Doctor Max, I'm gonna teach Faith a lesson she ain't never gonna forget." Keith gulped down what was left in his drinking glass.

"Come on, Keith, have a little more to drink. Stop being mad. When you mad you don't think right," Sal said, in an effort at getting Keith to focus on other things.

"There ain't nothing wrong with my thinking, Sal. I'm gonna make them both pay for putting me through this. Nothing and nobody gonna change my mind," Keith emphasized.

"I'm gonna order us a pizza from up the road. You had a rough couple of days. You need to eat something, and get a good night's sleep," Sal heartened.

Sal could clearly see that Keith was headed for destruction. However, there was very little he could do to convince his old friend that he was on a slippery slope. Rather, Sal tried his best to listen to

Keith's rant in respect to exacting revenge on Faith and her doctor friend. Every once in a while, Sal tried to share a little bit of common sense, but he realized that Keith was too far gone to listen.

***

"My brother took most of my dad's things away. My sisters took a few items and mementos, and I've already stored away the things I wanted to keep. So, everything else can go to the Salvation Army," Faith's voice wavered as she spoke to Max. "What time does the store on Alpine Road close anyway?" There was a forlorn, and a disconnected expression on her face.

"Six... But I called them earlier, and they know we're dropping off a few things," Max said demurely, as he finished packing some of James Langhorne's personal effects into boxes.

"Okay," Faith said absently.

It had only been a few days since the funeral, and Faith still found it difficult to speak. Her siblings, who had flown out to Seattle for the funeral, had returned to their respective homes. So, Faith was left to make sense of things in the wake of her father's death. Needing a few personal days in order to be there for Faith, Max had asked his work colleague and buddy Dalton Davis to oversee a lot of his responsibilities over at the hospital. That afternoon, Max was helping Faith with Mr. Langhorne's belongings.

Max had finished sealing up his last box with packing tape. Drifting over to Faith, he searched her face and eyes

compassionately. "How are you holding up?" He set his hand on
her waist and drew her into his arms. Crushing her to himself, he
buried his head in her shoulder. Inwardly, he was grieved over the
turn of events. In fact, Max had internalized Faith's anguish as his
own.

Faith immediately began to quaver in Max's arms, as tears
brimmed over in her eyes. She was so broken that it was trying to
verbalize any words. "I, I… He was doing better for a while, Max,"
she complained, presenting that argument. "We were so careful
about his health, and he *was* a lot stronger." Max's strong arms
sustained her. "He wasn't supposed to go that way," she said
mordantly. "He loved you so much and had hoped." She clung to
Max as she mourned.

"I know, baby, I know…" Max's heart rent in half, as he held
her acquisitively. "He *was* a lot stronger. You're right, baby, this
should not have happened. He and I had not known each other for
very long, but I loved him too." Max squeezed Faith devotedly in
support. "He was a good man, and he should not have been a
victim." Max could hardly breathe, as he expressed his heart.

Seeing Faith so shattered in the past few days had left him
undone. The worst part was the realization that there wasn't
anything he could do to mitigate the pain. Max prayed, and asked
God to strengthen them during this difficult time. Knowing that only
the power of God could carry them through, Max chose to stand on
God's word. Revenge was also something Max was tussling with.
Thoughts of finding Keith, and making the man regret the day he
was born consumed him.

And yet, Max knew that his anger wasn't in the will of God.
Furthermore, his outrage would serve as a poor example to Keith.

The Holy Spirit of God had reminded Max that Keith needed God's mercy and salvation above all else. However, Max was hardly at the place to submit to that. Seeing Faith so fragmented had in some way diminished him. What Max *did* know was that he was ready to do whatever was necessary to alleviate her suffering, but he had no idea how to go about placating her misery.

"Oh, Max, I just can't believe he's gone," Faith muttered. "He was the only family I had left out here."

"I know, baby. I know… I'm so sorry." Max sustained Faith and cried along with her.

"I must have done something very wrong, Max. Maybe, God hasn't been happy with me. I lost my mom, Matthew and now…" Faith's face wrinkled in misery, and she wept with abandon.

"You did nothing wrong, baby," Max countered, pulling away, and cradling her face in his hands. Delving her eyes, he emphasized, "Please, stop saying that. You didn't do anything wrong. You're like an angel. If anything, it's *because* you're wonderful and kind that this evil world has hurt you." Tears filled Max's eyes. "Please, stop saying you deserve hurt, loss and pain. It kills me to hear you say those things." Tears brimmed over in his eyes.

"You mean the world to me, and I can't stand to hear you talk that way. I know things are difficult right now, but I promise that we will figure it out together." Max cupped her chin with one hand. "I promise to remain by your side, until this horrible storm passes and clears." Max searched her eyes. "Losing your parents and your son…" He shook his head in the negative. "I know how shattered you've been over losing them… Faith, I may not be your family-"

"Max Kane, what are you talking about? You *are* my family," Faith said emphatically. "You *have* been my family. God knew just how much I was going to need you." She slipped her arms around Max's neck, reached up and bridged her lips to his. Collecting his face in her hands, she kissed him repeatedly. "I'm so sorry, Max. I'm so sorry for saying those things. I love you so much! You *are* my family."

"And you're *mine*. I didn't have anyone before you came along," Max admitted. His arms encircled her waist, and he gazed meaningfully into her eyes. "I was all alone and totally hopeless. So, I *know* what that's like, baby. I will remain by your side for as long as God lends me breath," he avowed.

"I promise to do the same." Faith breathed spasmodically and smiled through the tears. "Neither of us is alone anymore, Max. I don't know how I survived so long without you."

"Well, I ask myself the same about you, but this is for keeps, Faith. I'm not going anywhere. I love you so! Faith, you and I are going to get through this *together*. You don't have to try to figure things out on your own, alright?" Max delved her eyes. "As we walk this out and adhere to faith in God, we will make it through this dark chapter." He smiled through the grief and pain.

Faith nodded quiescently and buried her face in Max's chest. "By God's help and strength, and with you by my side, there isn't anything we can't accomplish." Faith hugged him meaningfully. "I love you so much, and I thank God for you, Max Kane!"

"You're my entire world, and *my* family, Faith Langhorne!" Max swayed her body in a gentle rhythm. "We're going to get through this, and life will make sense again. I promise."

"Because of you, Max, life *does* make sense. You mean everything to me!" Faith found a safe harbor in Max's arms. Anchored by such a great love, she realized that she wasn't alone by any means. God had allowed her to suffer unspeakable loss. Nevertheless, God had also blessed her with a love she never even dreamed was possible. Max *was* her family, and her new *home* out in Seattle. In him she'd found a haven she would cling to for the rest of her life.

***

"What a beautiful skyline!" Faith cheered, exploring New York City through an expansive picture window in a hotel suite. Skyscrapers and glistening glass front buildings, looked amazing against the pink and orange backdrop of the dusky sunset. City lights permeated the already picturesque setting, leaving Faith virtually breathless.

Max kept Faith wrapped in his arms, as they admired how gorgeous New York City looked at twilight. He had secured tickets to an event and had made dinner reservations for their first night out in NYC. Just a few days before Christmas, Max had surprised Faith by flying them out to New York.

Faith had been so distraught in the wake of her father's death, Max thought it to be a good idea to take her away from Castle Horn for a couple of days. His goal was to take her mind off of the sad set of circumstances. He and Faith had briefly discussed going out to New York to see the Rockets on Thanksgiving Day. And so, Max wanted to honor his word. They were scheduled to see the Christmas Extravaganza at Radio City Music Hall on the following night.

"This is pretty impressive, isn't it?" Max took in the sights from the window, squeezing Faith closer to himself. "You're not too tired after the flight?" Max explored her face and eyes, pertained.

"I *am* a little tired, but I'm equally excited to see New York!" Faith smiled in earnest. She cradled Max's face in her hands and stroked fondly on his cheeks. "Thank you for doing this, Max!" her voice wavered, as she doted on him.

"No thanks required, baby." Max admired how lovely she looked. "There *is* one thing I wanted us to do before having dinner later. Are you game?" Impishness danced on his face.

"Of course, I'm game. Max, are you sure that Doctor Davis has everything under control over at Fairfield? I feel as if my crazy life has pulled you away from your duties," she argued.

"Are you kidding me?" Max shook his head incredulous. "Faith, trust me when I say that everything *is* under control. I don't want you worrying about anything right now. If I'm here with you right now, it's because I *can* be." Max veered Faith's body towards himself.

Slipping his arms around her waist, he pulled her close. "The only thing you should be worrying about right now is what you're wearing to Radio City Music Hall tomorrow night." Max winked. "You're also allowed to obsess about all of the things you want to buy when we go shopping on Seventh Ave in the morning. Aside from all of that…" Max waved a disapproving finger and shook his head in the negative.

"Aside from that I'm *not* allowed to worry about anything," Faith ceded, smiling sentimentally up at Max.

"That's right." Max crushed her lovingly, and pressed kisses to her fragrant bed of hair. "I love you, and it's going to be alright. We're going to have the best time. I want you to focus on all of the things that make *you* happy." Tears shone in his eyes.

Faith squeezed Max fondly and closed her eyes meditatively. "I *am* focusing on all of the things that make me happy. I have everything that makes me happy in my arms," she said softly. "I love you too, Max! I love you so much! Thank you for being so kind. Thank you for taking me away from the familiar for a little while." She smiled encouraged.

Max pulled back enough to stare into Faith's eyes. "You're so welcome, my love! I can't wait to show you off to everyone in the city. From the gate, everyone's eyes at the *Gray Pearl Bistro* will be on my gorgeous girlfriend tonight."

"Well, I'm sure they're going to notice *my* incredibly handsome and *hot* boyfriend," Faith razzed, smiling up into Max's eyes. "Max, you still haven't told me where we're going before dinner," she pointed out.

Quirkiness and mischief danced on Max's comely face. Collecting Faith's face tenderly in his hands, he pressed his lips to hers. "I *know* I haven't told you. That's because you're not supposed to know," he quipped. "It's a surprise."

"Max…," Faith groused in the familiar way she did when she was exasperated by his antics. "You're *really* not going to tell me?"

"No, not at all… And don't you dare *'Max…'* me," he issued a farcical warning. Max loved teasing her about the way she said his name whenever she was incredulous over his capers.

"Max…?" Faith tried to argue.

"Uh-uh," Max countered, bridging his lips to hers. He took his time to explore every contour of her mouth, lavishing her in honey-dripped kisses. In between butterfly kisses, Max reminded her repeatedly of how much he loved her.

Max dressed warmly for his and Faith's first date out in New York. He and Faith had separate suites. Since James Langhorne's death, Max had seen to it that Faith didn't spend any time alone. So, Faith was staying over at his house in one of the guest bedrooms. The last thing Max had wanted was for Faith to be all alone over at her new place, grieving the loss of her father.

The circumstances were less than ideal, but Max was praying through them. He loved Faith more than life itself and was more than ready to propose marriage. However, the timing was off. Faith had recently lost her dad, and Keith was like a dark storm cloud hovering over them. Despite his best efforts, Max perceived that Keith would make one final attempt. So, Max could not afford to be lulled into a false sense of security.

Respecting his core values and beliefs, Max refused to compromise. Succumbing to anything which the word of God condemned just wasn't an option. Sex was meant to be enjoyed within the confines of a loving and committed marriage. He and Faith had discussed the matter extensively, and they were both on the same page.

Sharing separate suites at the *Platinum Pear Hotel* on the Upper East Side of NYC, was a mutual decision, but Max couldn't say that it was easy. Regardless, Max resolved to do what was right, and what was in Faith's best interest. The present set of circumstances were unconventional, but Max determined to ask Faith to be his wife just as soon as the time was right.

In the interim, Max would remain prayerful. His prayer was for a clear path, so that he and Faith could be together in a God-glorifying relationship. Every day Max celebrated the love God had *unsuspectingly* brought into his life. He had to laugh about the matter. All things considered, he could not have imagined finding the love of his life in the way he'd found Faith. Now more than ever, Max considered the mysterious ways in which God worked.

As he put on his winter gear, he celebrated the fact that he was completely and unremittingly in love.

***

The temperature was bordering freezing, as Max and Faith glided over the ice at the Rockefeller Center Skating Rink. The couple held hands, as they swirled on the slippery surface.

"I've got you, honey," Max reassured Faith. She'd stumbled, but Max had kept a firm grasp on her hand and had pulled her closer to his side.

"Max, this is amazing!" Faith delighted, taking in the lavish Christmassy décor. The happiness on the faces of the other skaters sparked joy in Faith's heart. Holding hands and floating across the ice was such fun. "I can't believe I'm here. I've seen pictures of this place in magazines and books…." Faith shook her head in skepticism.

"I'm glad you're enjoying it, my love." Max pulled Faith in for a brief kiss, but there was a rift as a result of their activity on the ice. "I didn't know you were such a natural." Max stared at Faith with a sense of dignity.

"Well, my dad…" Faith's eyes shone in affect, but she worked through the melancholy. "My dad used to take me out to *Meadowlark Fields* out in Seattle when I was a little girl. We used to go during the holiday season."

In a gentle way, Max shifted so that Faith could skate in front of him. He kept his hands on her hips from behind. "Guess what, baby? We can make *this* our new Christmas tradition," Max said, moving in closer to Faith.

Faith fastened Max's arms bout her waist. Pressing her back up to his chest, she veered just enough to establish eye contact. "I would love to create all kinds of traditions with you, Doctor Kane!"

Max continued to guide Faith along. In fact, the pair looked as if they were engaged in a skating competition. Setting his hands lovingly on Faith's hips, Max held her protectively, as they mapped their own course over the shimmering ice. "I think we've *already* begun to create our own traditions." He pressed a kiss to her cheek.

"Like...?" Faith rose playfully to the occasion.

"Like, coming out to the Big Apple before Christmas," Max whispered in Faith's ear.

"Okay, I *really* like that one." Faith beamed. She found herself smiling all the time around Max. He made her ridiculously happy. "Any others?" she goaded.

"Well, there's this..." Max pulled away for a moment but kept a firm grasp on Faith's hand. "There's pretending to be professional skaters at the Rockefeller Skating Rink," he razzed, and pulled faith playfully back to his side. "What are some *you* want to create?" There was a waggish expression on Max's face.

"Well..." Faith broke free and whizzed over the ice on her own. "You can take pictures of me while I make silly poses." She giggled.

"I can *definitely* do that." Max winked. Pulling out his phone, he took pictures of Faith, as she posed in silly and dramatic ways. He laughed because some of the patrons around them were chuckling over Faith's over the top goofy gestures. "Now, I like that pose. That's great, honey!" Max talked to Faith as if he were a real photographer, and she was a model engaged in a photoshoot. "Baby, you look like a bird about to take flight," he razzed.

"Now you," Faith prodded, sashaying back over to Max.

"Oh, no…," Max argued.

"Max, come on. *You* will look amazing. I don't think you're capable of taking a bad shot," she prompted.

"You really want me to make a total fool of myself on the ice in front of all these people?" Max asked in a hushed and reserved tone.

"Absolutely. It's our new tradition. So, you've got to honor it," Faith humored, snickering.

The smile on Faith's face made Max deliriously happy. She had suffered so much. So, Max considered it his responsibility to ensure that she remained at a good head and heart space. "Alright," he conceded. Max glided over the ice doing silly stunts. He parodied professional skaters by swinging his arms dramatically.

Some of the patrons stopped to watch Max be goofy, while Faith snapped pictures of him. He couldn't believe he was being so brazen. All things considered; it was more than worth it to see Faith laughing. "Are you satisfied?" he asked, feigning awkwardness, as he slid back over to her. "Now, all of Rockefeller Center has seen me make a fool of myself."

"I *am* satisfied," Faith quipped. "Look how awesome you look, Max!" Faith showed him the pictures. "Totally handsome and hot!" She reached up and pressed a kiss to his cheek.

Max blushed and took her hand in his again. "After being kissed by the beautiful Faith Langhorne, I can honestly say that it was totally worth making a fool of myself." Max chuckled.

"Ooh, Max, I have an idea. Come on." Faith tugged on his arm.

The couple wandered over to a spot where the grandiose and luminous Christmas tree was at the backdrop. "*This* could be our favorite tradition yet." Faith guided Max over to her side and positioned her phone to take a selfie with him.

Max pulled Faith acquisitively to himself. "What tradition is that, baby?" His face bridged lovingly to hers.

"It's kissing my baby at the Rockefeller Center Skating Rink with the Christmas tree in the background." Faith set her camera to video mode, as her lips fused to Max's. She captured their meaningful kiss against the wintery Christmas décor. As she and Max indulged in their confectionary kiss, Faith could no longer find sadness. She had suffered unspeakable loss and pain, but God had blessed her beyond her wildest dreams with an exceptional man who truly loved her.

***

"Yes, I want that policy implemented, and enforced on all of the wings of the hospital. Effective immediately," Max spoke over the phone. He'd just wrapped up a meeting with hospital personnel. However, the head of the OR wanted to confirm a few key points.

"Yes of course, feel free to call me again if you have any more questions. Actually, I'm working Christmas Eve, but I am off on Christmas Day," he disclosed. "Sure, of course... Merry Christmas to you and your family as well! Bye now." Max hung up. He'd been at the hospital since six a.m. Needless to say, that the day had been long and drawn out. He and Faith had gotten back from New York the day before. For a couple of *perfect days*, they'd shared a little quality time. Now, there was a sense of emptiness because they were apart again.

Max smiled contemplatively remembering how wonderful a time they had out in New York. The culmination of their trip was going to the Christmas extravaganza to see the Rockets at Radio City

Music Hall. It warmed Max's heart recounting how much Faith had smiled and laughed during their trip. That little respite was a much-needed excursion for both of them. Max appraised that it was all worth it, because it made Faith happy. And, making her happy was paramount.

Max was so excited about their future together. There were so many surprises he wanted to lavish on her. Just two days before Christmas Eve, and Max couldn't wait to start spoiling Faith. In fact, later on, he planned on surprising her with a very *special* gift. Max was on a happy cloud, when the knock came to his office door. "Come in," he called out automatically.

Ava discreetly opened up Max's office door, and popped her head through. "Do you have a minute, Max?" she asked politely with a faint smile.

"Ava!" Max said, surprised. Max stood to his feet, came from behind his desk, and crossed over to connect to Ava. He offered her an amiable smile. "How have you been?" Feelings of guilt and awkwardness instantaneously surfaced.

"I've been alright. How about you?" Ava stepped fully inside of the office, and gingerly shut the door. Max hadn't worked through the ER for a few weeks. In fact, she hadn't seen him since the night he'd stopped by her place for a moment on Thanksgiving.

"I knew I could find you in here." Ava's smile brightened. "Hospital responsibilities have *really* kept you on your toes." She explored Max's perfect face and found herself naturally gravitating closer to him. She'd missed him to the point of tears. It was obvious that Max was extremely busy, but she hoped that they could make time to reconnect.

"To say the least… I've been swamped lately," Max admitted. "I guess it goes with the territory." He smiled pleasantly at Ava. "I know that I haven't hung out with you guys down in the ER for a while. How's it going down there?"

"Well, you *know* how crazy busy it's gotten, Max. The influx of patients coming through the ED have multiplied since the implementation of **Rapha Nine**," Ava detailed. "That program has more than tripled the hospital's admissions."

"Yeah, I *know*," Max said with a faint smile. "I'm sorry, but that's what we wanted, right?" His face creased in uncertainty.

"Oh, absolutely," Ava concurred. "I'm not complaining. That program is keeping us *all* in pretty things," she razzed.

Max chuckled over her comment and shook his head nonsensically.

Ava reflexively drew closer to Max. "It's only been a few weeks since you've work through the ER, but it feels like an eternity. I've really missed you, Max," she confessed, taking Max's right hand in hers.

Max's face creased in uneasiness and guilt. "I've missed you too, Ava." Max cautiously reclaimed his hand from her grasp. "I'm so sorry I haven't been in touch." His eyes lowered intuitively into Ava's bright blue ones.

"About that… I wanted to ask what you're doing for Christmas. I realize that I'm asking last minute, but quite honestly, I was really hoping to connect after Thanksgiving." Ava's face grew sullen. Max seemed distant and even a bit aloof. Furthermore, he'd flinched from her touch.

"I'm so sorry, Ava. Things have been a little hectic. Not to mention the fact that I was out of town for a couple of days." Max's face creased apologetically.

"So, *are* you busy on Christmas day?" Ava asked, working through her tangled feelings.

"Actually, I *am*...so sorry, Ava." Max felt both remorseful and conflicted.

"Oh, okay...," Ava acquiesced, grieved. She suddenly stared up into Max's penitent gaze. "Max, I had hoped that we could go out again since the concert. I thought for sure that we would have. I had a great time that night, and I thought you did too," Ava explicated, with eyes shimmering in affect.

"I *did* have a great time that night, Ava. I am so glad you shared those tickets with me." Max searched her face and eyes in compunction.

"Max, I like you...I mean, I *really* like you," Ava admitted. "I had hoped that we would continue seeing each other."

Max gently took Ava's hand in his and explored her gleaming eyes. "I know, Ava. The truth is that I like you too." He sighed. "After we went out that first time, I *was* looking forward to a second date as well," he explained discreetly.

"Then, why can't we pick up where we left off?" Ava's face wrenched in frustration. "What's changed so drastically in the past few weeks?" she daunted, almost afraid to hear the answer.

Max squeezed her right hand caringly. "The truth is that I've met someone," Max said straightforwardly.

"You met someone in the past few weeks?" she queried in skepticism.

"I'm afraid so." Max's face wrinkled in concern.

"It's only been a few weeks, Max. My guess is that it's someone fairly new. So, it can't be all that serious," Ava rationalized.

"I'm afraid that it's *quite* serious," Max disclosed. "Believe me when I say that it wasn't something I planned." He smiled temperately. "Things just sort of played out that way."

"Oh, I see…" Ava hung her head in disappointment.

Max cupped her chin and made her look at him. "I'm so sorry, Ava. The last thing I wanted was to-"

"I'm fine, Max," Ava said shortly, veering away from his addictive touch. "I'm not hurt at all." She forced a smile. "We only went out once, so there were no *real* expectations," she justified, trembling. Tears blanketed her pupils like contact lenses.

"Ava…" Max sympathized with tears gleaming in his eyes. "You really don't need to…" Seeing how hurt and sad she was, Max drew her into his arms, and crushed her in comfort. Ava surrendered to crying in his arms. "I'm so sorry, honey. I'm sorry if you're hurt," he said cautiously. "I don't want to presumptuously assume that I *have* hurt you," he placated.

Ava guardedly pulled out of Max's arms, and her tear-filled eyes connected urgently to his. "I'm fine." She forced a smile and inched backwards towards the office door. "I'm really glad you found someone special, Max. You deserve to be happy." She guffawed with a sense of incredulity.

"Thank you so much for saying that, Ava. You are an amazing person, and you deserve to be happy as well."

"Well, thanks for saying that." The plaster smile remained on Ava's face, but she floated over to the door. "In any event, I'm glad we got to see each other before Christmas. We've truly missed you down in the ER." She tried to work past feelings of offense.

"I miss you guys too, but if you check the schedule, I'm on the calendar the first weekend of the New Year," Max detailed. His face wrinkled in conflict as he stared at her. There was no denying that Ava was hurt, and Max hated being the one who'd caused her pain. "Are you going to be alright?" he checked again.

"Yeah, I'm going to be great!" Ava said with an exaggerated smile. She turned and accessed the doorknob. However, she veered back towards Max. "Well, I guess if we don't get the chance to see each other before Christmas, Merry Christmas, Max," she extended cordially.

"Merry Christmas, Ava!" Max's heart twisted in knots over how hurt Ava seemed to be.

"Take care," Ava murmured.

"Take care, Ava." Max moved closer to the door.

He watched Ava open it up and step through it. However, for a moment Max stood in the doorway watching her amble down the hall. It hurt him a great deal to consider that she was heartbroken. How strongly Ava had come to care about him had eluded him. Max had liked her too and had seen her as someone he could potentially date.

However, that was before Faith Langhorne had stepped into the picture and had turned his entire world upside down. Max was so in love it was difficult to define. Even if he *did* feel somewhat guilty for having gone out with Ava once, Max was grateful to God for limiting their interactions. The last thing he would have wanted was to lead her on. So, in that respect, he was glad that he and Ava had stopped before they'd even gotten the chance to get started.

***

Later, in the evening, Max kept Faith blindfolded, as he walked her over to their appointment. Just a couple of days before Christmas, and predictability was something he tried to avoid. He was *that* guy who always went for the element of surprise. "We're almost there, baby."

"Max, I don't want to trip and fall," Faith complained, more intrigued than concerned about truly falling.

"Don't worry, I've got you." Max kept his arm firmly around her waist and continued guiding her along. "Besides, I will pick you up and carry you if the path gets a little too rocky," he reassured.

"Max Kane, why are you torturing me this way?" Faith protested, but an uncontainable smile covered her sweet face.

"I continue to torture you in this way, because I love you so much!" Max razzed on her, chuckling.

"I love you too, baby, but are we there yet?" Faith quipped-too excited to keep her wits about her.

"Almost, my love," Max told her. "Trust me when I say that I won't keep you blindfolded any longer than you need to be. Do you trust me?" he tested.

"With my life," Faith affirmed.

Max conveyed Faith up to the set of doors of the car dealership. He could tell that Faith had picked up on the fact that they were no longer outside. Max moved them over a few feet away from the entrance doors. Some of the car dealers stood by watching his interactions with Faith curiously. "Alright, are you ready, baby?" he quizzed.

"I'm ready, Max." Faith was anxious. "Can you remove the blindfold now?"

"Of course." Max was excited. He'd already paid for a new SUV for Faith. All she had to do was to pick out the one she wanted. *Castle Horn BMW* had a variety of foreign cars to choose from. So, Faith had the option of picking out a BMW, Mercedes Benz, Lexus or an Audi. Max was excited for her, as he cautiously removed the blindfold from off of her eyes. "Surprise, honey!" he acclaimed the moment he looked into her eyes.

Faith stared warily about. "Max, what's this? What are we doing here?" Bewilderment veiled her sweet face.

Max slipped his arms covetously about her waist and delved her eyes. "We're here to have you pick out your new SUV or a car…whatever you choose." Max's entire face lit up in celebration.

"What?" Faith's mouth gaped in shock. "What? Max, no… No, we're not," she argued with tears shining in her eyes. She cupped her mouth with both hands and began to tremble. Staring into Max's expectant eyes, she disputed, "Max, no. You can't do this." Her face warped emotionally.

"Oh *yes* I can, and I *have*," Max disputed, squeezing her closer to himself. "It's a done deal, my love. You're only here to pick out what you want," Max's voice was croaky, and he was getting choked up as well.

"But, Max, this is too much," Faith's voice undulated. She was incredulous and kept shaking her head in the negative. "I can't accept this from you."

"Evening, Dr. Kane," one of the managers of the dealership walked over to the couple.

"Good evening, Everett!" Max greeted properly. "Can you *please* tell my girl that this is a done deal? And please explain that all she has to do this evening is to pick out the car she wants?" Max prompted the gentleman.

"Whatever you say, Dr. Kane." Everett chortled. He moved in even closer to the pair. "You *must* be Faith," he acknowledged with a winning smile.

Faith smiled, and brushed tears away from her eyes. Nodding affirmatively, she extended her hand correctly to Everett. "Yes, I *am* Faith. It's nice to meet you!"

"It's nice to finally meet you, Faith! My name is Everett Descarles. I'm afraid Dr. Kane is right. It *is* a done deal. So, if you would kindly follow me. I will show you our selections." He smiled enthusiastically at Faith.

"Max, I can't believe you've done this." Faith shook her head nonsensically, as she and Max followed behind Everett. "You are too much." She stared at Max, marveling and skeptical.

Max hunched down and pressed a sweet kiss to her lips. "You mean the world to me, baby! There isn't anything you need that I want to see you without. Alright, babe? I know that horrible man took your car, so…" Max's face wrinkled in involvement. "Well, in any case, you need something to get around in," he established. He and Faith spoke quietly between themselves, as Everett Descarles guided them over to a vast selection of cars, trucks, SUVs and vans.

"Max, I'm overwhelmed," Faith said, cupping her mouth, as she browsed the selection of vehicles. "But everything's so expensive," she complained.

Max hunched down and silenced her again with another kiss. "Pick out what you want, baby," he coaxed. "Don't even worry about the price." Max pulled back, and allowed Faith to browse, following a few feet behind her. He was able to view the luxury vehicles through her eyes, and it warmed his heart. There wasn't anything he didn't want to do for Faith.

Max perceived that Faith had absolutely no idea how much he loved her. It was the first time in his life that he was *completely* in love, and the object of his affection loved him back. So, it wasn't something Max would ever take for granted. He wanted to show Faith every single day of their lives that she was the most precious thing on earth to him. And, having just lost her dad, he wanted her to know that they were family.

"You mean to tell me that I can drive off with it today?" Faith celebrated. She'd just picked out an admiral blue Lexus LX SUV. That particular SUV was the one she kept going back to after browsing a number of other selections.

Max chortled, tickled by Faith's excitement. "Of course, you can drive off with it today! I wanted you to have this before Christmas," he told her. Max kept a firm grasp about her waist. Wonder of wonders, in the past few weeks, he'd learned that he was the proverbial needy boyfriend. It was vital for Max to remain connected to Faith at all times.

"Really?" Faith's eyes shone in affect. This time they were tears of joy. She couldn't believe Max had just gotten her a new SUV-a Lexus at that. She kept shaking her head in disbelief. Turning towards Max, she draped her arms about his neck, inched up, and covered his face in loving kisses. "Thank you, thank you so much!" she praised. Faith buried her face in Max's chest, and crushed him meaningfully in her arms,

"You're so welcome, baby!" Max's voice broke, as he squeezed her devotedly in his arms. "I love you so much!" he whispered in their intimacy.

"I love you more!" Faith said softly, holding on to him for dear life. "Thank you, thank you, Max," she sang, as they swayed rhythmically in their fond embrace.

Everett cleared his throat just before he addressed the young couple again. He could tell they were very much in love, and it warmed his heart. One of his assistants followed behind him. Jessica Richards was more than ready to handle the paperwork aspect of the new automobile. "Dr. Kane...?" Everett tried to get Max's attention.

"Yes?" Max hesitantly pulled away from embracing Faith. "I apologize. You were saying...?"

"I was just saying that Jessica will finalize the paperwork, and we should have you and Ms. Langhorne out of here in just a short while."

"Awesome!" Max cheered. "Thank you, Jessica," he said amiably.

"You're welcome, Dr. Kane! And congratulations on your new SUV!" Jessica addressed Faith with a warm smile.

"Thank you so much!" Faith said, pressed up to Max's left flank, with her arms about his waist.

"You're welcome! Now, Dr. Kane, if you and Ms. Langhorne would kindly take a seat out in our reception lounge... Please, help yourselves to coffee, hot chocolate and to our Christmas cookies." Jessica smiled openly.

"Thank you," Both Max and Faith said in concert.

"I shouldn't be long," Jessica reassured.

"No worries," Max told her. "Faith and I will be in the lounge."

Max and Faith wandered away and slipped inside of the dealership lounge. The lounge looked more like someone's living room. There was living room furniture, a coffee table, and huge Christmas tree, embellished with seasonal décor. The couple took a seat and enjoyed the ambiance.

Jessica floated out to her office away from the showroom and shut the door. Most of the important paperwork had already been handled. The car was registered, had insurance and temporary inspection. It had only taken half an hour to get the car all set for Faith Langhorne to drive home. Now, the only thing left for Jessica to do was to put in a phone call. Jessica settled at her desk and accessed her cellphone. Autodialing a familiar number, she awaited an answer. "Hey, it's me," she announced.

"What's going on, Jess?" Keith's voice resonated over the phone. He'd met Jessica a few months ago at the post office. Soon after, he'd brought her over to his place. So, the two were well acquainted, and had been intimate quite a number of times. In fact, Keith had the pretty young blonde thinking that he was completely in love. So, there wasn't anything Jessica wouldn't do for him. The truth was that Keith could care less about her. She was only a means to an end. And, by virtue of the circumstances, the time and energy he'd invested into Jessica was about to pay off bigtime.

"Your *ex-girlfriend* is here with that Dr. Kane. Faith came in to pick out an SUV. Dr. Kane bought her a Lexus," Jessica detailed.

"So, she came in and picked out her ride…" Keith mulled over. "Well, I can't say that I'm not a little jealous, but what do you have for me? By the way, thanks for giving me Kane's address."

"You're welcome!"

"Did you place the tracking device under Faith's new car, so that I can follow her every move?" Keith cut straight to the chase.

"I *did*. The moment she made her choice, I slipped the device under the car. So, once she leaves the dealership this evening, you can start tracking her," Jessica informed. "They should be leaving in a matter of minutes, because I'm done with the paperwork."

"Jess, I can't thank you enough. You've come through for me bigtime."

"Does that mean you want me to come over to *your* place tonight?" Jessica quizzed, extremely eager.

"Yeah, sure, baby. What time are you getting off tonight?" Keith feigned excitement. Inwardly, he was celebrating *finally* being able to get to Faith. At last, he'd found a way to access Faith, and to get her away from Doctor Max Kane.

"Nine, but I can be by your place by half past," Jessica enticed.

"Sure, I'm looking forward to seeing you," Keith vamped.

"Okay then, it's a date."

"I will see you then, and Jess?"

"Yes…?"

"Thanks for coming through for me."

"No worries, Keith. You can *really* thank me later."

CHAPTER TEN

On Christmas Eve, Faith drove out to the local supermarket in her new Lexus. There were still items on her shopping list she needed to pick up. She and Max had made plans to cook a special breakfast, and a dinner to remember on Christmas Day. Faith was elated that Max had Christmas Day off, and she wanted to make their day exceptional. So, she was all set to cook up a feast of all of their favorites, and Max had promised to help.

Faith was on top of the world! Finally, her eyes were opened to the favor of God upon her life. For starters, God had used Max to bless her with such a beautiful gift! Such an expensive foreign automobile was something she'd never imagined driving. As she hauled her shopping bags into the trunk of the car, Faith teared up in acknowledgement of all God had done for her. She was also a bit nostalgic, because it was the first Christmas she would spend without her dad. However, God had not left her disconsolate. God had brought Max into her life at just the right time.

All set to leave the strip mall, Faith hopped into the automobile. She thought about going over to the hospital, and surprising Max with dinner, but changed her mind. She would wait to see him when he got home later. Surprising him over at the hospital was always a temptation, but Faith resisted the urge, because Max was extremely busy. Furthermore, he'd already taken so much time off for her. So, Faith refused to interrupt the vital work he was doing on a whim.

"Okay, Jesus," Faith sighed, "I have the ingredients for the dishes Max and I are cooking tomorrow." Her face wrinkled in introspection. "I just need to pick up some wine down the road. I've already gotten Max's gifts, I have our Christmas stockings all stuffed, and I also picked up cards for his coworkers like he asked…," she itemized.

Faith took a moment to thank God before pulling out of her parking spot. "Lord, I can't thank you enough for all of the wonderful things you've done in my life." Tears bristled over in her eyes, but Faith brushed them away. "You brought me out of an abusive relationship with Keith, and you brought Max into my life. I never thought that this kind of happiness was possible-at least not on this earth." She marveled.

"You *knew* how much I was going to need Max after dad died. I still can't believe my dad is gone, but I *am* thankful that you blessed me with Max." Tears meandered down her cheeks. "He's my *family* now. Lord, please work out our living arrangement. Max hasn't left me alone at the apartment since dad died. So, as you're well aware, we've been staying over at his house. But, that isn't ideal for us. I would want to be married, and I know that he wants the same thing. I thank, and I praise you for making that a reality for us. I can't thank you enough for all you've done, Jesus. I love you with my whole heart…"

Faith pulled away from the strip mall parking lot and cranked up Christmas music in her new car. She was floating on a cloud, so no one and nothing could bring her down. Despite the heartaches of the past, her life had taken an unexpected turn for the better. Faith would forever be grateful for all of God's blessings. She rolled out onto the main street and continued down the road. As she did, she noticed the overcast skies, and snow flurries dispersed in the wind. "Snow!" she cheered. "If *only* we could have a decent snowfall before Christmas!" She was all smiles, as the automobile careened down the path. The wines and liquor store wasn't too far away, and she was anticipating going home.

Keith had followed Faith out to the strip mall, and he was tailing her in a car rental. Jessica, the girl from the car dealership, had discreetly helped him rent the car. She had been kind enough to let him use one of her major credit cards. Keith was overjoyed, because he was getting closer to reclaiming Faith. He was outraged that Faith had been staying over at Max Kane's in the affluent area of Castle Horn. That night, Keith planned to surprise Faith in a way she'd never been surprised before.

Cautiously, Keith weaved, and wound his rented *Range Rover* tailing Faith. Only two cars stood between his and Faith's. Keith could hardly contain his excitement and anticipation. After Faith had spent weeks evading him, he was finally going to be in close proximity to *his* woman again. Yes, Faith would *always* belong to him.

It didn't matter how much she tried to convince herself that Max Kane was her guy. Irrespective of all of the near misses, Keith was more than ready for their reunion. Besides, he planned to teach Faith some key lessons she would not soon forget. He would also school her in regards to the repercussion of turning her back on him. Keith was determined to take Faith away, and he would never let her go…not ever.

In an unassuming manner, he watched Faith pull into the mini mall. Pausing for a moment, he waited for her to find a parking before he pulled up into the lot himself. Keith watched Faith step out of her illicitly expensive new SUV. Following her gait, he remained perfectly still, seeing her walk into the high-end wines and liquor store.

His plan was to precede Faith over to the house, and sneak in. Keith rationalized that he would encroach the residence, while Faith hauled her shopping bags into the house. He presumed that Faith would probably be able to bring in all of her purchases in two trips. In the interim, he would gain access to the house. When it was all said and done, he would recover what he felt to be rightfully his…Faith.

Faith pulled into the driveway of the house in the early evening. Her cellphone went off, as she killed the engine. She smiled expectantly because it was Max. "Hey, baby," Faith greeted, beaming. It was always such a joy to connect to the man she loved.

"Hello, sweetness!" Max's voice resonated over the line. "What are you up to?"

"I just pulled into the driveway, and I'm sitting in the car. I just gone done running all of those little errands we talked about for tomorrow's special day." Faith's face radiated with light and joy.

"Ah, how can I forget about our special Christmas feast?" Max cheered. "I can't wait, honey. This is our first Christmas together."

"I know, Max." Faith's eyes shimmered sentimentally. "I can't even remember what life was like before you in it, baby."

"I know exactly what you mean, my love. You've changed my life too-and definitely for the better. Faith...?"

"Yes, sweetie?"

"I want to make you forget all about the terrible things that happened before. That's all behind us now," Max affirmed. "I promise that you will never have to suffer that way again."

"Oh, Max..." Tears pooled in Faith's eyes. "I don't know what I ever did to be this blessed. Things haven't always been easy, but God has been so kind to me. He sent *you* into my life," she uplifted.

"Faith, you have no idea. You keep saying that I saved your life, but you *really* saved mine." Tears shone in Max's eyes, as he sat inside of his private office. He had a short break, so he was making the most of it by connecting to his love. "I didn't think I'd ever find love with anyone," he admitted. "Believe me, true love isn't something that a person finds very easily."

"I didn't think I would *ever* meet anyone like you, Max," Faith confessed. "I'm sure you already know that I wasn't having very much luck in the romance department until you came along. I love you so much, sweetie. Are you on break?"

"I love you more, babe. Yes, just checking in. I can't wait to spend the entire day together tomorrow. Merry early Christmas, my love!"

"Merry early Christmas, baby!" Faith's face creased in wistfulness.

"I'll talk to you a bit later. I love you!"

"I love you too, Max! Be safe, baby."

"You too. Faith, be careful okay. It's getting a little dark out now, so if you don't need to go out… Also, make sure the alarm system is activated," he reminded.

Faith nodded quiescently. "I'm not going out again. I promise to be careful and will definitely remember to activate the alarm system. Max, I'll be waiting up for you."

Max's smile was irrepressible. "I can't wait to see that gorgeous face! Bye, babe."

"Bye, Max." Faith cradled the phone, smiling.

Realizing that she needed to haul her purchases into the house, Faith immediately set the phone back into her pocketbook. Opening up the car door, she hopped out, and sauntered over to the trunk. Faith gathered up as many shopping bags as she could carry. Then, she tread up the house's walkway trying to balance them in her arms. She had already issued the command on her phone to automatically unlock the house doors. Now, she just had to find a way to twist the doorknob.

Setting her hand through the handles of her shopping bags, Faith allowed her wrist to balance the weight of the packages, as she turned the doorknob, and pulled open the storm door. Repeating the process, she did the same for the front door. Before long, she was inside of the house.

Keith had parked his Range Rover a good distance away and had walked over to Max Kane's on foot. As planned, he'd preceded Faith over to the house, and stood at a corner behind some shrubbery. He'd watched Faith talk on the phone, as she'd lingered in the car. There was no doubt in Keith's mind that the phone call was from Max Kane. The light on Faith's face attested to the fact.

It was a true exercise in restraint not to allow jealousy and rage to overtake him. Keith had made up his mind to hold it together until he executed his plan. Remaining at his post, he waited for Faith to step back outside to accrue the rest of her shopping bags. Keith was aware that she'd temporarily deactivated the alarm system. So, when she stepped outside, and wandered over to the trunk of the SUV to get her things, he would unassumingly slink inside.

If the outside was any indication, Keith estimated how expansive Doctor Kane's house was on the inside. So, it was his conclusion that he'd have plenty of space in which to hideout. Then, when Faith least expected it, he would make his presence known. Keith wasn't sure why his heart raced in angst. What he *did* know was that in upscale neighborhoods, there were always a crop of nosey neighbors watching everyone in the locale. Nevertheless, Keith would not allow that to deter him. His aim was to do what he set out to, and quietly usher Faith away.

His heart nearly popped out of his chest when Faith stepped out of the house again. Keith watched her hike back over to the SUV, and amble over to the trunk. It was the perfect opportunity. As Faith stalled towards the back end of the automobile, she was temporarily invisible. Keith counted on the fact that he was probably out of her range of vision as well.

As planned, he creeped over to the front of the house. Going up the stairs, he slithered through both sets of doors, which had remained partially opened. Keith felt victorious having infiltrated Max Kane's million-dollar home without setting off the alarm. He was certain that there were cameras everywhere, but he planned to move fast before there was any real trouble.

Keith drifted into the expansive house, which looked more like a mansion. It was the first time he'd ever been to such a luxurious place. Seeing the house made Keith hate Max Kane all the more. Keith burned with keen jealousy over the kind of life Max could offer Faith. It wasn't anything he could ever compete with. Regardless, Keith was there on a mission. He had to get Faith back. He couldn't offer her the indulgences Dr. Kane could. However, that was neither here nor there, because Faith *belonged* to him.

Keith wandered through the winding and vast house. Past the huge state-of-the-art kitchen, he wandered down the hallway. Staring all about the place, he assessed that he had a choice of different rooms to choose from. However, as he deliberated, he heard Faith coming through the front door again. Startled, Keith immediately turned the knob, and slipped inside the first available room. The room was the first one to his left-hand side. Delicately, he shut the door closed.

Even if the room wasn't very well lit, Keith could see enough to marvel. He assessed that this was *only* a spare bedroom, and yet it was extravagant. If a guest bedroom was so excessive, Keith imagined what Max Kane's bedroom looked like. This particular room appeared much too pristine to be currently in use. Again, assessing Max's wealth, made Keith feel all the more angry and inadequate.

Faith hauled the last of her purchases into the kitchen. She rested some of the bags on the counter, while she set others on the kitchen table. Stepping out of the kitchen for a moment, she strolled down the hallway to find her room. Once inside, she slipped off her coat. Then, stepping out of her comfortable UGG Boots, she strolled over to the dresser. Pulling out a drawer, she found a pair of black leggings and a comfortable gray sweatshirt. Faith found her fuzzy brown bear house slippers and wandered back over to the kitchen. Not wasting any time, she set out to put the groceries away.

Shortly after, Faith thought about seasoning the ham, but then changed her mind. She would first need to work on the homemade pie crusts for dessert. Faith walked over to the kitchen cabinet, which was positioned to the left-hand side of the refrigerator. Opening it up, she searched for and found vegetable shortening. Setting the can of shortening on the counter, she then reached for the large bag of flour. Faith made a sudden turn to set it on the counter but wound up dropping it on the floor.

White flour dust flew everywhere. Like a dense foggy night, the powder created a haze, but Faith remained frozen, and short of breath. She trembled as tears filled her eyes. Her heart thrashed so forcefully it felt as if it would pop right out of her chest. The level of terror she felt was unparalleled, as she stared into the face of the man she and Max had done everything in their power to avoid. Faith's entire body was electrified by fear and shock, and it was becoming harder to breathe by the second. Astonishment, incredulity and dismay veiled her sweet face. "Keith...," she said shakily.

"Hello, baby." Keith's expression was conniving. The devious look turned mocking, as he closed in on Faith. "What's the matter, baby? Cat got your tongue?" he derided.

"What are you doing in here?" Faith asked petrified. She willed her legs to move, but they felt cemented to the kitchen floor.

"What kind of question is that, baby? You *know* I'm here to see you." Keith eliminated the space between them.

"You need to leave. This is Max's house. There are cameras and a very sophisticated alarm system." The aghast expression on her face calcified. "You can't be here, Keith," her voice wavered. Faith shrank back, as the grim reality of the matter was staring her in the face.

"Don't worry, honey. I'm not planning to *stay*." Keith set his hand to the side of Faith's face and stroked it. "Oh, look at you. You are so beautiful! I missed you so much, honey. Did you miss *me*?" he asked throatily. Keith gripped Faith's left arm and began manhandling her. "Did you miss me, Faith?" he bellowed, aggressively twisting her arm.

"*Yes*, I missed you, Keith," Faith's voice undulated, as she grimaced in pain. Warily, she skimmed over the room in search of an object so that she could fight back, but she was completely frozen.

Keith violently pulled Faith into his arms and crushed her with a cobra-like grip. His voice was raspy, as he daunted her, "Now, you and I are going to play a little game. You're leaving here with me tonight."

"No, no... I'm *not* going anywhere with you." Faith shook her head in the negative. Tears looped over in her eyelids, as she quavered. "Please, leave me alone, Keith. I don't want to be with you anymore." Her face warped in misery.

"Well, guess what, baby? *I* want to be with *you*. Now, you're going to leave here quietly with me right now. Please, don't let me have to remind you what will happen if you put up a fight. You were *never* supposed to be here with Max Kane," he said irate, red-faced and eyed. "You were never supposed to be with him. You're sleeping with him right?" Keith's face and neck turned scarlet in outrage, and veins pulsed at his temples.

"No, Keith, we're not sleeping together. Max and I don't have that kind of relationship," Faith's language was choppy, as she breathed fitfully. "He isn't that kind of man."

"Unless he's gay-and I know he's not-he *is* that kind of man. Faith, don't mess with me. We're leaving now." Keith's clutch only tightened around Faith's body. "You're not going to make a peep as we leave this house. Do you understand?" He crushed her as if she were a piece of dough. "You're going to hug and kiss me at the door for effect as we leave. The neighbor's minds will be completely at ease seeing us so lovey-dovey."

Faith grimaced in pain. Panicked, she nodded frenziedly in compliance, but she couldn't stop trembling.

"Are we clear?" Keith roared, as veins pounded to the sides of his neck.

"Yes," Faith said quiescently, over-breathing, "we're clear." Revulsion shaded her face, as Keith guided her over to the front door. Surely, this was an out of body experience. Quite soon, she would awaken from the nightmare. In light of all of the measures she and Max had taken to distance themselves from Keith, the moment seemed implausible. However, Faith realized that Keith had been biding his time all along. He'd found a way to invade their personal space. The closer they got to the front door, the lower Faith's heart plunged into despair.

It was Christmas Eve. She and Max had made plans to have a wonderful Christmas Day together. The reality of the matter sunk in when the frosty air accosted Faith outside of the house. The wispy snowflakes she had noticed earlier on were picking up momentum. Faith kept thinking how much she would have enjoyed watching the snowfall on Christmas Eve. However, life had taken an unexpected and lethal twist.

"Now, give us a little hug and kiss, baby," Keith ordered, forcefully pulling Faith into his arms again.

Traumatized and still dazed, Faith involuntary set her arms about Keith's neck, and allowed him to squeeze her. As she pulled away, his lips fused with hers, and he kissed her violently. Faith scowled, and blinked back tears, because he was already beginning to hurt her.

"Didn't I warn you about that? I'm not playing games, Faith. You better put a smile on that face, or else it will be a lot harder for you once we're alone," Keith threatened, squeezing her right wrist in his maliciously strong hand.

"Alright, Keith, alright…" Faith wailed in pain. "Okay, I'm smiling." She pasted a smile to her face.

It occurred to Faith that without her phone, there was no way she would be able to get in touch with Max. She continued to blink back the tears of despair welling up in her eyes, as Keith led her over to a dark blue Range Rover.

Keith opened up the passenger's side door and ushered her inside. "Keep smiling," he threatened.

Similar to someone lost out in the woods during a terrible snowstorm, Faith couldn't stop shuddering. In her despair, a passage of scripture came to mind. Faith had recently read from Psalms 50:15. It reads, "Call upon Me in the day of trouble; I will deliver you, and you shall glorify Me. (NKJV). Inwardly, she kept praying for God's intervention and his deliverance.

Faith believed that God would help her, despite the hopelessness of the circumstances. Keith had already begun to drive away from the area. Internalizing just how deeply her sudden disappearance would affect Max, made Faith cry all the more. Max would be devastated, and he didn't deserve that kind of pain.

Keith had been a thorn in her side for the past two years, and Faith knew that *she* had to find a way to stop the cycle of abuse in her life. Depending on the intervention of her Heavenly Father, it was either Keith killed her, or she found a way to escape his cruelty. Faith was praying for the latter, because she could no longer go on living in fear.

***

With just a couple of hours left on his shift, work was the last thing on Max's mind. He'd spent a great deal of time on the hospital's East Wing handling a few matters. But now, he was headed down to the ER. Max had to check in on a few patients being admitted down in the ER. And yet, his thoughts were a thousand miles away. All he could think about was Faith. He had called her a number of times since they'd spoken in the early evening, but Faith wasn't answering her phone.

As Max plodded down the hallway headed over to the ER, he was about to turn a corner, but instinctively pulled back. Seeing his buddy Dr. Dalton Davis chatting with Ava Thorne, caused Max to shrink back in surprise. Max retreated all the more, and kept his back pressed up to the wall, so that he wouldn't be detected. He smiled contemplatively, because of the way Dalton was staring at Ava. Dalton's face flushed red, and he seemed a little awkward and even reserved around Ava.

Max also evaluated the novelty and excitement on Ava's face. From their facial expressions and body language, Max concluded that the two they liked each other. Moreover, it seemed as if Dalton was in all likeliness asking Ava out. Max shook his head in amusement over the scene. He had no idea that Dalton was *into* Ava. Seeing the two interact was the highlight of Max's night. Still, he was much too distracted to fully enjoy the moment. *Why on earth was Faith not answering her phone?* Max knew that Faith had been bustling about in preparation for their special Christmas plans, but it was unlike her not to return his calls and messages.

Max's face creased in jeopardy, and his internal alarm went off. Maybe, something terrible had happened. However, Max tried to convince himself that Faith was fine. She said she would stay home for the remainder of the night and promised to activate the alarm system. "Lord, please let Faith call me. Not hearing from her like this is making me totally crazy. I *know* we're not supposed to worry, but please watch over her for me. Please, let her respond to at least one of my text messages. I just need to know for sure that she's okay," he prayed.

Max saw Ava saunter away and reenter the ER, while Dalton stared hard after her. As soon as the coast was clear, Max emerged from the corner of the hallway.

Soon enough, Dalton heard footsteps. He turned and saw Max making his way over. "Maxi!" Dalton exclaimed familiarly. "What's up, man?" He beamed.

"Hey, Dalton!" Max acknowledged with a faint smile.

"I'm glad you're on tonight. I had *hoped* to see you before Christmas. Thanks for the gift!" Dalton expressed with a grateful smile, and patted Max on the arm.

"Oh, yeah, sure." Max had paid for Dalton's entire gym membership for the year. "I appreciate yours as well," Max said, distracted.

"You haven't opened it yet?" Dalton's brows furrowed in bewilderment.

"Well, we're *not* supposed to open up gifts until Christmas," Max pointed out, shaking his head nonsensically.

"Yeah, well, I guess I got bored." Dalton chuckled.

"Are you hanging out with us peasants in the ER right now?" Dalton razzed.

"No, not tonight, Dalton. I was actually about to check in on some of the hospital's admits." Max's expression was strained. "Listen, Dalton, can you do me a favor?" Max set his hand on Dalton's shoulder.

"Sure. What's going on, Max?" Dalton frowned in concern.

"I'm worried about Faith. I need to get home right away. Can you finalize the admission orders for me on the patients down in the ED? I will text you the instructions in a little while.

"Sure, Max," Dalton agreed right away. "Are you okay... Is Faith okay?" he asked, pertained.

"I'm not sure. I just need to get out of here. Maybe, I'm just freaked out for nothing, but it's unlike her not to answer her phone or return my messages."

"Sure, go on... Get out of here. I will handle things on this end."

"Thanks, Dalton."

Max tried not to worry, but he found his heart hammering in his chest. He didn't want to think the worst. However, given Faith's terrible history with Keith Wendt, it was difficult not to. It seemed implausible for Keith to have found a way to get to Faith. Even so, Max couldn't dismiss the possibility.

Without saying another word, Max veered away from Dalton, and took to running.

"Max," Dalton called out after him.

Almost to the end of the hallway, Max turned in order to acknowledge his friend and colleague.

"Keep me posted okay. Send me a text as soon as you can to let me know Faith is okay."

Max nodded in agreement and zipped out of that part of the hospital like lightning.

***

When Max pulled into his driveway, he was totally relieved to see Faith's SUV. Seeing her car was a total load off of his mind. However, until he saw Faith, he would remain unsettled. "Maybe, my baby took nap. She *has* been running around all day." Max smiled anticipating seeing Faith. He would take a quick peek into her room to see if she *had* indeed fallen asleep.

Over at the hospital, he'd check the door alarm icon on his phone, so Max wasn't too surprised to see that the door was already opened. He rationalized that Faith had made several trips to and from the car, and had forgotten to activate the system. "Faith…," Max began calling out the moment he stepped inside of the house. "Faith, baby, where are you?"

Max drifted past the living room and the formal dining room. "Faith…," Max called out again, as he entered the kitchen. However, his heart dipped to the floor in angst when he saw the bag of flour scattered all over the kitchen floor. "Oh my God, Faith…" Max rushed out of the kitchen. He made a dash over to her room. "Faith…" Max knocked frantically on her door. "Baby…?"

Hearing no response, Max opened up the bedroom door. Finding the room empty, he examined the state of the bedroom. Faith had her coat resting on the bed, and Max noticed that she had taken off her comfortable boots. So, he knew that she'd been inside of the house. "Oh, God, oh, God…" Max cradled his head in jeopardy. "God, where's my Faith…?" It felt as if someone had just taken a sledgehammer to his heart.

"Oh, God, no. No, this is not happening…" His face wrenched in jeopardy and turmoil. Racing out of the bedroom, Max immediately dialed 9-11, while simultaneously checking the alarm censor video feedback.

"9-11, what's your emergency?" the voice pealed over the line.

"Yes, I'm Doctor Max Kane. I just got home, and my live-in girlfriend is gone. It seems as if she's vanished, and her ex-boyfriend is abusive. He's hurt her many times before, and I'm afraid she was taken out of the house against her will," Max explained.

"Okay, Doctor Kane, we're familiar with the case. I will inform the head detective, and I am alerting the police as we speak."

"Okay, thank you. Please, hurry."

"The police should be coming to your area shortly," the young lady said temperately.

"Thank you."

Tears brimmed over in Max's eyes, and his heart throbbed in pain. Tremulously, he stepped into his private office to play back the video feed. With quavering hands, he rewound the video to approximately the time he and Faith had spoken. Undoubtedly, at around 6:15 that evening, Faith's SUV had pull into the driveway. Max then fast-forwarded past their phone conversation. He watched Faith open up the trunk of the SUV, haul her packages out, and carry them into the house.

Moments later, he saw Faith go outside again to accrue the rest of the shopping bags. However, what Max saw next threatened his sanity. He saw the man slip inside of the house, while the front doors were ajar. Max cringed in horror and regret. The man who'd slipped inside of the house was undoubtedly Keith Wendt. Guilt rumbled on the inside like a machine, as he internalized the implications of what had occurred.

Max trembled and wept with abandon, as he watched the footage. He fast-forwarded until he saw Keith ushering Faith out of the house. Keith had his hands all over her, and he forced a kiss on her. Max slammed his clenched fist on his work desk in frustration. "He took her away, and he's probably hurting her right now. I don't know where he took her, and I'm not sure what to do. Oh, God, please help me." Max rammed his fist on the desk again, feeling powerless.

Based on the video, Keith had taken Faith across the street from the house. However, the range only went but so far. It was obvious that Keith had conveyed her away from the block. So, the miscreant could have dragged her anywhere. Perhaps, he had a car parked quite a distance away. And, in light of what Max had witnessed, Keith had made Faith put on a happy front. "My poor baby looked terrified out of her mind." Max supported his head in his hands, so that he wouldn't lose it.

"Lord, we're not supposed to worry. And, we're certainly not supposed to let anger get the best of us. That said, you're going to have to help me with that right now. I depend on you, and I know that without you, Jesus, I can't do anything at all." Max's face warped in sadness and dismay. "Faith means everything to me. Lord, I've done everything in my power to keep her safe. I've tried so hard to make sure she'd never be in this situation again.

"I promised to keep her safe, and I've let her down in the worst way. I've never felt more powerless in my entire life. Please, protect her, Father. Don't let that horrible man put his hands on her again. I'm relying on your power, and on your strength to keep her safe. She's already gone through so much." Max's eyes were crimson, and tears were caked on his face. The thought of Keith hurting Faith again was driving him completely over the edge. He had to pull back for a moment and seek the face of his Heavenly Father. Only God could step in and change the circumstances. Max also prayed for self-control, because there was no telling what he would when he saw Keith.

***

No longer able to sit still, Max stormed out of the house moments later. Uncertain as to what recourse to take, he knew he had to get moving. There was a dusting of snow blanketing the streets, which littered the front of the house and the lawn like glistening crystals. The snow reminded Max that it was Christmas Eve. He and Faith had made plans to spend a peaceful Christmas day together.

However, those plans had been overturned. Max paced agitatedly as he waited for the police to arrive. His thoughts were racing. There *had* to be something he could do. Maybe, it was time he took a trip over to the apartment out in Somerset Ridge. He was just about to dismount the steps, when someone pulled up in his driveway, and it wasn't the police.

Max recognized the Escalade as his neighbor's a few houses down. Harry Chapin was a middle-age retired professor who lived close by. Harry had been the first one of his neighbors to welcome him when he'd first moved out to Castle Horn. Max alighted the steps in order to get to Mr. Chapin's automobile. Uncertainty and bewilderment wrinkled his features.

Harry Chapin stepped out of the vehicle, and rushed up the walk-in order to connect to Max. "Doctor Kane," Harry addressed Max out of breath, "I didn't have your cellphone number. So, I called the hospital, but they told me that you'd already left. I'm so glad you're here."

"Is everything alright, Harry?" Max face creased in angst.

"I saw your girlfriend earlier," Harry cut to the chase.

Max's heart nearly popped out of his chest. "You saw her? Did you see her leave with someone?" Max demanded.

"Yes. That's exactly what I was coming over here to tell you. She was with a man."

"Did you see where she and this man went?" Max's voice was croaky, and fresh tears gleamed in eyes.

"She didn't seem to be in any danger. In fact, she and the stocky Caucasian man seemed pretty friendly. But, I sensed something was off. I've been watching the two of you together. I *know* how fond you are of each other. And, the *man* who took her away, I've never seen before…"

"Did you see where he took her?" Desperation rang in Max's tone.

"They walked off together and turned right at the corner." Harry pointed up the block. "That was as far as I was able to see. I wanted to follow, but I didn't want your girlfriend thinking I was the creepy neighbor." He frowned in concern. "What's going on, Doctor Kane?"

Max's heart drummed, as he mulled over everything the man had said. Mr. Chapin had witnessed Keith dragging Faith away. "This man is her ex-boyfriend. He's abusive, and I'm afraid that he's taken her against her will," Max's voice broke, and tears escaped the corners of his eyes.

"I'm so sorry, Doctor Kane. If I'd known who he was, I would have called the police right away." His face contorted in remorse and empathy.

Max guffawed in incredulity. "You had no way of knowing. Thank you for trying to reach me over at the hospital. That was very kind of you."

"You're welcome! Have you contacted the authorities?"

"They're on their way over now," Max said distracted. The temperature had dipped, and the snow was picking up momentum. It was almost ten p.m., and the howling winds were crying along with Max.

"I'm happy to hear that the police are on their way. I'm so sorry this is happening, Dr. Kane," Harry offered sympathetically. "If there's anything I can do…"

"I'm afraid not," Max said, with a sense of disconnect. Max was in a different headspace. Images of Keith hurting Faith played in his head like a terrible movie trailer. The thoughts were a source of torment for Max. So, he kept praying through them.

Moments later, police cars overtook the locale. The cars were silent, but the flashing lights permeated the entire block. Max and

Mr. Chapin watched the police cars come up the road. Max dashed over to connect to the police right away. Three police officers stepped out of their vehicles in order to have word with Max.

"My girlfriend was taken against her will this evening. I saw the video footage, so I know for sure that her ex-boyfriend Keith Wendt took her away. However, my neighbor over there, Harry Chapin, actually witnessed Wendt taking Faith away," Max detailed. He veered to look over at Harry who was standing feet away. "As you're well aware, Wendt has abused her in the past," Max readdressed the police.

"So, you saw the man take Ms. Langhorne, Mr. Chapin?" one of the police officers asked Harry.

"Yes, I *did* see the gentleman leave with Ms. Langhorne," Harry affirmed, crossing over to stand next to Max.

"Did she look scared? Was the man hurting her in any way?" the police questioned.

"She didn't look scared per se, but she did seem uncomfortable. Also, I found it curious that she only had on leggings, a sweatshirt and house slippers in this weather," Harry added.

Max was livid. Not only had Keith forced Faith out of their home, but she was inappropriately dressed for the brisk weather. "Is there a point to all of these questions?" he suddenly asked, irate that the police were asking Harry Chapin a number of other inane questions. "Can we just start looking for my girl? She's in real danger, while we're standing here chitchatting," Max said, grated.

"Dr. Kane, we understand your frustration, but we've got to try to piece things together."

"Alright then. Thank you for coming. You can stand here asking questions, but I'm not sticking around." Max dashed away and jumped back into his SUV.

"Dr. Kane, where are you going?" two of the officers demanded, racing over to stand by the driver's side window.

Max lowered the window. "I'm going to look for my girl. I would appreciate it if *you* started looking for her as well. You're more than aware of Keith Wendt's abusive history. Find him," Max demanded. "In the meantime, I'm going to look for Faith. I can't stand here playing twenty questions, when that monster has her."

"Dr. Kane, we would ask that you not take matters into your own hands," one of the officers warned.

"My only concern is finding Faith. When the time come, I will let *you* do your jobs. However, in the meantime, *I* would appreciate it if you got out of my way." Max pulled out of the driveway and drove away like a man on fire.

Harry Chapin and the police remained outside of the house. The police were baffled and confused that Max had taken such initiative. However, Harry wasn't the least bit surprised, neither could he blame Max Kane for taking matters into his own hands. Harry tread back up to the house, hopped up the stairs, and checked the house doors to ensure they were closed.

His heart went out to the young man. He'd observed Max Kane's activities since Max had moved out to the area. The young man lived an exemplary life. Harry estimated that someone as good-looking and successful as Max, could have chosen to live a different lifestyle. However, Max had chosen to live a life of integrity. Harry admired both his success and his humility.

Descending the steps, he crossed back over to the police. "Do you have any more questions for me at this time?"

"No, not at this time, Mr. Chapin. Thank you for your statement," one of the officers said.

"Of course, … I sure hope you find that terrible man," he added.

"We're certainly working on it," the same officer stated.

CHAPTER ELEVEN

Max pulled up into the parking lot of Faith's old place out in Somerset Ridge. Jumping out of the car, he plodded through the powdery snow, and rushed over to the building doors. Not bothering to wait for the elevator, Max took the steps by leaps and bounds. Standing in front of the apartment door, he began pounding on it. "Look, I *know* you're in there. You'd better open up this door, or I will knock it down.

"Open up now." Max positioned himself to kick the door down.

"What's going on out here?" a middle-aged Caucasian gentleman came to the door, scowling in exasperation.

Max baulked in shock and embarrassment. "I apologize. I thought Keith Wendt lived here."

"Well, he doesn't anymore. From what I understand, he's been staying with a friend across town," the man said grudgingly.

"Where across town?" Max asked, with an anxious and hammering heart.

"*Morning Mill* or something like that. I don't know exactly. *Why* are you here at this hour?"

"Keith Wendt abducted my girlfriend from our home a few hours ago, and I *need* to find him," Max explained impatiently.

"Oh, I'm truly sorry to hear that." The gentleman's face softened in sympathy. "Let me think…" His face wrinkled in introspection at that point. "He came by here to pick up a few things a couple of weeks ago. I asked if he planned to move to another apartment through this complex, he told me he had a friend,

Paul…no, Sal. He said he would be staying with his friend Sal in *Morning Mill*."

Max kept expecting the gentleman to offer up an address. However, he realized just how fortunate he was to have gotten any information from the man at all. "I'm so sorry that I was rude a moment ago. Thank you so much for your help. I truly appreciate all you've told me," Max said, still dazed and distracted. The gentleman was about to say something else, but Max raced away like a machine. Taking the steps back down to the main floor, he resolved to find this *Sal* person. What connection did Sal have to Keith, and now to Faith?

***

"Please let me go, Keith," Faith begged, as Keith dragged her into the hotel room.

"Let you go? Faith, you *belong* to me," Keith yelled, as he thrust her onto the bed, and shut the hotel room door. Keith figured that the landlord for his new place had run a background check. So, the deal had fallen through. Not only had he not found another place, but he was no longer welcomed over at Sal's in the town of *Morning Mill*. So, for the time being, this cheap hotel room was going to have to do.

Faith sat up on the bed with her arms draped over her shoulders. She was clearly traumatized, and unable to stop trembling. Furthermore, she'd cried so much that the tears had caked on her cheeks. Keith had dragged her away without a coat or proper winter attire. All she had on was a sweatshirt, tights and house slippers. He had shoved her into a car and had driven them over to this *sketchy* hotel. "Keith, I've told you that it's over. I don't want to be in a relationship with you anymore," Faith disputed, with a wavering voice.

Keith instantaneously pounced on Faith, and forcefully held her by the shoulders. His acid eyes speared through hers in rage. "If you say that one more time, I promise it will be the last time you ever speak," he admonished, shaking her vehemently. "You had no right to walk away from me to begin with, Faith." Keith's crushed Faith's shoulders in a malevolent grasp. With venom in his eyes and in his voice, he threatened, "You're going to pay dearly for running off with that doctor."

"Keith, please," Faith entreated, breathing irregularly. "I'm sorry that I walked away," she back-pedaled, realizing that it was the only way to placate him. "You're right. I shouldn't have left you to be with Max." She flinched and shuddered in anticipation of Keith's first punch.

"No, you shouldn't have. You should have *never* walked away from me, Faith-leaving me for someone like him. Do you have any idea how that made me feel?" Keith's lower virtually burned a hole through Faith. The level of his outrage was such that he was ready to erupt like a volcano. "You humiliated me with that Max Kane. You watched him beat on me, and you didn't tell him not to."

Faith cringed, knowing what would come next. Keith always started with the *woe is me* rant before he hit her. "I'm truly sorry, Keith. I didn't mean to hurt you."

"But you let Dr. Max *protect* you, right? Isn't that right, Faith?" he hollered in her face.

Faith cowered under Keith's aggression. "I didn't… I didn't mean for things…," her words were fragmented at that point.

"What…? You thought Dr. Max would be able to keep *me* away from you?" Keith derided. "Is *that* what you thought, Faith?

You really thought some stupid piece of paper from the cops would keep me away from you?" Keith yelled, and jostled her even more aggressively.

"I didn't think anything, Keith." Faith's face contorted in distress. "I just didn't want…" Faith recoiled as Keith's crushed her shoulders. "Keith, please… You're hurting me."

"Does *that* hurt, baby?" Keith mocked, as his cobra grip intensified.

"Keith, please…," Faith cried, wounded. "Please, stop hurting me." She tried to shove away, but Keith yanked her forcefully into his arms, and refused to let go.

"We're going to deal with what you did to me in a little while. You're going to learn not to walk away from me ever again," his voice softened. "But first…" Keith cogently bridged his lips to Faith's and began to kiss her.

Faith couldn't bring herself to react, as Keith's hard mouth pressed to hers, and tried to pry hers open.

"I missed you, baby. Did you miss me?" He pressed forceful kisses to her neck.

"Yes…," Faith stammered, knowing that if she answered any differently, she would push the monster keypad, and Keith would fly into a rage.

"Kiss me, Faith," Keith said, guiding her back over to the bed.

Disgust and shame shaded Faith's face, as Keith continued to touch her. She kept asking God to help her get away from him. The thought of Keith touching her in that way again was such a foreign concept. Faith had turned her life over to the Lord, Jesus Christ, and she had given her heart to Max. Max was the *only* person she wanted to be with.

"Baby, please don't leave me again…," Keith said, as his kisses grew more intense.

"Keith, I'm tired. I've had a really long day," Faith squeaked. However, she was almost certain that Keith hadn't heard a word she'd said. "God, please don't let this happen. Max and I belong to each other now. You brought us together, and he's the only person I want to be with. Please, deliver me from this situation," she implored.

Just then, Keith's cellphone went off, startling them both.

Even if the ringing phone surprised Faith, she was grateful for the intrusion. Keith immediately shoved away, and sat upright on the bed. Faith wasn't sure why she'd expected the caller to be Max. She realized that it was only wishful thinking on her part. Nevertheless, she was certain that Max probably knew that Keith was the one who'd taken her away.

"Yeah, what's going on? No, Sal, I ain't got twenty bucks to lend you. I gotta pay to stay in his hotel, since you don't want me over at your place. Yeah, I'm still at the *Golden Grand*. What difference does it make?"

As Keith talked on the phone, Faith subtly began to inch away on the bed. She was almost to the very edge, when Keith turned, and gave her a menacing look. The death stare told her that if she even breathed too loudly, he would be all over her. So, Faith sat up on the bed too terrified to move. Something had to be done before Keith tried to touch her again. The very concept repulsed her.

She kept staring all around the room for an object-anything she could use to fight back. However, Keith was on to her, because his eyes remained glued to her the entire time.

"No, Sal, quit wasting my time. What?" Keith's face wrinkled in jeopardy. "What do you mean you seen me on the news?"

"Keith, they say you kidnapped Faith, and the police looking for you."

"Nah, you lying, Sal. The police ain't looking for me," Keith argued. Watching every move Faith made, he slid over to the nightstand, and got a hold of the television remote control. Keith turned on the television and accessed the local news.

"He told you that he's *still* at the *Golden Grand Hotel* out in *White Strand*, right?" Max quizzed Sal. With the help of the authorities, they were able to find out exactly who Sal was. Sal was Keith's friend who'd served time in prison for manslaughter. Sal had helped Keith make bail when Keith had been arrested a while back. Max was on the phone with the police and had preceded them over to Sal's place. Max had offered Sal five thousand dollars, and the man was singing like a canary.

Sal nodded in the affirmative to Max's questions. *"Emphasize* that the police are looking for him, and that they're on to him," Max ordered Sal to say over the phone, even if it wasn't true. Max wanted Keith to be totally freaked out.

"Keith, the police is looking for you. You got Faith over there?"

"Why you asking me all these questions, Sal? I don't see nothing on the news so far. So, I'm good."

"Listen, Keith, if you got Faith over there, you need to let her go. I don't want to see you wind up behind bars like me. It ain't worth it, man. Let her go." Sal made eye contact with Max, who was standing right in front of him inside of his cramped studio apartment. He nodded in the affirmative at Max in confirmation of their suspicions. Keith was definitely keeping Faith over at the hotel against her will.

"Sal, I gotta go. I don't like being short with you, but you getting on my nerves right about now. So, I'll talk to you later," Keith settled, and shut down the phone.

Keith then turned towards Faith. "Faith, don't even *think* about fighting me. You'll only make things worse for yourself. I think I've been pretty decent to you considering all the stuff you put me through." Using his right index finger, Keith motioned for Faith to come sit beside him on the bed.

Faith couldn't stop shaking, as she hesitantly inched in closer to Keith. She was afraid to do or say the wrong thing. The wrong move or word could possibly activate the detonator. If Keith exploded, Faith realized that he would beat her within an inch of her life. So, she had to tread cautiously.

"Yeah, he got her over at the hotel," Sal confirmed, taking the check Max handed to him.

"That's what I figured. Thank you for doing that," Max said, as he dashed over to Sal's front door. Max rushed out of the building like a man being pursued and hopped back into his car. He'd told the police about the *Golden Grand Hotel*. However, Max had to call them back to let them know that Keith was probably holding Faith there. Regardless, Max refused to wait around, because he needed to find Faith. Setting the address for the Golden Grand Hotel in his GPS, Max rushed away from the town of *Morning Mill* on a mission.

He had promised to protect Faith, and he would honor that vow at all costs. Max also resolved to teach Keith a lesson. Max had already begun to school the man in respect to putting his hands on Faith. Now, Max concluded that it was time for finals and graduation. Max prayed for God's guidance and wisdom in dealing with the situation. In the event Keith decided to do things the hard way, Max hoped that there wouldn't be another escalation of violence. It was his prayer that the matter be handled with wisdom and in peace.

"Dr. Kane, please do not approach Keith Wendt without backup. For all you know, the man could be armed and dangerous. Please, wait for our assistance," Detective Fennimore spoke over the phone with Max.

"There is reason to believe that Keith Wendt *is* keeping Faith over at the Golden Grand Hotel. I *am* requesting assistance. My girlfriend is in serious danger. Every second she stays with that maniac is a matter of life and death. Please, meet me over at the hotel. I can't sit still for another minute. He could be hurting Faith as we speak," Max's voice broke. Not even waiting for a response, Max shut down his cell.

***

Moments later, Max pulled into a parking space at the Golden Grand Hotel. Hopping out of his SUV, he stormed into the small, cramped-obviously cheap hotel-and rushed up to the front desk. There were two people working the clerical desk. "I'm looking for a Keith Wendt?" he addressed the young woman at the desk, not bothering to mince words.

"*Keith Wendt?*" the young lady asked, perplexed. "I will check our logbook."

Max tapped his right foot on the cut-rate green carpeting and drummed his fingers on the wooden desk in agitation.

"Sir, we don't have a Keith Wendt, but we do have a Keith Wentworth on the second floor."

"Yeah, I'm sorry," Max redirected, "I meant to say *Wentworth*." He was almost one hundred percent sure that Keith had used Wentworth as an alias.

"Oh, that's alright. People mistake last names all the time-"

"Can you please give me the room number?" Max asked abruptly.

"He's in room 241F," she informed, startled by Max's lack of decorum.

"Thank you," Max told her plainly. "Where are the stairs?" he turned back to inquire.

"Over there, Sir." The young woman pointed to a gray door at the very end of the hallway, positioned to Max's left-hand side.

"Thank you for your help," Max tried to sound a bit more civil.

"You're welcome-"

Max was already at the end of the hallway. Pulling open the heavy gray door, he speedily hiked up the stairs. His heart lashed in agitation on his way up. At the very top of the second set of stairs was yet another gray door, leading out to the second floor. Max yanked it open impatiently. Before long, he was out in the hallway checking for room numbers. Max moved like lightening. "236, 238...," he read off the numbers off on the doors. Moments later, Max found himself standing in front of room 241F.

He was tempted to start pounding on the door, but then rethought the matter. He had to play it cool. Rather than behaving impetuously, he paused in order to detect activity taking place inside of the room. Max perceived very little activity through the dense hotel room door. He had to figure out a way to get inside without setting Keith off. Faith would surely pay the price if Keith felt in any way threatened. As Max deliberated in front of the door, he saw a housekeeper strolling by with her pushcart.

Slinking away from the door, he shifted over and addressed the woman. Max kept a finger over his lips indicating that they keep their voices down. "Ma'am, if you would be so kind as to go over to that room over there." Max gestured. "Please, knock on the door and say 'Housekeeping.' That's all I'm asking," he pleaded with glistening eyes.

"I don't understand," the woman said, with a bewildered expression on her face.

Max sighed. "Please, just knock on the door, and tell the party you need to clean up. Please, ma'am. The man in there is holding my girlfriend against her will. All you have to do is to knock and say that you're from housekeeping. *I* will handle the rest." Max's face creased in jeopardy. "Please...," he petitioned.

The *forties something* Caucasian woman reluctantly agreed. "Okay." She took her rolling cart, and walked ahead of Max. Max followed quietly behind her.

When they came to the door, the woman issued a gentle knock.

Keith was startled by the knock on the door, and his hands fell away from the ministry of crushing Faith in his arms. He'd been trying to pick up where he'd left off, after having gotten off of the phone with Sal. Connecting to Faith in an intimate way was the goal.

Faith sighed in relief. Inwardly, she thanked God for the interruption. Keith was in process of trying to force her to sleep with him. She was about to make a sudden move when Keith menacingly gripped her right arm. "Faith, don't test me tonight." His scowl was lethal, as his toxic eyes impaled hers.

Faith winced in pain, because Keith had handled her so forcefully.

Keith tugged on her arm yet again and admonished, "Don't move…" His brows furrowed ominously as he squeezed her. "I mean it, Faith. Do you understand?"

"Yes." Faith shrank back, overwhelmed.

Keith drifted over to the door, and guardedly opened it up.

"I'm here to clean your room," the woman said, with a wavering voice, and a terrified expression on her face.

"You can't clean my room right now. You need to come back in the morning," Keith snapped.

At that moment, Max shoved into the room, and tore into Keith. "*I'm* not coming back in the morning, you sleaze."

"Max!" Faith's said, shocked, amazed and relieved. She cupped her mouth, as she watched the men tussle.

The woman from housekeeping left her cart to the side of the hotel room door and rushed down to the main floor in order to get help.

Max had Keith on the floor as they scuffled, and punches flew everywhere. "Faith, baby, are you alright?" Max handled Keith by the collar and punched him in the face.

"I'm fine, Max. Please, be careful." Faith said, panicked.

"I'm going to teach you a lesson you won't soon forget, Doctor. I'm so fed up with your nonsense. I've been waiting for this moment ever since our brawl over at the hospital parking lot." Keith pushed up and struck Max in the face.

"Stop it. Please, stop…," Faith cried. Instinctively, she hunched down, and checked under the bed for a shoe or anything she could use to stop Keith. Faith found Keith's boots. Taking a hold of one of the boots, she hit Keith over the head repeatedly, as Max subdued him.

"You're gonna be sorry you did that, Faith," Keith veered to look at her.

"No, *you're* the one who's going to be sorry you ever put your hands on her," Max railed, and gave Keith yet another defining blow to the jaw. "I guess you don't learn, do you?" Max stood back and watched Keith's legs give way from underneath him. The man fell to the floor harder than a chopped tree out in the forest.

"Max!" Faith cried out and rushed over to his side.

"Oh, baby…" Max held Faith protectively in his arms. "Are you okay?" He cradled her face in his hands and explored her tear-filled eyes. "Did he hurt you?"

"Not really. He didn't get the chance to. Are *you* okay?" Faith's face wrinkled in concern, seeing the bruises forming on Max's face.

"I'm fine, baby. I'm fine." Max kissed Faith on every corner of her face. "I was so scared that I wouldn't get to you in time." Max squeezed her lovingly in his arms, and thanked God he'd found her. "I'm so sorry this happened. I'm so sorry, baby." Tears shone in Max's eyes. "I promise that this will *never* happen again."

"Well, you can't make those kind of promises," Keith's gruff voice infiltrated the air, dousing the flame on Max's and Faith's reunion, and short-lived victory.

Max and Faith were startled, and on the defensive, when they saw the gun Keith had pointed in their direction.

"Baby," Max said urgently, "stand behind me." His heart whipped in angst and trepidation. Max wasn't concerned for himself so much as he was for Faith.

"Keith, you *don't* have to do this," Faith pleaded.

"Oh, *yes* I do have to do this. If I can't have you, I'll be damned if *Dr. Love* here will. I'm so sick and tired of your mess, Max Kane." Keith agilely made his way up from off the floor, cautiously keeping the gun pointed at the couple.

"Keith, please," Faith pleaded, taking her place behind Max, as he'd told her.

"You really don't want to do this, Keith." Max held his hands out in a halting manner. "The police are already on their way. You don't want to go to prison for murder on top of everything else. You're going to be brought up on charges for violation of the protection order, and for taking Faith away against her will," Max reasoned.

"Let *me* worry about what *I* want to do, Doctor. You're going to pay dearly for all the times you thought you could shove me aside. Well, I'm not going to lose Faith to you. She belongs to me. I don't think you quite get that."

"Keith, please, put the gun away," Faith entreated.

"Shut up, Faith. I'm *not* leaving this hotel without you this morning."

Max skimmed the room through peripheral vision trying to figure out a strategic way to get the gun away from Keith. "You *really* don't want to do this."

"Oh, yes I do," Keith argued, pointing the gun directly at Max. "So, you think you're better than me? You're better than me, because you can offer Faith the kind of life I never could. You're better than me, *Doctor?*" Keith harangued.

"I'm not better than you, Keith. I just wanted you to stop hurting Faith. If you love her as much as you say, you won't do this." Max kept his hands up in a halting manner.

"You don't get to tell me how I feel about Faith. She was mine long before you came into the picture and ruined everything." Keith's face reddened in indignation, with the gun viciously aimed at its target.

"If you want to hurt *me*, go ahead, but please don't hurt Faith," Max's voice was guttural. "Please, give her a chance to leave here this morning. If you hurt her, you'll never have her, because you'll wind up going to prison. Let's work this out man to man."

"Max, no," Faith pleaded quietly behind him. "Please, don't say those things. Please, baby," she petitioned

"Will you let her go?" Max bargained. "Your gripe is with me. She hasn't done anything wrong. *I'm* the one who took her away from you," Max explained courageously-all the while praying in his heart. God was there, and *God's* will, not the enemy's, would prevail. For Max, if it meant losing his life that early Christmas morning, he was prepared to. All that mattered to him was that Faith remained safe.

Keith kept shaking his head contrarily. "*No*, you don't get to bargain. You don't hold any of the cards this time, *Doctor*."

Max's hands were pushed out in front of him as he pleaded. "I know I don't. Like I said, you can do whatever you want to me, but let Faith go." His face strained in conflict. Nevertheless, Max positioned himself as a human shield for Faith.

Just then, the authorities stormed, and infiltrated the hotel room.

Startled, Keith reflexively pulled the trigger, and hit his target. Max was struck in the chest, and immediately fell to the floor.

"Max....," Faith screamed, and stumbled to her knees in horror. Faith wailed again, and cried inconsolably, as she saw the blood spread across the dirty beige carpet.

Having a clear target, the police took a shot at Keith's right shoulder, and closed in on him. Keith was down, and the police toppled over him, and cuffed him.

Everything was one big blur for Faith. There was a sense of disconnect from the activity taking place all around her. From a faraway place, she heard the police call for an ambulance. As if she were locked in a dream, Faith watched the cops drag Keith out of the room. There was a bullet wound to his right shoulder. Being struck by the bullet had reflexively made Keith drop the gun, and the police were able to move in and stop him for good.

"Why...?" Faith kept crying, as she held Max's lifeless body in her arms. Max wasn't responding, and the flow of blood was all-pervasive. "Jesus, please.... Please, don't let me lose Max." Faith had no more power to cry. "I've already lost everyone else. Don't let me lose him too. Please, Lord...

"Help! Somebody please help," Faith screamed.

Police officers rushed over to Faith's side. They helped her to her feet and ushered her away from Max's still body. They asked her not to touch him, while they were waiting for the ambulance to arrive.

"Help is on the way, Ms. Langhorne," they reassured her.

"Max...," Faith kept crying, as they restrained her. Faith couldn't process what had just occurred. It was Christmas Day, and things had gone terribly amiss. She and Max had made plans to spend the day together. They were supposed to be happy and *whole*, but things had taken a very dark turn. How had things gotten so terribly off course? Faith couldn't help blaming herself.

Her poor choices had tainted the lives of her loved ones. Her father had died as a result of Keith's abuse. And now, the man she loved was in danger-all because of her connection to Keith Wendt. As Faith rode along in the ambulance with Max, she felt indefinably numb. She was depending on God, but things weren't looking very good. It was difficult to put her jumbled emotions into words.

Amidst the turmoil, Faith was reminded of a passage of scripture Max shared with her all the time. Proverbs 3:5-6 (NKJV) "Trust in the LORD with all your heart, And lean not on your own understanding; 6. In all your ways acknowledge Him, And he shall direct your path." Holding on to God and His word was all Faith could do at the moment. Knowing that God had all power, and that nothing was too hard for Him, was her blanket of comfort on that awful morning.

***

"Ms. Langhorne?" Dr. Evan Andrews came out to the OR waiting area.

"Yes...?" Faith immediately stood to her feet and rushed over to connect to the doctor. Her heart whipped in angst. Max had been brought over to Fairfield Hospital. As the head of the hospital, he'd been given extra special care. Max had been rushed into the OR for surgery. The bleeding from the gunshot wound he'd sustained just after midnight that Christmas morning, had to be brought under control. Faith had been sitting out in the waiting area for hours.

Her heart skipped several beats, and her entire body tingled in angst, as she stared at the doctor awaiting a verdict. Faith's face wrinkled in jeopardy. "Is he…?" she questioned tremulously.

Dr. Andrews offered a faint smile. "He made it through the surgery just fine. Luckily, we were able to remove the bullet, and get the bleeding under control."

Faith sighed in relief. "Is he going to be alright?" she asked, direly needing to hear Dr. Andrews say the words.

"We have every reason to believe that he will be." Dr. Andrews's smiled brightened. "In fact, that's what I came out here to tell you."

Faith placed her hand on her chest expectantly, and her eyes widened in uncertainty.

"He's conscious. He's still very groggy from the surgery, and also very weak. He's also lost a lot of blood, but he's alert, and he's asking for you."

"Can I go in and see him?" Tears of joy and relief shone in Faith's eyes.

"Yes, but please try not to tire him out. I'm sure that seeing you can only do him good." Dr. Andrews set a caring hand on Faith's shoulder and gave her an affirming wink.

"Thank you." Faith's face warped emotionally, and she began to cry. She wrapped her arms around the doctor in celebration. "Thank you so much for taking such good care of him."

"Max is our *family* around here, and he's a great man. What can I say? Max is truly loved at this hospital." Dr. Andrews hugged Faith in return.

Faith slipped through the set of doors leading into the OR Recovery Area. Marching down the hallway, she drifted over to the private room they'd set up for Max. Before opening up the door, Faith said a prayer, and thanked God for His intervention. Through the glass slot, she could see that Max's chest was banded up. There was an IV, and other hospital-related monitors connected to him. Bravely, Faith pushed open the hospital room door. Her smile was as beautiful as a new rose, because Max's eyes sprung open. He seemed a bit loopy, but a lot stronger than she'd expected.

"Hey, baby." Max smiled faintly, and shakily extended his free hand out to Faith.

"Max!" Faith celebrated, and immediately rushed over to his side. Taking his hand in hers, she hunched down, and planted sweet kisses to the contours of his face. Suddenly, she broke down in tears.

"It's alright, baby," Max reassured, with a frayed but croaky voice. He caringly brushed his hand through her hair. "It's alright, my love. Everything's going to be alright."

"I thought I lost you," Faith muttered. Her tear-filled eyes connected to his. Max's eyelids wavered, and Faith could tell it was a struggle for him to keep his eyes opened.

"I wouldn't leave you, baby. I promised. I promised to take care of you." He swallowed the dryness in his throat.

"Hush… Dr. Andrews said that I shouldn't tire you out, so you don't have to say anything." Faith took Max's hand in hers, and pressed kisses to it. "I'm so sorry, Max. I'm sorry for all of it."

"Well, I'm *not*," Max managed to squawk out. "I'm not sorry that you came into my life, Faith. I love you more than life itself. I'll never be sorry for falling in love with you. So, don't you dare apologize to me, okay?" Max offered the widest smile he could muster. "Are we clear, Ms. Langhorne?" he teased.

Faith nodded quiescently and smiled. "We're clear, Doctor Kane," she told him. "I love you so much, Max!" She bent down and bridged her face with his.

"I love you more, baby! Merry Christmas, Faith!" Max laughed lightly.

"Merry Christmas, Max!" Faith reciprocated, trying not to laugh, but giggling all the same.

"You really shouldn't make me laugh, baby. It hurts," Max quipped, and tried not to chuckle, but it was no use.

"I'm so sorry." Faith shook her head nonsensically and chortled. "Oh, Max, I love you so much!" She pressed her lips to his.

"I love *you*, baby, and I always will. I thank God for bringing me back to you. And you know what?"

"What, baby?" Sentimental tears shone in her eyes.

"I'm not going anywhere."

"Promise?'

"I promise. God brought you to me so that I can take care of you," his voice broke.

"No, Max. God brought us together, so that we can take care of each other." Faith pressed her lips lovingly to his. "I love you!"

***

A year and a half later, Max sat in his office at Fairfield Hospital. He was in process of interviewing potential nurses to work through the hospital's East wing and also the ER. That afternoon, he'd interviewed with six potential candidates. However, there was one more person he had to interview with. The young woman would be his last interview of the day.

As Max waited for the applicant, he powered through paperwork. Smiling reflectively, he considered the whirlwind his life had been in the past year and a half. Max recounted meeting Faith in November of 2019. Max's world had turned upside down from the moment they'd met. He and Faith had endured a lot to be together. And yet, no matter how much he'd suffered personally, Max couldn't say he had any regrets. Knowing how much Faith loved him made him outlandishly happy. So, not for one second could he *ever* regret loving her.

After Kennedy Proctor-Bohm had concluded that he wasn't her person, Max had all but given up on love. However, God had changed the narrative altogether. God had stepped in and had shown Max that he was indeed capable of loving again. Moreover, God had exceeded his expectations. The love he shared with Faith was undeniably a gift from God. Aside from Faith, there wasn't anyone else Max could have shared such a special bond with. So, Max would forever be grateful to God. Despite the dangers and the difficulties, they would bask in the delight of a rare, once-in-a-lifetime kind of love.

The office phone rang at that moment, stirring Max from profound reflection. "Dr. Kane, speaking... Is that so? Alright then, I'm ready. Send her in," Max spoke over the phone. Apparently, his last interview of the day had just arrived-and right on time.

Max stood to his feet and went to get the door. Standing in the doorway, he had an irrepressible smile on his face as he waited on the applicant. His smile only brightened when he saw his *wife* making her way over to the office. Faith looked amazing in a periwinkle dress suit. Her hair was upswept, and she looked totally professional. Max smiled nostalgically to see a folder in her hand. Apparently, she had brought her resume and cover letters. "Hey, baby!" Max hunched down for a kiss, but Faith flinched back.

"No, Doctor Kane. This afternoon I'm *not* your wife," she settled, as she floated into the room, and stood at the center.

Max shook his head comically. Shutting the office door closed, he turned to face his wife. "Alright, you're *not* my wife this afternoon," he humored.

"I'm serious, *Doctor Kane*." Faith held both hands up in a restrictive manner and stared critically into his eyes. "I'm here to interview just like everyone else. I don't want any special treatment."

"Alright," Max assented, and made his way back over to his desk. "I will do my best to treat you just as I would *any* other potential employee." Nevertheless, Max found it challenging not to stare at his beautiful wife. He was captivated, and more in love than ever. Still, he would attempt to keep his feelings under wraps.

"I appreciate that, Doctor Kane," Faith said with a pleasant smile.

"Have a seat, Mrs. Kane." Max gestured that she take a seat in the armchair across from his.

"Thank you." Faith tried to keep a straight face.

It was difficult to maintain platonic interactions with Max. They'd been married for close to a year now. Not to mention the fact that Max had overseen her nursing program. Faith had obtained her nursing degree taking the comprehensive courses offered through the hospital. So, she now had the opportunity to work through Fairfield Hospital close to her husband. It was a dream come true, but somewhat of a mixed blessing. She had always imagined having her dad there when she reached that important milestone.

"So, Mrs. Kane, it seems you have very little hospital experience. *However*, undergoing Fairfield's rigorous nursing program is quite *impressive*," Max uplifted, taking a professional stance.

"Yes. The hospital's nursing program was very challenging, but I had a tremendous support system."

"*Did* you now?" Max's eyes bridged intimately to his wife's.

"Yes, the very best. My husband was the head coordinator of the program. There is no way I could have graduated without his support," Faith admitted, with glistening eyes. "He's been my biggest fan."

"Is that so?" Max's eyes shone in wistfulness. "Well, your husband probably knows you have what it takes to be an amazing nurse!" He winked at Faith. "You finished the course and graduated with high honors. Your credentials indicate that you would be an asset to any hospital. Is there a reason why you've chosen to apply to work through Fairfield?" Max pushed back in his armchair, and clasped his hands together, as he scrutinized his wife.

"Well, this *is* a great hospital." Faith smiled optimistically. "My husband is the director here, and he's also the chief of staff. So, I admire his work greatly. And…" she hesitated for a moment, as her eyes fastened timidly to Max's.

"Yes, Mrs. Kane?" Max prodded.

"Observing just what a compassionate caregiver and effective administrator my husband is motivated me to obtain my degree," her voice wavered.

Max nodded reflectively, and blinked back tears. He was stirred by Faith's words. It took restraint not to jump out of his armchair and scoop her up in his arms. However, for the sake of professionalism, he had one more question to ask his beautiful wife. Max's face sprinkled in mischief, as his puckish eyes linked to Faith's. "Are there any health concerns? Any reason why you won't be able to handle the fluctuating shifts?"

Faith's face wrinkled in perplexity. She opened up her mouth to speak but hesitated for a moment. "I don't think so. My husband conducted the physical himself. He cleared me for work. So, I'm sure I'm healthy enough to-"

"There *was* just *one* concern I detected after running a battery of tests, Mrs. Kane," Max said throatily, as his eyes shimmered in affect.

Faith's heart dipped to the floor, and she was bewildered. Placing her hand on her chest, she asked dubiously, "I *am* okay, aren't I, Max?"

Max smiled into her eyes lovingly. No longer able to keep up the professional role, he pushed out of his armchair, and walked around to connect to his wife. Extending his hand, Faith set her dainty hand in his, and Max helped her to her feet. Slipping his arms around her waist, Max cradled Faith securely.

"Max, what's going on?" Faith frowned, nonplused. "My tests all came out okay, right?"

"Uh-huh," Max said gutturally, bridging his face to hers. "All but one…" He pulled back in order to search her eyes. Max could hardly contain his joy.

"All but one…?" Faith asked warily.

"Yes, baby. I think you'll be able to work through the hospital's East Wing for a few months. Then, you're probably going to have to take it easy because of the pregnancy." Tears shone in his eyes.

"Max, I'm pregnant?" Faith asked, incredulous.

"Uh-huh, you certainly are, Mrs. Kane!" Max buried his face in her hair.

"Oh, Max…" Faith's face warped emotionally, and tears were in her eyes. "I haven't been feeling right, but I didn't think…" Her surprised expression connected to her husband's expectant gaze.

"Wow! I certainly wasn't expecting this so soon after graduating," she admitted. "How do *you* feel about it, Max?" Faith tested.

"Baby, I haven't been able to stop celebrating. I'm ecstatic!" Max gently picked her up from off of the floor and spun her around. "You have made me the happiest man in Seattle!" Tears bristled over in Max's eyes.

"I'm happy too, Max! It's such an unexpected blessing!" Faith cradled Max's face in her hands. "God has been so good to me, Max! There was a time I thought God didn't love me, and that he'd taken everything away." She shook her head contrarily. "I didn't know that he would wipe away my tears in such a wonderful way."

Max pulled back, and tenderly supported Faith's face in his hands. Gingerly, he brushed her tears away with his thumbs. "I know the feeling, my love. Sometimes, it rains for a very long time, but God always sends a rainbow." He smiled into her eyes and fondled her cheeks.

"What a beautiful rainbow He sent for me!" Faith reveled. "We're having a baby, huh?"

"It would seem that way, Mrs. Kane." Max covered her face in kisses.

"So, Doctor Kane, does that mean I'm being hired for the nursing position?" Faith quipped, feeling safe and secure in the folds of her husband's loving arms.

Max bent down, bridged his lips to hers, and kneaded them hungrily in a meteoric kiss. At intervals between their soft tender kisses, he asked, "Now, what do you think?"

"I'm hired!" Faith cheered.

"You are *so* hired," Max affirmed. In gentle and loving nuances, Max reacquainted himself with every contour of his wife's agreeable mouth and extracted sweet came from its source. Max's heart was full, and completely overwhelmed by love and gratitude to God.

Other titles from Higher Ground Books & Media:

Wise Up to Rise Up by Rebecca Benston

Of Love and Witches by Marjorie Joseph

Erin & Oliver by Marjorie Joseph

For His Eyes Only by John Salmon, Ph.D.

The Bottom of This by Tramaine Hannah

Saved by a Mystery by Deborah Randall

Out of Darkness by Stephen Bowman

Breaking the Cycle by Willie Deeanjlo White

Jack Kramer's Journey by Frank Adkins

Healing in God's Power by Yvonne Green

Chronicles of a Spiritual Journey by Stephen Shepherd

The Real Prison Diaries by Judy Frisby

My Name is Sam…And Heaven is Still Shining Through by Joe Siccardi

Add these titles to your collection today!

http://www.highergroundbooksandmedia.com

Do you have a story to tell?

Higher Ground Books & Media is an independent Christian-based publisher specializing in stories of triumph! Our purpose is to empower, inspire, and educate through the sharing of personal experiences.

Please visit our website for our submission guidelines.

http://www.highergroundbooksandmedia.com